'A fantastic debut – a funny and heart-warming comedy about love, fatherhood and being in the wrong places at all the wrong times' *Essentials*

'A very funny look at relationships' *Company*

'It's impossible not to laugh out loud at the Anglo-German quips and world-weary observations that tumble off the pages' *Guardian*

'Cracking' *Sunday Mirror*

'While books claiming to be 'laugh-out-loud funny' are legion, ones such as this that actually are are rarer than molars on a Rhode Island Red' Wendy Holden, *Daily Mail*

'A brilliant, thoroughly urbane hoot' *Big Issue in the North*

'Really funny' *Daily Express*

'A hilarious novel with a very different take on love. Not so much hearts and roses as hell and ridicule. Great fun' Adele Parks

'Guaranteed to raise a smile' *Irish News*

Mil Millington is the creator of the cult website www.things mygirlfriendandihavearguedabout.com and co-creator of www.theweekly.co.uk. He has written for the *Guardian*, the *Express* and various other newspapers and magazines. He was named by the *Guardian* as one of the top five debut novelists for 2002. Mil lives in the West Midlands with his girlfriend and their two children.

Mil Millington

THINGS MY GIRLFRIEND AND I HAVE ARGUED ABOUT

FLAME
Hodder & Stoughton

Copyright © 2002 by Mil Millington

First published in Great Britain in 2002 by Hodder and Stoughton
A division of Hodder Headline

A Flame paperback

3 5 7 9 10 8 6 4 2

A CIP catalogue record for this title is available
from the British Library

ISBN 0 340 82115 9

Typeset in Sabon by Palimpsest Book Production Limited,
Polmont, Stirlingshire
Printed and bound in Great Britain by
Clays Ltd, St Ives plc

Hodder and Stoughton
A division of Hodder Headline
338 Euston Road
London NW1 3BH

For Margret

ACKNOWLEDGEMENTS

Assuredly first, I'd like to thank Sidney and Eileen Millington who, recent scientific studies have revealed, were the best parents anywhere, ever.

Next up is Hannah Griffiths; an agent by trade, a groovster by nature – I'd pay ten per cent just to hang out with her.

A respectful nod to Mr Jonathan Nash, whose example persistently encourages me to try harder; a funny, clever man who has worked tirelessly to found a sanctuary where blind animals can go to be turned into low-cost insulation and pasties destined for export beyond the EU.

Finally, *huge* thanks to my fairy godsister, Helen Garnons-Williams. A wonderful publisher. A delightful human being. Not the world's greatest rock 'n' roll historian.

'Where the hell are the car keys?'

I'm now late. Ten minutes ago I was early. I was wandering about in a too-early limbo, in fact; scratching out a succession of ludicrously trivial and unsatisfying things to do, struggling against the finger-drumming effort of burning away sections of the too-earliness. The children, quick to sense I was briefly doomed to wander the earth without reason or rest, had attached themselves, one to each of my legs. I clumped around the house like a man in magnetic boots while they laughed themselves breathless and shot at each other with wagging fingers and spit-gargling mouth noises from the cover of opposite knees.

Now, however, I'm in a fury of lateness. The responsibility for this rests wholly with the car keys and thereby with their immediate superior – my girlfriend, Ursula.

'Where – where *the hell* – are the car keys?' I shout down the stairs. Again.

Reason has long since fled. I've looked in places where I know there is no possible chance of the car keys lurking. Then I've rechecked all those places again. Just in case, you know, I suffered transitory hysterical blindness the first time I looked. Then I've looked down, gasping with exhaustion, begged the children to please get off my legs now, and looked a third time. I'm a single degree of enraged frustration away from continuing the search along the only remaining path, which is slashing open the cushion covers, pulling up the floorboards and pickaxeing through the plasterboard false wall in the attic.

I do a semi-controlled fall down the stairs to the kitchen, where Ursula is making herself a cup of coffee in a protective bubble of her own, non-late, serene indifference.

'Well?' I'm so clenched I have to shake the word from my head.

'Well what?'

'What do you mean "Well what"? I've just asked you twice.'

'I didn't hear you, Pel. I had the radio on.' Ursula nods towards the pocket-sized transistor radio on the shelf. Which is off.

'On what? On stun? Where are the damn car keys?'

'Where they always are.'

'I *will* kill you.'

'Not, I imagine . . .' Ursula presents a small theatre of stirring milk into her coffee. '. . . with exhaust fumes.'

'Arrrrgggh!' Then, again, to emphasise the point, 'Arrrrgggh!' That out of my system, I return again to measured debate. 'Well, obviously, I didn't think to look where they always are. Good Lord – how banal would I have to be to go there? However, My Precious, just so we can share a smile at the laughable, prosaic obviousness of it all, WHERE ARE THE CAR KEYS? *ALWAYS?*'

'They are in the front room. On the shelf. Behind the lava lamp.'

'And that's where they always are, is it? You don't see any contradiction at all in their always-are place being somewhere they have never been before this morning?'

'It's where I put them every day.'

I snatch up the keys and hurl myself towards the door, jerking on my jacket as I move; one arm thrust into the air, waggling itself urgently up the sleeve as if it's attached to a primary school pupil who knows the answer. 'That's a foul and shameless lie.'

As my trailing arm hooks the front door shut behind me,

Ursula shouts over the top of her coffee cup, 'Bring back some bread – we're out of bread.'

It's 9.17 a.m.

The story in whose misleadingly calm shallows you're standing right now is not a tragedy. How do I know? Because a tragedy is the tale of a person who holds the seeds of his own destruction within him. This is entirely contrary to my situation – *everyone else* holds the seeds of my destruction within *them*; *I* just wanted to keep my head down and hope my lottery numbers came up, thanks very much. This story is therefore not a tragedy, for technical reasons.

But never mind that now, let's not get ahead of ourselves. Let's just stick a pin in the calendar, shrug 'Why not?' and begin on a routine Sunday just after my triumphant car-key offensive. Nothing but the tiniest whiffs of what is to come are about my nostrils. My life is uncluttered with incident and all is tranquil.

'Dad, can we go to Laser Wars?'

'It's six thirty a.m., Jonathan, Laser Wars isn't open yet.'

'Dad will take you to Laser Wars after he's mowed the lawn, Jonathan.'

It appears I'm mowing the lawn today, then.

'Mow the lawn! Mow the lawn!' Peter jumps up and down on the bed, each time landing ever closer to my groin.

'Dad – mow the lawn. Come *on*, quickly,' instructs Jonathan.

There's very little chance of my mowing the lawn quickly as we have a sweat-powered mower, rather than an electric- or petrol-driven one. Ursula was insistent – not that she's ever non-insistent – that we got an ancient, heavy iron affair (clearly built to instil Christian values in the inmates of a Dickensian debtors' prison) because it is more friendly to the environment than a mower that uses fossil fuels to protect one's rupturing stomach muscles. Almost without exception, things that are friendly to the environment are the sworn enemies of Pel.

Still, out there grunting my way up and down the grass, my children laughing at the threat of traumatic amputation as they circle around me, girlfriend calling out from the kitchen, 'Cup of tea? Can you make me a cup of tea when you're finished?' – it's a little picture of domestic heaven, isn't it? You never realise the value of wearying matter-of-factness until it's gone.

'Have you finished?' Ursula has watched through the window as I've returned from the lawn heaving the mower behind me, placed it by the fence, made to come into the house, caught her eye, gone back to it and wearily removed all the matted grass from the blades and cogs, made to come into the house, caught her eye, returned to sweep all the removed matted grass from the yard and clear it away into the bin, and – staring resolutely ahead – come into the house.

'Yes, I've finished.'

'You're not going to go round the edges with the clippers, then?'

'That's right. Precisely that meaning of finished.'

'I really can't understand you. You always do this kind of thing – why do a job badly?'

'Because *it's easier*. Duh.'

Ursula is saved the embarrassment of not being able to dispute the solidity of this argument because the phone rings and she darts away to answer it. In a frankly shocking turn of events, the kind of thing that makes you call into question all you thought you knew, the phone call is actually for me. The phone has never rung in this house before and not been for Ursula. She must be gutted.

'It's Terry,' says Ursula, handing me the receiver with the kind of poor attempt at nonchalance you might display when nodding a casual 'hi' to the person who dumped you the previous night. Terry Steven Russell, by the way, is my boss.

4

'Hi, Terry – it's Sunday.'

'A detail I didn't need. Listen, have you got some time to talk today?'

'I suppose so. Apart from going to Laser Wars in an hour or so, I don't think I'm doing anything all day.' (Across the kitchen I note Ursula raise her eyebrows in an 'Oh, *that's* what you think, is it?' kind of way.)

'Laser Wars? Great. That's perfect, in fact. I'll see you there. 'Bye.'

'Yeah, 'b . . .' But he's already hung up.

'What are you thinking?'

'Nothing.'

'*Liar.*'

Ursula appears to have an, in my opinion, unhealthy obsession with what I'm thinking. It can't be normal to ask a person, as often as she asks me, 'What are you thinking?' In fact, I know it's not normal. Because I'm normal, and I virtually *never* ask her what *she's* thinking.

I'm apparently not allowed, ever, to be thinking 'nothing'. Odd, really, when you consider the number of times – during an argument over something or other I've done – I'll have 'I don't believe it! What was going through your head? *Nothing?*' thrown over me. The fact is, I find thinking 'nothing' enormously easy. It's not something I've had to work at, either. For me, achieving a sort of Zen state is practically effortless. Perhaps 'Zen' is even my natural state. Sit me in a chair and do nothing more than leave me alone and – dink! – there I am: Zenned.

However, this – I think you'll agree – incandescently impressive reasoning would ching off Ursula into the sightless horizon like a bullet off a tank. 'Nothing' is simply not a thing I can possibly be thinking. For a while I did try having something prepared. You know, a stand-by. A list of things I could fall back on when caught with my synapses down. Thus:

'What are you thinking?'

'I was wondering whether we will ever, truly, get a unifying theory in physics. Or whether the divisions between Newtonian principles, relativity and quantum mechanics will always defeat attempts to craft a mathematically complete, always applicable whole.'

'*Liar.*'

So, another idea arcs into the waste bin, then.

However, on this occasion – sitting there on the sofa catching a few minutes' solitude before Jonathan and I go off Laser Warring – I have to admit that 'nothing' wasn't really what was shuffling around in my brain, kicking at pebbles. What was actually in residence was 'You know, nothing much, really'. Meaning, I was vaguely half-wondering what Terry Steven Russell wanted to see me for, when he'd be seeing me at work tomorrow anyway.

'OK, so what *am* I thinking about, then?' I plead defensively.

'I don't know, that's why I asked. Are you thinking about that house we looked at?'

'Yes.'

'No you're not.'

I exhale very slowly and for a long time. Too long, actually. It starts off as a weary sigh, but when it's hit a certain length I realise that, when it finishes, I'm going to be expected to say something. So I keep it going until I'm having to clench my stomach muscles to force the last bit of air out of my lungs. Finally, as if surfacing from a dive, I snatch a quick breath and use it to power 'What do you want for tea later?' My chances of this working are, admittedly, pretty poor.

'We were talking about that house.'

'No, we weren't.'

'Yes, we were.'

'No, we weren't. You just asked me if I was thinking about it.'

'And you said you were.'

'And you said I wasn't.'

'Well, were you?'

'I can't remember now.'

'You *liar*.'

Ursula and I can pass a whole day like this (and yet she complains we don't talk enough. Pfff – go figure that one out). As luck would have it, however, the phone rings to the rescue again. Ursula makes an impressive attempt at staring at me fixedly with an aura of 'Yes, that's right, the phone's ringing – so what? Let it ring. I'm trying to talk to you' determination about her. It is, however, *the phone*. She lasts three rings before cracking and dashing off into the other room to answer it.

I sharpen my ears to catch the defining first moments after she's picked up the receiver.

'Hello.' Then, again, '*Hello*.' But the second one, in addition to being coloured with recognition, also has a German intonation. One of Ursula's German friends has called her on the telephone. Phew. Edison? – I could kiss you.

So, then; Ursula. Fold your tray back on to the seat in front of you and ensure that all luggage is secured safely in the overhead lockers – here's Ursula.

Ursula comes from southern Germany – close to Stuttgart – and is five foot, eight and a half inches tall. Quite lengthy for a woman, I think. In my smokily recollected, pre-Ursula life, I'm sure I recall girlfriends routinely being happy to halt around the five-four, five-five mark. According to Ursula, this is merely because I was lazy and cowardly enough to go out with English Women ('English Women' to be ejected from the mouth in the manner one imagines Trotsky would utter 'strike-breakers'). She is solid in the opinion that five foot eight and a half is a perfectly average height for a woman – a little on the short side, even – and that English Women, quite transparently, stunt their own growth deliberately so as to appear all the more simpering to English Men (drunks and wasters, the lot of them).

As Ursula is my girlfriend of many years, I naturally rarely look at her any more. I register that her outline is there rather than actually *looking* at her. Purely for your benefit, however, I'll go rummaging around in the untidy basement of my memory to see if I can find where I left her features.

Ursula has blue eyes. Not the kind of chilling blue that art editors of women's magazines are scamperingly keen to paint on their cover models with Photoshop (so that it's hard to go into WH Smith's without feeling as if most of the Village of the Damned is staring at you from the shelves), but as blue as, say, some types of lavatory cleaner.

Below Ursula's eyes, as is the fashion nowadays, is her nose. A small thing, small and round. I can visualise Ursula's nose quite clearly. Possibly this is because I spend such a great deal of time with her looking at me down it.

Matching function with form, Ursula's mouth is large. She has extensive, pale pink lips behind which lies a great rank of the whitest, most flawless teeth not made in California by orthodontic craftsmen at great personal risk. You know those American beauty-queen mouths? The ones that appear above a bikini and say something about wanting to take blind children to the zoo before snapping into a smile that burns three layers of skin off the faces of all the onlookers? Well, get one of those and stick French actress lips on it and you have Ursula between nose and chin.

So, as a blissfully silent photograph, there's Ursula for you. A tall, blue-eyed blonde with a *Baywatch* mouth.

Not my type at all. But, well, that's not a big issue (I'm deep enough not to be put off a woman just because she's objectively attractive).

'Is it time to go to Laser Wars now? We've been waiting for a thousand hundred hours.' Jonathan is standing before me with a look of pained seriousness on his face. He is wearing red plastic wellington boots, Hawaiian shorts, the top from his Batman costume, a policeman's helmet made for a child at least four years older than he is, a cape he's constructed himself from two metres of floral curtain, and is holding a lightsaber. His small size merely adds weight to the impression that someone has conducted a terrifying scientific experiment aimed at compressing the Village People into the tiniest possible space.

'Yes. I think it probably is. Go and change into something less conspicuous.'

'Why? I'm a Jedi.'

'OK, then. But lose the cape. You'll fall over it and your mother will blame me.'

'Ohhhhh . . . I'll keep it on for now, but leave it in the car when we get there, OK? If I leave the cape here, Peter will get it and take my powers.'

'Wise, you are.'

Terry Steven Russell ('TSR' in general usage, incidentally) is pacing agitatedly about the foyer of Laser Wars when we arrive.

'You're late,' he says, astonished.

'Only by about two minutes, we . . .'

'Don't waste more time explaining – the time's gone, OK? Move on. Hello, Jonathan.' He glances at Jonathan's outfit. 'Well, if nothing else, we'll certainly have the element of surprise.'

It's a team-play game. On our side there's Jonathan, TSR, me and a pink-faced father with his two, pink-faced, sons. Frankly, I don't think they're going to be much help to us. Already they're bickering over who has which, identical, gun. Damn amateurs. When we get inside the arena proper, Jonathan immediately disappears. He's a sensitive child and much prefers to find somewhere to hunker down alone and

9

snipe at the enemy. TSR is crouched beside me, the Pink family off to our left – still quibbling internally.

'Will you *shut up*!' TSR hisses over at them. 'You'll get us all killed.'

Pink father frowns back at him. 'Steady on there. It's only a game.' A reply so staggeringly wrong headed that TSR and I can only stare at each other in disbelief and share a monosyllabic, head-shaking laugh.

Uh-oh, there it is – we're off. Keep it tight, soldier; this is for real.

An enemy child breaks cover and makes a dash for our position, firing wildly. Within a breath, a single laser beam spikes through the air and hits him right in the chest sensor. 'Awwwww!' he whines, disappointedly.

'Your mom,' Jonathan's voice calls out from somewhere in the darkness.

TSR and I are intermittently popping above the low cylinder we're using as cover, keeping the opposing forces pinned down with short bursts of fire. TSR drops back down from one of these harassing volleys and squints across at me. 'You know everything . . .' There's little point my denying this, so I merely raise my eyebrows in acknowledgment. 'What's the position with extradition treaties? Britain doesn't have one with Brazil, right?'

I jerk myself above the barricade and let rip with laser death at some attackers. One dives behind a box in panic like some kind of silly eight-year-old (admittedly, he does look about eight years old) but I catch his companion (who's eleven if he's a day) on the shoulder and take him down.

The defeated child is indignant. 'This sucks! I was never hit then – this sensor is rubbish!'

'Yeah, yeah . . .' I shout back from behind my cover. 'I own you.'

I turn again to TSR, licking my finger and making a '1' sign in the air. 'I think we do have a treaty with Brazil now. It takes *ages* for these things to get sorted, though. Even trying to extradite someone from America – where at least we speak, roughly, the same language – can go on for years. They just keep having endless legal arguments, and a missing comma in the papers means the whole thing gets put back another six months.'

'Mmmmm . . .' TSR hums in accompaniment to his thoughts. Our left flank is busy broadcasting how it'd lose badly to an army of Quakers. Pink Father's having some trouble with his gun of the 'pointing' kind. Pink Child One and Pink Child Two, meanwhile, have both decided to make a bolt forward at exactly the same time. The great god of ineptness smilingly accepts their offering; they run full into each other, there's a clash of heads, and they crumple to the floor in a wailing, clutching of noses.

'What about Asia?'

'Well, China doesn't have any laws. It just has whatever it thinks politically desirable that afternoon. Everywhere else has a sliding scale where the farther you get away from a major city the sillier the idea of a legal system seems.'

'I see. Do you know what the best form of defence is?'

'That, Major, would be "attack".'

'Indeed. WooooooaaaaaaaahhhHHHHHH – *cover me*!'

TSR commando-rolls out into the open area. I fling myself above the vinyl parapet and spit out savage red vengeance at any of the opposition who come into view. I'm not sure whether it's me alone or in combination with the icy sniping of Jonathan (who's still off somewhere, hidden, at one with the terrain), but TSR weaves across the field towards their position without taking a hit while mere feet ahead of him their men are cut down like gawping farm animals before they've had a chance to steady either their aim or their nerves. It's the kind of moment you experience perhaps only once or twice in a lifetime. I'm choking up now just thinking about it.

Needless to say, we won the battle. We were resoundingly

triumphant, in fact. Majestic, even. Our victory was slightly marred at the end by some nine-year-old on the other side weeping torrentially. It seems he'd been taken there for his birthday treat and then spent the entire time being killed unremittingly without getting more than about half a dozen shots off himself. But, hey, them's the breaks. It'll make him stronger the next time.

TSR fired a finger at us as we divided to go to our separate cars. 'Sterling work, gentlemen.'

After that, I saw him maybe two or three more times ever again.

THE CLEANERS WON'T LIKE IT –
I'LL TELL YOU THAT FOR NOTHING

Before the wall came down, you could go into the shops stitched around Friedrichstraße station in East Berlin and buy, well, crap: commemorative spoons, socialist toffee, 'My other car is an expression of effete, bourgeois dissolution' key fobs – that sort of thing. These shops were always staffed by heavy-set middle-aged women who looked like they'd spent the previous twenty-five years bludgeoning cattle to death in a state abattoir. They didn't own the shops, nor did it matter to them whether they sold two thousand novelty Stalinist purge fridge magnets each day or just sat there smoking Warsaw Pact-strength cigarettes among the same, unmoving stock until they were ready to collect their pensions. At a rough guess, I'd say their job motivation exceeded mine by about twelve-hundred-and-fifty per cent.

Look, there's no easy way to say this, so I'm just going to come right out with it, all right?

I work in a library.

There. There, I've told you, and I feel somehow cleansed. That said, I do need to press on pretty quickly and explain that it's not a public library. Ahhh, what a delicious dream that would be; old men with Thermos flasks quietly asleep in the newspaper section, erratically cut handouts for the women's keep-fit club at the local community centre, access to the lucrative Catherine Cookson reservation list – you could go gently mad in a place like that and never be bothered by anyone. Sadly, the cradling arms of such a library were not around me.

Presumably because I spent a previous life beating tiny

puppies with thorny sticks, I had been cast into the library at the University of North-Eastern England. 'UoNE' to its friends (which, at the last count, numbered the Vice-Chancellor, the Vice-Chancellor's personal financial adviser and the owner of the off-licence a dog's walk from the Vice-Chancellor's house).

As becomes its stature, the UoNE had its own logo (a Day-Glo orange 'UoNE' in shadowed blocks above the motto – written in ersatz, fast-flowing handwriting to convey a 'modern', 'pace-setting' feel – '*We take absolutely anyone*') and its own set of degree courses, including 'Scratch-card studies', 'Eggs and stuff you can do with them' and the groundbreaking 'Turning up'.

Yeah, pardon me. I jest.

I've said that I work in the library at the UoNE, but that was just me momentarily lapsing into the English language. Where I actually work is the 'Learning Centre'. A 'library', it came to someone as a particularly traumatic epiphany, evokes a place that holds books, whereas a 'Learning Centre' is a place that holds books and other stuff too; like computers, for example. You can see the problem. Go into a 'pub' that turned out to – what the *hell*? – provide a television showing satellite sports channels as well as selling beer, and all you thought you knew about semantics would spiral away into an unmappable chaos, yes? Equally, ask for the way to the library and some wag directing you to a learning centre instead could quite easily result in a shock that left you bald, skittish and unable to form satisfactory relationships for the rest of your life.

My job in the Learning Centre, on this particular Monday morning, was to be the Supervisor of the Computer Team. Please don't think that this makes me a techie, computer geek type. No, I took great pride in the fact that I really had very little idea what I was doing at all. A few key phrases will get you a long way in IT technical support. 'Ah, looks like a server problem', for example, has kept many a technician in paid employment for years. Another invaluable stand-by is to tut out a rueful smile and read aloud the name written on the computer in front of you – 'Yeah, the TX Series are notorious for doing this,' – that'll work for anything from the mouse pointer not moving to a minor fire. If you really want to get ahead, then a few minutes memorising the full meaning of a couple of dozen acronyms turns you from (let's say) some idiot with a degree in social geography and a mad German girlfriend into a powerful shaman. Casually let slip that the 'http' in web addresses is short, *of course*, for Hyper Text Transfer Protocol and your boss will infer that you have more than not the remotest idea whatsoever about how a hyper text transfer protocol functions – and then won't dare sack you for something as trivial as, say, none of the PCs in the building working.

The master of this kind of thing, the man uniformly regarded as the bullshitting giant of the IT industry, happened to be my line manager, TSR. TSR's diagnosis of some e-mail problem would form such a glittering and expansive vista of fabrication in front of the audience that many would leave not simply convinced but also genuinely moved. His capacity – at the click of fingers, mind – to weave a third of a fact, an eclectic selection of half-truths and deep pockets full of quickfire mendacity into a compelling argument was an inspiration to the Computer Team. Had he been on the *Titanic*, he'd have got all the lifeboats to himself and as he drifted away the people left on board the sinking vessel would have watched him from the deck, smiling and waving.

Unrelatedly, he looks like Satan.

Whether this look is deliberate is unclear. Some of it is just Nature doodling, but he did *choose* to wear a pointy-chinned beard and moustache combo of precisely the kind one sees attached to the Dark Lord of Torment in cautionary fourteenth-century woodcuts.

He is also the most impatient person in the history of the world. Terry Steven Russell has never, in all his life, heard the three beeps that tell you a microwave has finished.

We two, then, were the pulsating brain of the department's Computer Team. Below us sat a tier of genuinely frightening, semi-reformed hackers – Raj, Brian and Wayne. Each one of them impressed us at the interview stage by evoking in us the absolute certainty that if we didn't focus their energies within the confines of the UoNE, they'd surely end up sparking a computer-generated international missile exchange sooner rather than later. In all my time working with them I'd understood, in total, twelve to sixteen words they'd said. This is not only because they talk the most incomprehensible bollocks –

'Good weekend, Wayne?'

'Tuned my TCP/IP stack – *major* socket buffer tweakage was witnessed.' – but also because they couldn't, well, *speak*. They'd mutter, into their own chests. They'd trail off at the *beginning* of sentences. Every one of them was brilliant, no doubt about it. But it's lucky one can now order food over the Internet as I don't believe any of them could have entered a shop and conveyed 'I want a can of soup' with sufficient clarity to save them from starving to death.

Farther still down the chain of command were the Student Assistants. These were regular students who were paid at hourly rates to help out with the front-line technical support. Fortunately the desire to steal things from the storeroom ensured that they didn't fail to turn up for every single one of their shifts.

The expertly marshalled skills of the whole team were today focused on a crisis. The average IT support team in Britain has a major crisis about twice in any given eight-hour period. Here at the UoNE we flattered ourselves that we could regularly double that score. Today's mid-morning catastrophe was that the e-mail server wasn't working.

'Fix!' TSR directed our Three Wise Hackers, there being too little time in his universe for 'it'.

I followed up with an authoritative 'Ummmmm . . .' Which developed over time into 'Um . . . Um, what do we think the problem is?'

'I reckon it's aliens,' replied Wayne. 'SETI have been secretly destroying distress messages from outer space for years. It's payback time.'

'OK. Brian?'

'I reckon a server rack has blown.'

'Raj?'

'I agree with Wayne – it's aliens, all right.'

Behind me, I could hear TSR's breathing becoming ragged and erratic. I why-me'd my eyes heavenward then, with as much verve as I had to hand, listed out by fingers 'Right. Brian – go and take a look at the racks in the server room. Raj – find out if anybody else on the SuperJANET network is having trouble or if it's just us. Wayne . . . Wayne – check out the alien thing.'

They exited the office in a loping ribbon of KoЯn T-shirts, leaving TSR and me alone in our command centre.

'This place is a complete bloody circus,' he said, stabbing his finger repeatedly at the floor in front of his feet to stress the sentiment (though I assumed he meant the university as a whole, rather than just that particular piece of the carpet).

'Yeah.' I nodded, uncomfortably. 'And clowns are really scary, aren't they? I can't imagine how anyone ever looked at a clown and thought, "Ha! You've painted your face! Stop it – you're cracking me up." Maybe, when "a family day out" meant a public hanging, I can see how they could have been comedy relief, but their only function now is to frighten the crap out of me.'

'Can you see how you could have just replied "Yes" there, and not left me any worse off?'

'Well, of course, now you highlight it I can. And while

17

we're here clearing things up, what was all that yesterday about extradition laws?'

'What about them?'

'Yes, that's it; what about them? I know I don't have a very active social life, but I can count on one hand the number of times I've had a meeting at Laser Wars to discuss the international legal system.'

'I was just interested.'

'You were "just interested"? In extradition rules? On a Sunday morning?'

'Oh, come on, like you've never had that.'

'OK, OK, be enigmatic, see what it gets you.'

'Chicks. Chicks love enigmatic.'

'Ahhh, I don't need to invest in such cheap ornamentation any more. I'm out of that market. There's just Ursula and me, growing old together.'

'And that's better?'

'Yes. It's more efficient. With Ursula you get to grow old much quicker.'

'Yeah, well, whatever. I'm off to see Bernard. I'm not going to get dragged into faffing around, not now – I'll give Bernard a report on the situation so he's got something to tell the professionals when they start whingeing.'

Bernard Donnelly was our dysphoric Learning Centre Manager.

'What are you going to say?' I asked.

'Christ, how should I know? I haven't said it yet. Everything else is OK, isn't it? I don't want to be disturbed again.'

'Yeah. I think. I've got two Student Assistants who've swapped today's and tomorrow's night shifts. I think.'

'You think?'

'They're agricultural technology students from our Pacific Rim intake. I reckon I understand about one word in five they say, and I'm sure that puts me at about double the hit rate they have with my instructions. Anyway, they nodded and then sank back into that kind of silent, stoic misery that all the Pacific Rim students seem to favour, for some reason.'

TSR looked at me and said 'Yes,' to himself. 'Still, not our problem, eh?'

'Well . . .'

He'd finished listening and left the office; the effect was similar to someone turning down the gas under a pan of boiling milk. My natural condition, where I settle if not heated by events, is tepid. I'm happy to drift along at room temperature, equidistant from both Manic's crackling flames and Depressive's chill waters. TSR, however, is someone whose proximity alone is enough to double the volume on my nerves. Some people just 'give off' moods. That, I suppose, is what's called charisma. I don't have charisma. I *am* double-jointed – I can bend my thumbs back until they touch my upper forearms – which I like to think is pretty close to charisma, though.

After a few minutes, I noted from my PC screen – 'You have 217 new messages' – that the server must be up and running again.

Yo.

I wasn't allowed to enjoy the warming glow of apathy provoked by our success with the e-mail server for very long, however, because through the glass front of my office I saw the approach of Karen Rawbone.

Karen kindly gave you little time to become depressed by her approach by always scuttling right up to you at quite alarming speed – the hard thing, in fact, was to suppress your instinctive reaction upon noticing a body heading towards you at such a velocity and avoid protectively throwing your arms up in front of your face. A small woman with very tightly cropped black hair that made her head look a little like a used match, she was *just slightly* dumpy – nothing you'd even have noticed at all had it not contrasted so eerily with her fly-like speed. Her job was Learning Centre Student Liaison Officer (LCSLO). This meant that, though she was a librarian by training and psychology, she didn't have responsibility for a particular section but instead provided 'broad student support across all fields'. This didn't make her feel more important than everyone else. She already felt more important than everyone else, and her position just gave her a convenient excuse to express it.

'Pel,' she said.

'Karen, you've passed through the doorway. I thought vampires couldn't do that unless one invited them in?' I managed, after a fierce internal struggle, not to reply.

'Karen,' I said, instead.

'Pel, you're not going to believe this, hahaha . . .' She was one of those people who laughed at nothing. I wanted to seal her in a barrel with a litre of flesh-eating ants. '. . . but I'm going to run a student induction tomorrow over at the art faculty. So I'll need you to set up a laptop, projector, Net connection and display boards over there. There are about six boxes of handouts to take too. I kick off at nine in the morning – I'll be in one of the rooms on the second floor.'

'Witch,' I responded flatly, wringing a little pleasure from the homonym.

'24A – it's at the end of the corridor. Oh, can you carry some stuff up from Pierre's office too? Hahaha. He has a few sculptures contrasting the textures of lead and pig iron. The caretakers won't move them because the last time they did one of them cracked a vertebra and now the union's involved. They were getting all uppity about it. I said, "God, never mind, *Pel*'ll do it – problem solved." It's like they *look* for difficulties, it really is.'

Pierre was a lecturer in Dreadful Sculpture over at the art faculty. I'd only met him a couple of times but remembered he never broke eye contact and always left uncomfortably long gaps in his side of any conversation. I expect this made him 'intense'.

'OK, I'll go over there and set everything up tomorrow

morning,' I began to say, managing to get as far as 'O . . .' before the left-hand pane of my office window exploded inwards in a surge of spinning glass. The shards skidded across my desk, splintering and tumbling on to the carpet. I wasn't especially concerned about this because the bulk of my attention was focused on the two students who followed them, through the jagged hole in the window, into my monitor, across some minutes of a meeting about Consumables Purchasing and on to my lap. My chair being on wheels, the momentum caused all three of us to speed backwards across the room into a metal storage cabinet on the rear wall. The impact, in addition to making a noise a full three times as deafening as you'd reasonably expect the sound of three people in a swivel chair crashing into a huge metal storage locker to be, set the cabinet rocking and threw the brawling students from my lap on to the floor. Their departure was hugely fortunate, as a Hewlett Packard 840C printer that had been resting on top of the cabinet was tipped off and might have caused them serious injury had they not rolled away just in time to allow it to plummet into my groin instead. I took the opportunity to join them in writhing on the carpet.

After a few moments alone with my thoughts, I managed to push myself up on to all fours. The water in my eyes made the students a little indistinct; rather than a wrestling couple, they appeared to be a single, blurry, hyperactive amoeba rolling and bubbling across the office.

'You,' I squeaked. 'What are you doing?' I squeezed my eyes into my sleeve to absorb some of the tears and give myself a better view.

'This bastard deleted my essay!' shouted back the student on top, indicating the bastard he was talking about by punching him several times in the mouth.

'Fffmiminak!' countered the student on the bottom. An effective reply, as what he lacked in clarity he made up for by bleeding heavily. He did, however, then lose himself the unanimous sympathy vote by reaching out sideways to the broken printer lying on the floor and smashing his opponent across the side of the head with the sheet feeder. Still, that model is only made to hold fifty sheets, so it could have been worse.

At the edge of my vision I saw that Karen was still standing there, shuffling pieces of glass around with the toe of her shoe. 'It might be an idea to call Security,' I mentioned to her before turning back to the WWF qualifier. 'Pack it in. Pack it in, both of you – this isn't the Students' Union.' They shoved each other away and got unsteadily to their feet. I'd like to think it was my commanding presence, but it looked as if they'd both just run out of steam. 'OK, what's all this' – I waved an arm around at this – 'about?'

I was sprayed with the usual story, based on a disagreement about who had use of a PC. When I first joined the library, as it then was, it was open nine to five, had five PCs and usually eight students wanting to get on them. Now, with roughly the same number of undergraduates, the Learning Centre was open twenty-four hours a day, six days a week (twenty-two hours on a Sunday), had over 370 PCs and usually about 500 students wanting to get on them. Every single one of those 500 students was always fired up with the impatience that comes from not arriving to use a PC until fifteen minutes before their essay is due to be handed in. That's not to say they wouldn't be on the computers otherwise, of course, that's not the case at all. Sometimes they'd devote so much time to online chat that they'd barely have any left in which to play games or view pornography. They'd never come to type up and print their essays, however, until the fifteen-minute deadline has been reached. I think it's hormonal.

Inevitably, what would happen would be that a student doing his work would leave his PC for a moment to go to the toilet, have a cigarette, buy another packet of Pro Plus, or whatever. While that student was away, another student would become uncontrollably agitated by this 'free' PC, with its essay sitting idly on-screen, while knowing his own essay was due for delivery in fifteen minutes. He'd stomp over, log out the PC (losing the original student's essay entirely – that student wouldn't have backed it up anywhere), log in again and begin working on his own essay. The first student would return, there'd be an altercation, and they'd both end up crashing through the window of my office in a ball of shouting, scratching and biting. We did have a booking system, by the way, but the students regarded it as impossibly swottish to use it.

The current two were just finishing relating this tedious story to me when two men from Security arrived. The security staff had all recently attended the course on People Skills, run by a bubbly young woman with a whiteboard from Personnel Services. Therefore, they wisely avoided giving off any aggressive signals that might otherwise have inflamed the situation by sauntering slowly out of the lift with their hands in their pockets, chatting about the football scores.

'Tsk,' said one of them, looking around the office. 'Come on, lads.' And they all slowly ambled away together.

'So, it'll all be fine for nine a.m. tomorrow, then?' Karen asked.

'Yeah. Leave it with me.'

She walked from the office, shuffling past Raj, Wayne and Brian, who were just returning from successfully fixing the mail server and neutralising the alien threat. The three of them gazed about the shattered room, wide eyed, for a good dozen seconds before Wayne finally spoke.

'Cool!'

The top of First Born's head is an almost perfect oval. Spread across it, a film of bright blond hair – his mother's hair; thinner than overly thin strands that are fools for the lightest movement of air and flash iridescent when the sun stumbles into them. I have a picture in my wallet that shows his face. I refer to it from time to time, just to refresh my memory. I never see it directly any more as First Born (Jonathan – 'Jon' to his posse) is six years old and has had his face craned over his Game Boy at a permanent 45 degrees since a little past his fifth birthday.

The top of Second Born's head (Peter, aged three) is rounder. His hair is even more frighteningly blond than First Born's, but more confident. It rejects the submissive, fly away quality of his elder brother's and instead asserts itself away from his head at odd angles and in rebellious arabesques. I only see the top of *his* head because he's so small. He's a scampering thing that darts past me, constantly in urgent need of being somewhere else in his buttock-level world.

In temperament they are so different that, meeting them without background information, you would imagine Jonathan was the offspring of one of the Lake poets while Peter was raised by wolves. Jonathan is emotional and introspective, Peter carefully focused on learning how to kill a man with his thumbs. I see myself and Ursula clearly, clearly and equally, in both of them. Ursula herself says they're both just like me; whether she more often whispers this with a smile or bellows it angrily while jabbing a finger is too close to call.

Ursula, Jonathan, Peter and I lived together in a two-bedroomed Victorian terraced house. As the location of this house has 'some bearing' on what was about to happen, I'd better explain how we came to live there.

A little over eight years ago, Ursula and I had just returned from Germany, where we'd been living. She'd walked pretty easily into a job – she's a physiotherapist. Britain, at that time, was short of qualified physiotherapists and German ones were seen as especially attractive, being completely free from squeamishness about the twisting of the limbs of sick people in painful directions that is the physiotherapist's *raison d'être*. Quite remarkably (given a social geography degree and a CV in which playing guitar in a pub band was the high point), I too had found someone ironic enough to employ me. I was working in the medical library of a training hospital.

The only difficulty was that Ursula and I were living in different places. And not just metaphorically this time. Ursula had managed to get a room in the nurses' accommodation at the hospital where she worked. I tried this at the hospital where I worked, and encountered an impassable wall of knowing looks. So, I ended up lodging with some friends of mine, Martha and Phill, who were just buying their first house, could do with the extra income and also, I'm sure, felt like more of a family by having me there sitting on their sofa eating fish-finger sandwiches and (remote control readied at the TV) asking, 'Is anyone watching this?' Clearly, Ursula and I needed a place of our own, a gladiatorial arena in which we could grow.

I had a look around and discovered this: houses are dead expensive. No, really – they cost *thousands* of pounds. I spent a lot of time peering through estate agents' windows and sliding a blackening finger down the property pages of newspapers, hoping I'd bump into 'Three-bedroomed, detached residence in much-sought-after area. Owner has gone mad owing to a pituitary condition and will give house to first person who turns up with a bag of worming tablets and some wire wool.' The daily disappointment at not finding such a thing aged me.

Finally, in classic English fashion, I met a bloke in a pub. The bloke in question was an impressively barefaced pool cheat but, more relevantly, he was a builder working for a housing association. The government was providing grants to repair houses that would otherwise be left to fall into deeper and deeper dereliction and collect more and more urine from bored youths. They encouraged private companies to buy these houses, make sure the electrics, gas, etc. were better than potentially fatal, slap a bit of paint on the walls and tack factory-closure carpets on the floors, then sell them at cost. They made their money from the grant, not the sale of the house. So – a house you can just walk into without even having to decorate: £18,000. Thank you very much, I'll have one of those.

I tracked down the housing association and arranged a visit to a place they'd just finished. It was a fresh, sunny Wednesday afternoon when I first gazed upon what was to be our family home. The road itself was unremarkable; facing rows of terraced houses with tiny front gardens rolled out in a straight line. In the clear sunshine, it looked like the street where Mr Benn lived. The houses ended when the road decided to curve around a hospital. A huge Victorian hospital. Victorian architecture was designed to say this: 'We are the Victorians. And we're here to stay.' This place looked like God Himself had smashed its dark rectangle into the earth. A big, black, coffin of a building the weight of which made your shoulders sag just looking at it. In the other direction the houses were divided by two shops, facing each other. One was a standard, open-till-ten, urban newsagent's/off-licence/food store, while the other was a standard, open-till-ten, urban newsagent's/off-licence/food store. How did they both survive? I have no idea.

The man from the housing association (I forget his name, but let's be devils and call him 'Sexton') was waiting for me outside number 74 St Michael's Road when I arrived. He was in his late forties and possibly always had been. Too tall for his psychology, he hunched over the way the timid and lengthy sometimes do, fearful that his height might make him an uncomfortably conspicuous target if he didn't keep his head down.

He took me through the front door into the house, babbling things he'd clearly spent the journey there thinking he must mention, then half forgotten. Inside, it was a palace. A pristine palace crafted in woodchip wallpaper with magnolia emulsion and off-blue carpets so carefully free of any natural fibres that walking across just one room charged you up with enough static electricity to power every microwave oven in northern England – by the time I'd reached the living room I had an Afro.

'If you like it, we can keep it until you have a mortgage sorted out,' said Sexton. 'We'd need a deposit, of course.' He bit at his lip nervously. 'A hundred pounds.'

I tried for a wary 'Hummm . . .' It passed from my mouth as an excited little yelp.

'I've found our home,' I told Ursula. I was careful to say 'home' instead of 'house'. Women respond to that kind of thing.

'Where is it?'

'Really close to the city centre. You could go out and buy a blender on the spur of the moment.'

'Has it got central heating?'

'There's a place for it.' I took some milk for our tea from the fridge in the communal nurses' kitchen, using the felt pen I carried for the purpose to redo the mark on the side of whoever's bottle it was. 'We can just move right in and sit down in front of the TV. Everything's decorated. There's electricity, windows, the lot.'

'How do we pay for it?'

'Pfff – eighteen thousand pounds. We'll be lucky if we're

not outpaced by inflation. Ask for a five-year mortgage and they'll think we're dragging our feet.'

I could see Ursula was starting to think about the implications of what I was saying. Always best to nip that kind of thing in the bud.

'It's got a really big bathroom too,' I continued. 'Absolutely massive. We could hold parties in it.'

'How many bedrooms?'

'Two. But it feels like three.'

'In what way, may I ask, can two bedrooms feel like three?'

'On an emotional level.'

'Ah.'

'Look, the bottom line is it's a nice place and it's eighteen thousand pounds. Eighteen. Thousand. Pounds. There are some houses that are actually on fire that cost more than that. Come on. What do you say?'

'Oh . . . OK. OK, let's do it. But I want you to know that if anything goes wrong it'll be your fault.'

'Nothing will go wrong.'

'I mean it. I'm holding you responsible.'

'Just so long as you're holding me, my darling.'

'Get off me, you're spilling my tea.'

The stuff from Ursula's single room in the nurses' flats filled the entire house. Unpacking each of her boxes was like opening a parachute; I'd cut a piece of string and be immediately engulfed by an explosion of personal effects. Every last one of them a staggeringly useless piece of crap, incidentally.

Ursula is not like me. I believe effort is a finite resource, something to be used only when no other option is available. For me, half-heartedness is a full quarter too hearted. She, on the other hand, heaves herself into everything she does with the unreserved exertion of a sprinter lunging for the tape. My plans for the house stretched to buying a sofa and sitting on it, whereas Ursula's seemed to involve building on an extra wing.

First of all there was the garden. I hadn't even bothered to look out of the windows at the rear of the house to examine the garden when Sexton had originally shown me round. I'm not a garden person. When we'd gone to view the house together and, at Ursula's command, I did glance outside it was clear that bringing it under control would be best achieved not by a mower but by several months of strategic bombing.

'OK,' I said, knowing that the job couldn't be avoided, 'I'll machete everything down then I'll lay some Astroturf.'

'Don't be stupid.'

'I'm not. It doesn't cost much more than normal turf.'

'I want proper grass.'

'Astroturf is better than proper grass, it's designed specifically to be better than proper grass. It has only one reason for existence, and that's to beat grass at its own game.'

'You just want something you don't have to mow.'

'And that makes me what? An Evil Genius?'

'How unlike you to add the word "genius" there. What it makes you is idle. But we knew that anyway, and I am still not having a garden with plastic grass, it's not natural.'

'Who wants natural? *That* . . .' I made a theatrical sweep of my arm gardenwards. '*That's* natural. And, frankly, I fear what creatures may lie within its dark interior. Anyway, what's wrong with not wanting to have to keep mowing the lawn? I didn't make a thing about buying a washing machine. I didn't say, "You just want to get out of beating our clothes against a rock, you lazy tart," did I?'

'Don't call me a tart.'

'I wasn't calling you a tart. I was saying how I, unarguably, hadn't called you a tart, if anything.'

'We're having proper grass.'

As a compromise, we had proper grass.

The inside of the house was more of a long haul. There

was, for example, a bed and a refrigerator to buy, which I'd expected. I didn't know, however, that when you get a house you also need to buy monstrous amounts of pointless rubbish. Toilet-roll holders, lampshades, a trio of candlesticks of cleverly diminishing height and Mondrian-themed coasters. There's a thin line that divides the man you were from the person shuffling around Ikea with a stupid big yellow bag and dead eyes.

Eventually, though, we reached the stage where we were treading water more or less comfortably. I had my games console set up, Ursula had her phone, we'd meet at the microwave and exchange information over the gentle domestic hum of a warming lasagne. Even with the car insurance (given the area, it approached four figures to insure our VW Polo), we weren't too badly off money-wise because our mortgage was so low. When it rained heavily the water did come in under the kitchen door, but we could afford sturdy shoes and thus our spirits remained unbroken.

We strolled along like this for some months. Then, one Saturday afternoon as I was sitting on the sofa circling programmes in the TV guide, Ursula came into the room. She stopped, standing directly in front of me, as she does sometimes when she wants to say something from a position where she can block my escape. I carried on studying the guide for some time before glancing up at her (there are rules, after all). When I did so she spoke with spirit-level evenness.

'I'm pregnant.'

'Phew, thank God. I was beginning to think all of that sex was for nothing.'

She clicked her teeth. 'That's good. That's really good. Because all the times I've played this moment out, practising it in my mind, that's always been precisely the reaction I hoped for most dearly.'

'OK, come in again and try it. I'll faint or something. I'm really pleased – I mean, obviously, I'm most, most pleased.

We were trying, though – well, I was certainly trying extremely hard, and I remember you being there – so, it's not like it's just come out of nowhere.'

'Excuse me and my run-of-the-mill conception.'

There was a slight pause. I think I coughed like people do before the show starts in theatres.

'Well?' she asked. 'Are you going to hug me any time soon, or what?'

'No problem.' And I hugged her.

Hugged her as the music swelled, I thought. She obviously filed the moment away, however, because three years later she announced the approach of Second Born by coming into the room and saying, 'I'm pregnant. And it's not yours.' You've got to admire a woman who can spend three years preparing to make a point, haven't you?

That's the history of how we came, all four of us, to be living here. Ursula, however, was forthright in her opinion that *here* isn't where we should be living at all. As you might have guessed, the catch with our cheap house was that it was in an area of the north-east of England so dire that the Government was applying for a grant from the European Union to pay for it to be placed under martial law. It was good for the shops, which was enough for me, but Ursula took exception to the joy-riders, break-ins and occasional street riots. Naturally, I'd hate to admit that Ursula is ever right about anything, but one of her points was that it wasn't a good place in which to bring up children. She did have the appearance of rightness here, I'd have to concede (give the kids a cardboard box with wheels drawn on it and Jonathan would excitedly say to Peter, 'OK, you be the one who hot-wires the engine, I'll be the one who breaks the steering lock.').

Ursula had again mentioned, over the course of some forty minutes, her desire to move during breakfast. I was weakly mulling this over in my head at work as I waited for the arrival of lunch. At 1 p.m. each day I had lunch with Tracey and Roo. It was simply a question of pulling myself through the morning by my fingernails until I reached that point. And it's surprising how draining giving the appearance of doing something can be too. Sometimes, by the time I broke for lunch, my face was actually aching from maintaining the furrows that hinted at complex calculations taking place behind them. Occasionally I'd snap and just have to do some work to wind down. It always led to terrible self-recriminations, though, because there were more than enough people in the university who were devoting most of their day to finding work for me to do; to begin searching it out for myself was surely just the kind of wasteful duplication of effort that senior management was anxious to eliminate.

These were the kind of dilemmas I had to wrestle with each day until lunch-time arrived. So, obviously, thinking constructively about moving house *as well* would have been too much for anyone.

'You can kill one person – who will it be?' I was carrying my tea and bacon sandwich over to the table where Tracey and Roo were already seated.

'The Pope and Zoe Ball,' a cloud of cigarette smoke from Roo replied.

'Technically,' Tracey squinted, 'That's two people.'

'Whatever. I'll play my joker. There's no way I could pick one or the other, it's a real Sophie's Choice situation. If I killed just the one, the nagging doubts and self-loathing would cripple me emotionally in later years.'

I spoke through half a mouthful of sandwich.

'I don't claim to keep up to date with movements in theological thought, as you know. But, you being a Catholic, wouldn't killing the Pope count as, well, a sin, really?'

'I'm sure it might if I *weren't* Catholic. If I weren't a Catholic it might well be seen as simply going after some old bloke in a hat. Killing some old bloke in a hat definitely *is* a sin – the Church is quite clear on that. But, as a Catholic, because my life is supposed to be directly affected by every wacky thought that pops into his head, I think it's simply my contribution to the debate.'

Roo worked in a comic shop close to the university. And before you start picturing person-who-works-in-a-comic-shop stereotypes, let me tell you that you're entirely correct on all levels. The people of the earth were just diaphanous cut-outs in the World of Roo. Perhaps we had real lives, families, a history – he wouldn't rule it out as a possibility. But we were clearly less substantial, less solid and less genuine than, say, the Preacher or Strontium Dog. Roo himself was aged somewhere between nineteen and fifty-two and extruded into his never-varying T-shirt-and-jeans ensemble was a frame constructed entirely of bony right angles; just sitting next to him gave you the uneasy feeling that your body fat was being sucked right out of you as Nature struggled to achieve some sort of equilibrium. Also, he'd decided to go prematurely bald. It's hard to map out the logical route in any satisfying fashion, but, like a good deal of men, Roo had decided to disguise the fact that he was losing hair by shaving all his hair off. His head was a large, etiolated, shoulder joint with a cigarette stuck in it.

'I quite like the Pope,' Tracey replied.

'And that has nothing to do with your liking to dress up as a nun, I suppose?' I narrowly beat Roo in replying.

'Nothing. I just think he's sweet. And he speaks all those languages.'

Roo sighed.

'Imagine a man is running along the street,' he said.

'What?' Tracey pulled a face at him.

'Imagine a man is running along the street.'

'Um, OK.'

'He's racing away, desperate to catch a bus that he sees is

two hundred yards ahead of him, its indicator already flashing to pull out.'

'Right.'

'The man sprints towards it for all he's worth – arms waving, loose change flying out of his pockets.'

'Yes.'

'But, while he's still a good hundred and fifty yards away, he stumbles over a small dog – a Yorkshire terrier, perhaps – that disinterestedly crosses his path. He falls. Spinning awkwardly on to the pavement into the cruel oasis created by other pedestrians leaping out of the way. Failure. Wasted effort. A jagged rip in the elbow of his jacket where it's hit the ground. Ahead, unknowing, the bus pulls away and he's missed it.'

'Uh-huh.'

'Now, instead of a man, imagine it's you, and instead of a bus it's "The Point".'

'Cheers for that. It's certainly cleared up a few worries I was having. Also, you're a twat.'

'Who cares if he can speak two hundred languages? He's *the Pope*. Polyglot bollocks is still bollocks. I'd prefer a Pope who only spoke Cornish, but talked less crap in it.'

'I'm afraid I have to agree with Roo on this one,' I admitted.

'You would. But – Newsflash! – atheists aren't allowed to choose popes.'

'Tsh. I'm not talking about the Pope specifically, I mean the general principle. It's completely irrelevant whether he's a super-linguist or not. Look, say there's this bloke . . .'

'If he's running for a bus, I'm leaving this table right now.'

'. . . and this bloke is the type who'll say, "Aww, I know I've got a particularly heavy day at work tomorrow, but to hell with it, I'll muddle through it somehow; let's the two of us just get utterly wrecked and go out clubbing!" Now, he's exactly the kind of person who'd make a great and valued friend. But is probably not someone you'd want to be performing your vasectomy. You see? Different roles, different requirements.'

'I'm starting to suspect that this is just jealousy. You're both bitter about the fact that you talk so much bollocks but no one's made either of you Pope.'

'I must admit that I'm surprised that no one's made Terry Steven Russell Pope yet. He's been talking bollocks at international level for years.'

'Maybe they *have* made him Pope. He is leaving the university, after all,' Tracey replied into her tea.

'Eh? TSR's leaving?'

'Yeah, he's got another job somewhere, I think.'

I looked across at Roo, who nodded confirmingly.

This was how things worked at the UoNE. Any information worth knowing surfaced in Patrick's Cafe long before you learnt it via one of the thousand project groups and campus teams set up to ensure rapid communication at all levels. You'd buy your food next to a couple of gossiping secretaries, sit at a table behind a huddle of staff from Pensions grumbling about some new initiative that was approaching – many people even arranged actual meetings there because it was neutral territory (and they could smoke). If the UoNE was World War II, then Patrick's Cafe was Rick's Nightclub in Casablanca. Because Tracey and Roo spent ages in Patrick's drinking coffee and lazily eavesdropping, they were both tremendously well informed – and Tracey didn't work for the university either. She was an assistant at a shop in the city centre that specialised in what's known as 'playwear': nurses' outfits, rubber basques and crotchless lederhosen – it was a pretty buoyant market, apparently. Who bought this stuff I couldn't imagine. I'd given up after just a couple of attempts at buying Ursula very mild, lacy affairs only to have them dangled in front me – gripped contemptuously between her index finger and thumb, in the fashion one might display a tramp's sock – and be asked, 'And somewhere in the pit of your mind you had the thought I might wear these, did you?' The sheer amount of playwear being sold means every third person you pass in the street must surely be hurrying home to slip into a latex air hostess's uniform, though. (A slightly disturbing thought, when you actually try to pick out the one in three it could be.)

'When did you hear he was leaving? Where's he going?' I asked.

Tracey shrugged. 'No idea where he's going, but it's been common knowledge he *is* going for, oh, a week or so.'

Roo, apropos of not the slightest thing, began talking about stuff he'd quite like to rub on to Anna Nicole Smith but, despite his conveying his thoughts with real enthusiasm and much evocative detail, I was only half listening. TSR leaving? He'd kept that quiet.

I tried to find him to ask about it when I returned to work in the afternoon. But he was unassailably unlocatable, and then a group of students trying to steal a fire extinguisher for a party accidentally set it off in the lift as they were leaving. The doors opened to reveal a kind of furiously angry Santa's grotto, and I got embroiled in a dispute. They argued that the fire extinguisher was unduly easy to activate and if the foam had damaged any of their property or clothing, therefore, they were going to sue the university and me personally for every penny we had. The legal arguments dragged on until I, regrettably, had to go home.

'How was work?'

Ursula was holding Second Born by the face as she brushed his teeth, the speed and vigour of the operation causing Colgate to foam out of his mouth, rabidly. He appeared to have completely given himself up to her grip, like a kitten being carried by the neck in its mother's mouth. I suspected he might just be practising the indifferent submission to facial manipulation he'll use while being stitched up by his coach when he's fighting to retain the title of Heavyweight Kickboxing Champion of the World for the fifth time, about six years from now.

'Oh, you know, same as always.'

'Uh-huh.' She heaved Peter over the sink and commanded, '*Ausspucken*.'

He ausspucked, some of the spit even going in the sink, and then his legs began to cycle in midair. Ursula set him down and they caught on the floor, sending him crashing hinge-splinteringly through two doors, laughing at the impacts.

'About now, a proper boyfriend would be asking me how *my* day was.'

'Even if that boyfriend had had the common decency not to bother his girlfriend with meandering and inconclusive descriptions of his own work? Even then?'

'Vanessa was a cow in the hospital finance meeting, again.'

'Right,' I said.

'You just don't care, do you?'

'Don't be stupid, I . . .'

'Don't call me stupid.'

'I wasn't calling you stupid, I was simply suggesting you should avoid *being* stupid about a specific thing.'

'That's the same.'

'No. "You are stupid" is the same, "Don't *be* stupid" is quite appreciably different. Now we've cleared that up, let's return to "Right". Which wasn't "Right" in its "I don't care" sense but in the more common "I see. But we've talked about this before, at draining length, and I don't feel there's anything else I can add to where we left off after the previous nineteen discussions, so maybe we should not do it all again and just let Pel go and watch the news in peace" meaning of the word.'

'You have no interpersonal skills *whatsoever*, do you?'

'Yes, I do.'

'No, you don't.'

'Yes – I do.'

'No – you don't.'

'Yes – I *do*.'

'*No, you don't.*'

'Let's stop right there, OK? Before this gets childish.' (I whispered 'I do' too quietly for her to hear.)

'Vanessa . . .'

'Vanessa. How *is* she these days?'

'Vanessa told me I'd have to resubmit all this week's details and stormed out before I could say anything. I don't even know why.'

'Because she hates you.'

'That's no excuse.'

'You arouse strong passions in people – trust me. But that's beside the point. The point is that Vanessa looks like a baboon.'

'Eh? No, the point is I'm fed up with it.' Ursula took a tub of coleslaw from the fridge. 'It just makes me want to give up work and stay at home with the kids.'

'Yes, obviously, but we've talked about that, haven't we? Do you recall the phrase "starving to death"? It came up a lot. Are you going to eat that coleslaw?'

'I am.'

'I see.'

'Meaning?'

'Nothing. Nothing at all. Predominantly onions and raw cabbage, isn't it? Coleslaw.'

'So?'

'I was just thinking about how we might have been having sex tonight.'

'And you'd planned on involving me, had you?'

'Well . . .'

'You know what I hate the most?'

'Oh, come on – I only asked you to do that once.'

'What I hate the most is not simply that you want to control my diet for your increased sexual gratification, but that you

38

don't just come out and say it straight. It's all "I see you're eating curry, then" and "Has that got garlic in it?" Like you're leaving me to take the next step and think, "Hold on – garlic! What *am* I thinking?" So, I'm just going to ignore you. I'm going to eat this entire tub of coleslaw, and if you love me it shouldn't matter.'

'Oh, the Love Is Stronger Than Onions defence. I'll tell you what I'll do; I'll wear these underpants for two weeks then get back to you on that, OK?'

'If I didn't do the washing, you'd *always* wear your underpants for two weeks and we both know it.'

Having kind of lost the mood, sex-wise, when Ursula and I went to bed later we assumed Angry Position Four. It's a sort of 'X' shape, each of us forming one side of the letter. It's not *quite* an 'X', though, because we're not joined in the middle. That would require our bottoms to be touching. None of the Angry Positions allow for any touching of body parts – that would completely ruin them. Sounds are certainly allowed, and in some positions they're pretty much mandatory. Take Angry Position Two, where one person is in the standard half-'X' shape (facing away) and the other is a rigid 'I'; lying supine, eyes wide open, staring at the ceiling. Here you lose points for style if the 'I' person doesn't let out frequent sighs and snorts in an attempt to get the half-'X'-er to ask, 'What is it?' No touching, though, ever.

Locked in my position, I eventually fell asleep. It took ages, of course. It always takes ages to get to sleep when you're in an Angry Position because you fight it. You want to stay awake just in case the other person makes some comment and you can respond to it by pretending to be asleep.

In the basement of an Amsterdam sex museum, Helena Bonham Carter is standing before me, breathless and glistening with honey. She had just sighed, 'I want you, Pel – I've always wanted you,' when Ursula dragged me by a shaking shoulder back to St Michael's Street and a gummy, deflating wakefulness.

'Did you hear that?'

'No.'

'I'm sure I heard the door bang.'

'It was probably just a dog somewhere.'

'Yes, because – at night – a dog barking is almost indistinguishable from the sound of a door being smashed open, isn't it? Idiot.'

'I didn't say a dog *barking* . . .'

'Quiet. Listen . . .'

I listened. I heard silence.

'Well, I can't hear anything.'

'Go down and have a look.'

'Oh, for God's sake.'

'Go on, you're the man.'

'Why do your feminist principles always vaporise when one of us needs to get out of a warm bed and clomp downstairs at three o'clock in the morning?'

'What if there's someone down there? Do you *want* me to be murdered?'

'Do you want *me* to be murdered?'

'Just shut up and have a look downstairs, will you. It– there! You must have heard that!'

I did. There was a definite sound of movement from somewhere below. I simply can't tell you how depressing this was. Someone had apparently broken into our house while we were asleep upstairs. The unavoidable conclusion was that Ursula was right. Bad enough simply that she should be right, obviously, but thinking about the rewards she would be able to harvest here made a gust of cold nausea rush over me. Every single time she suspected she heard a noise in the middle of the night from now on, I would *have* to get up and investigate it; all my weary protestations would be broken beneath the heel of 'Go on – you remember that time when . . .' I could have cried, I really could.

I tugged on some trainers from under the bed and crept towards the door. Yes, crept, for some reason. Lord knows why; the person downstairs should be creeping, I'm entitled to walk about quite normally – it's my house.

'Be careful,' whispered Ursula as I opened the bedroom door.

'And what is that supposed to mean? You know, *specifically*?'

'Just, "be careful", that's all. Be careful. There could be several of them down there, half mad on crack – they might have guns.'

'I see . . . But you still want me to go down there, right?'

'Yes, yes, hurry up, will you.' She pulled a single arm out from under the duvet and shooed me doorwards.

Resignedly, I stepped out on to the landing and squinted down the darkened stairs. I paused for a moment to gather my thoughts. But it didn't take as long as I expected because the only thought going through my head turned out to be 'Bugger'. As I moved down the steps, closer to the door leading from the stairs to the living room, the noises become more distinct. By the time I was at the bottom of the stairs, paused by the door, the sounds could even be divided into categories. There was some shuffling, a bit of scraping and a moderate amount of grunting. If forced to choose, I'd have had to say that my least favourite was the grunting. It was hard to think of anything that could possibly be going on beyond the door that was both the cause of grunting and also something I'd like to witness. Still, whatever was the other side, it was certainly going to be preferable to step out into it than to go back upstairs to Ursula if I didn't. I flicked the handle and strode through the door.

Jesus, what a mess. The living room was a scene of madness, with children's toys and magazines scattered all over the place. Precisely, then, as I had left it when I went up to bed. I would have taken comfort in this confusion and disorder if the edge of my vision hadn't registered a large shape moving out of the living room just as I entered it. It disappeared into the front room before I even had a chance to turn my head.

I quickly jogged across to the door between the living room

and the front room. There, a room's length ahead of me, I saw our microwave moving speedily out into the street in the arms of a stocky man in an unflattering shell suit. He must have heard me, because he jerked a glance over his shoulder and our eyes locked. I pushed my hand up into the air, index finger extended, as one might do when hailing a taxi.

'Um. Excuse me . . .'

Commanding, eh?

He was obviously not interested in what else I might have to say because he instantly sprinted forward through the front gate and began legging it down the road. I shouted out a general-purpose 'Oi!' and started to run after him. Clearly, Ursula had been following the movement of the sounds from above, because as I left the house she was leaning out of our bedroom window, directly above me, screaming at the escaping burglar, 'You *wan*ker!'

She continued to shout things along a similar theme as I raced down the path after the intruder. In addition, she hurled a heavy Birkenstock sandal at him. Which hit me on the back of the head. 'Cheers,' I shouted to her, without looking back, 'that helped.'

The bloke continued to plunge down the road, phasing in and out as he passed between those few streetlights that the community's children hadn't smashed during stone-throwing practice. I kept up my end of the deal by hurling myself along after him. 'Why?' might be a question worth asking, because Lord knows what I thought I'd do if I caught him. Plead for my life seemed the most likely prospect. He jigged off down a side street. I rounded the same corner just in time to see him cut sideways again, this time down an alley that ran between the houses. He was about twenty yards ahead of me when I made the turn, his feet making heavy, but rapid, heartbeat thumps on the hard-packed soil of the ground.

Now, perhaps I'd let myself go a bit. Perhaps, getting just a little more exercise wouldn't have been a bad idea, all things considered. This bloke couldn't run anywhere but straight ahead in the alleyway, but it hardly mattered, as he was clearly outpacing me. And, well, you know – he was carrying a microwave oven. My breathing, on the other hand, had started to include what sounded promisingly like a proto-death-rattle, while my legs seemed to have become drunk. My brain was definitely calling, 'Run – run like the wind!', but my legs were now just rubbery stilts swinging beneath me with no coordination and very little decency. It was time to stop. I flapped to a halt and folded myself over with my arms stretched out down to my knees, forming a large, wobbling 'P'. Looking up, I watched the burglar sprint away into the night. Exhaustedly, I shook a weary fist and, interrupting myself for gasps for air, coughed out a barely audible 'And don't come back.'

When I returned to the house, Ursula was standing on the doorstep, wearing one Birkenstock. 'What happened?'

'There was a car waiting for him,' I said, pointing somewhere.

I called the police and we all went through the ritual. It appeared that our burglar had made off with not only the microwave but also some spoons – the kitchen drawer was open, and the spoons were missing. Maybe later at their secret hideout he'd joined up with an accomplice who'd spent the night stealing soup. Who knows? The fact was, I couldn't see the North-East Police Force sweeping the area with helicopters on the basis of such a haul. We had to go through the process, however, because you need a crime report number for the insurance claim.

I was rather het up. It was a crap time of the night, I was holding a cup of cold tea (which was made worse by the fact that I took a sip then thought, 'Tsk, cold. I'll just give it thirty seconds in the microwav-ggnnhh-ack . . .'), and as she walked around the living room, Jonathan dozing over her shoulder,

Ursula was giving me looks – awful looks, awful, awful looks; I was thinking of begging the police to stay with me. Peter would sleep through a gas main exploding, but the talking and general commotion had woken Jonathan up. He'd plodded downstairs into the room with that look of pale and wobbly, semi-sentient puzzlement that children get when woken unexpectedly in the middle of the night. All sleepy, squinting confusion.

I was very angry indeed.

What our visitor had done to get into the house was to take a short length of scaffolding from some building work that was going on a little way down the road. He'd used this like a makeshift battering ram, slamming it, presumably at a run, right into the lock on the front door. This lock (and the others; we'd added a lock after each of our two, previous, burglaries in a little commemorative ceremony) had held together in itself but the wood had simply shattered in the door frame. The locks dangled uselessly from the open door, each one like the pathetically broken wing of a bird. The police had explained the subtlety of this to me, thereby revealing its commonplace, calculated coolness. It appears, and once pointed out it seems obvious, that breaking into a house in which people are asleep is far less likely to be successful if the burglar, say, crowbars the door open. That way you get a more drawn-out succession of splintering and snapping. If, however, you smash everything in one immense impact you only produce a single, if larger, noise. Because it's not prolonged or staged, the sleeping occupants are likely to register it through the blanket of their sleep but, because it has no follow-up, slip back into unconsciousness before they've even truly woken up. The wily thief batters open the door in one go and retreats. If no one appears after a few minutes he's fairly safe in assuming the danger has passed and he can just stroll into the house and go about his business.

Gazing at the evidence of such premeditated and maddening

aplomb is going to set the muscles in your jaw flexing under any circumstances, but I was inflammably angry beyond my body's capacity. Casually break into my house, while I'm asleep upstairs, and I'd quite like to arrange for your throat to be torn out by a swarm of small dogs whatever my domestic situation. It wasn't just me in this house, though. Ursula was there, for one thing. Unprepared in her knee-length, Guinness T-shirt with the holes in both armpits and odd-sized woolly socks; she might have been lying, unknowing, in bed while just a staircase away some bastard had the run of the house. Even worse – even worse by twice the length of my anger – were the children. That this person was inside while the boys, suddenly heart-rendingly small in my mind, slept open mouthed, curled and trusting upstairs, made me so furious that I felt as if I were running around inside my brain sticking frantic fingers into the popping civilised dyke that was bulging against the pressure of rage behind it. I made a token effort to pity the burlgar, of course. But the musing that started with 'social inequality' and 'lack of opportunities' drifted easily into a vision of him taped to a chair in some deserted warehouse while I beat him with lengths of electrical cable. Angry liberals, eh? Fear us.

Fortunately, as a conversation with Ursula was pretty much inevitable at this point, the police stayed for a good forty minutes taking down all the details, and my sizzling wrath had a good while to be muffled by formalities. Eventually, though, the two officers left. As she passed through the door the policewoman stroked the ruptured wood of the frame and glanced back at us. 'Why on earth do you carry on living in this area?'

'It's good for the shops,' replied Ursula. Directing the response not to her but to me. And adding a stare that only just fell short of igniting my hair. I closed the door (by pushing a chair behind it) and turned round to face Ursula's silence.

'I know. I *know*. OK?' I said.

I slunk off to make a quick call to our preferred emergency locksmith while she carried Jonathan upstairs and laid him down, asleep, in our bed. She was waiting, perched on the edge, arms folded in front of her in a viciously taut knot, when I crept into the room.

'I think,' I said seriously, 'that we're beyond where it's at all useful to start apportioning blame.' I was aware of my own breathing.

'All of us could have been bludgeoned to death in our sleep. And for you, by the way, that's still a real possibility.'

'These things happen. We were just unlucky. OK, I know that living in this area might have increased the chances of it happening, but . . .'

'No, just shut up the fuck . . .'

'That's "shut – the fuck – *up*".' (I can't stop myself, I really can't.)

'I believe,' Ursula replied, and I couldn't help but notice that she was beginning to make little fists, 'that my meaning was clear. Now – Shut. Up. *The fuck*. Do you understand?'

'I . . . yes.'

'This area, and it's your fault we live here, don't forget, is the unfashionable end of hell. I've had enough of it. And I'd already had more than enough of it. So *now*, I've . . . I've . . .'

'Y . . .'

'Complete my sentence for me and I'll rip your lungs out, I swear it. So, *now* . . . I've had enough of it. You are going to every estate agent in the city tomorrow and getting a list of houses for sale.'

'OK.'

'Then you are going to make appointments to see every possible one.'

'OK.'

'Because we're not living here a second longer than we have to.'

'Yes.'

'You're going to those estate agents tomorrow.'

'Yes, yes – this is the sound of me agreeing with you. You can stop now, I'm saying "yes".'

'You're going to them tomorrow.'

'Hghh – tomorrow, yes.'

'You *are* going, don't think you're not.'

'Will you stop it? I'll go, you can finish talking now.'

'And it's all your fault.'

'It is.'

'Because you talked me into our buying this house, so it's your fault.'

'Look, I've surrendered here. Yes, you're right. You're right. I don't know how I can make that any plainer. You are right, and I'm admitting it. What do you want me to do? Walk through the streets with a sign round my neck?'

'This is just typical of England. People don't get burgled in Germany.'

'Er . . . I think that might not be true.'

'It is. I was never burgled there, neither was anyone I knew. It's just something that doesn't happen.'

'Oh, sorry – I didn't realise you had the figures to back it up.'

'Tomorrow you're going straight to all the estate agents.'

'I thought we'd covered this?'

'I'm not going to let this go.'

'Yes, I'd picked up on that.'

'We went to see that house a while ago and then you faffed around until it was sold.'

'I didn't faff. That house was a non-starter. It cost a hundred and fifty thousand pounds. We couldn't have afforded a tent in the driveway.'

'But it was lovely.'

'So's Bali – let's buy that.'

'You're going to the estate agents tomorrow.'

'*Yes.*'

'Because, we're moving – point.'

'You mean "We're moving – full stop".'

'I'm going to hit you in the face.'

The next morning I called into work sick – you're allowed to be sick, of course, but being burgled is your own damn fault – so I could have the day off to sort out the locks and insurance. Also, I thought I might go to some estate agents.

All estate agents should be put on a decommissioned naval frigate which is then towed out into the deepest part of the Atlantic and sunk. It's rather unfortunate that, in recent years, estate agents have become comedy *bêtes-noires*. Rather like lawyers or double-glazing salesmen. Every time they mention their job they probably get people amusingly making the sign of the cross at them or are subjected to some good-natured, humorous ribbing. This has the effect of distorting what I'm trying to say here, which isn't in the nature of a smiling roll of the eyes and a 'Tsk, estate agents, eh?' but rather 'All estate agents should be put on a decommissioned naval frigate which is then towed out into the deepest part of the Atlantic and sunk'. Still, I went around the city centre collecting brochures from their offices – with their vile pastel carpets and their hideous tubular furniture. I knew too that I'd have to select one firm to further gorge its bloated body by handling the sale of our house at some point; the common wisdom is that you sell your own house before you try to buy another one so, I concluded, I'd have to gag down my emotions and pick one soon.

'Or,' I thought, rubbing my chin slyly, '*do I*?' Our mortgage was almost paid off. (We'd made several lump-sum payments. A particularly substantial one had come from Germany; Ursula had an aunt who'd died and left her several thousands pounds in order to spite her own children. I'm very much a supporter of cackling vengeance from beyond the grave.) The two main problems I could see with selling our house were: a) selling our house – who in their right mind would buy a house in our area? and b) an estate agent tearing hundreds of pounds from our hands for doing next to nothing then laughing brayingly into our upturned faces before striding away to push small children into canals. It seemed both of these problems could be swatted by renting out the house instead. That would provide a regular income that we could put towards our next mortgage and, though selling the house would require the intervention of supernatural forces, renting was much easier. We could rent to students. Students will live anywhere. It was the perfect solution. If I'd had sufficient privacy, I would have kissed myself. I made up my mind, right there – standing in the doorway of Leech & Sons Property Services – that we'd rent. I'd stick an advert on the student notice-board at the university when the time was right. Sorted. I like to be impulsive once in a while – it means I can spend the rest of the week picturing myself as a fiery genius.

Because of my all-round excellence, I had a couple of hours free to go back home and sit and watch soap operas set in carveries, struggling knitwear factories and so forth, with the vacuum cleaner resting beside me. Not having a key for the new lock, Ursula peered in the window from outside when she returned home. But I'd spotted her coming up the street and therefore was visibly so absorbed in the hoovering that she had to knock on the pane three times before she got my attention. I opened the door for her, blowing air between my lips and wiping the back of my hand across my brow.

'Did you go to the estate agents?'

'I *knew* there was something . . .'

After letting her stare at me in an unblinking, icy silence for long enough to be completely sure she wasn't going to giggle, playfully knock my shoulder and say 'Ohhhh – *you*,' I nodded towards the living-room.

'All the brochures are on the table.'

'Right. You go and pick up the kids, I'll go and choose some houses for us to live in.'

'I think just the one house might be enough for us, eh?'

'I'm making the decisions from now on, thanks.'

The next day I returned to work, charged by my little holiday with new levels of enthusiasm. After the initial disappointment of seeing that the Learning Centre had failed to burn to the ground, I set about catching up with things. In fact, however, I'd only just opened my e-mail ('You have 924 new messages') when the phone rang – internal ring.

'Hello, Pel. It's Bernard. Could I see you in my office for a moment, as soon as possible?'

'I'll come down now.'

When I entered, Bernard was standing there looking glum. There's nothing so heartbreaking as a look of misery on a man with a moustache – as if his face hasn't got enough troubles. Bernard had an on-going quality of sadness and oppression hanging about him in any case. He was born in County Down and, though his Northern Irish accent was now vestigial, an intimation, he retained a tendency to pronounce the 'o' in 'no' as a drawn-out, slack-tongued 'ueer' sound, especially during moments of stress. Falling back into his childhood, I suppose; a sort of halfway house before going foetal. Whatever his dialect, the oval-eyed look of a man wrongly condemned to a life sentence in a Moroccan jail was always about him.

'I've had a complaint,' he said.

'About what? From whom?'

'I'll come to all that in a minute. The telling thing is that I'm seeing you about this, rather than referring it to your line manager. Terry Steven Russell would normally be the one to talk to you, of course. But Terry Steven Russell has gone.'

'Gone? You mean left the university?'

'That's right. He was here yesterday morning and gone yesterday afternoon.'

'Did he say where he was going?'

'No.'

'Did you ask?'

'I didn't even see him. I got back from lunch and he'd left a Post-It on my door.' Bernard held up the sticky label for me to see. It read 'I resign. Effective from now.' Uncharacteristically larghissimo for TSR, I thought. 'I went to see him, of course,' continued Bernard, 'but he'd already left. His locker was cleared out and Wayne said he'd said a quick "'Bye" to everyone in the Computer Team and given each of them a stapler as a gift.'

'Wow.'

'Turns out they were Learning Centre staplers, of course, so I took them back and returned them to the stationery cupboard.'

'Quick thinking.'

'The point is, it leaves us in a bit of a pickle. I'll get on to Personnel this morning to sort out advertising for a replacement, but it's sure to be at least a month before we even interview. And that's being optimistic. If any of the three committees who need to approve the wording of the advertisement have problems with it then we'll have to begin again.'

'Naturally.'

'So, I was wondering whether you could act up and do TSR's job until we fill the position? We couldn't pay you the salary for that post, obviously, but it would help us out and be valuable experience for you.'

I wasn't entirely sure what the job required, but then TSR never seemed sure either and it hadn't appeared to trouble him. I'd clearly be a fool to turn down the offer of what was a promotion in all but permanence and money.

'What about the job I do now? Who'll do that?'

'Well, it's silly to shift anyone to it for just a few weeks, so could you just keep that on as well? The two positions are required to work very closely together, after all, so in some senses it'll help you out, communication-wise.' Bernard had obviously thought this one through.

'Oh. OK, then.'

'Splendid. Then you're the Learning Centre's new CTASATM.'

No one had ever come up with an entirely comfortable way of saying the acronym for 'Computer Team Administration, Software Acquisition and Training Manager' (a title devised by two departmental administrators over the course of a day and a half), so it was always pronounced letter by letter – 'C' 'T' 'A' 'S' 'A' 'T' 'M'. After a while you didn't think about it and it just flowed out as an unbroken stream, 'Seeteeayessaytee-em'. The important thing was clarity. Had they named it 'IT Manager' people outside the department might have made incorrect assumptions, but with CTASATM everyone knew what your position was.

Bernard shook my hand. 'Unfortunately, you're first job as CTASATM would be to have a serious word with the Computer Team Supervisor. But as that's you as well, I'd better do it, eh? As I said, I've had a complaint.'

'I remember. Carry on.'

'Well, it seems that Karen Rawbone had a demonstration to do over in the art department yesterday. She says she'd arranged with you for all the equipment she needed to be there, but when she arrived . . . it wasn't. She not only had to ask the art department's IT support team to provide her with IT support – which is clearly not their job; I've had a terse e-mail from their manager – but they were also unable to view Pierre's sculptures in the room because no one was available to move them. Everyone had to walk downstairs to his studio, apparently. She wasn't pleased, wasn't pleased at all. OK, I know you were off sick yesterday, but you really should have organised it so that someone caught it in your absence. We all have to design in double-checks and safety nets, don't we?'

Damn, I'd completely forgotten about that.

'I didn't forget about that,' I replied, hurt. 'I'd arranged for TSR to do it.'

'Oh, right. He must have forgotten about it – or he couldn't be bothered, in his rush to leave.'

'I feel awful.' I bit my lip. 'You should have called me, I'd have come in and sorted it out. OK, I had that nauseous migraine, but I have a pair of welder's goggles I could have worn, just for a couple of hours – they keep the light dim enough and also provide quite a bit of facial protection if I become disoriented and lose my balance.'

'No, no, it's not your fault. You couldn't have known TSR wouldn't be here either. It's just one of those things.'

'Still, I feel terrible. Poor Karen.'

'What do you wish you'd known at eighteen?' I asked.

'Not to get my hopes up,' replied Roo, sprinkling tobacco into a cigarette paper.

Tracey looked across the table at me as I climbed into my seat. 'We really ought to get him to record one of those inspirational cassettes, you know.'

I was wary. 'Mmmm, he has a messianic quality about him, though. I fear we might unleash forces we couldn't control.'

Roo lit his roll-up with a single, prolonged inhalation, then sat back in his chair and bloomed smoke. 'I've had something of an interesting morning.'

'Me too. Guess what's happened.'

Roo took another long draw. 'So anyway, my morning, then.' He knocked the ash off his cigarette into the ashtray, continuing to tap it even after all the ash had fallen away from the tip. 'The Woman came into the shop again. She was looking at a *Vampirella Monthly* number three limited edition.'

'Wow.' Tracey nodded thoughtfully. 'I can see how that would be pretty impressive to someone who knew what the hell you were talking about.'

'It has a cover by Jae Lee.'

'Stop, just stop right there – my head's swimming.'

'She's had a new piercing too, a kind of twisted ring through her nose. I was hoping she'd come to the counter, but praying she wouldn't too. I know I'd have made a total arse of myself. I was running through what I'd have said to her – "Number Three? Good choice" – but even in my head I started stuttering, got all the words wrong and knocked my coffee into the till.'

Tracey held her hands out, palms up, the way you sometimes see Jesus posed in paintings. (Only not holding a piece of toast.) 'I don't see the problem. Just ask her out, for God's sake. What's the worst that could happen?'

'That's right,' I agreed. 'In all probability she'll just say "no". You'll have a moment of agonising humiliation. Then you'll lie in bed every night for several months, replaying the moment in your mind, each time being flooded with searing embarrassment and pulling the duvet over your head just wanting to disappear and die. Every second you're in the shop you'll worry about her coming back in, then when she actually does you'll prickle with awkwardness and horror. She'll come to buy something, cripplingly self-conscious at the shared knowledge of your failed approach, you'll probably try to make some sort of joke to break the curse, but it'll fall flat and she'll look at you with a rich mixture of pity, contempt and amusement. With luck, you won't have to quit your job and spend a year in a blurry half-world of wine-deadened self-pity.'

'Oh, cheers. You've really helped him get this in perspective.'

'Well, yes, I have, actually. "What's the worst that can happen?" – Lord above, that's dangerously female advice

56

from which I need to protect him. Rejection destroys the strongest of men. Just imagine what it could do to Roo. I mean, look at the state of him now.'

'It's better to know the situation for sure,' Tracey stated.

'It *is not* better to know the situation. Absolutely anything is better than a woman you fancy saying she doesn't want to go out with you. Far, *far* better that he gives up hope without trying, or becomes delusional, or continues to simply dream about the possibility while alone in his flat in a nightly orgy of masturbation.'

'We're not entirely alone in the café,' Roo pointed out.

'You are a woman. You don't know what it means to have an advance rejected. I wouldn't put it past you, in fact, to be the type who'd reply, "Ahhh – that's really sweet." Having an approach rebuffed is maiming for a man – and being *dumped*, well . . .'

'Hold on, hold on,' huffed Tracey. 'If I can just interrupt this stream of bollocks for a moment, I think you'll find women are upset by being dumped too. I remember I was dumped once and I was absolutely distraught for about six weeks.'

Roo and I explosively laughed out loud.

'There you go.' I clapped. 'Your Honour, I need call no more witnesses. *Six weeks*. A man is bizarrely resilient if he's traumatised for only six *years*. Women have a damn good cry, a few chocolate-and-anguish-driven evenings with their friends, and then it's on with the rest of their lives. Men just implode. It's a fact that men who are divorced *die* younger.'

Tracey shrugged. 'That's probably a hygiene issue.'

'See how I laugh,' I continued. 'Being dumped, quite literally, kills men. You wholly fail to absorb how needy we are. Even if a man gets a mistress, he can't give up his wife – we're tiny, helpless, fragile creatures.'

'Oh, don't; I'm starting to choke up. I can't remember you ever speaking of how Ursula is the only thing keeping you from an early grave.'

'Well, she is. Which proves my point beyond all argument – it's true even for Ursula. For a start, she guards against any tendency I might have towards hedonism. Who knows what self-destructive activities I might fall back into if she weren't there to act as untiring sentinel. And anyway, Ursula wouldn't *allow* me to die until someone comes up with a cure for ironing.'

'I don't think I'll be asking The Woman out just yet,' said Roo. 'I'd like to thank you both for crystallising that idea for me.'

'See what you've done?' Tracey said to me.

'Not important,' continued Roo. 'I wouldn't have done it anyway. So, Pel – you said you'd had an eventful time?'

'What? Oh, yeah. We were burgled, TSR's left, and I'm doing his job now. It doesn't matter.'

Back at work, I needed to begin moving some of my stuff. As the Computer Team Supervisor my desk was in the IT support office on the fifth floor of the Learning Centre. The CTASATM, however, as befits a team manager, had a home in the office with the heads of the other teams. TSR's desk was between those of David Woolf, the head of the Librarians (or 'the Professionals', as they like to be called – no, really) and Pauline Dodd, who managed the Library Assistant team.

Pauline wasn't at her desk, being tied up all afternoon in a departmental meeting to discuss what type of cups should be provided for the water cooler. How she ever managed to snake her way into her seat at all was an achievement I'd long hoped to witness. Her whole area of the office was a squat for cuddly toys, Gonks, ornamental flowers, amusing signs of the type sold in shops called 'Bitz' or 'Nick-Nacks' and photographs of small children.

David was there, though. He generally got in to work at around 7.30 a.m. (the cleaners told me – I'd still be arguing with Ursula in the bathroom at such a time) and stayed until he had just enough energy left to shuffle back to his car.

'So, you're our new CTASATM, then?'

'Until they find a replacement.'

'But you'll be applying for the post?'

'Um, well, I suppose so. I didn't really think that far ahead.' I genuinely hadn't. I'm not really a thinking ahead kind of person. (Though, if you want someone to brood over the past, I'm your man.) 'The job spec could well ask for qualifications I don't have.'

'Or you could have all the qualifications, but they don't even short-list you, irrespective of the fact that everyone knows you're the best person for the job,' David replied. David had a history. I quickly turned off this road into a less dangerous side street.

'Did TSR have any kind of filing system? I see a filing cabinet here, but it appears long on the filing and short on the system.'

'I've no idea, but I'd imagine he was happy with chaos. He wasn't a professional, after all. Non-librarians generally regard efficient collation as a chore. In any case, Terry Steven Russell was very verbal. He always seemed to be discussing things on the telephone or going out to meet people – can't imagine what half of them had to do with his role here, either; he used to see the deans more often than I do, and I'm head of the Professionals. I doubt . . .' For the first time, David looked up at me from the rota he was arranging. '. . . that he took proper minutes.'

TSR's PC was on his desk, but it was blank. There wasn't even an operating system on it. He'd obviously formatted the hard disk before he left. A standard thing to do nowadays, of course. People spend so much of their work time downloading pornography from the Web or viewing e-mail attachments of questionable legality that it's far easier, when they leave, to wipe the whole computer. Locating and erasing all the evidence would take ages, not to mention quite a degree of skill, and there'd still always be the nagging doubt that something had been missed. (Naturally, as soon as a person leaves, the first thing his former colleagues do is swarm over his PC to try to find what he has on it. There's a terrible feeling of disappointment across the department if Old Bob's PC doesn't turn out to hold images that reveal a secret interest in cross-dressing.) The fact he'd formatted, though, was quite pleasing. I liked setting up PCs. To partition the drive, install Windows and load and set up all the standard software took the best part of a day, but demanded only the mental effort required to click a 'continue' button every so often.

I pulled out a boot disk containing CD-ROM drivers – a thing so precious to anyone working in IT support that I've known technicians who merely had to touch one to achieve orgasm – and slipped it into the A drive. I rebooted and began to load an operating system from the CD. While it whirred and clicked away (and screens flashed up to tell me how the software I was loading would change my life for ever and make things easier than I'd imagined possible), I began poking around in TSR's remains.

Only the top of the four drawers in the filing cabinet favoured the vertical approach. Folders in the other three – where there were folders at all – were simply thrown in one on the other. I supposed this meant the most recent things were at the top. The uppermost memo in the second drawer (an official reminder of the need for a health and safety assessment to be undertaken, in the top corner of which TSR had scribbled 'Yeah, right') was certainly only a couple of weeks old. The top drawer, presumably kept to impress visiting dignitaries, did have a more conventional arrangement of labelled folders running back along its length. However, a few seconds of inspection revealed that these labels weren't in anything so clichéd as alphabetical order. Most of them were also uninformative, being things like 'GH & HT' or

'Fid;12/09/97'. Some of the folders were, in any case, empty. One turned out to contain a Cadbury's Crème Egg.

The drawers of his desk contained similar jungles, but this time the bulk of it was apparently not work related. There were old copies of *Mojo*, Argos catalogues, discarded parking tickets, receipts from Foto Processing – seemingly anything that TSR had emptied in there because it was nearer than the waste bin. Only in the bottom drawer did I discover anything that was placed rather than just trashed. In that drawer was a small package, a Jiffy bag, with 'Pel' written across it. I felt its contents through the unopened envelope – because you have to do that with packages. (The idea is, if you can successfully guess what's inside before you look, then you can open it with a 'Yeah, thought so' instead of a 'Well – didn't expect that' and you manage to negate the surprise and are rewarded with a tiny disappointment instead. It's a way of bleeding a little pleasure from your life.) So, I squeezed the bag, did the shaking it by my ear thing and, none the wiser (it felt hard and failed to rattle distinctively), peeled away the sticky tape. Inside was a mirror. One of those tilting make-up mirrors you can find on the tombola stall at any school jumble sale or in shops that sell everything for a pound. I'd have thought TSR was suggesting I was vain as a jokey Parthian shot, but he was clearly making a different point. On the face of the mirror he'd used a felt-tip pen to write 'Watch your back. Terry.'

I wasn't sure whether to find this quirky or creepy.

For most of the next six weeks I held my head in my hands. As I was doing two jobs, I had to make some tricky time-management decisions. It was a constant balancing act, but in the end I managed to devise a system where I was, day in and day out, doing both of them really, really badly. While not getting to grips with the CTASATM job at all (I didn't even sort through TSR's dishevelled files) I succeeded in losing my grip in the Computer Team Supervisor area. Overall, not a good time for gripping. However, so long as you're one step or more away from catastrophic collapse, you're not failing in your duty. And if you *are* that single step ahead, going for any more just smacks of vulgar flamboyance.

The CTASATM post was advertised. It specified things like 'You will be a self-motivated, enthusiastic, team player', but I applied for it anyway. I mean, it said 'you will be', right? Not 'you are'. There's always the chance a person can change.

The application form asked for three referees. I put TSR as one, naturally; even though no one had seen him since he left and his home phone number was returning a dead tone. For the other two I put Tracey and Roo. Everyone knows that references – except, perhaps, for that annoying 'last employer' one – are nonsense. No one is going to put down a referee they suspect won't give them a reference absolutely obese with complimentary adjectives. As far as I know, personal referees can be quite blasé about their shocking mendacity too. Any problems and they can just say, 'Well, in the four years I've been his mother's bridge partner he's never defrauded *me* of close to two hundred thousand pounds. How was I to know?' Given, then, that references are a complete waste of everyone's time, you may as well nominate people who'd be quite pleased that you think enough of them to ask them to speak for you.

At home, Ursula was close to sexual meltdown. When she gets an Ikea gift voucher she flushes and her breath starts to come in accelerated rasps, so going shopping for a whole *house* – well, her eyes sparkled with an animal fire from the moment she woke up.

'These are the best forty so far,' she said one afternoon, placing a huge sheaf of papers on the arm of my chair when it must have been clear to the most casual observer that I was playing *Tekken*. 'I'd like you to look at them.'

'OK. In a minute.'

'Fair enough. You have one minute.'

'Oh, come on.' I looked at her imploringly. Well, I couldn't actually look at her because the action on screen was rather frenzied, but I did turn my shoulders in her direction and twist my head as much as the need to keep my eyes on the game allowed. Quite frankly, this distraction was the last thing I needed when my health bar was a mere sliver and I was trying to pull off a Cat Thrust & Bloody Scissor combo.

'No. I know your minutes. You'll still be here when we come down for breakfast in the morning.'

Ursula – and I'm trying not to be judgmental here – has 'poor perspective' when it comes to video games. She is extravagantly pitiful at all of them; always panicking, asking which buttons do what and making inexplicable comments like 'That wouldn't happen in real life'. It would be unforgivable to mock Ursula because of this – it's a terrible affliction, and the fact that she pretends to regard her risible video-game abilities as trivial is quite tremendously brave. I explained the situation to the children very early on – the last thing I wanted was for them to discover their mother's condition for themselves later, and for it to be a source of awkwardness or embarrassment. I must say they've been very supportive. Patiently demonstrating moves and explaining the objective of games to her over and over again. Children can be very strong if you just give them the chance.

Something that can still be a problem, however, is that a related aspect of Ursula's disorder means she is unable to recognise a video game as a whole. It's not a visual difficulty, she can clearly identify individual parts of a game, but she's unable to process the way these join together. Again, I'm enormously proud of the way Ursula makes light of this when, for her, even a simple racing game must be a disorienting and frightening experience. Yet it does lead her to mistakes like saying 'Stop that now. You've been playing it solidly for six hours.' She is, in a very literal sense, *unable to see how that's not possible*. For Ursula, turning off when you're two opponents' distance from fighting to be Tournament Champion is just the same as turning off at any other point.

Anyway, knowing all this, and my being just as committed as Ursula to finding a new house as quickly as possible, after only a couple more hours I cast Tekken aside and began looking through the houses Ursula had chosen. I quickly saw that the criterion she had used to select these properties as possibles was 'Are in this hemisphere'.

Ursula was sitting at the table in the other room, reading a magazine article about using curtains to make your room more something or other. The sheer gravity of the writing was clearly such that she was only able to move a spoon back and forth between a toffee yoghurt and her mouth very, very slowly.

'How harshly did you weed to end up with this pile of houses?'

'I used a different method from the one you used to find us a home in an area like this one, if that's what you mean. Basically, I asked myself if a property said to me "ideal location to doss down when not on remand" – and excluded it if the answer was "yes". Unusual, I know, but let's give my system a try, eh?'

'There's a difference between looking for a house in a better area and saying "Mmmm – what would Ivana Trump do . . . ?" Look at this one . . .' I held one of the pages up in front of my face so that only my astonished eyes were visible over the top. 'You could buy the whole of this street for that.'

'Something you'd probably do, if you were choosing.'

'We can't possibly afford this. We couldn't even afford to buy enough drugs to makes us hallucinate that we could afford it.'

'It doesn't cost anything to look at it.'

'Woah, hold on. You're telling me you're picking out houses just so we can *look round* them?'

'It will give us ideas . . .'

'Yeah, I'm having one now.'

'. . . and provide us with a comparison. How can we choose what we want if we have nothing to compare it to?'

'We could try not being insane, if that's still an option. What the hell are you talking about? It's not like we've never seen a house before. I've been in lots of houses. My friends live in houses.'

'That's different.'

'How is it different?'

'We're not buying those houses.'

'We're not buying *this* house' – I pointed to the sheet advertising the Earl of Gloucester's north-east retreat – 'either. And anyway, you can pretend you're buying a friend's house if you want to. We'll phone someone we know; ask for an appointment, tell them to say there's been lots of interest – we can even go outside for a while and stare at their roof tiles.'

'Or perhaps I could just take this spoon and use it to hurt you in the face? Look, you can say you're against any of the houses I've given you there. That's why I gave them to you, so you could go through them and we could discuss it as a couple. But if you want to reject any without even viewing them I'll need a damnly good reason why.'

I could tell by the challengingly erotic way she drew her lips around the upturned spoon that she wasn't going to be shifted from her position. So I took all the houses over to the armchair and slumped into it, grudgingly.

All house adverts from estate agents are the same; a list of facts and measurements, room by room, under a small photograph of the front. If people have done something especially extravagant and ill advised to their living room, there might be a small picture of this too. Ursula probably found it enjoyable to leaf through page after page of these things; I just felt as if I were in a police station trying to identify the house that was attempting to steal my wallet.

'I see you've applied for the CTASATM job?' said Bernard, who'd crept up behind me while I was pilfering someone's tea bag in the staffroom.

'Yes.' I attempted to be casual. 'I thought I'd better; just to show that I'm interested in moving ahead in the department, not just stagnating in the supervisor's role.' He nodded. 'Not that I'm not very keen to do the job in its own right.' He nodded again. 'Or that I think the supervisor's job is, erm, stagnant.' I thought about asking for my application form to be burnt and apologising for all the time I'd wasted.

'You know we'll be interviewing external applicants as well. It's a very important role at this location.'

'The past few CTASATM interviews were internal only, though, weren't they?'

'Yes, they were.'

'And the position here is paid at precisely the same scale as elsewhere in the university?'

'That's right, it is.'

'I see.'

'I knew you would. It shows just how highly we regard the position here that, though it's paid no more than anywhere else, we've made it a lot harder for existing staff to get it.'

'When you put it that way' – I want to drop car batteries on to your feet – 'I realise just how valuable you regard the position as being.'

Bernard put his hands deep into his pockets and smiled weakly. I scooped the tea bag from my cup and dropped it over the bin. Too late realising it was the swing-top one. The tea bag hit with a brown splash then slowly slid down the lid into the base leaving a streak of tea behind it. It was impressively evocative of someone having hurled a turd at a smooth white wall.

'I'll go and get a cloth for that.'

A house.

'This is my husband, Tony.' Tony is angled, straight legged, in an armchair watching a football match on the television, but he raises a hand in our direction. He favours the not nearly uncommon enough combination of tight one hundred per cent nylon T-shirt and immense beer belly. His beer belly, in fact, is one of those that appears to have surged forward faster than the skin can keep up. Rather than a flabby overhang, it's a smooth, tightly stretched affair. You feel that, if you were to go over and flick it with your middle finger, it would ring like a beach ball. I find myself looking at the front of his strained-to-a-shine T-shirt, inexplicably fascinated by the tiny hollow that indicates the position of his navel.

The downstairs room is not content with just containing Tony and the TV, but also has a music centre with smoked black glass doors (I glance at the CDs – mostly compilation albums) and a wall of shelves full of cups, shields and trophy statuettes depicting golden men lining up shots at snooker tables. There is a tropical fish tank and two massive plastic chests employed in the standard fashion of holding all the children's toys you shovel off the floor in the final seconds before guests arrive. It's a big enough room, but there is only the one. A single downstairs room is not really a comfortable arrangement for us. Clearly, when Ursula or I crown an argument by striding out of the room, crashing the door behind us with decisive finality, having to shuffle back in again a few minutes later to watch the TV is a poor state of affairs.

Ursula and Tony's wife return from the kitchen and, chatting, head off up the stairs. I still haven't moved, having been too deep in contemplative gazing at someone else's navel, but tag along with them now.

'This is the bathroom. The water heater's in this cupboard.'

'How old is that?' asks Ursula.

Tony's wife tilts her head slightly in the direction of the bathroom door. 'Tonyyyyyyy?! Tonyyyyy, how long have we had the water heater?!'

From downstairs comes a distant, distracted shout of 'Dunno'.

Tony's wife looks back at us. 'I can't remember, to tell the truth. About ten years, I think. Right, out here . . . is the main bedroom.'

Arrggghh! Quite honestly.

'There's built-in wardrobes along the back wall, there. We keep our clothes in those . . . Back out, and . . . oh, the loft's up there, but we just use it for storing stuff.'

'What kind of insulation is up there?'

'Ooo, never go up there myself. Tonyyyyy! *Tonyyyyyyyyy*! How's the loft insulated?!'

'What? Dunno. There's some stuff or something. In the . . .' There's a great 'ooooah!' crowd noise from the television and Tony breaks off into 'Oh, you *fucker*'.

'Tony doesn't seem to know either. We can check into that,

68

if you want. This is the kids' bedroom.' She opens the door on to two boys of about nine or ten. One is orchestrating a conflict involving soldiers, racing cars, Power Rangers, robots and dinosaurs while the other is reading a Pokémon magazine. He's lying on the bed on his stomach, legs bent upward at the knees so he can slowly clap his feet as he leafs through the pages.

'Ahh,' I say. 'Pokémon. My sons are both into Pokémon.'

He glances up at me. 'So?'

'As you can see, you can get two children's beds in here without too much problem . . . Back out again, and we've got the spare room.'

It contains an exercise bicycle and piles of old magazines. Ursula points up to the corner by the window where there's a jagged crack at the point the wall meets the ceiling.

'There's a crack there. Have you had any structural problems?'

'You know, I've never noticed that before. Tonyyyy! *Tonyyyyyyy*! How long's this crack been here?!'

'Dunno . . . What crack?'

'In the spare room, there's a crack in the spare room.'

'In the wall?'

'Yes.'

'Dunno.'

She turns back to us. 'Well, we're not sure how long that's been there, but we've not had problems with the house, generally. Nothing's fallen off it while we've been here, hahaha!'

I echo her laugh politely. I can feel Ursula looking at me with her 'What the hell are you doing?' face but determinedly avoid meeting her eyes.

'Do you want to take a look at the garage?'

We say we do. Turns out there's a car in it. 'There you go,' says Tony's wife, 'that shows you can get a car in it.' We have another laugh together while Ursula watches from the sidelines.

As we're walking back to the car the neighbour waves at us. He's about fifty, sleeves rolled up to the elbows, digging his flower-bed.

'Come to look at the house?'

'That's right.'

'Good, good. Just the two of you, is there?'

'No, we've got two young boys.'

'Oh, that's nice. Be nice to have another family there. The wife said some coloureds came to look at it yesterday. That's a bit worrying, eh? Neighbours can make a big difference.'

'Yes,' I reply. 'Yes they can.'

A house.

'How long has it been on the market?'

An estate agent jangles his car keys. 'It's only just become available for viewing, as it happens. The old woman who lived here previously died in the bath . . .'

'In this bath?'

'That's the one. It was a number of weeks before they found her, apparently – eventually the stench alerted the neighbours. There was a fair bit of cleaning up to do, as you can imagine, and then the owners held off until after the inquest. There had been a lodger, but it looks like he'd left well before the tragedy – at least, no one recalls seeing him for several months previously. Would you like to take a look in the attic?'

'No.'

A house.

'Are you in a chain?' asks a woman in a tracksuit and mules.

'A chain? What's that?' Ursula squints back.

'She means are we waiting for our house to be sold to someone who's waiting for their house to be sold, and so on,' I say. 'No, we're not. We've virtually paid off our mortgage.

We don't have to wait to sell our house before we buy. We might even rent our house out, in fact.'

'Might we?' asks Ursula, adding a look.

'Not now,' I say to her in German, smiling.

'That's good. I've had sales fall through before because of problems with chains. I've had sales fall through twelve times. I'm on tablets.'

'Do you think we could come in?' asks Ursula.

'You're not in a chain?'

'No.'

'Well, OK then.'

She leads us down a short hallway. 'This is the kitchen. I . . . oops, excuse me. It's probably best if you come in one at a time. As you can see, everything is within easy reach.'

'Is that the door to the back garden?'

'Yes. I don't use that. You can go out the front door and walk through the passageway if you need to go into the back garden. Through here – excuse me – through here we have the living room. This is where you can sit and watch the television.'

'Was this originally two rooms?'

'I think it was. It was like this when I moved in, but you see where the paint on the ceiling changes from red to yellow? I think that was where the original wall must have been.'

'Oh, yes.'

'Do you want to look upstairs?'

'Very much.'

'OK, if you follow me – mind that vase. It's from Portugal. Right . . . right. This is the landing. Over here is the bathroom.'

I reach for the handle, but she steps in between me and the door. 'I'd prefer you didn't go in there.'

'No problem.'

'And over here are the bedrooms.'

'Three bedrooms?'

'Yes. Well, two and a boxroom, really. You could still get a single bed in the boxroom, though.'

Ursula pushes her head into it and looks around. 'I don't think you'd be able to open the door if you did.'

'You could take the door off.'

'These windows? They're not double glazed, are they?'

'No, they're not. But I have been meaning to have them done.'

'Well, thank you very much for showing us around.' We begin to go back down the stairs. 'It's very nice.'

'You've got the number of the estate agent, have you?'

'Yes. They said they'd call us on Monday, to see how we felt.'

'I'm not accepting offers,' she says, opening the door to let us out.

'They said.'

'Well.'

'Well.'

''Bye. And thanks.'

'Goodbye. I'll wait to hear on Monday.' We smile back and she closes the door as we walk away. Ursula is striding purposefully down the path. I turn to her, quite excited.

'I liked it.'

'Get in the car.'

A house.

'I'm not going to deny,' says the estate agent, jangling his keys, 'that it needs a bit of work.'

A house.

'Mr Richards? Hi, I'm Pel, this is Ursula, we're here to view the house. Sorry we're a bit early, but we saw the car in the drive so we thought we'd . . . We can come back in ten minutes if it's . . .'

'No, no, it's fine. Please, come in.'

We walk through the door and are shown into the front room. The walls are lined with unfaded rectangles where pictures once hung. The room has the doleful, reflective hollowness of most houses bare because the former inhabitants have moved their possessions and their lives elsewhere, but is generally in quite a good state of repair. Something that Mr Richards isn't, I notice. He's wearing a suit, but the impression is that he was wearing it this time last month too and hasn't taken it off in the intervening period. He's gone two, perhaps three days without shaving, and his eyes float slowly on two dark bags of insomnia.

'This is the living room,' he says, spreading his hands wide then bringing them together with a clap. 'Central heating, as you can see. All the rooms have central heating.'

'When was it installed?' asks Ursula.

'About ten years ago, we had it put in just before our first winter here . . . Yes . . . But we've had it serviced every year. There've been no problems with it at all. Yes. That's lasted well enough. Next room?'

'Lead on.'

He takes us into a room with a startlingly horrid fireplace and French windows that look out on to an overgrown garden.

'This is the dining room. There's the fireplace, you see, which is quite a nice feature.'

'Very nice.'

'It's not quite as big as the living room, but it's still fairly sizable.'

Ursula peers out of the windows at the three-foot-high grass. 'You moved out some time go, then?'

'Yes. Yes, a few months ago. I'm living with my brother and his family at the moment, until I find myself a flat. Need to sell this old place, of course, so we can divide up the dosh – divorce settlement.'

'Oh, I see,' says Ursula conversationally. I feel my stomach chill. I actually *feel* the inside of it plunge about 20 degrees Celsius in a single instant.

Most of the time I don't even remember that Ursula is German. We don't, quite honestly, go to a great many dinner parties and formal occasions so Ursula's distinctly German etiquette, with its unaffected, enquiring openness, doesn't make regular appearances to remind me. The English and German words are almost identical; 'tact' and '*takt*'. The cultural definitions, however, are about as similar as if they were 'goose down' and 'Blitzkrieg'. I'm staring right at Ursula's casually interested face, but I'm unable to speak or move. I see her lips begin to open.

'Divorced? Why is that, then?'

'I, um, my wife and I split up. About eight months ago.'

'No – I meant did you divorce her, or did she divorce you, or was it a mutual thing?'

Mr Richards clears his throat. I finally manage to raise my arm and say, 'The kitchen's through here, is it?' He doesn't appear to notice.

'It was a mutual thing. Though it wasn't really, of course; she was sleeping with some piss-wick from work, hahaha! Been going on for *ages*, apparently. Bitch. Still, we had an "irreconcilable differences" affair, to keep it civilised and grown up.'

'Could I look in the kitchen at all, do you . . . ?'

'Though I suppose opposite opinions about whether she should splay her legs for every tosser who wanders by with a few minutes to kill is a pretty "irreconcilable difference", don't you think?'

'I'm sorry,' says Ursula, compassionately. 'It must be very difficult to have one's marriage fall apart like that. Especially so for you, as you have to cope with the sexual humiliation as well.'

I don't remember a great deal about the rest of the house, having spent the next twenty minutes or so shuffling around it in a hum of raw horror. But, as we were leaving, Ursula wrinkled her nose at me and said she wasn't keen on the lack of a garage, so we never put in an offer.

Roo looked at me questioningly as I approached the table that he and Tracey had secured in Patrick's Café.

'Best sound in the world?' I asked.

'Posh women saying "fuck", obviously. Erm, are you aware that you're wearing a suit?'

'Tch – it's his interview today,' said Tracey, leaning forward and slapping him on the forehead.

'Oh, right, yes; TSR's job. Let me buy you lunch, then, as moral support.'

'Eat? Christ, I couldn't eat. My stomach's like a tumble-drier.'

'Phew. That saves us both the embarrassment of my having to borrow the money off you, then. What about a cup of tea?'

'Yeah, OK.'

'Trace? Get the poor man a cup of tea, will you?'

Tracey paused for half a beat before sliding Roo's tea across the table so that it was in front of me. 'I hear you're in with a chance,' she said.

'Really?'

'Yes. I'm not saying sit back and coast, but they reckon the external candidates aren't up to much.'

'What's your source for that?'

She shrugged. 'Some women from Personnel were in buying pasties earlier.'

'Ahhh . . . Good. I was rather hoping the special lure of rubbish pay would ensure that the people applying from outside the uni were a bit crap.'

Roo nodded. 'So, then, you can say, "Look, I'm about as crap as they are, but at least I know where everything is"?'

'That's basically my ace, yes.'

'You'll be fine,' smiled Tracey.

'Yeah, they know you're already broken. And it's only an IT job after all; one you're already doing, at that.'

'Yeah, I might be doing it, but I look bad on paper.'

'You look fucking awful in that suit too, but that's not bothering you.'

'It wasn't before I came in here, no. I meant that I've got no IT qualifications. My degree's in social geography, for Christ's sake.'

'What are you going to say if they ask you about that?' asked Tracey.

'I'm praying like hell that they don't.'

'It'll be fine. You'll be back in here tomorrow, and you'll be an IT manager.'

'CTASATM,' I corrected.

'Whatever. Some kind of high-flier, and we'll both have a new-found respect for you.'

'A "new-found" respect,' I repeated.

'"New-found." That's it,' confirmed Roo.

'You just march in there,' insisted Tracey, 'and lie and grovel like we all know you can.'

I was all fired up after Tracey and Roo's pep talk, but unfortunately I couldn't march straight into the interview. The person being interviewed before me was still there. She remained hatefully still there even when the official time for the end of her interview had passed. What's more, she was laughing. I could see her and the panel of interviewers through the glass front of the office. All laughing. All sharing some fantastic joke. About me, probably. All of them in there, laughing and bonding, and laughing and bonding, at my expense, while I sat outside pretending to read corporate literature in a stupid chair that was making my bottom sweat.

It looked like she was an external candidate. Certainly she was no one I'd ever seen around before. She had dark hair –

pulled back into a ponytail in a shamefully obvious ploy to convey an efficient nature – and was wearing a dark blue suit with a shortish skirt and sensible black shoes.

Um, nice legs, actually.

After what seemed enough time for her to have explained her experience, her personal strengths and the history of her family since the Crusades, there was finally the 'Anyone have anything else?' glancing around among the interview panel that signalled their mutual love-in was winding up. Yes, yes, everyone get to their feet, yes, shaking hands, smiling, 'Well – *hope to see you soon*', yes, yes, now fuck off, you tart. She strode confidently out of the office, glancing at me with a lack of any expression, which was a sure sign of derision and contempt. I knew that she clearly saw just how unpleasantly damp and intrusive my underpants had become.

That still wasn't the end of her, however. Her ghost stayed in the office for another ten minutes of nodding and scribbling before I was finally asked whether I'd like to come in now.

Job interviews are unfalteringly horrid, but internal ones emphatically more so. For a start, all the sustaining fabrication that is normally the essence of interview technique is denied you as everyone knows precisely what you're like. You're left with trying to pretend that everything you've done in the place up until that moment was just ironic or something. 'Yes, I've been here a number of years, but obviously I was only joshing with you good naturedly until now.' You're also wearing a suit – on to which it's been nothing but a terrifying challenge to avoid spilling things all morning – but aren't creating any smart impression; everyone knows you normally turn up looking like a week-old lettuce. You're condemned to wear it merely so as to confirm that you've 'made the effort'. I only had one suit, in any case, and wore it solely for job interviews and funerals – the choice of tie being down to whether I was burying someone or whether someone was burying me.

The interview panel comprised Bernard Donnelly, Keith Hughes (he looked after departmental logistics and was second-in-command, after Rose Warchowski) and a woman from Personnel who'd be there to ask the equal opportunities question.

'Take a seat,' said Bernard, gesturing towards the chair on the opposite side of the table to where the judges were sitting. 'OK. Well, Pel; me, I think you probably know . . .' We both had a little laugh at this clever joke. 'This is Keith Hughes, Senior Administrator of Learning Support; staffing, buildings and drainage . . .' Keith and I flicked up our chins at each other. We weren't old mates on the same intimate level as Bernard and I had reached, but we had shared a few stilted conversations and quite often passed each other in corridors. '. . . And last, but not least . . .' Laughter all round. '. . . Claire MacMillan from the personnel department.'

'OK,' said Keith, 'perhaps you'd like to tell us a little bit about yourself to begin with. What you're all about, why you're interested in this position, that kind of thing.'

'Yes, that's fine.'

'Off you go, then.'

They were all sitting with their backs to the window. It wasn't a sunny day, but the sky was one unvarying expanse of thick, pure white cloud, so the effect behind them was of a Phil Spector of light. I have eyes that were designed specifically to watch a TV at three in the morning in a room with no ambient light, so to me they might as well have been emerging from the spacecraft in *Close Encounters of the Third Kind*. I could feel my face squinting into an impression of Mr Magoo and tried to force my eyes open, which, of course, meant pulling my lower jaw down too, for some reason. I hadn't even said anything yet and they were already making notes on their clipboards; I assumed these read 'Possibly possessed by evil spirits'.

'I'm sorry,' I said, 'but I wonder if we could just close the blinds in here?'

'Er, yes, I suppose so,' replied Keith, rising from his seat and moving over to the window to pull the cord that released them.

'Thanks, thanks. Only the light's very bright.'

'Is it?' he said in a I-don't-think-it-is fashion.

'Yes, I find it very bright.'

'Do you have an eye condition?' asked Claire MacMillan.

'No.'

'No?'

'No. I've, um, taken atropine. You know, it dilates the pupils. They use it in eye tests.'

'You've just had an eye test?'

'Well, no. I was just saying that they use it in eye tests.'

'So why are you using it?'

'I . . . I was producing excessive amounts of saliva. Atropine counters excess saliva secretion.'

'Really?'

'And sweat, yes. Saliva and sweat both. It's a drug of a thousand uses. Hahaha.'

'I see,' said Claire MacMillan.

'That's very interesting,' added Keith.

'Just one of those things, you know. "Ooops – bit too much saliva about there, Pel," and you trot off to the doctor's for a bit of atropine.'

All three of them nodded. Very slowly.

'Still, as long as my eyes are fine – which they are – then . . . well . . . So, a little bit about myself . . . I've been the supervisor of the computer team here for quite a while now and over the past few months I've been acting up in the position of CTASATM . . .'

'If I could just butt in there,' Keith butted in. 'I see from your CV that your degree is in social geography. You don't have any IT qualifications. Isn't that rather a drawback in the role of CTASATM?'

'I'm glad you asked me that, Keith. In fact, I think my lack of computer "qualifications" . . .' I made little quotation marks with my fingers, the motion simultaneously waving goodbye to my immortal soul. '. . . is actually an asset.'

'How?' Keith asked me.

'I'm sorry – "how" in what sense?' I asked Keith.

'Well, in the "How is it an asset?" sense, really,' he clarified.

I nodded receptively. 'Well, I think that a danger in the CTASATM role is becoming entangled in technical issues. We're all very keen to make sure we fulfil the departmental mission statement, naturally.' I had not the remotest idea what the departmental mission statement said, but I did remember hearing somewhere that Keith had a big hand in drafting it. This was confirmed by his vigorous nodding response. He turned to Bernard, who nodded back even more vigorously, and then to Claire MacMillan, who stuck out her bottom lip to convey a supportive 'Whatever'. Encouraged, I continued, 'A danger – a real danger . . .' (That'd be a 'real' danger, there. I'm going straight to hell.) '. . . is that the CTASATM becomes diverted by practical issues and therefore fails to drive forward the overarching policies in a meaningful and proactive way. I think I'm far less prone to such a pitfall because I've avoided, educationally, focusing on the mechanics of computer technology.'

'Yes. That's a good point,' said Keith.

'And also,' interjected Bernard, chuckling, 'it's always good for when we're doing the crossword, isn't it? Useful to have someone around who knows what the capital of Ethiopia is.' We all chuckled together for a few moments. 'Um, just out of interest, what is the capital of Ethiopia, Pel?'

'I don't know. I did *social* geography.'

I had a little cough at this point.

'Yes. Yes, of course. Tell me – what would you most like to do if you were appointed CTASATM? What would be your highest priority?'

'Well, Bernard, I think continuity is important. But we must also be flexible and adaptive. We have to crystallise good practice and at the same time be responsive to change; in such a dynamic environment as this, quality – *real* quality – is only achievable if we combine our traditional skills with a welcoming attitude towards innovation; to drive that innovation ourselves, in fact.' I prayed this was entirely meaningless; it's so easy to tread on a mine if you're not careful.

'I think,' replied Keith, 'that's what we all feel.' Phew.

Claire MacMillan raised her pen. 'As you know, this university is committed to equal opportunities. Could you perhaps talk about some of the things we could do to achieve our goals in that area?'

There's a golden rule about the equal ops question; don't talk about race. If you talk about race, or gender, you're dead. Either you say 'everything's fine, nothing more needs doing', which is so clearly The Wrong Answer as to be actually provocative, or you end up implying that your colleagues are racists and bigots. Thank God, then, for the disabled.

'Well, I think that an important aspect, and one that's often overlooked, is the physical problems caused by building design. We only have one lift, for example, and when that's out of order access for wheelchair users is terribly compromised. Our Tannoy system excludes the hearing-impaired students, of course, and it's nearly impossible for a student to use a single-study carrel if he or she has a guide dog.'

'Yes, that's very true,' she replied, smiling, and I was thinking about punching the air while letting out an explosive little 'Yes!' when Keith joined in.

'While that's true to some extent . . .' What was he talking about? 'To some extent'? You don't use phrases like that around the equal ops question' the man was putting a rope around his own neck. Then I realised: Keith had departmental responsibility for buildings. Bugger. Buggering hell – I was being interviewed by Scylla and Charybdis. 'We have to acknowledge the limitations we face,' continued Keith. 'Budgetary restraints will, inevitably, prevent us from putting four or five lifts into buildings, for example.'

'Oh, yes.' I back-pedalled furiously. 'Of course. I think what I was saying is that we need to raise awareness of the issues.'

'I think I'm quite aware of them already.'

'No, no, noooo, not *your* awareness, clearly. I meant *general* awareness. If we can raise awareness, generally, in . . .' Careful, Pel, not too specific, you don't know how many budget allocation committees Keith sits on. '. . . in *England*. Well, then, perhaps we'll be provided with sufficient resources for the department to pursue a more comprehensive equal opportunities policy.' I scanned my eyes across them. Had I managed to move the goalposts far enough away that no one in the room had to take any responsibility for their maintenance?

'Yes,' replied Keith, at last. 'That's a key problem.' Claire MacMillan, bless her tiny nose, harmonised with a sad and solemn 'Mmmm'.

I continued to blow with the wind for around another ten minutes. There were a few shaky moments, but also a couple of masterful bits where I managed to paraphrase an opinion someone had just stated back at them as though I hadn't really noticed what they'd said but, as we were in the area, just needed to nail my colours to the mast concerning a point about which I felt very passionate. I also shoehorned in the phrase 'integrated learning environment', which gets you a triple word score. I was therefore feeling pretty good when they started to wind the interview up.

'Well, that's everything, I think. Thank you very much. Is there anything you'd like to ask us?' said Keith.

'No, I think you've covered everything.' Ugh. Not now, not as I was crossing the line. You *have* to have something to ask. It shows you've spent ages worrying yourself sick about the interview. They use the "what they asked" box as the tie-breaker, everyone knows that. 'Except, erm . . .'

'Yes?'

'Except . . . that shirt. Where did you get that shirt, Keith?'

'This? I . . . er, I don't know. My wife bought it for me.'

'It's very nice. I like the . . . blue. In it.'

'I can ask her where she got it from, if you'd like.'

'Would you? That'd be great. Thanks very much. Great.' OK, pulled that one from the fire. But had I done enough? 'When will you be letting people know who's been appointed?'

'We hope to have made a decision before the end of the day,' Keith said earnestly. 'So you should know by tomorrow morning, at the latest.'

'OK. That's great . . . Well, then . . . Great.'

I shook everyone's hands vigorously and, as befits someone interviewing for a managerial post, backed out of the office, littering my goodbyes with a series of little bows. The next applicant was sitting in the chair outside, nervously rubbing a thumb into the palm of his hand. This competitor I knew. He was a senior technician from the biological sciences faculty.

'Hi, Tony. You're up next, then?'

'Yes, I suppose so. I'm nervous as hell.'

'Psh – don't worry about it. You'll be fine.'

I walked away giving him an encouraging thumbs-up sign and failing to mention that his fly was open.

Being in a suit at work waiting for an interview is awkward and unpleasant, but being in one after an interview is several dozen times worse. It marks you out, even to the students, as having some career hopes left. In a suit, you feel naked. The most terrible thing, terrible beyond all words, is to not get the job yet still have to work out the rest of the day in your interview suit. It becomes a flag displaying your miserable defeat; your colleagues can't even bear to look you in the eyes if you're rejected and in a suit.

I went back to the office and tried to do something productive, but it was like driving in fog. Everything that I tried to focus my mind on imperceptibly but rapidly segued into fretting over what I should have said or said better. I'd open an e-mail and start to read a line in my head, but when I got to the end of it I'd realise my brain was actually talking about something else. I'd go back and try again, yet every time I reached the full stop I couldn't remember what I'd just read and heard only my own chattering thoughts.

I spent about two and a half hours sitting around bubbling with this kind of frenetic inactivity. Then the phone rang. Internal ring.

'Hello, Pel speaking.'

'Hello, Pel. It's Keith. Could you come down to the office for a moment, please?' There was nothing is his voice but flat formality.

'Sure. No problem.' I was enthusiastic and eager to oblige. Because, naturally, they might have decided to give the job to someone else but, hearing how upbeat and keen I was, overturn their decision – 'Wow! He said it was "no problem" to come down – let's give him the job after all!'

I got to the office, knocked brightly and, when Bernard opened the door, entered with a twinkling smile and friendly 'Hi'. (Because they might have decided to give the job to someone else but, seeing my chirpy nature, etc., etc.) Claire MacMillan had gone. Keith was still where he'd been sitting for the interview, looking through some papers. Bernard, after opening the door for me, didn't return to his seat but walked slowly about the office, hands in his pockets, making small 'pup-pup-p-pup' noises with his lips; I assumed from a tune in his head that wasn't worth humming.

I didn't know whether I was supposed to sit or stand – Keith and Bernard weren't giving a clear lead. After a couple of seconds of indecision I approached the chair and was beginning to take a seat when Keith looked up with a brisk 'So!' This threw my plan to the winds and I transformed my crouching movement into reaching down to scratch my ankle instead. I would probably still have captured the look of someone who was confident and in control had I not had my eyes fixed on Keith's suddenly upturned face. Instead, as I bent down, reaching for my foot, I overbalanced, toppled forwards and smacked my forehead against the top of the table, producing the loudest resonating crack the world has ever known.

'Ouch!' Bernard said vicariously. 'Are you all right?'

'Yes, yes, I'm fine.' I smiled at him from under my arm. Straightening up, I rapped myself on the head – 'Tsk' – with my knuckles to indicate how amusingly solid it was and how I hadn't felt a thing. Doing this hurt.

'Are you sure?'

'Yes, really. It's nothing.'

'So . . .' Keith began again. 'Pel, we'd – are you sure you're OK?'

'Never better.' I just knew there must be a great, red, throbbing weal growing out of my forehead at the rate of half an inch a second. From the line of his eyes, it was obvious that it was this, rather than me, Keith was addressing.

'Right . . .' he said to the welt. 'Pel, we'd like to offer you the position of CTASATM here.'

'That's great. That's fantastic, in fact.'

'Good – I'll take that as your accepting the offer. We're very pleased, and I know you'll be an asset to the Learning Centre in the post. You weren't a unanimous choice, of course, but that's irrelevant. The important thing is that we were all prepared to settle for you to get a quick decision. Congratulations.'

'Yes, congratulations,' echoed Bernard.

I turned my head round. 'Thank you.' I was feeling a little woozy and twisting to look at him didn't help.

'Are you *sure* you're OK?' He was squinting at me. 'Your pupils are dilated.'

Keith sighed. 'Keep up, Bernard. That'll be the atropine – remember?'

'Yes,' I confirmed. 'Aprotine.'

I swung my face towards Keith again. He was now leaning back in his chair and conducting his speech with a ball-point pen. 'We'll be starting you on the lowest salary point of the CTASATM pay scale and taking your start date as next month for annual increment purposes. I'm sure you see that it wouldn't be fair to the rest of the staff to do otherwise.'

'Naturally,' I agreed. Keith was starting to phase in and out. That didn't bother me initially, until I realised that it was probably me who was phasing in and out. 'What about the supervisor's post? I . . . sorry. Give me a second. I'm a bit . . . thrilled.'

'That's understandable. To answer your question, we thought we'd leave the supervisor post vacant for a while.'

'That's not just to save money, by the way,' Bernard said from around three-quarters of a million miles behind me.

'No.' Keith shook his head, pained at the thought. 'Because of the fluid situation, departmentally, and the fact that you already know the supervisor's job so well, we thought you might like to combine both roles for a while. For continuity. Just for a few months. Unless you don't feel you're up to that? If you think you're not up to that, just tell us. We'll understand – just tell us now if you think what we'd like you to do is beyond your capabilities and we'll accept your assessment.'

'No. Well. No, I can do the two jobs – I've been doing them until now, after all. And it's just for a little while.'

'That's right, it is just for a little while.' Keith beamed.

'A tiny while . . . tiny,' Bernard said, in the far, far distance.

'Good. Then it's all settled.' Keith reached forward to shake my hand through a contracting iris of blackness. 'You're our new CTASATM. I sure you'll be unstoppable.'

'Yes.' I smiled back. And collapsed sideways into a bookcase.

'Well, that's pretty much what I had planned for today.' Ursula was driving me back from the hospital and had reached the point where she felt she could no longer convey her feelings solely through the medium of savage gear changes. I suppose some people might think, as I was the one with the concussion and the dark blue swelling the size of a second forehead, that *I* ought to be the one who was a bit annoyed by events, but those people are going out with a different girlfriend, so what would they know about life?

It seemed that, after they'd dug me out from under a pile of procedures manuals and library suppliers' catalogues, Bernard had decided to call an ambulance. Keith, however, was more level headed. When the fire alarm is activated at the Learning Centre, it also rings immediately in the local fire station. If it turns out to be a hoax – students being amusing – then the fire service charges the university £80 for a false call-out. No one was sure of the facts, but there was a worry that if they called an ambulance and I turned out not to be sufficiently injured, then it could mean the university got billed. To be on the safe side, Keith had decided to call Ursula at work and asked her to come and collect me.

We went to the Accident & Emergency department of a local hospital (not the hospital at the end of our street, incidentally, which didn't have an Accident & Emergency department since the health authority closed it down to provide a better service). There I was seen within four minutes by a qualified nurse, after which I sat on a bench for five and a half hours with about thirty quietly bleeding people while we waited to see a doctor. In the end, I was taken to a cubicle and had been sitting there for only another ten or fifteen minutes when a captured doctor came in to see me. He looked so bad I offered him my seat. As he appeared not to have slept for around thirty-six hours, I imagine I'd caught him about halfway through his shift. We both knew he had no more idea of how many fingers he was holding up than I did, but he went about his business methodically; shining a light into my eyes, asking whether I felt nauseous, all very medical. In conclusion he diagnosed a minor concussion and said he'd like to keep me in for the night.

'What for?' asked Ursula.

'Just for observation. I'd like to keep an eye on him.'

'Oh – I'll keep an eye on him,' reassured Ursula. Reassured the doctor, that is, not me.

'Well, yes, OK then.' He turned to me. 'You get some rest. And don't operate heavy machinery or climb any high ladders.'

'But operating heavy machinery and climbing high ladders is how I relax, Doctor.'

'Very droll. Go home now.'

We had to go to my mother's house before we went back home because she had been looking after the kids while we were at the hospital. This is what my mother does: worries. Fair enough, she might do other stuff too, but it's incidental; her *raison d'être* is to worry – Born to Fret. I wasn't really looking forward to going into the house with an alarming head wound, but I couldn't possibly stay in the car – she'd imagine I was so disfigured that Ursula was scared to reveal me.

'Oh my God!' She steadied herself against the wall.

'Hello, Mother.'

'Oh my God.'

'I'm fine. They said I was fine, just a mild concussion.'

'*Concussion?* Did they take X-rays?'

'No, they . . .'

'You go back now and *make* them take some X-rays.'

'OK.'

'You go back there.'

'OK.'

'You're not going to go back there, are you?'

'I'll go and get the kids,' said Ursula, slipping by and making for the living room. I quickly followed her, leaving my mother still by the door, the back of her hand pressed against her forehead in the manner of a silent movie actress in great peril.

The children were lying on the floor, looking up at a cartoon that was playing on the VCR. Their mouths were slightly open and their eyes coins of transfixed awe. That didn't provide any clue as to the actual quality of the programme; they're able to watch any kind of television with the same single-minded intensity.

'Hallo, *Kinder*,' said Ursula, to no reaction whatsoever. She sighed. '*Hallo . . . Kinder*,' she repeated, jabbing them each in turn with her toe as she gathered their coats.

'Nh-yh,' they both replied.

They continued to watch the television as she lifted them to their feet and began feeding them into the coats. 'Your father got a new job today.'

Jonathan glanced over at me, paused for a second, then returned his eyes to the television. 'Did you have to fight for it?'

'I didn't have to, they just said I could if I liked.'

Having got them dressed, Ursula pulled Jonathan and Peter towards the door. They kept their eyes targeted on the screen until the angle made it completely impossible, then both let out a heart-rending 'Awwwww, Mom!'

'You can finish watching it the next time you come to Grandma's,' Ursula said, but this comment – showing as it did a casual attitude to the terrible severity of the situation – only intensified their agony. Peter fell, prone, to the floor, overcome by anguish.

'What's happening?' my mother appeared in the doorway to ask.

'Nothing, Mary, they're just tired.'

'I'm not tired,' wailed Peter.

'I'm not either,' said Jonathan.

'Well, I certainly am.' I picked up Peter and carried him under my arm out to the car. Ursula followed with Jonathan, and we each fastened a protesting child into its safety belt. Ursula had the easier job as Jonathan was mostly just trying to shame her into stopping by arguing the cruel injustice of her actions. Peter, on the other hand, was twisting and jackknifing and trying to climb back out of the car over the top of my head. On hearing the glorious click of the restraining buckle on his child seat, I leapt round into the passenger seat – Ursula was already revving the engine.

My mother waved us goodbye as we started away and shouted, 'Phone me when you get in so I know you haven't crashed on the way home!'

'When do you start your new job, anyway?' asked Ursula. I was lying in bed, exploring my bump with my fingers. It appeared to be even more colossal than it had earlier. I hoped it was the same phenomenon as probing a hole in your tooth with your tongue – in a mirror, barely visible; using your tongue, a vast cavern twice as large as your mouth. Ursula was padding around, naked, throwing clothes into the washing basket. She picked up a pair of my underpants from a chair and pressed them to her nose to see whether they were clean or not. I love to watch her do that.

Um, that's probably a bit weird, right? Let's forget I mentioned that.

'Well, I'm doing it now, so in that sense I've already started,' I replied. 'Why?'

'I need a holiday.'

'Why's that?'

She stopped collecting washing and wordlessly stared at me.

'OK,' I said, 'whatever.'

'We could have a couple of weeks in Germany. Maybe go skiing.'

'Yeah, I fancy a bit of skiing . . .' I snaked my hand out in front of me, twisting it elegantly from side to side. 'Pwsshhh! Pwshhh-shh-shhhhhh!' I noticed that Ursula was hunched over the washing basket. 'Are you laughing?'

'No,' she squeaked.

A house.

Jangling his car keys, the estate agent led us briskly up the path. It was a tidy semi-detached out on the edge of the town. The woman who lived in the adjoining house was standing in her doorway, surveying her garden as she sipped a mug of tea. I'd say she was about one-hundred-and-eighty-seven years old. 'Good morning.' I smiled.

'Here to look at the house, are you?'

'Yes, that's right.' The estate agent was fumbling agitatedly with the door key.

'It's a lovely place. Doris took real care of it – very house proud, she was. It's a terrible shame, really. It is a lovely place, but people get one whiff of the sewage farm behind the trees back there and they don't bother about anything else. Silly. You might say I'm not one to speak – my sinuses went during the Blitz – but the people round here will all tell you that you don't even notice it after a couple of weeks. We have a laugh about it. The neighbours will have friends come to visit and they'll say, "My God – what's that terrible stench?" and we'll say, "What stench?" Because we don't even notice it, you see. Some days, apparently, the wind's in the other direction and you can't smell the place at all – *then* everyone here'll prick up their noses and think something's wrong; yes, then they will. Some of the neighbours do like to go away for a month at the height of summer, but that's not really because of the smell, that's more down to the flies.'

'Shall I open the door?' asked the estate agent.

'No,' I said. 'Thanks anyway.'

I'd decided to make an assault on TSR's filing cabinet. Part of me said that I should leave it for a year. The logic being that, if I could get through a year without sorting it out, then I could probably go for all time without doing so. In which case, forty minutes and half a dozen bin-liners would put it behind me for ever. I knew that this, fittingly, would have been TSR's way of doing things, but, despite the briefly tempting urging of the inner voice, I knew that it wasn't mine.

I always have the feeling that everyone else knows loads of stuff I don't. That I'm the only person who hasn't seen that film or read that book. That everyone but me knows the numbers of all the elements in the periodic table, the name of the Italian Foreign Minister, and the year the internal combustion engine was invented. It's a constant worry to me. I open a newspaper and there is a discussion of the latest round of talks about European agricultural policy – passing references are made to agreements forged at previous meetings, there are wry asides about the chief protagonists; clearly, everybody is talking about this all the time, it's commonplace common knowledge, but I simply don't have a clue. Chives? What quotas? When? If I threw the contents of TSR's filing cabinet away, I knew that the very next day I'd be in a meeting, wishing I hadn't. 'Everyone knows more than me' has always been my feeling. (Which, come to think of it, makes it odd that I was so surprised to discover later that my feeling was right.)

I tried to sort things into piles: 'Definitely rubbish', 'Definitely not rubbish' and 'I have absolutely no idea'. After about ten minutes it was clear the final category was going to dwarf the others. Fortunately, both Pauline and David were out (a carpeting meeting), so I could spread out across the whole office – it's surprising how much space you need to make little headway. It wasn't just a question of deciding what something might be, but how it related to other things. Papers were rarely dated and almost everything described whatever it was talking about simply as 'it'. Was the 'it' that could get problematic if not dealt with quickly the same 'it' that was going to be hosed down with some bleach? Who knew?

I would have loved to have asked TSR for a little guidance. In fact, a couple of weeks previously – having reached the point where my shoulders were beginning to ache from responding to questions by shrugging – I drove round to his flat. His phone had been dead for ages and I'd fired off a few e-mails to his personal address without getting a response, so I couldn't think of any other option. It turned out he was no longer living there. The man who rented the flat above arrived while I was leaning against TSR's bell. 'After Terry, I see.'

'Yes.'

'He doesn't live there any more, I'm afraid.'

'When did he leave?'

'Oh, some weeks ago now. Just upped and went. The landlord asked me if I knew anyone who'd like to take over his flat quickly; said he'd slip me a few quid if I could find someone right away. We pay the rent a month in advance, you see, and Terry had gone with almost a full month's in hand; if the landlord could've found someone else, he'd have been, in effect, renting the place twice over for the month. I didn't know anyone, though. The place is still empty, as far as I know.'

'Do you know where he moved to?'

'Not the faintest. He told the landlord he was moving abroad. But it's always a good idea to tell landlords that, isn't it? Stops them turning up at your new place with a handful of unpaid utility bills and a few points to make about the state you left the bathroom in.'

'Mmmmmm.'

'Anyway . . .'

'Yes – thanks.'

So, that was that. Naturally, when someone asks you, out of the blue on a Sunday morning, about extradition treaties and the next thing you know they've effectively disappeared, you start to think. The trouble was, I'd thought this – 'Um'. I would have liked to have thought something more along the lines of 'Ah-ha! The final piece of the puzzle. At last, everything falls into place and, additionally, I'm vastly wealthy and all women desire me!' but I didn't have anything to work with. TSR had gone, that was it – even in Patrick's no one knew where or why.

I didn't expect to discover a clue to TSR's evaporation among the pile of papers in his filing cabinet, and so, obviously, that's exactly what happened. It was a wonderfully dramatic moment, marred only by the piffling technicality that I didn't have any idea whatsoever that I'd found anything of importance, and so I squinted at the piece of paper for a second, sighed again, shook my head again, and moved on. In fairness to myself, a scribbled note containing just a date, '874440484730' and '100,000 (HKD)' is hardly going to get anyone slapping their forehead in abrupt realisation. I fleetingly wondered who 'HKD' might be, but, in the IT business, the TLA (Three Letter Acronym) is a famous pestilence, so I knew it might well not be a person at all – perhaps it was a High Kilowatt Diode. 'K' is often used as shorthand for one thousand too; 'HD' is an abbreviation for 'hard disk', so it could be some type of hard disk with a thousand . . . somethings. I didn't know, and it was too late in the day to begin learning about computers, thanks all the same. Into the 'I have absolutely no idea' pile with it, then.

I continued to sort the items carefully until the time of my appointment to see Bernard for my first meeting as official CTASATM. At that point I gathered all the piles together and threw everything back into the filing cabinet. Going through

TSR's papers for an entire morning had revealed nothing to me other than to confirm how heavily he was into Mott the Hoople.

David and Pauline were returning from their project group as I left. She was saying, 'But I think pink is a very welcoming colour,' miming 'Come *in*,' with her hands for emphasis.

He, lecturingly, replied, 'It is not the business of the Learning Centre to be *welcoming*.'

'I'm going to a meeting,' I said, to no one in particular.

Bernard looked across the table at me and smiled his sad smile.

'Well, I really don't know where to start, so I suppose we'd better get started.'

'Yes. That's . . .'

'So, we . . . sorry?'

'Pardon?'

'What?'

'I'm sorry. What?'

'Were you about to say something?'

'No, I was . . . wasn't.'

'Sorry. My, um, so then. So, *then*.'

'Yes. *Yes*.'

'*Yes!*'

We were fired up now and no mistake. Bernard forged ahead.

'Yes,' he recapped. Then, after the briefest of pauses, 'Yes, well, I think we ought to talk about the new building. They'll be starting work soon so there's a lot to do.'

The Learning Centre was being extended at a cost of something horrific. I wasn't sure where all the money for this was coming from, probably a combination of sources – that seemed to be the general way of things. The university itself, local government, central government, industry, all sorts of places seemed to fund all sorts of things. This wasn't just a university habit; you can be driving down a road in the North-East and suddenly have a sign alert you to the fact that 'This traffic island was built partly with a grant from the European Community'. This is the truth. Somewhere in Brussels sits a subcommittee with the power to decide whether the construction of a small mural at a railway station on a branch line will go ahead or not. I defy anyone to prove they don't decide all the applications each morning by tossing a coin then spend the rest of the day arranging wheelie-chair races around the office.

I knew that the new building (it was really an extension of the existing Learning Centre) was going to reach out into what was currently the central courtyard area. I knew that everyone agreed it was necessary – the existing Learning Centre couldn't satisfy demand – and I also knew that everyone dreaded it, because it meant a great deal of work. The professionals tended to talk of 'disruption' a lot too; 'disruption' is to librarians as, let's say, salt is to slugs.

'The contractors will be starting to dig up the courtyard fairly soon now.' Bernard took a blueprint down from one of his shelves and spread it out on the table. 'This is the layout I've got from the architects. It won't look like this, of course.'

'Why not?'

He looked at me, surprised. 'Because this is just the plan.' He shook the astonishment from his head and continued. 'The exterior walls we can take as being pretty much on target, though, which is the important thing when we're considering where the foundations will be.'

'Right. That starts soon, then?'

'Hopefully. There's still final clearance to get. You know that this was the site of the city's mental hospital in the Middle Ages, I suppose? Well, the area we're building on was possibly the graveyard. Apparently, there are all sorts of laws about digging up graveyards. The builders have been given a provisional go-ahead, but it'll all have to stop if it turns out it really *is* a burial site – there are legal requirements, the historians will want to examine the area, etc. You can imagine.'

'Yes. I've seen *Poltergeist*.'

'Pardon me?'

'*Poltergeist*. It's a film. They build on a graveyard and this girl gets sucked into the television.'

'Really? Oh, nueer. Have you told anyone about this?'

'It's just a film. It didn't really happen.'

'You're sure?'

'Well, I mean, it's impossible, isn't it?'

'Yes . . . Yes. Yes – let's hope you're right. So, anyway, the building work will start before long and we can expect noise and inconvenience. TSR was on a few committees that were set up to oversee the project, and you might want to get up to speed by attending future meetings.'

'Isn't Keith in charge of buildings for Learning Support?'

'He would be, normally, but he handed this over entirely to me, as part of his goal of devolving control of projects to the people closest to them.'

'Gosh.'

'Yes. And I handed it entirely over to TSR.'

'Mmmm.'

'The other thing we have coming up is the annual Improvement Day.'

'Do we have a date set for that?'

'I've set one, yes. I won't be making it known, though, to avoid a repeat of last year.'

Improvement Day was a time set aside for all the Learning Centre staff to meet without the pressures of day-to-day work. The idea was to spend it making things better right across the board. Staff who hardly met during the normal course of their work could get to know each other better. It was an open forum for ideas that anyone, at any level, might have for improving the running of the service. There were little workshops and seminars on enhancing customer care, or best practice in specific areas, or general work management skills. It was the one time the whole of the Learning Centre could come together, without distraction, and make things better. Everyone despised it with a sulphurous passion. Last year, because the date of it had leaked out in advance, Bernard arrived to find almost everyone had called in sick or reported they had a domestic crisis they must attend to or that – curses! – the gearbox on their car had disintegrated. It seems (I wasn't there, being confined to bed with food poisoning, at a go-karting racetrack, with TSR) that only Bernard and David had actually turned up. Any improvements were minor.

'I'd had two hundred ham sandwiches done by Catering,' Bernard recalled, ruefully. 'I picked at them all day, but one man can't make much of an impression on two hundred ham sandwiches.'

'One hundred. Surely? David was there too.'

'It seems David is vegetarian. He had to go out to buy sandwiches.'

'Ah.'

'It didn't create a very positive atmosphere.'

'No.'

'So, this year will be different. I thought some role-play, perhaps? Get people involved.'

'Mmmm, I don't think people like that, Bernard.'

'They don't like role-play?'

'Or getting involved, for that matter. Perhaps something that . . .'

'Yes?'

'Well, I don't know. Something that kind of *washes over* them.'

'Not quite with you. Tell you what – you organise it. That can be your first official project as CTASATM; organise the structure of the Improvement Day. You can do that, can't you?'

'Christ.'

'What?'

'Sorry – sorry. I meant to say "Yes" and *think* "Christ" . . . I mean, I meant to say "Yes" and *think* "Christ – yes!" No problem. Improvement Day . . . Christ! Yes!'

'Did they do X-rays at the hospital?'

'No.'

A house.

'Are we . . . ?'

'Not at all – come in. Please, come in. I was just collecting a few final things together.' He was called Mr Beardsley and he pulled the door invitingly wide. We knew his name and something about this house already because we had not come here through an estate agent.

Ursula – and it's not something I approve of – talks to everyone about everything. If I happen to drop by her work for some reason, I can be pretty confident the receptionist will say, 'So, is your diarrhoea any better now?' or something equally uplifting, while Ursula's closest friends could effortlessly give lengthy presentations on my sexual technique. (At least, I hope they'd be lengthy.) However, it's simply her way, and I smile affectionately at how this trait adds a little carbonation to our relationship which, of course, is otherwise the stillest of waters. Any slight irritation I might occasionally have is soon soothed by simply sitting alone in the car for a few hours and screaming and screaming and screaming.

Because Ursula talks to everyone, she picks up a lot of stuff by word of mouth. I talk to very few people and watch TV a lot. Together, not much slips by us. Ursula might be unaware that Britain is at war with Canada, while I could have not the smallest suspicion that the eighty-a-day smoker directly across the road has taken to stockpiling petrol in his living room, but, between us, we stay current. On this occasion, Ursula's chattiness had unearthed the existence of a friend of a friend whose sister had a father-in-law who had a house for sale. He was selling it himself; that is, without going through an estate agent. This was because he despised estate agents, so, right away, I knew he was someone with a proper sense of right and wrong. Ursula got further details via her complex web of informants and we made an appointment with him to have a look around. The time had arrived and around was how we were now looking. Mr Beardsley went to take a box of things to his car, telling us to begin viewing the house on our own.

'It's *gorgeous*,' said Ursula as we walked into the front room. I peered about the room, trying to find what she was looking at.

'What is?' I asked finally.

'The room, it's *gorgeous*.'

I stared around more frantically. It was a reasonably sized room, not what you'd have called large or anything, but not troublingly smallish either. Reasonably sized, then. It had a bay window, an old-fashioned one with some coloured glass in the top panes – it wasn't double glazed – with a central heating radiator below it. It didn't look as if the central heating was at all recent, but it did at least exist. The floor was wood; not impressive wooden flooring, just rough wood over which a carpet would need to be laid. There was a fireplace. That would have to go. The walls were covered in wallpaper that had been given a coat of white emulsion not long ago and the ceiling was also painted white. It was a room. It was, you know, a *room*. Clearly I was missing something.

'*What's* gorgeous?' I asked.

Ursula looked at me with disbelief. 'Look at the light.'

'The *light*? Look *at* the light?'

'Yes, it's *gorgeous*. Can't you see the light.'

'Well . . . there's light *in here*. I'm certainly able to see *with* the light but I've been able to see with the light in every house we've been to.'

'No you haven't.'

'I think, in fact, I have, Ursula.'

'No, no. What about that one last week, for a start? There was no light in the living room there, they had to switch on the light.'

'And then there was light.'

'Not real light, that was electric light.'

'Sorry. You've lost me. Electric light isn't light?'

'Of course not.'

'So that's what's gorgeous? The room has light coming in the window? During the hours of daylight, light comes in. What can I say? Wow!'

Mr Beardsley returned from his car and joined us in the room, rubbing his hands together to clean them.

'Ah, you're in the front room, then. Nice room this. Good light.'

'It's *gorgeous*,' said Ursula. I felt like I'd stumbled upon a cult.

'Yes,' Mr Beardsley continued, 'I've given the walls a new coat of paint, as you can see – I've done the whole house, in fact. My father hadn't decorated for a while.'

'It was your father's house, then?' asked Ursula, her voice unusually melodious – clearly she was still intoxicated by the Power of the Light.

'Yes. Well, it still is, really. I'm afraid he's become ill in his old age . . . senile. It became too dangerous for him to live here on his own any more.'

'He was starting to become forgetful and so on?' I asked sympathetically.

'That's right. Forgetful. Confused. Began starting fires. Shall we look at the dining room?'

'Yes!' burst Ursula.

'Fires?' I asked, but they'd moved on.

'Oh, this is lovely,' Ursula was saying when I caught up with them. Again, I couldn't see anything especially lovely – it was just another reasonably sized room. I didn't say anything, though, for fear of them both looking at me as if I were simple and saying with a sigh 'Tsk – the *air*' or something. This room had French windows leading to a tiny, semi-conservatory affair, beyond which lay the back garden. On the back wall was another fireplace. Which would also have to go.

'I can just imagine eating breakfast in here.' Ursula beamed. 'Can't you just imagine eating breakfast in here?'

'Hold on . . .' I said. 'Yes,' I confirmed after closing my eyes to concentrate for a few moments, adding, in German, 'Can you imagine having frantic sex in the hallway?' Ursula shot me a glance that indicated she probably couldn't.

'OK. Just through here is the kitchen . . .' Mr Beardsley opened his hand towards a room housing the most terrible collection of savagely red cabinets in England. It was a sight people pray they don't live long enough to witness.

'We could get a new kitchen suite for there,' mused Ursula, dreamily. It was the moment I knew she'd embraced madness. 'Pel does most of the cooking,' she said (unaccountably trailing off before adding 'and all of the washing up'). 'We could get a new suite for this kitchen and it'd be perfectly fine, wouldn't it?' I peered deep into her eyes, trying to locate the tiny spark of humanity I longed might still be there. There was nothing.

'Yes. Or we could just eat out at the Savoy.'

Beyond the kitchen there was a utility room and a toilet. The utility room was empty apart from damp, whereas the toilet ingeniously blended being technically inside the house with somehow managing to evoke the distinctive horror of an outhouse. Ursula became even more excited when she saw these two areas, however. The toilet she ranked as a great asset, as the children could use it if they were playing in the garden and would therefore not have to traipse filthily through the whole house. I assumed 'the children' were some other children she was even now planning to secure from an Internet site – there was no way *our* children would use it; it was musty, cold and probably teeming with insect life. My grandmother had an outside toilet and it appears in my dreams even now as a symbol of the sinister unknown. The utility room stimulated Ursula to enthuse, 'We could put the fridge in there!' Quite obviously, to see a room and know that it's of such quality that you could put a refrigerator in it is high praise indeed. I was beginning to become anxious about how much more of the house Ursula could take without the relentless euphoria pushing her into a debilitating hysterical trance, or perhaps causing her to black out entirely. We'd only seen the ground floor so far, and I briefly considered asking Mr Beardsley whether we could come back and do the upstairs another time, after I'd protectively loaded Ursula up with a couple of bottles of Temazepam. However, I decided that it was best to try to get through it in one go. For one thing, I couldn't face doing this again.

Mr Beardsley took us up the stairs (which were 'lovely', it seemed, in a way so charming and subtle that most people would see only a run of wooden steps that allowed you to walk between one level of the building and another) and into the bathroom that was directly ahead.

Ursula said, 'We could get a new bathroom suite for here, it'd look great.'

I opened my mouth, but nothing came out.

There were three bedrooms; two similarly sized main ones and a smaller one at the front of the house. Ursula spontaneously called the small one 'The Guest Room' and – without pause, mind you – pointed to a wall and said, 'We could put our bookcase there, couldn't we?'

'Yes. There . . . or there . . . or in another house . . . It's that kind of bookcase.' She wasn't listening.

The first of the two larger rooms contained a fireplace. That would have to go. It also contained more of The Light that had been downstairs in the living room. Possibly the same Light, possibly Light merely similar enough to be spoken of in the same terms at this stage, I didn't know. There was another bay window (where, as any fool could see, you could 'sit in the summer') and some suspiciously DIY electrical wiring. The other large room overlooked the garden. I was pleased to see that it was well kept, rather than back-threateningly overgrown, and it was nicely secluded as most of the outside of it was planted with high conifers.

'That could be paved quite easily,' I observed.

'No, no it couldn't,' replied Ursula. 'Look at the flower-beds, look at the perfect size of the lawn . . . Can't you just imagine sitting out there in the summer?'

'Well,' I said sorrowfully, 'I'd rather set my heart on spending the summer sitting in the bay window in the other room.'

I would have thought that such an array of splendour would have been enough for anyone, but Ursula spotted a panel in the ceiling of the landing that revealed the existence of an attic. Mr Beardsley conjured up a stepladder and Ursula scurried up it with a torch. I waited below while she made several 'Oooh's and an 'Ahhhh' into the loft space, then she reversed back down and handed me the torch before pushing me up to have a look for myself. As the opening was only big enough to allow access for my head and one shoulder, it wasn't very easy to look around, but I was able to confirm to my own satisfaction that it was a staggeringly dirty hole with no floorboards, into which mote-saturated light sliced from between the feltless roof tiles.

'Isn't it *huge*?' Ursula called up my legs.

'Um . . .'

'What do you think?'

'That I'm actually quite frightened.'

'We could have a loft conversion. It'd be fantastic.'

'Yes. We could get another bathroom suite and another kitchen suite for up here too.' Ursula laughed and I smiled to myself in the semi-darkness.

'Tsk – not a kitchen suite,' she replied. And I stopped smiling.

I descended the ladder, impressed that under a minute had been sufficient time for the loft to hammer the vilest filth into every pore of my face. Ursula chatted excitedly to Mr Beardsley and was assured about such things as the plumbing being a traditional and genuine period feature, just like none of the doors shutting properly. As we made our way back to the front door, Ursula caressing every surface with her fingers as we went, I pointed out to Mr Beardsley a few of the questions marks that, for me, hung over the house. He ignored me with great gentleness. Finally, standing in the doorway ready to leave, we said our goodbyes.

'We'll have to think about it quite hard. The asking price seems rather steep considering all the work that needs to be done,' I said, taking up my negotiating position.

'How soon could we move in?' Ursula asked, taking up hers.

'The house is empty now, as you can see,' replied Mr Beardsley (to Ursula). 'My father has already moved into a residential home so, really, the only delay would be with the legal technicalities. Once those are done, you could move in right away.'

Ursula jumped up and down. I swear it, she jumped up and down.

'As I say, we'll have to think about it,' I sternly reiterated, dragging Ursula towards the car.

I got in and started the engine, but Ursula remained outside, gazing back at the house. I turned the engine off again and waited. I was at the 'reading the rules and regulations on the back of the old car park tickets on the dashboard' stage when she at last opened the passenger door and sat down beside me. Her eyes were wide and glistening.

'I like that house.'

'Really? Well, you had *me* fooled.'

'We've got to have it, Pel, we just *have* to.'

'Every room needs something doing to it and the roof is semi-transparent. We wouldn't be buying a house, we'd be buying some walls.'

'But . . .'

'If the sentence coming next has the word "light" in it – don't. Just don't.'

'It has so much *character*.'

'Character is what graveyards have. I was aiming more for electrical wiring you don't have to be afraid of. He's clearly asking about ten thousand pounds too much for the place – and I don't know how much he'll come down after you did everything bar tonguing the keyhole.'

'Do not lose this house, Pel. I'm warning you. If we don't get this house you will never have sex again.'

'That's rational. Buy a building or never have sex with you again.'

'You're not listening. I didn't say "with me". If we don't get this house I will make it my business to ensure you never even go the bathroom without one of the kids being with you.'

Her eyes didn't flicker.

I started the engine. 'We'll go to the bank on Saturday.'

'You *what*?' Ursula looked across at me from her chair as she said this. The inflection (and I rather suspected the metaphor ran deep) was reminiscent of a rollercoaster going over the lip of a terrifying drop; slowly reaching up to the crest on the 'you', teetering, almost stationary, for a fearful extended moment on the 'wwww', before plunging rapidly down into the chest-constricting frightfulness of the 'what'.

'It's . . .' I was falsetto. I cleared my throat and tried again. 'It's not on the market. You knew that . . . We talked about this. And everything.'

'No we didn't.'

'Yes we did. I said how it might perhaps be better to rent our house out.'

'Oh, I remember the "perhaps". Because when you said that "perhaps" I made *this* face.' Ursula made the face. Oh dear. 'And just because you had raised that as a – stupid – possibility and hadn't put the house on the market *yet*, I didn't think you'd decided not to advertise it *at all*. I mean, if I'd thought that I would have injured you, wouldn't I?'

'Ursula . . .'

'And what about the times I've asked you if there'd been any enquiries about the house?'

'I thought you meant enquiries about renting it.'

'Did you?' Her voice was viciously flat. 'Did you really?'

'Look, it's a simple misunderstanding. Let's move on.'

'You impossible wanker. You have the mind of a six-year-old child. A monkey child. I cannot rely on you to do a single thing, can I? You are a monkey child. Say it.'

'Ursula . . .'

'Say you're a monkey child. Go on, say it.'

'Erm, perhaps you two can discuss this later – we'll just assume a hundred per cent mortgage.' The bank's mortgage adviser spoke from the other side of the table. She glanced up at the clock. 'I do have another appointment in fifteen minutes.'

'I'm sorry,' said Ursula. 'I apologise for the delay caused by having an infant primate for a boyfriend.'

'It was just a misunderstanding.' My eyebrows pleaded towards the mortgage adviser.

'Monkey child.'

'Interest rates, then – Ms Krötenjäger, Mr Dalton. I think you'll find we offer very competitive interest rates.' She tapped a few keys on her computer. 'This will print out an example of the monthly repayments you could expect to pay based on the house you're looking at. There are several options – you can choose the mortgage that you feel suits you best.'

The print-out revealed standard mortgage arrangements. There were lots of figures detailing various interest calculations, tax modifiers and so forth. These were canonically impenetrable (I stroked my lips as I read them and nodded 'I see'), but it didn't make any difference as almost everything ended with an asterisk that linked it to a footnote that said, in essence, 'This could change to something wildly different at any second; our company takes no responsibility for customers who foolishly fail to dismiss everything we've just said out of hand.' Only two columns were important. The first displayed an example of (asterisk) monthly repayments and made you look at your shoes in an effort to calculate whether you could get another twenty-three years' wear out of them. The second showed what you would end up paying the bank, in total, under different options, and ranged from maddeningly obscene usury to diabolical ravings in the style of a murderous, crack-addicted, loan shark.

The mortgage adviser said, 'We like to build a proper relationship with our homebuyers here. So we produce this information pack. It gives you details of our mortgage options, but also has booklets with general information that's very useful when you're buying a home.'

'Thanks,' I said, 'that's great.' I took the folder so I could file it later with the information packs every other bank had given us. The sprawling pile of glossy photographs of couples smiling at each other up and down stepladders as they painted walls in the curtainless sunlight now occupied about twenty per cent of our bedroom.

'Does that include cover if one of us should die?' asked Ursula, looking at the print out.

'It gives the standard insurance – payment of balance in the event of death – that's required, yes, Ms Krötenjäger.'

'Good,' Ursula said.

'It was just a *misunderstanding*,' I pleaded.

'Monkey child.'

'I'm not . . .'

'*Say it.*'

'Well – Ms Krötenjäger, Mr Dalton – I think we've covered all the major points.'

'Yes,' I agreed. 'Do you have a card?'

'I . . . no. It's OK, you can speak to any of my colleagues here. Helen, say. Ask for Helen Reeves. Helen's very good. Ask for Helen.'

We said our goodbyes and were asked to leave by a side door.

I sat in the living room with Jonathan and Peter. We were going through Jonathan's homework together to give Ursula some 'Me Time' alone in the dining room, growling to herself and laying the table by hammering every single item down with measured, clunking violence. I don't remember having homework at Jonathan's age. I don't know whether that's because educational demands have risen generally or because Jonathan went to a nice Church of England school that was among the top three in the local league tables, while I had gone to a string of shrieking asylums that were little more than holding areas for the nearest borstal. Whatever the reason, Jonathan always had a spelling test to prepare for or sums to do or a book to read or some activity we needed to perform together. He was unwavering and passionate in his opinion that homework was 'not fair', but – as he was vocal about the unfairness of around eighty per cent of the world as it related to him – he was keen that so blunt a weapon should not be his only defence against the many-headed cruelty of it. Thus, within the overarching unfairness, each section of homework had specific, unattractive qualities. Spelling, for example, was 'stupid' while maths was 'sad'. Reading was 'harsh' and history 'fat'. I listened to his position with a sympathetic ear each time he argued it and, each time, I made him do his homework anyway. To be honest, Jonathan's case wasn't helped by corruption in the judiciary. Educational considerations aside, I simply loved doing his homework with him. I loved discussing it with him, explaining things, going off on interesting tangents. More than anything else, I loved finding a grammatical error in the teacher's instructions. Jonathan will outpace me one day. He'll reach the limit of all I know and just race on. I'll have to cup my hands and shout after him for instructions on how to take each half-step forward and – with a kind of benevolent amusement, and without stopping – he'll call the answers back over his shoulder. And I won't understand a single word he says. That's in the future, though; right now I'm omniscient. I may sometimes have to fudge the odd stinker – 'Who decided that "blue" should be that colour?' (a question which, obviously, is *not fair*) – but it is still indisputable that I know everything. One day Jonathan will discover that I *don't* know everything. And I want to be right here to hold back that day as long as possible.

The homework before us was a poem that he had to learn for the school assembly. It's important to have a routine, so our session began in the same way it always did.

'Homework time. Jonathan, put down the Game Boy. Peter, can you climb off my head now, please?'

Jonathan let out a wail that conveyed the most abrupt and distressing emotional collapse imaginable. Peter, his face upside down as he peered at me over the top of my head, tentatively asked for confirmation of what he scarcely dared allow himself to believe.

'Jonathan has to do his homework?'

'Yes.'

Peter commando-rolled down the side of my body, coming to rest sitting upright on the sofa pointing a pistol-like finger at his brother.

'Jonathan! Jonathan! You've got to do your homework!'

Jonathan's tiny body was thrown to the floor by another wave of torment.

'*Noooooooooo.*'

Peter was calm. 'Yes you have.'

'Come on, Jonathan. The sooner you do it the sooner it's done.'

'But I still have to *do it* – can't you see that's the important bit? It's harsh – ultra, mega-harsh.'

'Look, you're doing it now, OK? This is non-negotiable.'

'What's "non-negotiable" mean?'

'It means I'm not going to change my position, it's fixed. May I remind you that this house is not a democracy? I am the boss here and what I say goes.'

'Dad's the boss,' confirmed Peter, pointing me out to Jonathan.

'That's right. Now just come here and . . . Peter! Peter, come back here. You weren't going to tell your mother that thing about me being the boss, were you? Promise, now. Good boy. Jonathan, let's get going.'

The photocopy the school had sent gave a short poem of the 'God made everything' variety. I had Jonathan read through it, then try to remember it couplet by couplet. We practised saying it together and finally he recited it a few times on his own, from memory. It wasn't a difficult thing – a boy who can remember the details of over 150 Pokémon isn't going to have any trouble with sixteen lines of verse – but I did suck my teeth a great deal throughout for other reasons.

'You know God didn't *really* make flowers, don't you, Jonathan. That's just a myth.'

'Like the Greek myths? Like those stories you read to me? Like Justin and the Argonauts?'

'*Jason*. Yes, like that. People believed those at one time, but they're just fairy stories really. Some people still believe all this God malarkey, but it's just a story. The world is interesting and wonderful and amazing, but there's not really any such thing as magic. Magic just makes nice stories.'

'No magic at all?'

'No. You be careful of people who tell you that magic is real, they're trying to get you to believe things that aren't true and the truth is very important.'

'I see.'

'Good, that's good.'

'So there's no such thing as magic *at all*, then?'

'No, not at all.'

'But what about Father Christmas? He's magic.'

Damn.

Damn, damn, damn, damn, damn.

'Ahhh, well, that's a bit different . . .'

'How? He must use magic to bring presents to all the children in the world in one night.'

'Not magic, no. No. Erm, he's . . . You see . . . No. No, Father Christmas simply has access to some extremely advanced technology.'

'What kind of technology?'

'I think the tea's ready . . .'

'No, I can still hear Mom saying things to the plates. What kind of technology?'

'Oh, you know, essentially it's a combination of high-yield fuels and intensely efficient engines. For his sleigh.'

'I thought the reindeer pulled his sleigh?'

'The reindeer? Oh, the reindeer are just there for decoration, to make the sleigh look nice. In fact, it's driven by ion engines, that's how it can go so incredibly fast.'

'How fast?'

'Incredibly fast.'

'How fast?'

'How fast? Nearly the speed of light. Yes, that's right. It travels at nearly the speed of light and, as objects approach the speed of light, time slows down for them relative to other objects. So, *to us*, it appears that Father Christmas does all the visits in one night but, from his point of view, he has a whole year to do them all.'

I admit to punching the air at this point.

'And that's not magic?' asked Jonathan.

'No, that's the theory of relativity.'

'But how does he carry all the presents?'

'That really is the tea ready now . . .'

'No it's not.'

'OK, have you heard of Heisenberg's Uncertainty Principle?'

'No.'

'Well, it's that.'

'How?'

'It's to do with observation . . . and the presents not being there until we see them.'

'Eh? How?'

'Like I just said.'

'But *how*?'

'Shall we have a pillow fight?'

'OK, then.'

'Arrggghh!'

'Aeeiiiii!'

'Agh! Agh! No! Peter – put the stool down.'

Sometimes I think I should have been a teacher.

'You can only take one CD to a desert island, what is it?'

'David Bowie's *Tin Machine*,' Roo replied swiftly.

'*Really?* You'd want to listen to that more than anything?'

'*Listen* to it? I thought you meant take it to a desert island and leave it there.'

'I like your style – let's be friends.'

Tracey snorted a little laugh into her coffee.

'You know what amazes me?'

'All-purpose glue?'

'The speaking clock?'

'No . . .'

'Instant tea?'

'Stripey toothpaste?'

'In fact, no. What amazes me is that such definitive nonentities as you two can constantly sit around rubbishing the famous and talented.'

'I'm going to have to dispute "talented" at this point,' interrupted Roo. 'The subject was, after all, David Bowie.'

'It doesn't matter who the subject was. You pair haven't got a good word for anyone.'

'I . . .' Roo was cut short.

'I'm not counting porn actresses – I think we all agree that they're in a special category. But if virtually anyone else is popular or successful, you two will hate them.'

'It's the English way.'

'That's right,' I added. 'And, moreover, it's a duty too. From each according to their abilities, to each according to their needs. They get to be rich and famous and refer to Anthony Hopkins as "Tony". While, as nonentities, we get the right to judge them.'

'Judge them,' clarified Roo, 'and find them wanting.'

'Precisely. Given that we will never be part of their world and, additionally, have absolutely no influence whatsoever, we are in a uniquely disinterested position from which to declare them false, self-inflated, unjustly fortunate or ugly.'

'That actress in the *Bad Girls* movie . . . Oh, what's her name?' Roo closed his eyes and tapped his head in search of the memory.

'That's right,' I confirmed. 'She's all four.'

'Tsk. *You've* just been promoted to a "managerial position", Pel. That's just the same as some actor who works their way from soup commercials to starring in the next Spielberg movie.'

'The difference between being CTASATM at the University of North-Eastern England and being Nicolas Cage is subtle, Tracey, but, nevertheless, very real,' I said, adding, speaking to myself really, 'For a start, I bet he has someone to field the phone calls from nutters.'

That morning I'd had a phone call. I was sitting in the office preparing some student usage figures that were part of the department's monitoring process (these are rather important for planning purposes, so I was putting quite a bit of effort into inventing convincing numbers) when the phone rang its external triplets.

'Hello, University of North-Eastern England, Pel speaking.' There was a pause. No, not quite a 'pause', just an extra beat of silence before the reply, which stuttered the normal bouncy rhythm you have at the opening of a phone call, when everyone usually knows their lines.

'Where TSR?'

'I'm sorry, but he's left the university.'

'When he return back? What time?'

'No, I mean, he no longer works here. I'm the CTASATM here now – perhaps I can help?'

'You have replaced TSR?'

'That's right.'

'I understand. My name Chiang Ho Yam.'

'Hello, Mr Chiang, what can I do for you?'

'I am Hung.'

'That's . . . nice. That's, um, you know . . . "nice". I'm happy for your good fortune – I'm only averagely endowed myself. I still don't see how I can help you, though, I'm afraid.'

'You know the arrangement?'

'Well, I imagine I could picture it if I tried. But I don't really lean in that direction. I didn't know TSR did either, for that matter.'

'You straight with me?'

'I am, yes. Sorry.'

There was a pause – a proper pause this time – and he put down the phone.

I thought for a moment or two and then called the switchboard.

'I've just received an external call. Could you tell me the number of the person who called?'

'Hold, please . . . No, I'm afraid I can't. It was an international call.'

'I see. Thanks anyway.'

I looked across at Tracey and Roo and blew on my tea.

'Have you ever heard anything about TSR being gay?'

'Gay?' replied Roo. 'Not unless he thought there was money in it.'

Tracey shook her head decisively. 'No, he's definitely straight. We bumped into him at a club not long ago – remember, Roo? We saw him when we were at Groovy Al's?'

'Oh, yeah, that's right,' Roo confirmed. 'Though I don't see how that means he must be straight.'

Tracey tutted. 'No one who's gay could possibly dance that badly. What makes you think otherwise, anyway, Pel?'

'Oh, no reason.'

'Ha! Nice one.' Tracey laughed, tilting her head to a knowing angle. 'Like you can say that and we'll let you move on. Spill.'

'I don't know, it was probably just a crank. I got a phone call this morning from some bloke who seemed to want me to talk dirty to him.'

'Did you?'

'No. As it happens, no I didn't. The university hasn't sent me on that course yet. Anyway, quite apart from anything else, I think I've forgotten *how* to talk dirty.'

'You don't talk dirty with Ursula? What a shame.'

'Good Lord no. We've been together far too many years. Ursula does talk during sex, but it's mostly to ask me what colour I think we ought to paint the kitchen or something.'

'He's fishing for sympathy again,' Roo said to Tracey.

'Yes.' She nodded. 'Probably trying to justify why he's resorted to gay phone-sex.'

'You're both very funny people and one day, long after you're dead, the world will realise that.'

Tracey patted my hand.

'So, what did this bloke say?'

'In essence, he asked for TSR and I said I'd taken over the role. He told me he had a large knob, I replied that I didn't, and he hung up.'

'Well,' replied Tracey authoritatively, 'I think *I* can see the point where you went wrong in that conversation.'

'Yep,' added Roo. 'You could have lied about your size; he'd never have known over the phone.'

'My size is quite adequate for me, thanks very much.'

'For you?' asked Roo.

'Leave the poor man alone, Roo.' Tracey put on a thick German accent and spoke into her coffee as she stirred it. 'Oh, Pel! You are so . . . adequate.'

'So, to recap,' I said, 'TSR "not gay" we reckon, then?'

'Nah, crank call,' said Roo.

'Or a set-up.' Tracey looked at him. 'Like that call I answered at your flat the other night.'

'Yeah. Someone called "Bill" obviously has a similar number to me. I often get calls at three a.m. just saying "You *wanker*, Bill" or whatever. Bill must have annoyed someone.'

'And we can be sure that TSR annoyed lots of people,' said Tracey. 'Maybe one of them set up a prank call, not knowing he'd left.'

'The bloke didn't know he'd left, that is true. Yeah, maybe that's it.'

David Woolf and Pauline Dodd were both in the office when I returned after having lunch. David was reading through a print-out of the minutes of some meeting. Every few seconds he'd exhale a great, weary sigh, scratch at something on the print out with a red Biro and then make furiously heavy notes in the margin. Pauline was combing the hair on a Gonk. I began going through the TSR information tip once more. There was the general chaos to work on, but I was also trying to find some note that might provide a subtle clue to confirm one of the theories about that morning's incident – 'Tsk; *this* is going to provoke crank calls' perhaps, or 'I am secretly gay!' I was spectacularly unsuccessful on all fronts.

'Oh, Pel, I've just remembered, love; Bernard left a message for you,' Pauline said after about fifteen minutes. 'He said he'd been talking to the VC and could you give him a call.'

'Give Bernard a call?'

'No, the VC.'

'Why on earth would the Vice-Chancellor want *me* to call him?'

'He didn't say.'

David looked across at us from his minutes. 'If the VC is continually going to talk directly to the CTASATM, then I think that's wholly inappropriate. They always said that he and TSR knew each other outside work and that's why they were in contact so much, but if it's going to be the same with *every* trumped-up – no offence, Pel – with every trumped-up CTASATM that comes along then it's just very, very inappropriate. The Professionals are quite clearly on a line between top-level management and technical staff. This just makes a mockery of the whole organisational structure.'

Pauline smiled. 'Oooh, you old misery guts, you. He probably just wants to congratulate Pel on getting the job.'

'The VC? Congratulate Pel? On becoming CTASATM? You do a very important job here, Pel, don't get me wrong, but it's like the Prime Minister wanting to meet someone and shake their hand for successfully becoming a lavatory cleaner. Have you even spoken to the VC before, Pel?'

'There was a university restructuring consultation meeting last year and I asked a question. So I suppose, technically, we have spoken.'

'Maybe your question made an impression, love. You could have stuck in his mind as a sharp one ever since,' Pauline offered.

'I doubt it. I just asked if there were any more biscuits.'

'The whole point about this, Pauline, is it shouldn't be about personalities anyway.' David was really quite angry. As he spoke, his index finger was rapidly jabbing in the air, as though he were doing a hand shadow of a woodpecker. 'You cannot run an organisation successfully unless you adhere to the proper structures.'

David had issues in this area. He'd gone for the Learning Centre Manager's job a few years ago when the previous incumbent, Janice Flowers, had retired owing to ill-will. He hadn't got it, of course, it was given to Bernard. (Bernard was an external candidate, having come from an industry background; he'd been the corporate librarian for a large fertiliser company – David was wont to paraphrase the description 'Bernard's background is fertiliser.') There was no doubt David was capable of doing the job of Learning Centre

Manager, so its being given to an outsider would have been a bit of a blow to anyone. As this was the sixth time David had applied for the post, however – killing one previous manager so the position became free, the other librarians joked – it was even worse. It was clear that someone simply didn't want David in the Learning Centre Manager's position. Because he was blatantly and hellishly efficient, this could surely only be down to a clash of personalities. Obviously, then, David had a particular interest in things being done strictly by the book without personal sensitivities being allowed to interfere.

'You *are* going to be tidying all that up, aren't you, love?' Pauline asked me, clearly keen to change the subject to something less likely to detonate David.

'Yes. I'll put it all away. I just need to spread it out right now to sort through it.'

'Only I've been doing a reading of this room – feng shui, you know. And, according to the layout we've got, we're all going to have terrible bowel problems. I think a load of papers scattered all over the floor would just make things even worse.'

I immediately began shovelling the papers back into the filing cabinet.

That completed and, I prayed, our looming intestinal troubles now of a size that wouldn't require calling in the army, I gave the VC a ring. He wasn't there, but his secretary said she'd tell him I'd called. She was afraid she didn't know what he wanted to speak to me about. I assured her she wasn't nearly as afraid as I was.

I wonder whether the person who invented shopping trolleys had the slightest idea about the impact they would have. Was it merely a memo passed across someone's desk – 'People sometimes want to buy more than a couple of baskets' full of stuff. Please advise, Derek' – to which a busy executive had carelessly replied, 'Build big baskets with wheels on'? Or was it the result of a Manhattan Project-style endeavour involving the finest minds in retailing? Culminating in the first prototype being wheeled out in front of a hushed clique who instantly knew the world would never be the same again. How did students get home from the pub before shopping trolleys? What did people throw into bodies of water back then? Without shopping trolleys, huge superstores catering almost exclusively for car-driving shoppers would be impractical – hitting both the retailing and the building industries – and the cross-fertilisation of checkout workers and undergraduates stacking shelves overnight would remain the stuff of Marxist fantasy. Without the shopping trolley, the sixties might never have happened.

I was in a hypermarket, without a shopping trolley. This was because we were only passing by to get a few things. I'd been in favour of using a trolley anyway, but Ursula had given me a stare that said 'You are not having a trolley, because you'll only hunch over it and propel yourself along the aisles, skidding your feet out to the side to make it change direction or hot-dogging with pirouettes or doing store-long thrusts to pull up right by the cereal you wanted and then looking really pleased with yourself'. She'd handed me a basket. The kids were also miffed about the lack of a trolley but I wasn't too bothered about that – they'd only have played around on it.

Because it was a flying visit and we only had to buy a few specific things, we'd been in there for well over three minutes before we lost each other. Jonathan was with me but Lord knows where Ursula was (I'd raced along all the aisles, peering down each one as I passed, but couldn't see her; she'll often hide at the end of the bays or crouch behind other shoppers or disappear into the jungle of the clothing section). I just hoped with all my heart that Peter was with her. If Jonathan gets separated from us while out shopping it will frighten him. The second his attention melts from whatever drew him away he'll feel abandoned and scared; in the couple of minutes before you find him again he'll have become understandably distraught. Peter, on the other hand, thinks only 'Free!'. I used to watch him; before he broke me in, I'd occasionally use the dawdling-child threat 'Right, that's it. I'm off now. If you don't come along I'm leaving you here', after which I'd determinedly march away, just out of sight, to spy on him from behind a hide of soup cans or a wine rack. There was never even a brief moment of indecision. Never. He'd just be off, racing in the opposite direction, climbing into the 'reduced to clear' bins, putting anything he passed that was remotely hat-like on his head and beaming right across his face. I'd have to rush after him and drag him back; there's little Peter can be taught about controlling the balance of power.

'Can I have one of these?' asked Jonathan.

'No.'

'Awwww. But I *want* one.'

'Jonathan, it's cheese. We have cheese.'

'Not like this.'

'That's round and in a red wrapper and expensive, but otherwise identical to the cheese we have.'

'I *want* it.'

'No.'

'*Awwww*, it's not fair.'

'Life isn't fair. Hypermarkets exist to teach us this.'

I threw a selection pack of low-fat crisps into the basket with the yoghurts and kiwi fruit and led my heartbroken son away from the processed dairy products. A couple of own-brand diet lemonades and a rechargeable battery later, we were heading for the checkout. I collided with another shopper as I came out of the bottom end of the aisle and we were just about to apologise to each other profusely when I noticed it was Ursula and Peter.

'God – watch where you're going!'

'I *was* watching where I was going, you're the one who wasn't watching,' responded Ursula, testily.

'You *were* watching? So you saw me, and just walked into me deliberately, then?'

'That's the wrong battery.'

'No it isn't.'

'It is. I said an AA.'

'You didn't. You said an AAA.'

'I did not. You obviously weren't listening. Again.'

'If I wasn't listening I'd have thought you said either an "A" or nothing at all. How can I possibly have been not listening and heard an *extra* "A"? Eh? How?'

'Because you're an idiot.'

'No, I'm *not* an idiot, in fact. *In fact*, you're a wrong battery asker; you don't know your batteries, that's the problem.'

'Shut up and give it here. You start queuing at the checkout while I change it. Peter, go with Dad.'

Peter indicated that he'd prefer another foray into the fascinating plenitude of the store, rather than coming to stand with me in the checkout, thusly:

'Nooooooo! Noooooooooooooooooooo!'

I caught his eyes flicking towards the freezer section; he was wondering whether he could make it. 'I'm three years old, but Dad has got a basket and Jonathan to slow him down . . .' I *saw* the thought flash behind his eyes. Instinctively, I acted – whipping out a hand and grabbing his arm before he could make a break for the wire.

'Nooooooooooooooooooooooooooooooooo-ah-ah-ahhhh!' (I suspect that Jonathan and Peter are practising this together when they're alone – 'That's *quite* good, Peter. But you need to convey more of a sense of utter desolation as the vowel sound begins. Let's try it again – and from the diaphragm, remember . . .')

The end checkout was in sight and I headed towards it. The shopping basket was hooked, painfully, over my left arm with my hand beyond it, clasping Jonathan's. He was ice-skating his feet along the floor, using me to provide half of the energy. Peter was dangling from my right arm. He'd just flopped like a protester and I was having to drag him along behind me. In what can only be considered a stroke of improvisational genius, he was tearfully casting his eyes around at the other people in the store and plaintively wailing: 'Help me! *Help meeeee!*'

By the time I'd hauled my offspring the few yards to the checkout I knew for certain that every parent in the place regarded me as contemptible and the store manager was in the process of collecting the CCTV footage to send to the police. Jonathan was grumbling like a poorly tuned radio, so that only the occasional word rose through the stream of mumbling with volume and clarity: '. . . mmmnnmnmmnm Me mnmnmnmn Cheese mnmmnmnm Not fair mnmmmnnnnn . . .' Peter was merely a limp and yawling ball of snot. I stood at the Eight Items or Less line, which, as always, sent a shiver of fury through me at the grammatically incorrect use of 'less' instead of 'fewer'. I choked this ferocious pedantry back but succeeded only in slipping into the other great Eight Items or Less line pitfall of counting the items in the basket of the person in front and becoming mutely hysterical because there were more than eight. On this occasion, however, the righteous anger was diluted with incredulity. Nine items will make you annoyed, ten to twelve and you *really hope the person on the checkout sends them away*, any more than twelve is simply a work of unimaginable Evil. The woman in front of me must have had over twenty items in her basket.

What happened next I can, even now, scarcely believe. I sometimes think I must have dreamt it, the memory being really nothing more than an especially vivid recollection from a fevered nightmare.

The woman in front of me took some separators from their special slidey groove along the edge, laid them on the conveyor belt . . . *and divided her shopping into three eight-item-or-less chunks*. It was one of those things you appear to watch happen in slow motion. I could not believe what I was seeing. I stopped breathing, I literally stopped breathing and stood, a whining child on each arm, staring at the items with my mouth flopped open.

The woman working on the checkout, her eyes only flicking between the conveyor belt and the cash register, went through the first lot of items, took payment and moved on through the next lot.

'That'll be thirteen pounds and . . .' Glancing up. '. . . are these yours *as well*?'

'That's right,' said the demon, brightly.

'Um, well, you, um . . . Thirteen pounds eighty-two pence, please.'

The demon paid and moved down to the end of the checkout to begin putting her shopping in carrier bags. The checkout cashier moved through the third pile of shopping and then looked up at me.

'Seven pounds exactly, please.'

Expressionless, I shook my head thrice and then made a single nod towards the demon ahead. There was a queue behind me now. We were all, massed, just a tiny shred of Englishness away from beginning to chant 'Kill! Kill! Kill!'

The cashier turned round to the demon.

'Excuse me, are these . . . ?'

'Oh, yes, they're mine. How much?'

'Seven pounds. Exactly. Please.'

'Seven pounds . . . seven pounds . . . There you go. Thank you.'

I watched her pack the rest of her shopping into bags and leave. There's a hypnotic quality to insouciant depravity on this level, and the cashier had to call out my total several times before it registered in my head. I was still in a daze as I walked away from the checkout. Which, I suppose, is why

I walked in front of the trolley that drove enough supplies to keep a couple fed and washed for a month into a single point right on the side of my knee.

It was the type of knee impact that is so sudden and unexpected that, initially, you think you've got away with it. 'Oh, my knee has been in sharp collision with a hard and unyielding object,' you think. With the slightest of pauses, you further reflect, 'And, gosh, there doesn't appear to be any pain. What a happy and pleasing phenomenon.' This smoothly segues into 'Arrrrrrrghhh!'

I crumpled to the floor, clutching my knee with both hands. Shopping splashed in every direction and went gambolling away into the distance. Jonathan stared down at me in alarm. Peter stared down at me for an eighth of a second before making a dash for the car park. I released my knee with one hand and clawed it out in an arc, trying to catch his ankle, but he was already out of range.

'Jonathan!' I shouted. 'Capture your brother!'

Jonathan flung himself out to the side and wrestled Peter to the ground. They rolled around on the floor, Jonathan trying to pin down all of Peter's many limbs, Peter beating Jonathan over the head with our family pack of low-fat crisps.

Having thus brought the situation under control, I looked up at the driver of the trolley.

'Hello, Pel,' said Karen Rawbone.

Karen was with her husband, Colin. I can't say how the two of them originally got together, but I'd be very surprised if it didn't involve a satanic ritual at some point. Colin was a person who clearly took personal grooming very seriously indeed; he looked like a forty-something gigolo. (Though, tragically, with the hair of a sixty-something gigolo.) Moreover, Colin also haunted the UoNE; he was the careers agent. In fact, he wasn't employed by the university directly, but worked for an independent agency that leased him, full time, to us as an adviser. This arrangement probably made sense to someone, somewhere. (Obviously. I mean, otherwise it would just be madness, right?)

I continued to hold my knee in my hands, rocking to and fro on my back like a wobbly child's toy cast in the shape of a stricken shopper.

'Hi, Karen. Hi there, Colin.'

'Are you all right?'

'Yes, fine. I think it's only chipped the bone.'

Colin nodded towards the children.

'No self-consciousness have they, children? Not nowadays. We'd have never behaved like that when were young, eh, Pel? Parents wouldn't have stood for it. But what can you do? Hahaha.'

'Yes – ow, *owww* – kids always get wound up shopping. I suppose that's why they call them *hyper*markets.' Not the cleverest of gags, admittedly, but I was hoping that the lying on the ground in agony might have sold it.

'No,' replied Karen, looking down at me, bemused, 'I think that's because they're really big.'

The best thing that could have happened at this point would have been Ursula not arriving.

'Why the *hell* didn't you wait?' said Ursula. 'You *knew* I'd just gone to get the proper battery. Why didn't you wait for me to get back so we could have paid for everything together? I had to go and join another queue. I had to stand in another queue to buy a single battery, just because you didn't wait for me . . . What are you doing down there?'

'Aerobics.'

'Get up. You look stupid.'

I used the Rawbones' trolley to pull myself wincingly upwards and, holding on to it to keep my balance, stood like a crane.

'This is my girlfriend, Ursula. This is Karen and Colin Rawbone – we work together.'

'Though not closely – I'm a Professional,' smiled Karen.

'And I'm a careers agent. The university leases my skills from a specialist company,' added Colin.

'Hello,' said Ursula. 'We're just doing a little shopping. It always seems to lead to an argument, I'm afraid.'

'Of course. It's only natural.' Karen glanced across at Colin. 'I mean, we see it a lot. I don't think Colin and I have *ever* argued, though. Hahaha! Isn't that strange? We just don't, do we, Colin?'

'No. I think it's because we're very similar – same likes and dislikes, same temperament, same way of looking at things. There's very little to argue about when you're so alike.'

'It's almost as if we share the same brain.'

'Yes, that's right. Sometimes we'll complete each other's sentences, or just look at each other – just *look* – and we each know what the other one is thinking.'

'That's wonderful,' I said. 'I don't think Ursula's ever let me complete a sentence, have you, darling?'

She smiled at Karen and Colin. 'Ha-hahh. Pel thinks he's funny. Is he like that at work too?'

'Yes,' replied Karen and Colin, in unison. They laughed at the precision of the harmony and pointed at each other and went, 'Ahhhhh.'

'Well . . .' Karen sighed. 'I don't want to keep you – we have things to do. See you at work, Pel. Nice to meet you, Ulrike.'

'Ursula.'

'Yes.'

They pushed the trolley away, together, and I began limping around to collect the spilled shopping.

'Before they decided to share a brain, they ought to have asked if it was big enough for two,' I hissed to Ursula.

'They seemed nice enough to me.' Ursula took the carrier bag from my hand. She started off towards the car, pointing down at Jonathan and Peter – who were still squirming around for dominance on the floor – as she passed and calling back to me, 'Sort out your children.'

MAYBE IF I SPEND A LOT MORE TIME
PULLING AT IT

I phoned the Vice-Chancellor's office before doing anything else the next morning. My thinking was that the best chance of catching him was very early, before he had to attend any meetings or got drawn into any other business. So, one second after nine, I called his number. His secretary answered and said he hadn't arrived yet. She also said she'd told him I'd called and that though she couldn't say what it was about, he was very anxious to talk to me. She was going to phone me anyway, as soon as the VC arrived, to ask me to come over. I thanked her, confirmed I hadn't got anything unavoidable in my diary, and said I'd wait for her call and go over as soon as the VC got in.

Sure enough, at a little past eleven, the phone rang and the VC's secretary said he was in and waiting for me now. I immediately began making my way over to his office. The university is organic in structure. It wasn't designed to be a major higher education centre catering for tens of thousands of students. Before it had become a university it had been a polytechnic, before that a college, and before that, quite possibly, a newsagent and tobacconist's. All through its life it had grown as its student body and specific needs demanded; newer buildings being tacked on to older ones, height and design matching the spirit of the times. Rounded blocks thumbed along the edges of streets; long walkways often connected the buildings where the university had leapt a road in expanding. But sometimes there were outposts – departments that had been marooned, or escaped, across the city, hiding among the retail sector. Since it had become a university the amount of real estate it possessed had enlarged with special haste. It had bought up property all around the city centre and converted it to the business of education. That it was the city's biggest employer was unremarkable, but how suddenly it had become *visibly* so, its seemingly instant ubiquity, that was startling. The VC's office, naturally, didn't lie out on one of the university's spiral arms, it was in the centre – not all that far from the Learning Centre but in a much older building.

Rather than go outside, to get to the building that housed his office and enter it, I'd decided to thread my way through the multi-levelled warren of corridors and arrive without ever having to venture out into the air. The university is so vast and erratic that no one knows anything beyond their own department and its environs; you can often come across one of the finest minds in hydroponics wandering lost and frightened in some echoing passageway. As I'm almost completely senseless when it comes to direction, it was hardly unforeseeable that I would get comprehensively lost. I've been lost many times in the university and I don't mind it in itself. I do mind people knowing I'm lost – because you feel such an idiot, and you can sense that everyone you pass somehow sees you're wandering around befuddled and disoriented. Some time ago, however, I made sure that I was never without a piece of paper in my pocket during work hours. Walk down a corridor with a piece of paper in your hand and you're instantly cast in a different light; focused, in control, if not in a position of authority then quite possibly heading towards somebody who *is* in a position of authority, bearing a piece of paper. When you've got paper in your hand, people take you seriously. During my scenic route to the VC's office, I did have one unfortunate moment when I paused by a coffee machine, nodded to the few people standing there blowing into their Styrofoam cups, glanced around the five possible exits and then strode off purposefully down what I guessed was the most likely one. Some twenty seconds later

I rounded a corner to stand before the same group of people, still blowing into their cups. They looked at me wordlessly. I nodded to them again, this time – 'Pfff, eh?' – waving my bit of paper in the air, and walked away down another exit with important speed. Eventually, after only some six or seven times what it would have taken me to walk around the outside of the buildings, I found myself standing in the office of the Vice-Chancellor's secretary.

'Hi, my name's Pel – we spoke on the phone. I'm here to see the Vice-Chancellor.'

'Yes. Take a seat. I'll just call through to him.'

I sat down long enough for her to say 'Pel Dalton's here for you . . . Yes' before getting up again and being shown through the door into his office. She closed it behind me and went back to whatever she was doing outside.

The room was large for an office, by UoNE standards. Apart from a computer, it was free of the usual furniture of a work room; there were no filing cabinets and the bookshelves held proper books – that is, books designed to be of interest, rather than procedural manuals and folders of regulations and the various other official documents that were interesting to no one whomsoever. The walls were bare of the standard collage of Blu-Tacked memos, timetables and rotas. All around the room, glass-doored cabinets held plaques, cups, vases, statues (in spite of myself, I couldn't help looking for one of a man bent over a snooker table), carvings and all manner of improbable gifts and awards. Along the back of the office, a broad, high window framed a view of the city's impressive central park, whose well-maintained area of lawns and gardens was, even now, dotted with semi-conscious men in huge overcoats clutching bottles of cider. In front of this window was the Vice-Chancellor's heavy wooden desk. Behind the desk was the Vice-Chancellor himself, looking rather like he'd been savaged by dogs.

'Chrrrist – I feel like my head's been sodomised,' he said,

holding a hand on either side of it as though he feared it would fall into pieces if he didn't.

George Jones had been the Vice-Chancellor for a little over three years. Previously he'd run a southern university, the name of which I (and also quite probably he) can't recall. He was a squat Welshman crashing around somewhere in his mid-fifties; jet-black hair still thick on his head, broad shoulders and a neck of above average circumference. His look was of a man who'd probably been, if not athletic, then definitely possessing a bulldog-like virility in his youth but, as time had progressed, what he'd lost in years he'd gained in pounds.

'Headache?' I asked, because it felt as though I should say something.

'The Bitch Queen of headaches, man. Went out for a few beers last night, woke up this morning with my temples throbbing like an oil rig worker's wedding tackle.'

'I could come back another time?'

'God, no – my problem, don't you bother about it. So, you're TSR's replacement, then? "Pel", right? That's a bit of an odd name, isn't it?'

'Is it? I suppose, um, no one's ever mentioned it before.'

'Doesn't really matter, though, does it? Doesn't matter what you're called. Your parents could christen you "Shitey" and it'd make no odds – it's not like we have to grow up to fit our names, is it? Grab yourself a seat, man. Can't have you standing around like you're in the headmaster's office. Did you know TSR well?'

'Moderately.'

'Don't know where the bastard's gone, do you?'

'No, sorry. No idea, I'm afraid.'

'No. What a tosser, eh? Sorry – would you like a drink? Tea? Coffee?'

'No, thanks. That is, not unless you're having some any-way.'

'Chrrrist, not me. Wouldn't dare put anything down my throat. I'm slopping about up to *here*, man – I damn nearly heaved in the car coming. But you worked with TSR, right? How well do you reckon you know all the things TSR had to do for us?'

'Terry and I worked very closely together. We conferred on almost all the areas of the CTASATM's work. Naturally, the final decisions were always Terry's, but, in terms of familiarity with on-going projects, I'm entirely comfortable with everything.' I could have added, 'As I said, verbatim, at my interview, having practised the spiel the previous night in front of a mirror.'

'Everything?' he asked, the inflection fishing for confirmation of something or other.

'Oh, yes – *everything*.' I had no idea what he was talking about, but I could do inflections of my own well enough and thought this was the best policy to cover my wholesale ignorance.

'Good. Good for you. So you're a sound bloke, then, eh? Realist. Someone I can rely on the way I relied on TSR. Except for the bit where he suddenly goes bouncing away like spit off an iron, of course – not got his itchy feet, have you?'

'Me? No. Anyway, I couldn't, I have a family.'

'Family man, are you? Good for you. Got some proper work out of your sperm, eh? That's great. Chrrrist, my mouth tastes like I've been eating dog-ends out of a urinal – ahhhhhhhhh. Look at my tongue – ahhhhhhhhh. How's it look?'

'Well . . .'

'No, you're right, don't tell me – best not to know. Anyway, Pel, enough of the pleasantries, we need to have a little chat about some pressing work matters.'

'Fire away.'

'OK. First off there's this bloody new building we've got coming up over at the Learning Centre – building a library over a graveyard; spot the difference, eh? The contractors, being contractors, are a pack of bastards. TSR was keeping them in line, so you take over there. Don't take any crap from them. They'll try and play one hand off against the other if they can, so you just deal with them direct, OK? You're God as far as they're concerned, man, you understand? If they get to thinking you can't wipe your arse without getting a vote on it in a committee first they'll walk all over you. Keep me informed, of course, but don't waste your time weaselling a consensus out of a prat-filled Action Group when you should be kicking the contractors' arses into gear. Do you know Nazim Iqbal?'

'I know *of* him, but we've never met. He's the uni's marketing director, isn't he?'

'That he is. Full of shit, but that goes with the territory. He knows his business and he can't be panicked. TSR and he always kept in touch – everything is image nowadays. If it starts raining crap then Nazim is the man with our umbrella. I'll let him know you're the new CTSAATM . . .'

'CTASATM.'

'Whatever. I'll let him know you're our new man. Next up we have the recruitment of Pacific Rim students. *That's* a shit-storm at the moment, as I'm sure you can guess. I don't know if the people over there know about TSR skipping out – we'll play that down. They'll be getting jittery, though. You'll have to do some sweet-talking there.'

The mention of the Pacific Rim and TSR brought it up in my mind – subconsciously, the phrase 'sweet-talking' probably contributed too – so I thought I'd chance my arm with a question, hopefully without giving away how clueless I was about all these new CTASATM responsibilities.

'Do you know Chiang Ho Yam?'

'Chrrrrist, has he been in touch?'

'He phoned me. Well, he meant to phone TSR; I told him I'd taken over.'

'What else did you say?'

'Nothing, really.'

'Good work. Chiang Ho Yam's one of the men we deal with over there, he's Hung.'

'So he said.' My God, how well endowed was this guy? Had I missed a documentary or something? 'I wish I could say the same.'

'What?'

'Um, "hung". You know.' I looked down at my crotch to indicate.

'*What*? No, he's "Hung" with a capital "H".'

'Right, I get the picture. The man has a serious appendage.'

'What are you . . . ? Chiang Ho Yam's *Hung*. He's a member of the Hung Society; our Pacific Rim recruitment people. I thought you knew about all this?'

Oh, arse.

'No, that is, *yes* – I do. I was making a joke. You know Hung, *hung*. See?'

'Where did you get that bump on your head?'

'Playing squash. Collided with a racket.'

'Did it need X-rays?'

'God no. Barely noticed it at the time. Just kept playing. Won the game forty to love.'

'Forty to love? I didn't think you scored like that in squash. I thought you played to nine points.'

'We play Egyptian Rules – sudden death. Yes, so, the Hung Society, of course. Look after our Pacific Rim student recruitment; TSR and I discussed that. Often.'

'Right, OK. Sorry, Hung/hung, I see it now. Very funny. This hangover's sitting its fat arse on my sense of humour today, obviously. Anyway, the building work and the Pacific Rim recruitment, those are the top priorities right now – the P. Rim recruitment situation especially, that could turn nasty if you don't get on top of it. Clearly, keep things tight – just me, you and Nazim. We don't want every dog and his fleas getting involved. I'll tell Christine to put you straight through if you call. You're The Man now. Any questions?'

'No. Well, just, it does seem rather a high level of responsibility for a CTASATM. David Woolf was saying recently . . .'

'Chrrrist, man, what does David Woolf know? What was he asking about?'

'Nothing, nothing *specific*, he was just saying how a CTASATM dealing directly with the Vice-Chancellor seemed inappropriate.'

'See? This is what I mean, this is why we have to be so careful, the slightest little thing can have Lord knows who on your back. You just keep tight lipped right across the board, man – need-to-know basis. Who knows you're here seeing me now?'

'Um, Bernard Donnelly, I suppose. David knows, and so does Pauline Dodd.'

'Who's Pauline Dodd?'

'She's manager of the library assistant team in the Learning Centre.'

He shook his head to indicate he still wasn't any the wiser.

'Red, frizzy hair,' I said. 'To about here. Freckles . . . mid-thirties . . . inclined towards Indian-print cotton dresses . . .'

'Oh, *yes*, I'm with you now, man. Not a bad looker? But you suspect she'd chant about bloody crystals or something while you were doing the business? She's probably harmless enough, but, like I say, you just keep it tight between us. If David Woolf starts asking you about work practices, well, just . . .'

'Yes?'

'Just tell him to fuck off. Things need to get done, that's the bottom line. We managed to keep this place on track with TSR, now you need to take over.'

'Mm,' I replied.

'You are *sure* you're up to this, Pel?'

'Yeah. No problem. George.'

'Good man. Good man. Right, better let you get to it, then. Off you go.'

I stood up and began moving towards the door.

'Thanks,' I said. For some reason.

As I was halfway out of the door he called after me.

'Just remember . . .' he said, finishing the sentence by tapping the side of his nose. He then slumped his head back into his hands to the accompaniment of a carefully enunciated 'Chrrrrist!' and I closed the door on him.

'So – how can I improve my life by fifty per cent without doing anything that requires any effort?' I asked as I moved around behind Roo to take my seat in the café. He waited until I'd sat down then pointed at me with two fingers, his cigarette smoking in between them.

'Reject the tyranny of socks.'

'Ahhh, I see.'

'No you don't.'

'No, I don't.'

'It's a mindset. Socks are a mindset, and you must reject it.'

'If you're suggesting I stop wearing socks then I have to point out that's crazy talk.'

'No, socks are good.'

'He's probably going to advise against putting them on your feet, though,' interrupted Tracey. 'Stuff them with newspaper and push them down the front of your underpants, I bet that's where he's heading.'

'I am not heading for his underpants.'

'You're not heading for his underpants?'

'Yes, that's it. What I'm saying it that we've been brainwashed by socks. How much time, Pel, do you spend with a sock in your hand, frantically searching for its partner?'

'Weekly?'

'Let's say weekly, yes.'

'Quite a bit of time.'

'There you go, "quite a bit of time". And do you know how long that adds up to over the course of a lifetime?'

'No.'

'No, of course you don't, no one does. No one is even *trying* to calculate how many hours are lost searching for the second sock, no one even thinks about it – we're letting the socks set the agenda here. Not only that, but there's also the sheer frustration and anger of looking for the other half of the pair. And when is this most likely happening? *When?*'

'Go on – I'm transfixed.'

'First thing in the morning, that's when. It's setting you up in a bad mood right at the beginning of the day. You arrive at work, possibly late or having had to skip breakfast . . .'

'The most important meal of the day.'

'The most important meal of the day, as you rightly observe, you feel you have no control and you're furious and bitter. Well, I say, "No." Simply let go. Pull two socks out of the drawer, and put them on. If they match, fair enough, if not, don't give it a second thought. It's quite unlikely anyone will notice, or even see, your socks and, if they do, you can always play the "interestingly quirky, me" card.'

'I feel . . . *reborn*,' I gasped.

'I don't have any socks,' said Tracey. 'So I just feel left behind.'

'Ah, you can extend the principle. Women should always wear black stockings and suspenders.'

'What? *Always?*' asked Tracey.

'Well, except . . . No – no, in fact always,' replied Roo.

'Christ,' I said. 'He's really thought this through.'

'I suppose it's irrelevant now it's all been sorted, Pel,' Tracey said, 'but why do you want you life improved by fifty per cent anyway? I thought things were going pretty well; promotion, you've found a new house and, erm, well, that's two things. You can't sniff at two things – don't you even begin to say it, Roo.'

'Well, for a start, I haven't really been promoted to a new job yet, I've just got a new job *as well*; they've still got me doing the supervisor post too. Not only that, but I saw the VC this morning. Now I realise there's about three times as much stuff I don't have the faintest idea about. I was just getting comfortable not understanding the CTASATM's job and all of a sudden I have spread my cluelessness much, much farther. I don't know how long I can keep bluffing. They're sure to find me out soon.'

'Unless they're bluffing too,' replied Tracey.

'Oh, yeah, *right*.' I sniffed. 'You're saying that everyone at the uni, right up to the Vice Chancellor, doesn't really have any idea what they're supposed to do?'

'He finds that somehow difficult to believe,' Tracey said to Roo.

'Yes,' he sighed back to her sadly. 'I think we may have lost him.'

'So, that's work,' I continued, ignoring them. 'We have got the mortgage for the new house sorted out, that's true. But we have to rent the one we've got now – I put a card up in the Students' Union the other day.'

'You *are* renting, then?'

'Yeah. Ursula and I discussed it at the weekend. We weighed up the pros and cons, looked at all the options, I spent a few nights sleeping in the bath, and that was it – sorted. The fact is, it'd take ages to find a buyer for the house, but we should be able to get students to rent pretty quickly. There's loads of work to do on the new house, though, and I just know that's going to lead to trouble. Doing stuff is always a flashpoint with us.'

'I think it's romantic, moving into a place together. Don't you, Roo?' Tracey said.

'Depends on the place. I suppose it's OK if it's a good place.'

'Tch, no, it's *better* if it isn't a good place,' Tracey went on. 'If it's a good place it's boring. It's only romantic if it's run down and you have to work on it together. Painting the walls, fixing the doors, no furniture or fittings – only an electric kettle to make each other mugs of tea as you go along. Work all day then snuggle up under the duvet on a mattress on the floor; just a candle for light and each other to keep you warm.'

Roo and I peered at her in silence for a moment, before he asked, 'Why can you only use a candle for light if the electric kettle works?'

Her reply was to dip her finger into his coffee and flick it at his face.

'Anyway,' I said, 'you brushed over the bit about the two howling children. Did I tell you the kids put on a tremendous show for Karen and Colin Rawbone at the weekend?'

'No,' Tracey said, sucking coffee off her finger. 'Where was that?'

'Out shopping. We were just doing a quick bit of shopping – with all the screaming and violence that involves – and we ran into the bloody Rawbones. Kids rolling over the floor, Ursula and me rowing, and there they are watching with their trolley full of crisp vegetables and sparkling spring water; I bet it's the closest Karen's ever got to an orgasm.'

'What did she say?' asked Tracey.

'Oh, "Isn't it interesting how great we are when juxtaposed with how rubbish you are? Hahahaha" basically covers it. *They* don't have arguments, it seems, and they like exactly the same things.'

Roo shrugged. 'It's hardly a great surprise that they don't argue. I think you'll find that to have a personality clash people need to have personalities.'

'Well, Ursula and I certainly both have strong characters.

Um – it still counts as a character even if it's made up entirely of flaws, right?'

'Your imperfections make you perfect for each other.' Tracey beamed. 'Jane Austen – "Our imperfections make us perfect for each other" – it's from *Emma*.'

'I don't think it is, actually,' I grimaced.

'It *is*. The bloke says it, what's-his-name, erm – Jeremy Northam.'

'Oh, right. That's in the film, but I don't think the line is in the book.'

'Oh, for Christ's sake! I get one chance to look clever and knowledgeable by doing a quote and you have to go and shoot me down.'

'I'm not shooting you down, I just said it wasn't in the book. If it ever comes up again, you can simply say "As Mr Knightly said in the film of *Emma* . . ." and your erudition will blaze just as brightly.'

'No it bloody won't. You have to quote from books to look clever. You can't quote from *films*. If you quote from films you just look like a geek.'

Both Tracey and I were unable to prevent our eyes briefly flicking towards Roo.

'You talkin' to me? You talkin' to *me*?'

'That's nonsense, Tracey. Movies are *at least* as valid as books, intellectually speaking. Anyone who says otherwise is just a tiresome pedant.'

'Then why did you correct me and say it wasn't in the book?'

'I was just, you know, making conversation.'

'Not as refreshing as you'd think it'd be, is it?' Roo said to me as the flicks of coffee ran down my face.

'Getting back to the point,' said Tracey, 'you and Ursula are a far better couple than Colin and Karen Rawbone. I've been round your house, remember – seen Ursula desperately trying to look angry when you and the kids walk in dripping all over the kitchen floor after a water fight in the garden. There's genuine love there; the Rawbones make you feel they're together because it's no trouble and they both go well with their wallpaper. *You* wouldn't have Ursula any other way . . .'

'Well . . .'

'Don't say it – you wouldn't and you know it; you *want* her to be opinionated and determined. And Ursula loves you too. You're attractive – not in a sexual way, of course . . .'

'Cheers.'

'Attractive because you're kind and clever in no useful way and just a bit weird and always look like there's something slightly alarming going on in your head we can't quite guess at and, most of all, for Ursula, because you love her not because she's a *just like you*, but for who *she* is.'

'Pel . . .' stuttered Roo in a hushed voice. 'I'd really like to hug you right now.'

'While *Roo* here,' said Tracey, 'is a complete fucking twat.'

Roo laughed. 'Don't try to deny it, babe – you're irresistibly attracted to the "slightly alarming" things that are going on in my head.'

Tracey laughed too. And stuck her tongue out at him.

'Anyway,' Roo said, 'dragging the conversation back down to our usual level of gossip and smut, has your big penis man phoned again?'

'Big penis? Oh, right, no. Misunderstanding – it's not important.'

'Big penis not important?' gasped Tracey. 'Now it's my turn to correct *you*, Dalton.'

Jane Austen quotations didn't feature a great deal during the following twenty minutes.

Some things purchase good real estate in your mind; sturdy, resilient, conveniently situated near the front of your consciousness. As in life, the residents with the means to afford such homes generally get it by being shits. Tracey's – well, *paean* seems the only word – Tracey's paean to vast penises was still hanging around, unwanted, in my brain that evening when I took a shower before bed. Gazing down, I could shrug, 'Pah – foreshortening due to my perspective' as often as I wanted, it didn't banish my pernicious doubts for a moment. It wasn't that I felt it was irrefutably 'small', it was rather that I felt no urge to preen because it was 'imposingly big'. I had to face life while carrying the knowledge that I had a so-so penis, and I wasn't sure I had the spiritual strength. Simply because it's so much easier to kick someone when he's down, a second realisation came in with its foot swinging. Still staring sadly at my groin, I noticed that I had a stomach. Not a sagging sack filled with years of fish-and-chip suppers, you understand, not a bulbous mound meaning I had to lean forward so as to be able to peer at my indifferent penis, but a visible stomach nonetheless. Last time I'd glanced in that direction, I had no stomach, just a vertical drop from ribcage to crotch. Now a small, but identifiable, structure had appeared between the two areas. I couldn't imagine where this had come from. I didn't eat a great deal; in fact, my appetite was very light because I sat in front of a computer most of the day and never took any exercise, so I did nothing to provoke an appetite. It seemed impossibly unfair. This stomach certainly wasn't a useful store of energy – chasing that burglar had clearly shown that my reserves were designed merely to carry me over the twenty-five yards that separated my initial burst of speed being used up and some people arriving to revive me with a defibrillator.

As my body clearly had it in for me, I wasn't in a buoyant mood by the time I'd finished in the shower. Ursula was already in bed and I slid in next to her. She was reading a book, *Über alle Grenzen verliebt – Beziehungen zwischen deutschen Frauen und Ausländern* (*Love over All Borders – Relationships between German women and foreigners*), pausing every so often to underline sentences with a pencil. She'd been sent the book in one of the frequent Red Cross packages her family made up for her. Every month or so she'd get a parcel about twice the size of a shoebox from Germany. In it her parents, siblings, friends and well-wishers would have placed all the things they knew she wouldn't be able to obtain in England. Biscuits, for example, and soap, chocolate, candles or tampons. Sometimes they'd also slip in a photocopy of a European Union report on the state of Britain's beaches, or a newspaper clipping from the *Süddeutsche Zeitung* about how all English meat products are made from decaying dog carcasses in the lightless basement of a sewage farm by a cadre of sex criminals specially chosen for their open sores and explosive dysentery.

It's banal even to mention that England since 1950 has put its greatest efforts into developing the fields of hooliganism and litter. Germany is cleaner than England, the standard of living is higher, both its government and its people are generally better educated, more conscientious, harder working, more polite and, quite simply, kinder. All across the board Germany is better than England – apart from the area of popular music, where England still has a special talent and, gratifyingly, Germany is almost frighteningly rubbish. I recognise this, and am the first to shout it at anyone still clinging to ludicrous World War II clichés and pathetic, ill-informed nationalism. So, naturally, whenever our German friends and relatives – more in sorrow than in anger – look at England as a proto-Third World nation I get *incredibly* defensive about it and rant hysterically about how you can't get a proper loaf of bread in Germany and the banks are closed all the time and the traffic lights are unnecessarily confusing, etc., etc. I like to think that it's just such paradoxes which give the relationship between Ursula and me the type of unpredictable, self-sustaining vitality one can sometimes glimpse at a food riot or a fight in a pool hall.

I moved closer to Ursula and hooked my arm around her, bringing my hand up to stroke her hair.

'What do you want?' She squinted at me suspiciously.

'Want? Nothing.'

She let out a not entirely convinced 'Mmmmmm . . .' but squirmed herself lower so she was resting her head on my chest, looking down at the book now propped up on her stomach. I continued to brush my fingers through her hair as I scanned the pages. My, let us say, 'functional' German just made it frustrating; understanding a third of something is far worse that understanding nothing at all.

'What's "*Duldung*" mean?'

'Toleration.'

'Right . . . What about "*einklagbare*"?'

'Um, recoverable – recoverable by law.'

'Oh . . . Do you think my cock is big enough?'

'Where's it say that?'

'Humour. Nice one. I'm just asking, do you think my cock is big enough?'

'Don't use that word. Can't you say "dick"?'

'I don't like "dick". "Dick" is childish or comic – "cock" is raw and primal. A cock is what you use during thrashing, panting, delirious, consciousness-threatening sex. A dick is what twelve-year-old girls snigger about; it's just a small step from "dick" to "willy", and once we get there we might as well do everything with test tubes. Anyway, it's my cock, so I think I should be able to choose – you make me say "breasts".'

'Because "tits" is just vile.'

'You are mistaken. Tits is just pure sex; the t's a voiceless, lingua-alveolar stop plosive – aspirated too, I think – you go *right* in with that, but finish on the strong fricative "s" whose sibilance you can extend for pretty much as long as your nerve holds out.'

'Oooh, stop it, you're getting me hot.'

'Whereas "breasts", on the other hand, merely provide infants with milk.'

'Nonsense. "Breasts" are beautiful, "tits" are what English women pull out and wave around at parties.'

'You're wrong. It's not your fault, of course, but you're wrong.'

'Saying "you're wrong" is survivable. Introduce that bastardly, head-patting "it's not your fault" crap and you're simply asking me to punch your face until you die.'

'They're English words. Your English is superb; your understanding is astonishing and you only make the odd mistake . . .'

'What mistake?'

'Just the odd one.'

'Which odd one?'

'Um, I can't think of one off the top of my head.'

'Humph.'

'OK, OK, so you never make any mistakes – Jesus – but the point is you can never really *feel* the language. Not at a completely instinctive level.'

'We both prefer "cunt".'

'Yes, that's true, but you'll sometimes slip in a "vagina". That's terrible. Horrible. It's a medical term; your using "vagina" at a crucial point can have a very detrimental effect on me.'

'Why didn't you say?'

'It never seemed to be the right moment.'

'Fair enough, then.' She closed her book and placed it on the bedside table. 'I'll try to remember not to use a "vagina" in future. Goodnight.' She kissed me on the cheek and turned off the light.

'Hold on. What about my cock?' I said, turning the light back on. 'You didn't answer me – are you trying to avoid the question?'

'What?'

'I asked you if you thought it was big enough.'

'Oh, yeah. It's fine. Can we go to sleep now?' She turned the light off again.

We nestled closer together, facing the same way so my arms were around her and my nose was nuzzling against her ear. We lay among the warm, steady waves of our breathing for a minute or so.

'You're not just saying that?' I whispered.

'Eh? Oh – no, I'm not just saying it. Really, your dick's fine.'

'OK.'

I squeezed her hand and let things lie for quite a while before, for clarity, I whispered, 'What do you mean by "fine"?'

'Mmmm?'

'I said, what do you mean by "fine"?'

'I mean your dick's "*fine*". It's "*fine*".'

'Yes, I know that. It's just not a very emphatic word, is it? Fine? It's the kind of thing you'd say about a soup you didn't like, just to be polite. It's not like "great" or "fantastic" or "splendid".'

'Who the hell says "Your dick is splendid"?'

'Who the hell says "Your dick is *fine*"?'

'Oh, for Christ's sake. You asked me if it was big enough, and it *is*. What do you want me to say? It *is*; it's not very small, it's not very big – it's . . .'

'Hold on – "not very big"?'

'Yeeees, it's not very big.'

I put the light back on and sat up.

'So what you're saying – I just want to be clear about this – is that I haven't got a very big cock?'

'Yes, yes; that's a good thing.'

I stared at her in silence for what I estimate was about a million years.

'Nope. You have *completely* lost me there.'

'Why would I want it big? It'd just be painful. What's the point of it looking impressive but being awkward to use?'

'So it's unimpressive? I have an unimpressive penis. Perhaps you'd like to stab a pair of scissors into my chest now?'

'I'm moving in that direction . . . Look, I didn't say your dick was unimpressive – it's fine . . .'

'Yes, of course, "*fine*".'

'. . . it's fine. It's *splendid* – I could just sit staring at it for hours, I really could – but the point I'm making is that it's of a size that suits me, physically, when we put it to use, that's all. I personally wouldn't want it any bigger.'

'Great. So you do think it's tiny. It's tiny, but at least it's not uncomfortable to sit on. Fantastic. Great. I've got a "convenient", "pocket-sized", won't-spoil-your-appetite-style penis – I can just see all the women in the world *really* getting fired up over that; "Oh, look – a Travel Penis."'

'Wait a damnly minute. What does is matter how other women might feel? What are you saying, exactly?'

'Oh, don't try to turn it around. I'm not having you twist the argument. Remember when you came back from the hairdresser's all miserable about the way it'd turned out? And you asked me whether I thought it looked terrible, right? And I said it didn't matter whether you looked attractive or not because I loved you anyway and it wasn't important what other men might think any more. Remember? Yes, that's right – you went off like a bloody hand grenade, didn't you?'

'What the . . . How is that *remotely* the same? Your dick isn't on your head, is it? We were talking about my hair, for Christ's sake. It's a very public thing. It affects how I feel about myself. You don't have to have your dick on show to everyone you meet all day. Not unless your new job includes some responsibilities you've been very cagey about mentioning to me.'

'But a penis is far more important to your self-esteem than your haircut. God, there's no comparison. For a start, a penis is forever. You can't choose your penis out of a magazine. I can't walk into a shop with a picture of Errol Flynn and say,

"I'd like it like that, please." I can't look down at it gloomily and think, Oh dear, that's too short to suit me – still, it'll grow out. This is the unchanging definition of my manhood we're talking about here, that's why they call it your *manhood*. It's absolutely vital to my self-image; I *am* my penis!'

'You need emergency psychiatric help. I cannot believe I'm having this conversation. What's the time now? My God – *look at the time*. I have to go to work tomorrow, I need to get some sleep, and instead I'm having an argument with a case study; Patient M – the man who thinks he's a penis. Let's just forget the whole thing, OK? I need to get some sleep. Imagine you asked me about your dick, I said, "Pel, your dick is gargantuan," and we can both get some sleep.'

'Don't be stupid. There's no way I can pretend you didn't say all that stuff. My tiny penis is out of the bottle now, we can't put it back. I just have to live with it. For ever.' I reached up and turned out the light again then heavily shuffled the duvet around myself, curled up and facing away from her.

I heard Ursula sigh into the darkness.

'You're sulking now, aren't you? You're going to be sulking for days.'

'I'm *not* sulking.'

'Right. You're not sulking.'

'I'm *not* sulking.'

Ursula made a tutting noise and moved up behind me. She kissed the back of my head, said, 'Goodnight,' and lay there, her breathing gradually smoothing into the relaxed rhythm of someone going to sleep.

I lay completely silent (except for the occasional – involuntary – long, afflicted sigh) and bore my horrible torment uncomplaining. Asking for nothing but wordless solitude in which to face my pain alone. That'd teach her.

'Are you *still* sulking?'

'No.'

Breakfast successfully navigated, then, I went to work. I decided to visit the troops to bolster morale. Concentrating on not making any headway in the CTASATM position had meant I'd rather neglected being ineffectual as the Computer Team Supervisor for a while, so I marched into the office to encourage the workers and show them I still cared.

'Hi there! How's it going? Everything moving along well?'

'Nmmm.'

'Mmm.'

'Hnnn.'

'Good. Good. So, no problems? Shininess all round? Eh? Is it? Wayne? No problems?'

'The new net cache system displays a single address, externally, to subscription servers using IP verification.'

'Excellent.'

'No, that's bad.'

'Of course it is – I meant excellent that you've told me about it. Tricky one. I can only think of three or four workarounds for that. What would your suggestion be, Wayne?'

'I've already fixed it. I had a word with the sys admins – we're using cookies to verify through the browser now.'

'That would have been my top choice too.'

'What were the other ways?'

'That's not important.'

'I'm just interested.'

'Oh, you know, really fiddly things. Really, really fiddly Windows hacks.'

'But only the local machines are Windows. Our server is running UNIX.'

'Shut up now, OK?'

He shrugged.

'We need to focus, that's the important thing.'

'Focus on what?'

'Not *on* anything, just *focus*. We need to keep ourselves *focused*, yes? There haven't been any other problems, then? Hardware faults? Student troubles?'

'Only the usual amount.'

'How's the league table?'

'We got another four complaints from students about other students using mobile phones yesterday. That takes it up to seventy-four this month, which means it's just overtaken complaints from students about our telling them not to use their mobile phones.'

'How many used the word "fascist"?'

'Fifty-six per cent. Slightly down. There have only been three cases of students being caught having sex in the study rooms so far.'

'Any captured on video?'

'Just the one.'

Raj cut in. 'Bill the security bloke has the tape at the moment, and then it's me. I'll put your name down on the rota if you want, though.'

'Thanks, Raj. Wayne, what about pornography?'

'Online chat is much more common that downloading porn at the moment; we think maybe due to seasonal factors.'

'Damn.'

'Your points do get a boost from the sixteen students whose dissertations were lost due to disk faults, though, because of the number who'd made a back-up copy.'

'How many?'

'None.'

'Yessss!'

'The health service workers on short courses are still the most clueless, of course, though Brian is saying we should drop that category.'

'That's right.' Brian looked pained. 'For a start it's subjective – it's just a matter of opinion that the nurses and so on are more clueless.'

'Oh, Brian – they're wilfully inept. They're proud of it, even. I don't think you have a case there.'

'Right, OK, I'll give you that; but it's still not fair. I picked the art students out of the hat. They never use the PCs in here until their final week. They're just as useless with computers, and just as self-satisfied about it, but we simply don't get to see them. It distorts the figures.'

'Fair point. Perhaps we'll drop the 'hopeless' category next season.'

I must admit that I was quite uplifted by the team meeting. Wayne, Raj and Brian seemed to have responded extremely well to the greater responsibility that had been placed on their rounded shoulders by my absence. On a couple of occasions they even glanced away from their computer screens to look at me when replying; by their own efforts they'd discovered social interaction. On top of that, naturally, was the fact that I'd gained quite a few points in the league table and if just one more student said, 'So, you're saying a Mac and a PC are *different*, then?' I was sure of winning the *Blade Runner* Director's Cut DVD at the end of the academic year.

Hyped up by my success, I telephoned the contractors lined up for the new building. They were due to start very soon and I wanted to make sure I spoke to the person in charge – a Bill Acton – before any work began. He wasn't in, but his secretary gave me his mobile number.

'Hello,' he crackled, barely audible on the poor connection above an angry hum of engine noise. I stuck my finger in my ear to cut out any background sounds and squinted to . . . well, I don't know why I squinted – you just do if it's a bad line.

'Bill Acton?' I shouted.

'Yes.'

'Hi, there, I'm . . .'

'Why are you shouting?'

'Because I can't hear you very well.'

'Well, shouldn't *I* be the one shouting, then?'

'Er, I suppose, yes.'

'How's that?'

'Better. Thanks. My name's Pel. I'm from the University of North-Eastern England. I've taken over from Terry Steven Russell.'

'Oh, right you are, squire. We're going to be— Oi! Get over, you idiot! Can't you see me coming through here? Tch. Cretin. Sorry about that, Pel. Yes, we're going to be starting work over at your place very soon.'

'Good. Excellent. That was why I was calling, really.'

'Yes?'

'Yes. I was hoping we could meet before you began the work.'

'Why's that? Fine by me, squire, don't get me wrong. Just seems a bit unnecessary.'

'It's because I want to get myself up to speed before it all begins. I've come late to this.'

'Ah, but TSR did talk to you, right? I mean . . . Hold on, I'm going under a bridge.' He disappeared into a roar of static for a few seconds. 'You still there?'

'Yes, I'm here.'

'As I was saying, you do know everything about the set-up, yes?'

'Well, yes . . . of course. I've been following the project closely – of course – it's just a few details, really.'

'Like what?'

'I can't say. I can't say . . . because . . . I'd need to draw pictures. To convey the ideas properly.'

'You're the boss, squire. Tell you what you— Oi! Watch where you're going! Moron! Yes, and you, mate! Sorry. You're the boss, Pel. You're in the Learning Centre, right?'

'Yes.'

'Well, I'll pop over soon and we'll have a chat, OK?'

'That'd be great. That's great. I'll let you go now, don't want you having an accident – it's a bit dangerous to use a mobile phone while you're driving.'

'I'm not driving,' he replied, puzzled.

The Computer Team not imploding and an arrangement to meet the person in charge of the contractors; two successes in one day. I couldn't remember the last time that had happened. I coasted for the rest of the week.

The following week I had another conversation with Mr Chiang Ho Yam. In a parallel universe where Pel is going through life with a breezy competence the telephone call probably allowed him to move up a gear; here in my world I got the sound of trying to change gears without the clutch. The phone played its external riff.

'Hello, University of North-Eastern England. Pel speaking.'

'I Chiang Ho Yam,' Chiang replied in his careful, steady voice.

'Hello there, Mr Chiang. Sorry about the confusion last time you rang. I didn't realise who you were. My secretary's fault, I'm afraid.'

'You know now? I Chiang Ho Yam, I am Hung.'

'Indeed. Yes, you're involved in the recruitment of our Pacific Rim students. How can I help you?'

'I am pleased you are ready to help, Mr Pel. We are concerned that the arrangements are not being followed. I am 415, Mr Pel, it falls to me to ensure that arrangements of this nature are properly executed.'

'I see.' I didn't, clearly.

'The 14K have worked hard to provide you with the number you required for the coming year. The paperwork is with you. It is in order, is it not?'

'More or less,' I conceded brightly. As I had almost no idea whatsoever what the hell he was talking about, it seemed churlish to disagree.

'Good. That is good. So may I ask why the funds have not been transferred as usual? I – and my superiors – are very concerned about this. The delay has now become worrying.'

'And your anxiety is understandable, Mr Chiang.' (For a start you're talking to someone who hasn't a clue what's going on – that's enough to be concerned about, right there.) 'But let me assure you that everything is under control. We had a computer problem.' Thankfully, there's little if anything that you can't blame on a computer problem, so I felt pretty safe even though I didn't know what I was actually blaming on one. 'That has prevented us moving forward at the speed we would like. Things are back on track now, however. In fact, I was just going to speak with someone about your situation this morning. I'm sure I can get things moving.'

'I hope so, Mr Pel. Because of this matter our 438 in 14K, with whom I have conferred, has insisted we contact some of our people in your country. They have been asked to visit you and ensure the situation is resolved.'

'I look forward to meeting them. Do you know when they'll be coming?'

'Not precisely, no.'

'Well, I'm usually here in the Learning Centre. They can drop in and find me here.'

'It would be best all round if they did find you there, Mr Pel. If they had to go searching for you their mood would almost certainly deteriorate.'

'Probably best they telephone first, then, Mr Chiang, to warn me they're arriving.'

'I will suggest this to them. I'm sure they will find the idea amusing.'

'Anyway, as I say, I was *just* about to speak to someone about your situation. Leave it with me, OK?'

'Thank you.'

'My pleasure – nice to speak to you again.'

My heart didn't exactly sink, but it did start taking on water. Student funds, even straightforward ones, were always a hellish maze to get through. In this case, I wasn't even sure what funds he was referring to. Foreign students, certainly the Pacific Rim ones, are generally funded privately. They don't get money from our Local Education Authority – our LEA is famously against giving money to its own students, let alone any others. Where were the funds he was expecting coming from? If it was their own countries, surely he was better placed to deal with it than us?

I knew I'd have to ask someone. The VC seemed the obvious person, but I couldn't think of a way to ask without making it clear I didn't know – and thereby tarnishing my, up to now, excellently on-the-ball image. Fortunately, another option barged into me without my even having to look for it.

Bernard came into the office while I was still sitting in quiet, managerial thought.

'Hi, Pel. I was just passing. I wondered if you'd done any work on the preparation for the Improvement Day?'

'Oh, yes, lots.' I *knew* there was something.

'That's great. Because I was thinking of having it soonish. What kind of things have you planned, exactly?'

'Gosh – I don't know where to start . . .' This was the absolute truth.

Bernard opened his mouth and the phone rang – the timing really was that precise, as though they were connected; either his mouth had set the phone off or his voice had been replaced by ring tones.

'Sorry, Bernard, let me get that . . . Hello, Learning Centre, Pel speaking.'

'Pel! Hiya, guy! Listen, this is Nazim, right? George tells me you're the man who talks the talk and walks the walk now TSR's disappeared.'

'That's right, I'm the new CTASATM here.'

'Magic. Listen, can you get yourself over to the conference room in Chamberlain Block?'

'What, *now*?'

'If you could, yeah. There's a meeting about the new Learning Centre build. I arranged it late last week – meant to call and tell you. Forgot. Sorry, guy. It's the last one before work starts, though, know what I mean? It'd be good for you to be here.'

'Um, yes, right, OK. I'm on my way over now.'

'You're a star. Kick-off's in ten, right? See you here.'

'Yes. 'Bye.'

I turned back to Bernard as I rose from my seat in something between a fluster and a tizzy.

'I'm really sorry, Bernard, but I have to run – there's a meeting about the new building just about to start.'

'No problem. We can discuss the details of your plans for the Improvement Day when you get back.'

'Oh, no need, Bernard, really. I've got it all in hand.' I rushed out of the door. 'Don't worry about it,' I called back to him as I began racing down the stairs that zigzagged down to the exit.

'Really? Well, good work.' He was coming down the stairs after me – surprisingly sprightly for a senior librarian.

'Just doing my job.' I quickened my pace further, jumping down the last four steps on to the first landing and skidding around to begin hurling myself down the next flight.

'I'm very impressed, all the same.' He had speeded up to match me. Though, instead of taking multiple steps with each stride, he was taking each one incredibly quickly, his knees flashing up and down and his voice being given a warbling quality by the combined impact of each tiny descent.

'Thanks.' I plunged through two sets of doors so I was now outside in the car park.

'It's all off pat, the . . .' Bernard said to the air when he emerged perhaps three seconds after me. 'Oh.' He peered left and right, clearly trying to see which way I'd gone. 'Oh.' He shrugged his shoulders and walked back into the building.

I stayed crouched down for a moment; eyes just high enough to see the door to the building through the back windows of the Ford Sierra I was hiding behind. I reflected that earlier in my career I might have just stood up without waiting to be sure Bernard wasn't going to reappear, but now I had a managerial position I was a lot more measured in my actions. After a few seconds I was pretty sure it was safe and I raised my head up a little higher. Idly glancing to the side along my shoulder, I caught my own reflection in the glass of the driver's door. I froze with alarm at the unexpected set of my features and the dispassionate eyes, only inches away, staring back at me. Until I realised it wasn't my reflection, but rather David Woolf's face, on David Woolf's head, atop David Woolf's body, looking out at me from the driver's seat of David Woolf's car.

With a gentle hum, the window moved down from between us.

'What are you doing, Pel?'

David's voice had only the slightest inflection and his eyes remained completely unblinking and inexpressive.

There was a noise like wind rushing in my ears. It filled my head and swept away my fragile thoughts as David and I looked at each other for a period of time whose length I couldn't even guess at. It was still there as I replied; I heard my own voice speak indistinctly under its roaring blanket.

'It's a secret.'

*   *   *

I was short of breath when I got to the room in Chamberlain Block. It wasn't all that far, but I'd run flat out the entire way for all sorts of reasons. The door to the conference room was open – I could see lots of people, none of whom I knew, sitting round the table inside drinking catering-style cups of tea and coffee and chatting with pre-meeting brightness. Just outside, to the right of the door, stood a man laughing into a mobile phone. He was in his early to mid thirties and wearing a blue suit clean, recent, uncrumpled and stylish enough to make it obvious he couldn't possibly be a member of the academic staff. His build was light – slightly too thin, even; as though he'd been perfectly proportioned, then unexpectedly grown another six inches. Well-cut, shortish hair bristled from his head and he had flat sideburns running down each cheek; narrow triangles, tapering to a sharp point. He didn't have any children. No one with the time to shave their sideburns like that every morning could possibly have children. If this wasn't Nazim Iqbal, then it ought to be.

I walked over and stood uncomfortably in front of him, looking around – at nothing; the ceiling, my fingernails, the panels on the door – with great interest to make it clear I wasn't trying the exert any pressure on him to finish his call.

'Yeah . . . Yeah . . . *Yeah* . . . Haha – yeah . . . Yeah . . . OK, cool. Speak to you soon, yeah? Ciao.' He flicked his phone closed and grinned at me, holding the mobile up by the side of his head so it faced me, like an actor in a television commercial showing you a new model. 'Sorry, guy. Never ends, you know? I'm 24/7 international. Right now, I'm guessing you're Pel, yeah?'

'That's right. You're Nazim?'

'All day, every day.' He shook my hand with debilitating enthusiasm. 'So, Pel, let's get in there, guy.'

'About that . . . I'm not really one hundred per cent, totally up to speed on the new building situation yet.'

'No sweat. In fact, less sweat than that. You sit yourself

down and look bored – let me do all the talking, OK? This is just cosmetic stuff. We hold a few meetings and then people can't say they weren't consulted. You and me are running the show really, right? Let Nazim work his magic and we can get on with it without anyone on our backs.'

'Whatever you say.' I was pleased that someone was offering me the opportunity of not having to think.

'Great – let's do it!'

We walked into the room, Nazim catching the eyes of everyone around the table and giving them a smile or a wink or a wave. It reminded me of an American presidential candidate walking up to give a fund-raising speech or a Vegas casino owner playing the punters – 'Hey, Joey! Get my friend Ralph here whatever he wants to drink, on the house.' He sat down at the head of the table. He either offered me the seat next to him, or placed me down in it, it was difficult to tell.

'Great! OK. Everybody here?'

'Amanda couldn't make it,' replied a woman in a vast floral dress. 'She's got her ankles again.'

Nazim's face was immediately a thing racked by sorrow and concern.

'Oh, that's a shame. Send her my best wishes.'

Nazim's face recovered.

'I saw Rose Warchowski this morning,' he continued. 'She sends her apologies, but she has an especially vital SCONUL meeting to attend in Cambridge this afternoon and can't be with us. We do, however, have Pel Dalton here . . .' He gestured towards me – *voilà!* 'Pel is the new CTASATM at the Learning Centre.' At the other end of the table, a different woman in a different vast floral dress pointed her ear at me.

'*Mel*, did you say?'

'No, *P-P-Pel*,' I answered.

'Pel? That's rather a strange name.'

'Really? Maybe it is, now I think about it. No one's ever said before.'

Nazim cut in, probably anxious to get on.

'My fault for not speaking clearly. Can everyone down there hear me OK now? Everyone? Drusilla?' Everyone nodded. 'Great. Well, a *very* quick, final, meeting today, I hope. I'm just here to report that things are all on track and work is due to begin very soon indeed. The feedback from the Stakeholder Consultations has been addressed and our responses seem to have satisfied all concerned . . .'

'Sorry. Sorry, Nazim, but I'm not sure I've seen those responses. When were they circulated?' fidgeted an unhealthily thin, middle-aged man in thick black-rimmed glasses.

'They were put up on the intranet, Donald. Some weeks ago.'

'Oh, I see. Do you have the address, at all?'

'Can't remember it off the top of my head, Donald – sorry. But you can navigate to them from the top-level menu via Departments, Estates, Capital Projects, On-going, Consultations, Documentation, Departments, Learning Support, Consultations, On-going, Capital Projects, Learning Centre . . . and so on.'

'Oh . . . Thanks.'

'No problem. Anyway, as I say, the Stakeholder Consultations are now complete. I've received the reports from both Focus Groups, all six of the Action Groups and eighteen of the nineteen Report Groups.'

'Which Report Group hasn't reported back?' asked Donald.

'Carpets. A cause for some concern, obviously, but luckily we can go ahead with the new build without waiting for that to be resolved.'

'What about the Signage Report Group?' I got the impression that Donald lived for these meetings.

'They gave in their report a few months ago, Donald.'

'I thought that was the Signs Report Group?'

'No, sorry, a misunderstanding – my fault, I'm sure. The Signs Report Group reported last month on the *signs* they thought the new building required. They wouldn't have been able to do this had not the Signage Report Group laid down clear guidelines on *signage*. They've both reported back now, though, no problem.'

'Have the reports been circulated?'

'They're on the intranet.'

This was masterful stuff. I'd have begun taking notes on Nazim's technique if I'd brought along any paper, or a pen.

'Right!' he continued. 'Great! As I said at the beginning, there's not really very much to tell you. All we can do right now is hope the contractors carry out their instructions efficiently – which I'm *sure* they will . . .' He crossed his fingers on both hands and waved them in the air, rolling his eyes. The room was swept by relaxed, knowing laughter. '. . . and thank all of you for the, quite unbelievable, amount of effort you've put into this endeavour. Without your expertise, commitment and – laugh at me for saying this if you want, but I have to say it anyway – your *friendship* over the whole period . . . well, I would be sitting here now as chair of a very different project. The success we're witnessing right now is down to you, to all of you. On a personal note, let me say how proud, how quite simply *proud*, I am to have colleagues whose tireless desire to see the UoNE maintain its position as a regional university of outstanding quality is, well, simply off the scale. Thank you. *Thank* you.'

Nazim closed his eyes and, taking a deep breath, clasped his hands together.

I, for one, was beginning to choke up.

'Well! Great! I know you've all got lots to do, so I'll let you get back to your departments without having to listen to me *blabbing* on any more. You know how to contact me if you need anything. Thanks again and take care – 'bye!'

He was somehow out of the door. He'd risen from his chair, moved fluidly across the room, and was gone without it ever looking as if he was running out of the door. I was thrown for a second. Then I got up and ran out after him.

Nazim was poised just outside the staff toilets. He flicked his head towards them and disappeared inside. Half a second later, some of the others began to drain out of the conference room, chatting to each other and glancing at me standing, dead footed, in the middle of the corridor.

I smiled back at them.

'I think I'll go to the lavatory,' I said, some eight times louder than I intended.

They all stopped talking and looked at me.

I pointed to the toilets, and clicked my teeth.

The moment now seemed right for me to stroll over into the Gents without attracting attention.

'I thought that went pretty well,' said Nazim as I entered. He was standing at a urinal, staring down into it as he spoke, but I assumed he was talking about the meeting.

'Yes,' I replied. 'I was talking to the contractors, they said everything was ready and they'd be starting soon.'

'*Did* they? God. Well, that's great – good work, guy.'

'Oh, I thought you knew they were about to start . . . you know, from what you said.'

He laughed and shook himself finished (not laughed *because* he was shaking himself, I hoped, with a vaguely uncomfortable feeling).

'No. I haven't spoken to the contractors for an age, I just made that up. You don't get anywhere if you let yourself get bogged down in practicalities. Anyway, guy, that's your show, I wouldn't dream of sticking my oar in. I'll sort out the publicity, sure, but you're The Man when it comes to the important stuff.'

'What publicity?'

'Oh, whatever, the usual. A breathless piece in the in-house newsletter, picture in the paper, maybe a little piece on the local news if we can think of an angle – the standard routine.'

'I see. Yes, of course. Um . . .'

'What? What's on your mind, guy?'

'Well . . .'

Nazim's mobile phone rang at this point. The rapid arpeggio ring tone (it sounded as if it was probably some dance track, but I couldn't name it) was even more jarringly unpleasant because it reverberated back from the amplifying tiles all around. He looked down at it, made an amused sniffing noise then silenced it with a few key presses.

'Tch, like I said – 24/7 international. Anyway, what were you going to say about the new build?'

'Oh, nothing, I'm sure that'll work out fine. I was just wondering if you knew anything about another matter. I'm not *totally* sure I've got all the details about this one . . .'

'Fire away.'

'It's about the Pacific Rim student recruitment.'

'Oh, riiiight, gotcha. The Hung Society is probably keen to get things back on track, yeah?'

'Yes. That's seems to be it. I think maybe I need a few of the details filling in – I worked very closely with TSR, of course, but he dealt with *the details*.'

'Yeah, didn't he just?' Nazim laughed.

I laughed in response. I didn't know what the joke was, but I thought I might as well give the impression that I did. Fly the flag of competence for just a final couple of seconds before going ahead and asking someone I'd known for under thirty minutes how to do my job while standing in a gentlemen's lavatory.

'So, then – stop me if I'm getting this wrong – Chiang Ho Yam is our contact with the Hung Society. We've got an agreement with them to coordinate the student recruitment in the Pacific Rim area, right?'

'Yep, we use them to find students for us in that area, that's right.'

'They *find* them, that's right. They're not just an administrative body, they actually go out and promote the university to prospective students . . .' Nazim didn't interrupt, so I carried on. 'Then they have some sort of involvement in processing the students' funds . . .'

'Do they? Yeah.' He laughed again. 'I wouldn't be surprised if they take a cut there, as well as our money.'

'Right – our money – right. We have to pay them for their work, naturally.'

'Well, even TSR didn't have the moves to get the Triads to work for free.'

I passed a moment in wordless reflection. Then continued, enunciating my words very precisely.

'Did you say "the Triads" there, Nazim?'

'Huh? Well, yeah, guy – the Triads. You know, the Hung Society – the *Triads*. We deal with the 14K Triad, because they're so strong internationally, don't we?'

'And by *the Triads* we're talking about the criminal gangs in Asia?'

'My understanding is that only a very small percentage of Triad members are actively engaged in criminal stuff, the rest are just people, well, "networking", basically; like being a member of the golf club.'

'So our Triads aren't criminals?'

'Oh, Christ, *ours* are, sure. We're talking about people who need to get students for us. In a world full of universities, to get students – from all across the Pacific Rim countries – to come to *us*. The Triads have people in all the regions and are probably very, um, proactive about recruitment.'

'So we're paying an international criminal gang to get students for us?'

'We're paying them when TSR doesn't sprint off with the money, yeah.' Nazim laughed again.

'Bloody buggering hell! How many people know about this?'

'Well, we were under the impression that *you* knew about it, for one. George, TSR and me are the only people who know, *really* know; but I suspect a few others have an idea. Naturally, as it works out good for everyone, even if other people do have suspicions, no one's making noises. You aren't going to be noisy, are you, guy? I don't think that would be helpful to anyone.'

'But this Chiang character wants his money! He thinks *I've* got the money for him . . . Fiery shit! He said he's got some people coming to visit me!'

'Don't sweat it, it's no problem.'

'They'll kill me – I judge that to be problematic, OK? Perhaps it's my fault for being unprepared. Maybe the job description said "manage Computer Team, develop training materials, be killed by Triads . . ." and I've failed to prioritise; don't recall seeing it, though.'

'Chill out, Pel. Keep your voice down, yeah?'

'I'm going to be hacked to death . . .'

'No you're not.'

'Because . . . what? You've got me lined up for job share with Jackie Chan? They're coming to me for the money and TSR's scarpered with it. That's what you said, didn't you?'

'Sure he's taken the Hung money – that, and a good deal besides – but we have more; TSR didn't take *all* the cash we have available. We'll just get the funds to you to pay them – we're only talking a few thousand pounds here, guy.'

'*Me* pay them? *You* pay them if you have the money. I don't want to get involved with this.'

'Well, you sort of *are* involved now. If I were you, I wouldn't want to give Chiang Ho Yam the impression that you're a boy scout who stumbled into this by accident, right? This really isn't a big deal. The university gets paying students, without spending significantly more than we would on publicity. The students get an education. The Hung Society gets its money – possibly helping local economies all over the Pacific Rim. It's not as if we're buying heroin off them or anything, right, guy?'

'But we're still paying a criminal gang. And how do the *students* feel about them as recruiters?' A realisation abruptly jumped up and shook me by the brain. 'Oh my God – no wonder all the Pacific Rim students have to share the same eight words of English and constantly look pissed off about everything.'

'Pch – what's "criminal"? The Allies used the Mafia in Italy in World War Two, yeah? And who does it help if the students go to Craphole Tech., Minnesota, because we didn't use the most efficient organisation available to recruit? The Triads might, technically, be illegal, but we're not asking them to *do* anything illegal. It's just business. See? If you pay them as usual there are good vibes all round. If you go into a mood, it's bad for everyone, you included.'

'I . . .'

'That's it, guy! I knew you were a solid player, I *knew* it.'

'But . . .'

'I'll get the cash to you, it's not an issue, just leave it to me. There's a bank account it needs to be paid into. TSR always took care of it, but I can find out the details, I've got them somewhere. Whether you do it the usual way or hand over the cash to Chiang Ho Yam's local guys is up to you – whatever you think best, you're The Man.'

Nazim placed his hand on my shoulder and gave it an amiable shake.

'Contact me, any time, if you need anything.' He moved to the side and checked his hair in the mirror. 'I'm here for you, guy, OK? We're buds, right? Christ, look at the time. I've got to go – speak to you soon, OK?'

He bounced out of the door leaving me standing, in at least two senses, in the toilet.

I might easily have stood there, motionless, for a number of years had I not suddenly grabbed at something while swatting at the thoughts that were swarming around in my head. It kicked me back into life and I rushed out of the door.

Minutes later, panting like a spaniel, I crashed into the office back in the Learning Centre and raced across to the filing cabinet. David Woolf, fighting a smile, looked over at me.

'What's wrong, Pel? Are you "it"?'

I ignored him and began digging around in TSR's papers. I scattered them across the floor (Pauline Dodd tutting with increasing volume behind me) as I glanced at, then flung away, each reject. At last I found what I wanted.

There it was; the slip of paper containing the date, the number and the Three Letter Acronym. The date, it was a fair guess, was when the payment had been due. The number would probably be a bank account. And '100,000 HKD' must surely mean one hundred thousand Hong Kong dollars. I sat down at my computer and went to one of the currency conversion sites on the Internet. At that day's exchange rate 100,000 HKD was about nine and a half thousand pounds. This was both alarmingly big and curiously small.

Nazim had dismissed it as 'a few thousand pounds'. If nine and a half was 'a few', then I must remember to ask him to jump down a few stairs. Clearly the money available for this kind of thing was sizable (at least it was nice to know someone in the university had a decent budget). However, the other thing, oddly, worried me more. That sum of money was nice to have stuffed in your pocket, but would certainly not tempt you to take it and run to Brazil; you'd be able to live the champagne lifestyle for about three weeks. TSR would never have skipped out on the temptation of that alone. I remembered Nazim saying he'd taken 'lots more besides'. How much? I wondered. This troubled me no end. TSR would sell you a car with a reset mileometer and pigeons nesting where the engine should be, but I didn't think he'd just *steal* money; it simply didn't seem 'him'. Not unless the amount was absolutely *huge*, not unless it was irresistibly enticing. More important, why had he been concerned about extradition? The university was obviously not going to go to the police complaining he'd run off with their slush fund. He would be very keen on not being found, but surely he didn't imagine that the North-East Police would be the people doing the looking?

I slipped back into a pensive coma.

'What's wrong?'

The exhausting daily barrage of threats and bribery having finally moved the children through eating specific, arbitrary and disparate portions of their tea, they were now in the living room battling with makeshift swords. Ursula and I were sitting together in the postwar chaos of the table eating in the artificial peace before we had to toss a coin to decide which of us would have to get them to brush their teeth.

'Nothing,' I replied, mutilating a potato without appetite.

'Oh – *nothing*; of course. It's Pel's chronic Nothing Affliction again, is it?'

'OK, "nothing you can help with", then, how's that?'

'You could tell me anyway. I tell you things that are bothering me whether you can do anything about them or not.'

'I am very much aware of that.'

'Let's put it this way, then: either tell me what's wrong, or stop doing the brooding hero. It might be attractive when Al Pacino does it in the movies, but in real life it's just going to get you a turkey nugget pushed up your nose. Are you still sulking about your tiny penis?'

'No. It's work stuff. It's just . . .'

'God, don't start me on work stuff – do you know what Vanessa did today?'

'Got you into a bit of a pickle with the Triads?'

'She lost a pile of my reports and then blamed *me* for it. I was so angry I couldn't speak.'

'I've never seen you that angry.'

'I really am going to have to get a job somewhere else. It's unbearable – I have no idea why she seems to pick on *me*.'

'Because she's ugly, obviously. She's very ugly, and every time she sees you it brings it home to her just how wincingly ugly she is. She doesn't see why you should walk around being happy when she has to walk around being really, really ugly.'

'Every time I think I've heard the stupidest thing you're ever going to say . . .' She clicked her fingers in the air. '. . . you open your mouth again and top it. She blamed me for losing the reports because she's *ugly*? Is that what you're saying?'

'Yes.'

'And this, what? Came to you in a dream?'

'It's obvious. I mean, first of all, she's ugly. Right?'

'Well, um, that's just a matter of opinion, isn't it? Erm, she has, um – she has a good bone structure.'

'On to which God built a punchably ugly face. So; she's ugly, you're not, it makes her angry, it comes out as complaining about reports. It doesn't take a genius to see that.'

'Was I arguing you were a genius? Can I just point out that saying four things in a row doesn't show they're related.'

'It's just a woman thing.'

'You know you're dead now, right? You do know that?'

'I'm not criticising, I'm just observing. I'll give you an example; I was going out with this woman once, and she threw a fit at me about some shelves. There I was, watching TV, not bothering anyone, and she came in and started raging on about these shelves and how they were useless and why didn't I get off my arse and do something about them and it's typical and so on. I was completely thrown – where the hell did *this* come from? I didn't see that the shelves were a big issue, especially ten minutes before the end of the movie

I was watching, and we ended up having a huge row about shelves. Turns out the *real* reason she was upset was because she was worried about her mother. But – even if I'd known – had I said at the time, "You're worried about your mother. It's coming out as shelves. Forget about the shelves, OK?", she'd have said I was patronising her and trying to diminish the validity of her shelf opinions. Women seem to do that. Men are much more in touch with their emotions. A man would say, "I'm worried about my mother and you're just sitting there watching TV. You cow." The relationship between the feelings is more direct.'

'Except, you wouldn't say anything at all, you'd just sulk for a week.'

'I don't sulk.'

'And the point you're missing is that, though I may well have been worried about my mother, *the shelves were still crap*. This is just the "What's *Really* the Problem?" line you fall back to when you can't defend the position you're in. If I were shouting at you because you'd let the bath flood the house while you were out betting every penny we had on a greyhound after you'd got a tip from a stripper you'd spent the night with, you'd say, "Have you got your period?" – stop grinning.'

'I wasn't grinning, I was just . . . stretching my mouth.'

'I'll stretch your lips up over the top of your head if you're not careful. Anyway, back to the point. I think I'll look for a new job – "Good pay. Flexible hours. Colleagues not ugly" – and, whether I find one or not, I *have* to have a break. I'll give Jonas a call, see if I can fix up some skiing.'

I suppose I ought to have mentioned the situation at work to Ursula. The trouble with telling Ursula stuff, though, is she'll always end up hassling me to do the right thing. If I tell Ursula I've got toothache, she'll badger me to go to the dentist, which is the last thing you want to have to deal with. If I told Ursula about the problem she would fail to grasp the complexities of it and advise me to go to the police, I could just see it coming. Where would that leave me? There was no certainty that George and Nazim and Chiang Ho Yam couldn't simply deny everything at least effectively enough to make it impossible to convict anyone (except perhaps me). Everyone would hate me for being a squealer and messing about with student recruitment – thereby threatening their jobs – and they'd manufacture some way to fire me in the blink of an eye; I didn't want 'getting myself sacked' to be the very first thing I did after being promoted. Most of all, I *very* much doubted that the Triads would be happy about my disrupting the nice little set up they had. Going to the police, therefore, appeared to be the best option for the kind of person who quite fancied being hated, unemployed and dead. Whereas if I dealt with it in my own way – that's to say, let things continue in the hope that it would all sort itself out and be fine – then I was sure everything would sort itself out and be fine. No, I simply couldn't tell Ursula about having to pay the Triads for overseas students for the university. I'd never hear the end of it.

I like to think that, in *Deliverance*, I would be the Burt Reynolds character. While everyone else gives in to fear or panic or confusion, I would remain calm and clear thinking and do what needs to be done. I know this assessment of my make-up is pretty much on the mark. I have, after all, watched no end of Party of Normal People in Peril movies and every time I've identified with the 'Damn it – pull yourself together. Do as I say and we'll all get through this' hero. Surely, if I were built otherwise, I'd be more emotionally drawn to the advertising executive who tries to save himself by selling out everyone else and ends up being eaten by sharks in a plummeting lift. Were he to find himself in the same situation with the Triads, then, I have no doubt that Pel played by a younger, leaner Harrison Ford would have spent the morning sitting wordlessly in front of his computer making little horses out of Blu-Tack.

Fortunately, up until now I had been left to do this in peace. Pauline was in the office but was clearly scouring the Internet for cheap flights to Málaga. She wasn't having much success, mostly getting sites themed around 'Spanish fly' (causing her, with great, disapproving sighs, to note things down on a small pad), but obviously didn't want to ask me for help as it would alert David, who couldn't, from his seat, see her screen. David himself had started off the day going through some HEFCE (Higher Education Funding Council for England) reports, but, for a change of pace, had then moved on to going through JISC (Joint Information Systems Committee) reports.

This office calm was fractured, however, when the door

whipped open and in swirled Jane, the political sciences librarian. Jane was gaunt, about two-hundred-and-forty years old and owned one, or several absolutely identical, paisley print dresses. She had the kind of enviable, endless vitality that often goes hand in hand with being old and mad. Ignoring Pauline and me, she went straight over to David.

'Have you got a moment, David?' Her voice was furiously measured.

'Yes, I suppose so.' He put down his papers and swivelled to look at her.

Pauline and I slipped into 'transparently pretending not to listen with delight' mode.

'Well, David, I feel I must talk to you about . . .'

At this point Brian, the subject librarian for economics, sailed through the still-open door. Brian had a head of rich, auburn hair. It was quite clearly someone else's hair, but everyone played along with the charade. A rotund, waistcoated, almost Dickensian figure, Brian walked determinedly through the dying embers of his forties. Despite his spherical mould, he was birdlike in his movements; shooting out limbs in unexpected directions and taking rapid half-steps backwards and forwards being the closest he could manage to standing still. The unnerving exception was his head. On a couple of occasions I'd seen him become overexcited, flick his head round in the manner of the rest of his body and have it looking off at forty-five degrees while his toupee remained facing forwards. To avoid such unfortunate episodes, while below the neck he was dancing to an arrhythmic, staccato beat, his head generally made only the slowest, most languid of movements. Just watching Brian walk around some chairs was an eerie experience that would haunt you for days afterwards whenever you closed your eyes.

'Ahhh, Brian,' mocked Jane when she saw him appear. 'Perhaps you'd like to tell David what you just said to me, and the tone in which you said it?'

'I'd be happy to, Jane. Let me begin by informing him what you have been doing this morning.'

'I have been doing precisely what I do every morning.'

Brian snorted. 'Yes, I won't argue with you there.'

'Can I just hear what's happened, from the beginning, please?' asked David.

'I was sitting at my desk just now . . .' began Jane.

'*That's* not the beginning. It began when I came into the office today,' interrupted Brian.

'No it didn't,' snapped back Jane.

'Did so,' replied Brian.

'Oh, "did so", that's *very* mature.'

'*I'm* not the one who's come running to teacher telling tales, Jane.'

'I'm glad you see making complaints through the proper channels in that way, Brian. It explains a lot.'

'Can I just hear what's happened, please?' David asked again, more pleadingly.

'He called me an idiot!' said Jane.

'She broke my pencil!' responded Brian.

'First of all, it's not *your* pencil, it's a university pencil. And second of all, I did not break it. The lead was broken already because you'd been drumming on the desk with it.'

'It was a university pencil I took from the store for my own, personal use, and they don't use lead any more, they use graphite.'

'I think . . .' began David, but no one was listening.

'Taking something "for your own personal use"? I believe that's what they call "theft", isn't it?'

'Not when you only take it to your desk. Theft is when you take it home. Like that word-processing software I saw in your bag the other week, for example. Perhaps I should write a letter to the *Library Association Record* concerning appropriate behaviour of professionals with regard to software licensing?'

'And I'll write one about the ethical implications of colleagues spying on the contents of other colleagues' handbags!'

'Not with my pencil you won't!'

'Let me just . . .' David tried again, but this time he was cut short by a voice from another source.

'Woooh! Looks like I've walked into a war zone, eh?' laughed Nazim as he came in through the, still open, door.

This caused everyone to look in his direction. And David to notice that all the other librarians had gathered in an excited little huddle outside, peering in at Jane and Brian's exchanges.

'All of you!' David shouted out to them. 'Get back to work – there's nothing to see here.'

They started at being caught, then darted away chattering.

'Hiya, Pel – have you got a moment?' Nazim asked me cheerily.

'Yeah,' I replied, trying to feign the same happy and relaxed attitude but sounding more like I'd just sat on something unfortunate.

'OK,' Nazim replied. He didn't move from by the door. 'Great.' I realised he wanted to talk to me alone.

'Let's talk while we walk, OK?' I said, getting up from my seat. 'I need to go and do some things. Now. Things that are in other parts of the building and need doing.'

'No problem, guy.'

I walked out with him and pulled the office door closed behind us. I saw, through the glass, that as soon as I shut it Jane and Brian burst back into life, assaulting each other with words I couldn't hear. Nazim and I began walking away together.

'So, how are things, Pel?'

'Well, I haven't been killed gangland-style yet so they're going better than I expected.'

'Ha! You crack me up, you really do. It's a tonic just to

talk with you. Speaking of which, is there anywhere we can have a few words in private?'

'Um ... We have a room dedicated to the history and achievements of the university. No one ever goes in there – we could try that?'

'Lead on, guy.'

I took him up a couple of floors to the room. Naturally, no one was in there, but I took the precaution of closing the door and locking it behind us. (Now I was CTASATM, and thus part of the Management Team, I had been given a master key that worked with every lock in the entire building. Apart from the three members of the Management Team, the only other people allowed master keys were the Learning Centre Manager, Security, the cleaners, and Maintenance. Though there was a spare one in a biscuit tin in the staffroom, just in case.)

'Great,' said Nazim.

'Is what you have to tell me going to be upsetting?' I asked.

'Ha! Not at all. I'm here to help.'

'Uh-huh.'

'I know you were concerned about these Hung guys wanting their payment ...' He reached into his inside pocket and brought out an envelope, then reached in again and brought out another. '... so I've come to set your mind at rest.'

He handed the envelopes to me. They weren't sealed, just folded shut, and a quick look into them revealed that they were both full of £50 notes.

'There's ten thousand there.' Nazim waved a hand at them, to indicate he wasn't talking about any other ten thousand pounds I might have about my person. 'That's more than we agreed, in fact. I've rounded up in pounds from the figure we agreed in Hong Kong dollars. Tell them we've paid extra to apologise for the inconvenience, eh? You'll be in their good books right off.'

'I'd rather not be in any of their books, to be honest.'

I held the envelopes nervously in my hands. I was terrified that, standing still, in a locked room, I still might somehow manage to misplace them. It was, by a vast distance, more money than I'd ever had in my hands. The very act of holding it seemed to change the nature of the world; it was now a place constantly buzzing with the potential of frightening loss. Nazim smiled and shook my shoulder in his matey fashion, and I wanted to head-butt him in return. It came to me that I didn't quite know what to do with the envelopes; Nazim obviously had a jacket smartly tailored to carry thousands of pounds in cash without any problems, just the thing for the fashionable courier-about-town. I wasn't wearing a jacket at all and could only stick a packed envelope into each of the pockets of my trousers. They stuck out like ears. So much, I thought, for money making you more attractive to women. Here I was suddenly carrying more cash than ever before in my life and I looked an utter graceless dolt.

'Have you heard anything more from the Hung people?' Nazim asked, moving towards the door.

'No, not yet.' I had to temporarily remove £5,000 from my pocket to get at the master key. 'Actually, I don't even know Chiang's phone number.'

'Ah, right. Can't help you there, guy, sorry. I did have it, but I know he favours mobile phones and changes them every few months. Only TSR would know what number he's using at the moment.'

We walked out on to the main floor. I kept my hands resting on top of the envelopes in my pockets, fearful they'd drop out and instantly vanish. It reminded me of the way a gunslinger might move. If he were cautiously making his way past shelves of geography textbooks. With envelopes instead of guns. Intent on looking like an idiot.

Nazim flicked his cuff back away from his watch.

'Well, stuff to do, guy, stuff to do. I'd better be off. You know where I am if you need anything, right? Know you won't, though – you've got this cracked, am I right? Yeah, you've got the knack – duck to water, guy, I can tell.' He checked his watch again, for effect. 'Jeez, better get a move on – 24/7 international. Catch you later, OK?' and he headed towards the lift. Keeping my hands on the contents of my pockets, I walked swiftly (combine these two elements, by the way, and you get a form of movement widely known as 'mincing') towards the service stairs on the other side of the building. I descended them as fast as I could and, on the ground floor, went straight to my locker. I opened it, stuffed the money inside, locked it again, and checked that it was locked. Then I rechecked that it was locked. After which I checked that it was locked again. With a sigh of partial relief, I began walking back to my office, and not until I was at the door of it did I return to my locker and check that it was locked. Which it was. Definitely. I checked it again, for confirmation.

I got through the rest of the day without problem by the simple method of checking my locker every seven minutes. In fact, I didn't stay at work for the entire day – I left early because I wanted to go shopping. The good thing, pretty much the only good thing, about working at the Learning Centre was that it was in the city centre, so popping to the bank or the shops simply meant a walk of a couple of minutes. I decided to leave early so that I could go to the shopping mall and buy a jacket. I had a jacket, of course, but it wasn't a jacket I could trust with £10,000 (and I certainly felt happier keeping the money on me). All the jackets I had were half hearted in the pocket department. Some had no pockets at all, others shallow or (unbelievable as such a thing may seem) fake pockets. If I was going to stuff great wads of £50 notes into them, I wanted big pockets. Big, *fastenable* pockets. Pockets that could be sealed with formidable zips. A big, stupid jacket with big, stupid pockets. Fortunately, these were in fashion so there wasn't a shortage of them on offer.

I don't like shopping for clothes. Getting a new pair of trousers is generally a simple matter of going to the place I bought the last pair of trousers and buying them again. Ursula's method, incidentally, is to try on every pair of trousers in every shop in the city and return home without buying any trousers. You might think that this means I'm a better shopper than she is. The simple fact of my returning home in forty minutes with what I went for, while she spends eight hours changing in and out of trousers all across the city only to return with a new-trousers score of zero, might make the unskilled observer believe I'd won on points. Ursula would vigorously refute this, however, on the basis that my good marks for content are eclipsed by my abysmal performance in the style category. I am, Ursula frequently declares, no fun to shop with. I'm not especially stung by such a judgment of the less than riotous way I exchange money for goods or services. If she said, 'Bah, you're no fun to buy life assurance with' I'd be devastated, of course, just as I'd be cut to the quick were she, more in sorrow that in anger, to lament, 'Pel, setting up a direct debit at the bank with you simply has no spark.' But as, whenever Ursula insists I go shopping with her, I'm unhesitatingly aware I'm having no fun whatsoever, I feel able to accept her decision with an embracing calm.

Had Ursula been there on this expedition, however, she would no doubt have pronounced me the Mr Fun of shopping, because I tried on no end of jackets in a whole series of shops; even returning on a couple of occasions to try on the jackets a second time. It seemed a false economy to cut corners on a jacket I was buying specifically for its £10,000-securing abilities, but at the same time I didn't want to pay the earth for something I wouldn't dream of wearing when not waiting to pay off the Triads. Besides price and sturdy, sealable pockets, I decided that it was also best to go for a jacket that was so unrepentantly bulky and protrusive that you could stuff two envelopes of cash into it without it emitting any clue. I eventually found two jackets that seemed agitatedly keen to meet all my requirements, but unfortunately one – presumably being aimed at teenaged girls – was only available in a string of sizes all far too small for me. So, in exchange for my credit card's promise of £70.99, I walked away from a factory outlet with a creation in acrylic. It was host to a biblical plague of pockets, placed irregularly about it and all of them having heavy zips (rather giving the impression that, in its youth, it had been badly and repeatedly scarred in a duel). Puffy diamonds of anything up to about eight inches in thickness made up the surface of the jacket, and while the lining (containing three huge pockets) was a matt-green colour the outside was a shiny and vivid orange. I put it on and fastened the envelopes in its womb-like innards immediately.

A normal man might have been satisfied to have secured this garment alone, but, as it happens, I made another purchase during the outing. In one of the shops I'd been to earlier, the racks of clothes were laid out so they met the areas set aside for garden-related products and exercise equipment; so as better to serve the shopping public calling in for a shirt, a rowing machine and a couple of sacks of peat. The jackets there were pathetic things one might wear for appearance alone, and I was actually leaving when I noticed what must be the greatest invention ever conceived, manufactured and put on sale for £54.75. It was a machine that exercised for you by the clever use of electrocution. A small thing, no bigger than a woman's handbag, connected by wires to half a dozen rubber pads, it stimulated the muscles to contract using little pulses of electricity. This, then, was the BodyBox personal toning device. A conveniently stored fitness programme for the unalterably idle – that I should be fortunate to live to see such a thing! Breathlessly paid for and in a plastic carrier bouncing at my side before two minutes had passed, it was a new stomach in a bag.

'Oh, Pel, you've only just been promoted,' Ursula said as I walked through the front door wearing my new jacket. 'Do you really think now's the right time to pursue a career in rap?'

'Have you ever thought of "not saying things"? I really think it's an option we should explore.'

'Jonathan! Peter! Come and look – Dad's wearing a dinghy!'

The children scampered out of the dining room and stood by Ursula's side, staring at me with a mixture of curiosity and bewilderment.

'What's that in the bag?' asked Ursula, peering.

'Nothing,' I replied.

'Why you wearing a dinghy?' asked Peter.

'Ohhh, *Peter*.' sighed Jonathan, 'It's not a *real* dinghy, it's just a silly-looking jacket.'

'I've bought myself a jacket, OK? I have no interest in trivial fashions, it's simply utilitarian; is that fine with everyone?'

'What's "utilitarian" mean?' Jonathan asked.

'It means being purely functional, Jonathan,' Ursula said, looking down at him. 'Having a use that is more important than other considerations. You see, he may look funny, but Dad is now completely unsinkable.'

I pushed past them to go upstairs.

'Dad, why you wearing a dinghy?' repeated Peter.

Jonathan sighed with increased irritation.

'It's *not* a dinghy, Peter – it's a utilitarian.'

When I got to the bedroom I took the jacket off and stuffed it under the bed. There seemed no point taking the money out, but I didn't want to hang it up on the coatrack given the frequency with which burglars wandered around our house.

I also pushed the BodyBox under the bed, on my side, and covered it with some old magazines.

Ursula and the kids were sitting at the table eating *spätzle* (a Swabian speciality that required the kitchen be left looking like the site of a horrifying medical experiment) when I came back downstairs. As I took a seat, Ursula skimmed a letter towards me.

'It's parents' evening at Jonathan's school next Wednesday. Can you ask your mother to babysit?'

'She won't be able to. She's going to stay with her sister in Devon, I remember her saying.'

'Is she? What are we going to do, then?'

'It's OK. You can stay here, I'll go.'

'But I want to go too.'

'It's not a big deal. There's nothing special happening, it's just a routine event. They'll say everything's fine, and I'll say, "Good." Then they'll ask if I have any specific questions, and I'll say, "No." It'll all be over in ten minutes.'

'*I'd* have some questions.'

'We're not going to ask to see their teaching qualifications again, it's embarrassing.'

'In Germany teachers have to be properly qualified, here they give the job to anyone who says they're prepared to have a stab at it. I want to know the teachers have undertaken the proper studies.'

'In Germany children don't even start school until they're six. The teachers here might not have to study so rigorously, but they get to work on the kids for more years to make up for it. We've discussed all this.'

'I still want you to find out everything that's happening. I'll expect you to be able to tell me when you get back.'

'Of course. I'll grill Mrs Beattie mercilessly.'

'Miss Hampshire,' Jonathan said, without looking up from his plate. 'My teacher's called Miss Hampshire.'

'Since when? What happened to Mrs Beattie?'

'She blew up.'

'No, Jonathan, I'm serious.'

'She did blow up,' nodded Ursula. 'Gas leak in her flat.'

'Oh. Right.'

'My friend Louis says they only found her shoes.'

'I see. That's very sad.'

Jonathan shrugged and carried on eating. 'These things happen.'

'Oh,' said Ursula, 'I called my brother, by the way. He's going to see if he can arrange some leave from work so we can go skiing together. Probably stay with my folks for a bit, then go skiing for a few days with him and Silke.'

'Fine, whatever.'

'You'll be able to get leave too, right?'

'I don't think it'll be a problem.'

'Good. Because I *have* to have a holiday. Did I tell you what Vanessa's been doing at work?'

'Not for almost a day. The uncertainty has been playing on my mind.'

'Well . . .'

'Doc, Dopey, Sneezy, Bashful, Sleepy, Happy, Grumpy.' I placed my burger down on the table and shuffled into a chair behind it. 'If you were the eighth dwarf, what dwarf would you be?'

'He'd be "Wanky",' grinned Tracey.

Roo gave her a flat, ersatz laugh.

'Ha . . . Ah-ha. In fact, I think I'd be . . .'

'Creepy?' ventured Tracey again. 'Bleary?'

'. . . I think I'd be "Picky". I often get called "picky". Which is fine by me as it's obviously just what the unsophisticated call those with higher standards.'

'True.'

'And, talking of standards and their relative heights, Pel, please won't you tell us the story of that jacket?'

'*Humpf* – it's just a jacket.'

'Oh, no, it's certainly not *just* a jacket. It goes far beyond the point past which a jacket would dare not tread. Is it perhaps . . . what? An emerging nation?'

I'd thought about this quite a bit. Should I tell Tracey and Roo about the Triads and me? I wasn't worried that they might tell me to do the right thing as Ursula would. First, because they were my friends and, as such, had no history of giving me sensible advice and, second, because, even if they *did*, they weren't Ursula and so ignoring them was a viable option. Finally, by a thin margin, I'd decided not to tell them. It was such excellent gossip that it was too much to ask of anyone not to spread it. To tell them about the Triad situation, then insist they didn't talk about it to anyone, was an inhumanly cruel thing to do; an awful way to repay Tracey and Roo after we'd eaten all those lunches together. In any case, clearly, the fewer people who knew about it, the better. I could keep the secret to myself; I was sure I wouldn't crack under interrogation. That is, I was sure I wouldn't crack under interrogation until I realised I was having immense trouble not shouting the whole thing out in the middle of the café when provoked by the fact that Roo was taking the piss out of my jacket. Maybe that's how the Soviets used to break spies during the Cold War. Methodically make fun of the agent's clothes until he spat back, 'Well, *of course* my shoes are funny, damn you – they're stuffed with microfilm.'

'It's just a jacket. I needed a jacket, this one was on sale.'

'It was on sale or it had set sail?' laughed Tracey.

'You two should be on the television, you really should. Evening news report, "Bodies found", something like that.'

'I'm sorry,' replied Tracey, still laughing, 'we're just having a bit of fun.'

'Yeah, well, there's too much fun in the world.'

'God, *hardly*. For a start, look here . . .' She pointed at Roo.

'I meant fun as a thing that people want all the while. Take sex . . .'

'Taking sex is my speciality.'

'This fundamental axiom of popular culture that "Sex should be fun". What a load of toss.'

'I think sex *should* be fun,' replied Tracey, with some conviction.

'And me,' said Roo. 'I think you ought to be able to get it from dispensers on the wall too. In fact, if I could make sure it was fun *and* available from dispensers on the wall, I think I'd be invited to form the next government of this country.'

'Having a laugh in bed together is great. It's, um . . . just great,' Tracey added.

'I'm in bed with Tracey here, Pel. We're for fun sex.'

'No, no, no, no, *no*. Sex should *not* be fun, OK? Sex can be lots of things – thrilling, romantic, scary, mindless, dirty, dangerous, frantic, forbidden, freaky – but if you're finding it "fun", you're doing it wrong.'

'I don't think I a . . .' began Tracey.

'Yes you are. Shut up. There is no place for laughter in sex. Sex can survive almost anything else: guilt, the bleak spectre of our own mortality, odd noises, imperfect weather conditions, ill-placed components of car interiors. Massive doses of alcohol and drugs which render you utterly unable to perform even the most basic procedures are not only no hindrance to sex but, in fact, increase its likelihood no end. The one thing guaranteed to stop sex dead in its tracks is a laugh. Everything nowadays tries to be a bit of a lark – "The *Fun* Way to Learn", "The *Fun* Way to Diet", "The *Fun* Way to Bank". Well, arse to that. Most stuff isn't fun; the world is eighty per cent misery, suffering, injustice and gnawing existential bleakness. A further seventeen per cent is sheer, suffocating boredom. That leaves us with a couple of minutes of stolen "fun" a week, tops. Far better we spend that fun, I gently suggest, somewhere other than ruining a potentially serviceable bout of sex by guffawing the erotic frisson away. If you want a head-spinning whirlpool of desire, hunger, madness and ecstasy, then let's have sex – if you want a bit of fun, play bleeding Pictionary or something.'

There was a pause at the table. A staring silence. Then Tracey leaned forward towards me.

'You've got a bit of lettuce between your teeth . . . no, just there.'

'some chinese guys want 2 c u,' said the Post-it stuck on my monitor. The handwriting looked like Wayne's, but I wasn't completely sure. I didn't see a great deal that he or Raj or Brian had handwritten; they much preferred using a keyboard.

'How long has this been here?' I asked, nervously sweeping my gaze from David to Pauline and back again.

'One of your . . . "staff" put it there as he was leaving for lunch,' said David.

I pounded up the stairs to the top floor as fast as I could and lurched into the office. Wayne wasn't there but Brian and Raj were. They appeared to be playing against each other on their computers; as I entered Brian chuckled at the same point as Raj groaned – apparently having been killed by decapitation, his screen filled with a picture of his own, headless, corpse and the message 'Brian says: You are my bitch'. Catching sight of me they both stabbed at keys and Excel spreadsheets jumped up on to their monitors.

'Uh, hi, Pel,' mumbled Raj.

I shook my hands about, to indicate I wanted to say something urgently but was far too short of breath to make any sounds. I waited for a few seconds for some oxygen, then began.

'Hhhhav . . .'

At which point I realised I hadn't caught my breath at all; it had made good its escape.

'What?' asked Raj.

I shook my hands about again, then reached into my pocket and pulled out the Post-it. I gave it to him.

'Oh, yeah. Yeah. Some Chinese guys wanted to see you.' He nodded.

I indicated 'Yes, I *know* that, you twat' by use of the I-have-your-neck-in-my-hands-and-I'm-strangling-you mime.

'Hold on . . .' He got up from his seat and walked to the door of the office, scanning the computers outside on the floor. 'They're still here. It was those two over there.' His finger pointed at two men standing by a PC over on the far side of the computer suite. I gave him a thumbs-up of thanks.

I bent over, head dropped, and took some deep pulls at the air. After about half a dozen, I thought I might be able to form words successfully, so I sprang up and headed towards the two men.

'Hi,' said Bernard.

'Argggh!' I replied, unexpectedly seeing his face right in front of me.

He jumped backwards – on to a handbag a student had placed on the floor as she waited for a computer. It made a crunching noise.

'Oi!' she said.

'Oh, nueer, I'm sorry. Is everything OK in there?'

She pulled out a handful of broken plastic with a battery dangling from it.

'You've smashed my rape alarm, you wanker. Look at it. Completely fucked. You know what that is? That's reckless endangerment – you've exposed me to an increased threat of assault through negligence.' I made a guess she was a law student. 'I'm going to sue you to fucking *death*.' Yep.

'Oh, nueer. I'm dreadfully sorry. Raj? Raj? Will you get a replacement personal alarm from the store for this person, please? Right now. Thanks.' (We carried a supply of personal attack alarms so that they were available to all the staff. It was that kind of university.)

'I want fucking *two*,' said the student.

'Raj? Make that two, please . . . I really am terribly, terribly sorry about this.'

'Good.'

Bernard backed away from her, trailing apologies, and turned to me.

'So, Pel, "Hi." Um, new jacket?'

'Yes.'

'Are you very cold?'

'No, I'm fine.'

'OK. Only it seems like the kind of jacket you'd usually leave in the cloakroom.'

'Look – sorry – but I'm *really* busy right now, Bernard. I have to go and talk to some people.'

'Righto. No, that's fine. I just wanted to have word about the Improvement Day. The things you've got planned and so on.'

'Oh, that's all sorted, like I said. Don't worry about it.'

'I know. I was just wondering if we could talk them over.'

'I haven't got time just at this moment, I'm afraid.'

'Of course, of course, no problem. Perhaps you could pop into my office later?'

'Yes. Sure. Whatever you want. It's just that now . . .'

'I understand – no peace for the wicked, eh? Haha.'

'Haha . . . I have to go now.'

'Fine, fine. Off you go. I'll see you later.'

'Yes, later. We'll have a chat.'

He plunged his hands into his pockets and turned towards the stairs – heaving his leg round in that direction as though by the force of his arm. I forced out a smile, then hurried over to the two Chinese men.

They were talking to each other in low voices.

'Hello. I'm Pel, I'm the CTASATM here. I understand you were looking for me?'

'You boss?' asked the one closest to me, seriously.

'Yes, I'm in charge of the Computer Team.'

'We need thing.' He pointed at me. 'You help, perhaps?'

I patted my pockets. 'I think I might have what you need. I . . .' Suddenly I became conscious that there were people all around. 'Is this something that it might be better for us to do in the toilets?'

You can tell a lot from an expression. From the expression on their faces I knew, knew instantly and with complete certainty, that these were not the men from the Triads. I made a stern face and continued.

'Because, if it is, I have to tell you now I'm not interested. We're trying to stamp out toilet meetings in this university; we have meeting rooms for meetings, there should be no reason to use the toilets for that. The toilets are for . . . well, you know what the toilets are for. So, what are you telling me? I need to be clear about this.'

'We no want to go to the toilets with you,' said the farthest one. His friend nodded with unrestrained vigour.

'That's good. Good. I had to check, you understand.'

They both nodded.

'So, now we've cleared that up, how can I help you?'

'We student. We need thing. Thing to make Chinese typing on these computers. You have?'

'No, they have that in the languages department, I believe. If you use their computer lab you can type with Chinese characters. You know where the languages PC lab is?'

'Yes.'

'Good. Is there anything else?'

'No. Thank you.'

'Don't mention it.'

I returned to the Computer Team office, went into the storeroom and closed the door behind me. I then put my head in my hands and made this noise: 'Aaeeeeiiiiiiiiiiiiiii . . .'

MAYBE NEXT YEAR DAVID COULD
ORGANISE IT?

I simply couldn't face being at work for any more of the day, so I told Raj and Brian I was taking time off in lieu.

'And when Wayne gets back please inform him that if he leaves a note for me about Chinese students he should write Chinese *students*, not just Chinese *guys*.'

'What else would they be besides students?' Brian asked with a puzzled look.

'They could be anything, anything at all. They might be . . . well, *anything*. This university doesn't exist solely for the benefit of *students*, you know.'

I went home and entered the unnatural quietness of my house. It always seemed a different, alien place when Ursula and the children weren't there; too still and lifeless. Even the clicking off of the kettle as I boiled water to make myself a cup of tea seemed loud and harsh in the emptiness.

I took my tea upstairs and sat down on the bed. For what must have been the thirtieth time, I took the envelopes from my jacket and counted the money to check it was all still there. Carefully laying out note after note induced a slightly surreal feeling. They began to lose their sense of value, like when you repeat a word over and over again it starts to sound ridiculous and meaningless. A stray thought went through my head saying, even if I did lose the money, I could say to the people, 'Well, it was just *paper*, really, wasn't it? In a sense, what was it actually *worth*?' The thought that followed this saw me in a deserted area of woodland, being raked by automatic gunfire.

Having made sure that none of the cash had wandered

off, I returned the envelopes to my pockets and laid the jacket under the bed. I pushed it securely back and my hand returned holding the BodyBox. There was a picture on the front of the box of a man such as you might find in any Olympic decathlon or exhibition of homoerotica. The electric stimulation pads of the BodyBox were placed on his alarmingly shiny body and, finger resting on the controller, he was laughing at something outside the frame of the picture – something amusing that his perfectly toned wife was doing, perhaps. Naturally, only a hopeless fool would think that this man had gained his physique simply through the use of the *BodyBox*. He probably played tennis or something too. That hardly mattered, however, as I didn't wish to reach a state where I could perform at hen nights; I just wanted a moderate, effortless workout to remove my slight stomach.

I opened the box and read the instructions. They contained various warnings which didn't apply to me (the 'can only promote weight loss as part of a calorie-controlled diet' rider that appears on pretty much everything sold since the 1970s, for example) and a set of diagrams showing where to place the pads to target specific muscle groups. There was one for the leg muscles, and I briefly wondered whether, with practice, it would be possible to rapidly alternate the impulses between your left and right legs and so effect walking without having to resort to the usual tedious exertion. That was a project for the future, though, I concluded; best to take one thing at a time. I removed the little pads from their plastic bags and attached them to the control unit with the colour-coded wires, then connected the unit itself to the mains. After that, I quickly removed my shirt and, carefully following the diagram, I used the belts provided to fasten the pads to my torso. They were really quite chilly when they first touched. Still, I thought, 'no pain, no gain'. Despite having no stomach, the man in the diagram seemed to have far more stomach *area* than me; he had a neat array of pads, I had a nest-like tangle of wires.

Whatever. The instructions said to set the timer (I selected the 'full workout' of thirty minutes) then slowly ramp up the intensity until you could feel it 'tingling'. Quite obviously, this was written for people with too much time on their hands. I couldn't sit around for thirty minutes of tingling, I needed to get right to the serious exercising. So I pushed all the sliders up to about eighty per cent as soon as the unit started up.

'Hngh!' I said, involuntarily, as a spasm tightened all my stomach muscles into a sudden, straining grip such as one might encounter in the darkest days of constipation. The clenching continued for a few seconds, before abruptly stopping and allowing my stomach to slump to its natural position. There it lay, startled, until a few seconds had passed and – 'Hngh!' – another burst of electricity hit.

The inflicted clenching, and the pauses waiting in uneasy anticipation for the onset of the next inflicted clenching, kept me entertained for a while. Then my interest in the electrical constriction of my own abdomen began to wane. It seemed that, even when you removed the extra horridness of effort, this was still, like all exercise, deeply, deeply boring. I couldn't really do much because, as I was plugged into the mains, I wasn't able to wander about freely. I flicked on the clock-radio by the side of the bed (deliberately set to a chart-based station at sleep-frightening volume), lay back, closed my eyes and listened to a parade of boy bands occasionally broken by girl bands while my stomach got on with it alone.

I lay like this for perhaps fifteen or twenty minutes, until a slight rustle of movement made me open my eyes. I profoundly hoped I'd open them to see another burglar, but I wasn't so lucky. Standing at the end of the bed, looking down at me with a look of shock, dismay and horrified awe, was Ursula.

'Oh my God – you're having a mid-life crisis.'

This, I don't mind admitting, stung. Not, as you might think, because I could justifiably claim to be rather too young to be having a mid-life crisis; quite the opposite, in a way. As I understand it, a mid-life crisis is when you feel that your life is slipping away from you; you've achieved nothing and Death is starting to tap his foot impatiently. Well, I've felt like that since I was about seven years old. I am immune from a sudden attack of mid-life crisis, because I've been having one since before I hit puberty.

'What – Hngh! – what are you doing home? It's only four – Hngh! – o'clock.'

'My last appointment cancelled so I decided to leave early. How long has this been going on? Is this . . . this . . . *this* what you do every afternoon?'

'Oh, give me a – Hngh! – break. I just thought that it would – Hgnh! – n't do any harm to get a bit fitter.'

'Why don't you buy a bike? You could ride a bike to get fit.'

'Don't be stupid.'

'What?'

'Riding a – Hngh! – bike is really tiring.'

'Heart and lungs; that's what getting fit is, heart and lungs.'

'Oh, boll – Hngh! – ocks. You can get transplants for those. It – Hgnh! – makes more sense to work on the bits you can't – Hngh! – get fitted.'

'It's a mid-life crisis, that's what it is. You're after your lost stomach – failing self-image. This, the hip-hop jacket . . . Christ! I bet this is where that whole penis episode came from too! It's the same thing. That machine's tied up with your dick, isn't it?'

'In fact – Hngh! – no. If we're using metaphors now, I – Hngh! – find that living with you is nearly the – Hngh! – same as having electrodes strapped to one's – Hngh! – genitals.'

'How much did that thing cost?'

'What's that matter?'

'How much?'

'I – Hngh! – bought it with my money.'

'Just tell me how much.'

'Fif – Hngh! – teen pounds forty-nine pence.'

'Show me the receipt.'

'I don't have it any more. Hngh!'

'Where did you by it from?'

'I can't remember.'

'Crap. Where did you buy it from?'

The BodyBox made a little series of beeps to indicate it had finished hurling my stomach about. I began removing its pads from my body.

'It's completed the cycle. Those beeps meant it's finished now.'

'What – you mean it beeps *too*. Wow.'

'By finished, I mean finished this session. You have to do it every day for six weeks for it to have the full effect.'

'Really?' Ursula gestured, astonished, towards my stomach. 'It doesn't stop there?'

I put my shirt on.

'Naturally it takes time. This isn't some kind of gimmick, you know,' I said. 'Anyway, are you going to pick up the kids from the childminder or shall I do it?'

'Nice try at steering me away there, but I haven't forgotten I asked you where you bought it from.'

'Didn't I answer that?'

'No.'

'Yes, yes I did. I said I couldn't remember.'

'Oh, don't misunderstand me, I completely accept you had to try that line but, well, it never really had much of a chance, did it?'

'No, really, I can't remember. I bought it . . . from . . . the Internet!' I blurted out "the Internet" with rather too much of a 'Aha! Yes! *That's* it!' inflection. Cleverly, I rubbed my stomach to give the impression it'd had some sort of spasming flashback, and said it again, more nonchalantly. 'The Internet.'

'The Internet?'

'That's right.'

'Where on the Internet?'

'That's the point; I can't remember. There're so many similar URLs, it's just impossible to recall the specific one.'

'Right. Right . . . so I'll check the credit card statement when it arrives.'

'I paid cash. They didn't have online ordering, so I sent off the money.'

'You sent money to an address you found on the Internet.'

'Yes.'

'The address of a company you can't remember.'

'That's right. So, shall I pick up the kids, then?'

'If I find out you're lying you can imagine how bad that will be for you, can't you?'

'Why would I lie?'

Ursula just stared at me.

'Right. I'll go and pick up the kids, then.'

The childminder, who lived a short car journey away, looked after Peter for most of the day (he also attended a nursery for a few hours) and Jonathan between the time he finished school and when Ursula and I finished work. I collected the children from her and fought them into their child seats. They both walked out of our door each morning with spotless faces and presentable clothes; each teatime they returned dishevelled, sticky and smeared with filth. I didn't let this bother me. I think it's a dangerous thing to try to control your children for effect. To make them be a certain way purely out of a self-centred belief that how they appear reflects on you. No, it's far better, if cornered, to say they're not yours, you're just looking after them for the afternoon.

I edged out into the traffic, Jonathan and Peter chattering to each other about something in the seats behind me.

'What did you do at school today, Jonathan?'

'Nothing.'

'Really? Again? Is that a project you're working on? What did *you* do, Peter?'

'I made a poo.'

'Did you? Impressive.'

'Are we moving to a new house soon?' asked Jonathan.

'Yes, soon. We're just waiting for the solicitors to finish everything, then we can move in.'

'What do the solicitors do?'

'Mostly, they do nothing. But we have to pay them lots of money to do it. Perhaps that's what they're teaching you at school, to be a solicitor.'

'I don't want to be a solicitor. I want to be a Jedi.'

'Well, you certainly can't be both.'

'Dad? Here . . .' (Peter was at the stage of giving me things. He'd come racing into a room with a breathless 'For you', and I'd have to go 'Thank you! A clothes-peg! That's great.')

'What is it?' I reached one hand behind me, round the side of my seat. I kept my other hand on the steering wheel and my eyes on the road, by the way. I mention this because, if it were Ursula driving, she'd have stared fixedly at him in the rear-view mirror or possibly turned right round to face him. In fact, there's a good chance she'd have just jammed the accelerator with a stick and climbed into the back seat herself to collect whatever it was.

'Here,' repeated Peter, placing the object in my hand. I snaked my arm back round my seat to examine the gift.

'Ugh! Where the hell did that come from?'

'Up my nose.'

It took multiple attempts to finally flick it out on to the road. I think the car behind me thought I was signalling; he certainly started gesticulating emphatically at me through his window.

'Put the radio on,' said Jonathan. I poked at it. Debbie from Mansfield was phoning in about the bins. 'Oh, not talking. Talking's sad – find some music.' Another stab landed on a channel playing a timeless rock classic that had been sampled and was now being talked over by someone anxious I should know that he was very good in bed.

'We'll be going to Germany soon, Jonathan. We'll do some skiing – you can go sledging, Peter.'

'I want ski *too*.'

'You're still a bit young, Peter.'

'I'm not.'

'Yes you *are*, Peter,' said Jonathan. 'You can't ski. I can ski, but you can't.'

'Yes I can.'

'No you *can't*. I can and Mom can and Dad can a bit, but you can't.'

'What do you mean, I can ski "a bit"?'

'You're not very good, are you?'

'Yes I am.'

'You're not as good as Mom.'

'Mom's been skiing a lot longer. She grew up in Germany so she got to spend much more time skiing. I couldn't go skiing when I was growing up.'

'What did you do instead of learning to ski, when you were growing up?'

'Um, ride a bike I suppose.'

'Mom can ride a bike.'

'Not as well as me, she can't.'

'How come you never ride a bike, then?'

'I don't have the time any more.'

'I can ride a bike,' said Peter.

'No you *can't*,' replied Jonathan.

'Yes I can.'

'Only with stabilisers on. That doesn't count. Oh, listen, it's Britney Spears. Do you like Britney Spears, Dad?'

'No, Jonathan, I despise her and everything she stands for. Of course you can ride a bike, Peter. We'll be taking off those stabilisers soon.'

'If Mom was skiing and you were riding a bike, who'd win?'

'I would.'

Let it never be said I don't try to provide my boys with an effective role model.

Everyone was giving me despising looks, so I knew something was up. Usually they just ignored me, but this morning I got to work to find my colleagues had designated me Learning Centre Judas. I would probably just have thought 'Oh well' and got on with things – the librarians could have any number of reasons for hating me and the library assistants were a volatile and idiosyncratic group whose actions one couldn't predict; perhaps they were being sponsored to hate me for Children in Need or something, who knew? – but I then bumped into Bernard and everything became clear.

'Pel! Well, *there* you are.' Bernard pointed to where I was.

'Morning, Bernard.'

'I was worried, what with your not coming to see me yesterday and everything.'

Ahhh, yes, I was supposed to have gone to see him after talking to those Chinese students who'd been impersonating Triad members. I'd completely forgotten about that. There was no option but to confess.

'Sorry, Bernard, I had a stomach problem.'

'Oh, nuuuu – are you OK now?'

'Fine, thanks. Just one of these sudden twenty-four-hour bugs, I reckon.'

'That's lucky. Anyway, I wanted to speak to you again about what you'd prepared for the Improvement Day . . .'

'Like I said, don't worry about it, Bernard, I've got it all sorted.'

'No, I mean *yesterday* I wanted to speak to you about it – because we're going on it today. Now.'

'Oh shit.'

'You *do* have it all organised, don't you? I have asked a couple of times before and you've said . . .'

'No, it's all sorted.'

'You're sure?'

'Yes, what's the . . . Oh, I see – the "Oh shit" thing. Internet slang; it means "Oh, shit".' Unable to repeat the words with anything but the same inflection of sagging hopelessness, I did add two thumbs-up signs as I said it this time. 'You know, like "Let's go".' I did the thumbs-up signs again. Bernard nodded. I could see he wanted to find this convincing, he really *wanted* to. 'Oh shit,' I said with thumbs one more time.

'I've never heard that before,' said Bernard.

'It's a recent thing.'

'Interesting.'

I could see he'd made a decision to give credulity a go and felt a little burst of triumph, for the picosecond it took to remember that I had done no preparation whatsoever – nothing, absolutely nothing at all – for the Improvement Day. Bernard and I were enjoying the pregnant pause together when a call came across the Tannoy.

'Could Pel Dalton come to the issue counter, please?'

'I'd better go and see what that's about,' I said, flicking a hand in the rough direction of the counter.

'Of course. Be quick, though, the coach is waiting for us outside. We're off in ten minutes.'

The coach would be taking us to the location Bernard had booked for the day – probably a lecture theatre or conference room in one of the bits of the university across town – while a skeleton staff from another department would look after the Learning Centre for the day (they would do so exceptionally badly to make the point that they didn't like being dragged away from their important work to do it, and their poorness would, naturally, be further played up on our return to make the point that running the Learning Centre was a skilled and complex job that only we could perform effectively). It needed to be done, however. Bernard would say that it was to ensure we were allowed time away from the centre, where we couldn't be interrupted; the real reason was that bussing us to another location made it more difficult for people to escape.

I jogged around to the issue counter. Geraldine, one of the library assistants, looked at me with the kind of expression you'd make at a child molester who'd just knocked a tin of paint into your lap on the way to your wedding.

'Sorry to bother you. I'm sure you were busy getting things ready for us . . .'

'I didn't know it was today, Geraldine,' I said in a low hiss. 'Bernard gave me the job. I'm . . .'

'Just following orders? You don't have to make any excuses to me, Pel. God will judge you. Will you just have a word with these people. They insist it's important.' She indicated two Chinese gentlemen standing at the counter eyeing me levelly, and I let out a groan that started at my knees.

'Thanks, Geraldine,' I said. 'Thanks *a lot.*'

I walked – well, more 'plodded' – over to them. There was still a tiny, tiny voice in me whispering in the storm that they might just be another pair of students, but even the most optimistic parts of my brain weren't really listening to it. Age is no indicator of who's a student at the University of North-Eastern England, because we have so many mature students, people doing short courses paid for by their employers, etc. But there is a certain minimum level of scruffiness that all students adhere to, regardless of age or background. These two people were far, far too well dressed to be students here.

'May I help you?'

'Are you Mr Pel Dalton?'

'I'm afraid so.'

'Good. I believe our superior, Mr Chiang Ho Yam, told you we'd be coming to meet with you.'

It seemed that only one of them would be doing the talking. He was slightly smaller than his companion, and that was really all there was to notice between them. They both wore similar impeccable suits and similar implacable expressions.

'Yes, he did. I've been expecting you.'

'Could we go to your office, perhaps?'

'Um, actually, now's not a very good time.'

'That's very disappointing. I'm disappointed about that. Have you ever felt the pain of disappointment?'

'It's just that I have to go somewhere now.'

'Where might that be?'

'I don't know.'

'I see. Life is uncertain, isn't it?'

'No, I mean, I don't know specifically where it is. It's not far. I'm not fleeing the country or anything.'

'Perish the thought.'

'I have the . . . thing you need – you can have it now if you . . .' I reached towards my pocket.

'No.' He held up a hand. 'I'd prefer somewhere a little more private.' He casually glanced in the direction of the CCTV camera covering the counter area. 'Unfortunately, however, we are only here for a limited time.'

'Why's that?' I asked.

He shot a look at his companion. 'It's awkward with the trains, apparently,' he said. Companion looked down briefly at his shoes.

'Right. I see . . .' I did some nodding. No one joined in. 'I can find out where I'll be. I'm sure my boss won't mind telling me the location, but I'm likely to be tied up there a lot of the time.'

'Perhaps you could ring us to say you're free. I hope, as much as you, that this won't take long,' said Talker.

'Yes, that's a good idea.'

'Good. My mobile number is . . .'

'Ahh . . .'

'Ahh?'

'A lot of the phones don't allow dial-out access to mobiles, to stop personal calls.'

'Right. Of course. And you don't have a mobile phone yourself?'

I laughed. 'God, no. Mobile phones are for wan . . .' I stopped laughing. 'No.'

'No.' Talker turned to Companion and said something terse in Chinese. Companion looked as if he might reply, but Talker repeated it even more insistently and Companion sullenly reached into his pocket and handed him his mobile phone. 'You see this number?' he said to me, indicating an entry in the phone memory. 'That's my mobile. When you are free to see us, you ring this number, OK?' He handed me the phone.

'OK. Yes, got it. I'll go and find out where I'll be now . . .'

'Never mind. Ring and tell us. We'll make sure we are in a place where a taxi is easily available.'

'Good. Well, see you later, then.'

'Yes.'

I wasn't quite sure of the accepted way of ending a conversation with Triad heavies, but I noticed that Bernard was standing off to the side of the counter. He caught my eye and tapped his watch. So I took my leave of them with 'Gotta go' and a small wave. They didn't wave back.

All the staff were guided towards the waiting coach, Bernard at the head of them, David bringing up the rear watching that no one broke away. Once they were all inside in a grumbling mass, David was sent back into the building to check the toilets. He returned about five minutes later with Raj, Wayne, two library assistants and the social studies librarian, heads bowed.

We got under way, and as we drove along Bernard stood at the front telling everyone 'a little bit about the day'. This was pretty sketchy. Basically, he said I'd got lots of interesting things planned, and that we'd be away the whole day – until 5 p.m. – at Bunerley Hill; lunch would be provided. Bunerley Hill was an old primary school that the university had bought when it became surplus to the needs of the local council. It had been converted into a conference centre and, because of the reasonably extensive playing fields, was also used by the sports science students. It was only a journey of about fifteen minutes to get there. I took ten of those trying to think of what I was going to do with fifty-plus staff until 5 p.m. that would both Improve them and also not give the impression I'd thought it up in ten minutes during the coach journey to the venue.

In a depressingly short amount of time I found myself sitting in a hall with all the Learning Centre staff (I say 'with' – in fact no one would sit by me; there were empty chairs for three seats in both directions), knowing I'd have to take the stage in a matter of minutes. The entirety of my brain was empty. I bit my nails for a while, and then Bernard beckoned me with his hand. I looked theatrically at the people behind, then mouthed 'Me?' while pointing at my own chest. He nodded, and I shuffled to the front of the hall and followed him on to the stage. A mike had been set up.

'Everyone? OK? Everyone?' said Bernard, quietening the hum of chatter. 'Time for me to take a back seat now. I'm handing the day over to Pel.'

I walked over to the mike to the sound of a single person clapping very, very slowly.

'Thanks, Bernard. Well . . . Yes . . . Can you hear me OK at the back?' The people in the last row made a show of complete indifference to indicate that they could. Remarkable, really, as to me the PA didn't seem to be amplifying my voice very much at all (though it was picking up my breathing and turning it into a breathy tearing sound quite excellently). 'Good. Well, here we are at Improvement Day . . . Improvement Day . . . *Improvement* Day. What exactly do we mean by

'"Improvement Day"? Well, it's a day – a period of time – when we all come together to *improve* things – to make them better. To make them better . . . What exactly do we mean by "make them better"? Well, quite simply, to ameliorate them. Although we call this "Improvement Day", it could just as easily be called "Amelioration Day". And I think it's important to remember that.'

I expanded on this theme for about forty-five minutes.

Having defined both 'improvement' and 'day' to a degree that would have provoked Wittgenstein to take his own life several years earlier, there seemed only one logical place to go.

'So, what I'd like now is for you to split up into groups of five or six and discuss what "improvement" means *to you*. There are flip-charts around the hall. You've got, oh . . . let's say thirty minutes. OK?'

Having killed half an hour there, I killed another by having a spokesperson for each group take the stage and announce the essence of their group's findings to everyone. I then summarised the results for thirty minutes. Next I had everyone form different groups, write 'Where We Are' at the top of a flip-chart, 'Where We Want to Be' at the bottom and then fill in what they thought were the necessary and desirable stages in between. After that, I asked that people form different groups and roll a piece of paper into a ball. They had to form a circle and toss the ball to each other randomly. The ball was a student and whoever caught it had to express an improvement that a student might want, then throw it to another person who would address that concern – it alternated, but with every sixth throw the ball had to be either physically disabled or from an ethnic minority. Next – to free us all psychologically from the mindset of an old-fashioned library, in the hope that it would promote the suggestion of radical new ideas – I guided everyone through a twenty-minute session of Primal Screaming.

After this, a rather hoarse Bernard announced that it was time to break for lunch. I made it known I was looking forward to the afternoon, when we'd build on what we'd done so far.

'Thanks, Pel. That was very . . . *surprising*,' Bernard said to me as we all began to shuffle towards the buffet.

'Well, I wanted it to feel fresh – spontaneous. I didn't want it to seem like I was working to a rigid plan.'

'You succeeded,' David commented in a monotone.

'How long did you say we had for lunch, Bernard? An hour?'

'Thirty minutes. I didn't want to lose the momentum.'

'Right . . . right . . .' That didn't leave much time.

'I'll go and keep an eye on the people going outside for a cigarette,' chipped in David. 'See no one wanders off.' Great. Thanks, David.

'I think I'll pass on the food.' I patted my stomach. 'Still a bit unsettled. In fact, where are the toilets?'

Bernard pointed and I hurried over to them.

There were three urinals and two cubicles, none of them occupied. I quickly went into one of the cubicles and locked the door behind me. Thirty minutes wasn't long, but it was long enough to secretly meet up with the Triad duo, give them the money and get back, I reckoned. The toilets had obviously been refitted, but the basic building was that of the former primary school. I stepped on to the seat of the lavatory and from there moved up to stand on the cistern. The window above the toilet opened out on to the edge of the playing fields at the rear, but it was very small. There was no chance of my squeezing through it in my massive jacket, so I took it off and pushed it through the window ahead of me (conveniently, there was a small ash tree just to the side and I was able to hook it over the snapped-off end of a branch).

I threaded my arms through the window first then, using

a pulling, kicking, wriggling process, pushed and dragged the rest of me after them. I imagine that in California someone marketing it as rebirthing could make a fortune using just such a window frame and a tape of some whales moaning – I was finding it one of the most unrewarding experiences of my life, however. The opening was even smaller than I'd first thought, and my egress was further hampered by two more factors. The first was that the small metal peg on the window latch had, with hateful tenacity, hooked itself through my clothing in partnership with a series of tearing noises and an element of pain. But the second problem was the real killer. I'd reached a point where my hands had nothing to use to pull me forward and, behind me, my legs were now thrashing about in midair unable to make contact with anything that they could push against. You know that thing where you place your flat hands together, palms first, fold down both middle fingers, swivel your hands around then waggle the fingers about for the amusement of small children? Well, in essence, I was that scaled up.

I took a deep breath and decided that the only option left was to panic. I did this to the best of my ability; it involved some wild flailing about, cursing, strained, nasal whines of despairing self-pity – I drew deeply on all I'd learned during my life and was soon rewarded with the serenity of exhaustion. In this new tranquillity, dangling like a piece of spaghetti over an outstretched knife, I looked about me to see whether there were any brilliant ideas lying around. My eyes came to rest on my jacket, hanging from the tree. This wasn't close (I'd only been able to hang it there by twisting my arm out and using the jacket itself to extend the reach to the branch), but with a little straining I could reach it. The stub of a branch it was hanging on was small and dead; I wasn't at all sure it was strong enough to bear the strain of being an anchor against which I could bodily drag myself out of the window, but it was my only chance. With a groan of effort, I pushed out my left arm to grab it. The first time the shiny material slipped from my sweaty fingers as I pulled it towards me; my heart hit a wall as I thought the whole jacket might fall to the ground. It merely flopped back into its position draped over the branch, however, and a second attempt brought it back all the way until I had it firmly in both hands. The last thing I wanted, now so close, was for it to slip off its fastening as I pulled on it. So, I carefully twisted it round into a kind of very, very thick rope, forming a straight line between my hands and the peg that attached it to the tree. I took another deep breath, without any sudden jerks but with all my strength pulled on the jacket and . . . yes! I was right! The branch broke off! The stub also stayed wedged in the collar of the jacket long enough to fly forward and hit me in the face too, which I thought was a nice touch.

I held the lifeless jacket out in front of me and, with a coldness I'd never have imagined I possessed, cursed it to an eternity of the most sickening torments ever conceived. I stopped doing this only when a switch abruptly flicked on in my brain and, buzzing with a sudden hope, I scrambled into a pocket, triumphantly retrieving the mobile phone Talker had given to me. In moments I'd found and called the number I'd been shown.

A ring – 'Come on . . .' – a ring – 'Come on . . .' – a ring – 'Come *on* . . .' – and a voice, bare of any inflection, answered. 'Yes?'

'Hi, it's me! It's Pel. Come now, I need you to come right now.'

I explained my location (I was asked to repeat some details and confirm I wasn't elaborately insane) and I kept the line open for the creeping eternity it took them to get a taxi to where I was. I talked them through getting to the back of the building by foot and, when they eventually came into view, was more pleased by the approach of two Triad money collectors than I'd ever have thought possible.

'Thank God,' I sighed when they were standing in front of me. Because of the height of the window, I was about eighteen inches above them. This, combined with the vague feeling of being suspended in the air and the look of utter surprise and incomprehension on their faces, recalled to me some painting I'd seen of the shepherds being visited by the angel Gabriel. My subconscious never misses an opportunity to take the piss.

'You have what we require?' asked Talker.

'Yes, yes – just pull me out.'

'I'm not a man who jumps to hasty conclusions, Mr Dalton, but your behaviour is, let's say, "erratic". I'd prefer to get our transaction completed before we did anything else.'

'Oh, for Christ's . . .'

I stopped abruptly because behind me I heard the door to the toilets open and Bernard call out, 'Pel? . . . *Pel?* . . .' He rattled the, fortunately locked, entrance to the cubicle and called my name again. There was a little shuffling around, another 'Pel?' and then I heard the outer door open again as he left.

'OK, OK,' I said, darting into the pockets of my jacket. 'Here, it's all there. And a little extra for the inconvenience.' I handed the envelopes down to Talker. He fanned through them, nodded wordlessly and passed them over to Companion.

'Um, do you . . . do you think I could have a receipt?' I asked rather sheepishly.

'*What?*'

'Look, it's an awful lot of money.'

'You're not going to try to claim the tax back, are you?'

'No, of course not. I mean, I'm sure I can trust you, obviously. Obviously I can. But, just to keep things, erm, "proper", I'd feel better if I had a receipt. You know, look – say you're killed in a train crash tonight, right? I'd at least be able to show Mr Chiang I'd delivered the money.'

Talker looked at me without saying anything for a while. Then he reached into his coat and brought out a pen.

'OK, whatever . . .' He patted his pockets. 'I don't have any paper. Do you have any paper?'

'Hold on . . . I think I have a bus ticket somewhere . . .' I hunted through my jacket for it while Talker stood clicking the top of his Biro impatiently. 'Ah, yes – here.'

Talker scribbled some Chinese characters on to it. Lord knows what they meant, but at least it was something and I didn't feel I could push my luck any further.

'Thanks,' I said as he gave it back to me. 'Thanks very much. Oh, and here's your mobile. Do you think you could help me out now?'

Talker took the mobile phone and handed it over to his colleague.

'Well . . .' he began, but was interrupted – to the shock of both of us it seemed – by Companion.

'Je*sus* – it's switched on. There's no call time left. I only bought a top-up yesterday.'

'Sorry,' I said.

'What were you thinking? Mobile-to-mobile in the middle of the day? Why didn't you text us?'

'I . . .'

'It's your own fault for being on a different network,' Talker said, unmoved. 'It'd be a lot cheaper if you were on the same one as me.'

'Your line rental's too high.'

'Yes, but I get free call time included, so it makes up for it.'

'Only if you're a heavy user. I only carry it for emergencies.'

'Tch. You *say* that, but then you end up texting the whole time.'

'Sorry,' I cut in. 'Sorry; man stuck in window here! Do you think . . . ?'

I stopped because I heard the door to the toilets in which my rear half was located open once more.

'Pel?' called Bernard's anxious voice. '*Pel?*'

'Quick, *quick*!' I hissed down to Talker, stretching out my arms to be pulled. But it was too late. Behind me there was scrambling, a heavier scrambling than the last time, and now in the company of some grunting too.

'Pel?!' shouted Bernard, presumably at my buttocks. 'David? David, I think I've found him!'

Talker and Companion both heard this and began to make a run for it.

'No, come *back*!' I pleaded, but with entirely no expectation that they would.

Bernard's voice appeared closer to me; he must have climbed over the cubicle door and moved up to my side.

'Pel? Are you stuck?'

This struck me as a conspicuously stupid thing to say, and for a second I was heading towards shouting back, 'No, Bernard. Why do you ask?' However, I quickly realised that I wasn't in any position to be condescending. It was hard to imagine, in fact, *what* attitude might go with the position I was in.

I heard more voices begin to arrive behind me; a crowd of onlookers was obviously gathering. Bernard made a few tentative tugs at my legs. It didn't help. I think the way I'd become entangled in the latch made it far easier for me to continue outward than be pulled back.

'Oh, nueer. He really *is* stuck – you really *are* stuck in there, Pel.'

'Perhaps if we cut away his trousers,' offered David.

An encouraging murmur went through the crowd.

'No!' I shouted back. 'No, don't do that.'

'David, go and hunt out Maintenance for the building, would you? Perhaps they have some special tools . . . Pel? Try to stay calm, I'm coming round the other side.'

Down past my feet there was a rushing, chattering sound; like a swarm of locusts suddenly taking to the air. In the few dozen seconds of complete silence that followed that sound I'd like to say I prayed for a miracle. That, at least, would have shown some spirit. In reality, though, I just slumped over and hoped death might appear on the swiftest of wings.

It wasn't long before the fastest runners in the Learning Centre had rounded the outside of the building to where I was. Soon almost everyone was there. They formed a buzzing arc in front of me. Some out of breath, many chattering, all beaming with uncontrollable delight.

Apart from David, who was presumably getting Maintenance, Bernard was the last to arrive. His face was typically anxious, perhaps growing a little more so when he saw how high up the wall I was on this side. He looked up my nose and asked how I was feeling.

'Oh, you know.' I shrugged.

I tried not to make eye contact with anyone, but in the same way as covering your eyes is far easier than not peeking through the cracks in your fingers, the nearness of horror sucked at me. It was inevitable that the magnetic pull of self-destruction would slowly, but inexorably, drag my head up so that I connected with Karen Rawbone.

A grin slashed her face in two. I wondered whether it were possible to literally die of ecstasy, but sadly concluded it probably wasn't. She tried to impose a faux seriousness on herself as she spoke, just for effect, but it was asking too much.

'So, Pel . . .' She paused and put her lips through a series of rubbery contortions to hold back giggling collapse. 'So . . . What's happened here, then?'

I sighed with exasperation and rolled my eyes.

'Isn't it *obvious*?' I said.

A hush fell like a heavy blanket over the crowd. The intensity with which they reached out for what I was going to say next was surpassed by only one thing, and that was the intensity with which *I* was reaching out for it. No one spoke. No one even breathed. I let it go on, and on, and almost reached the point where I thought the new wordless atmosphere might prevail until people slowly drifted away in ones and twos.

'Er – no,' replied Karen, edging forward slightly to crown herself the voice of the mob.

'Oh, for God's sake. Clearly – *clearly* – I came into the toilet . . .'

'Please, go on.'

'*Clearly*, I came into the toilet . . . and there was nowhere to hang up my jacket. So, seeing this tree . . .' I pointed. '. . . outside the window, I reached out to hang my jacket there. But became stuck.'

That explanation did contain a sliver of truth. I didn't fool myself that this would help at all. My best defence, my only defence, was to gaze around with a look that suggested that anyone who didn't see the prosaic, logical nature of this chain of events must be some kind of simpleton.

It was a pivotal moment. Bernard ended it by hurling himself on the side of the scales opposite me.

'Nueer,' he sang, with an empty innocence. 'There *was* somewhere to hang your coat inside – I saw the hook on the cubicle door just now.'

'Oh . . . I must have missed that.'

Some people's legs buckled from laughter. All cheeks ran with tears, and the woman who worked in Inter-Library Loans slumped into the arms of her friends hissing, 'I can't breathe, I can't breathe.'

To this day I don't know who it was who called the newspaper, but a reporter and a photographer from the local daily arrived well before Maintenance had devised a way of freeing me. They only managed this, in fact, by removing the window frame with chisels. (They were quite happy to tug me free by brute force, they stated, just as long as the most senior person present took responsibility if my spine came apart. Bernard declined.) Even when I was lifted down, I still had a window frame around me like a wooden tutu until it was sawn free.

Sitting at the table amid shouting children and broccoli, Ursula spun her head towards me as I shuffled through the door.

'Sort these kids out,' she demanded, stomping away into the other room. 'I've had enough – I had a *crap* day at work.'

I WONDER IF YOU'D DRY THAT SEAT
WITH PAPER TOWELS BEFORE YOU GO?

I took some time off work, using the marvel that is self-certification to sign myself out sick for a few days; I put down 'stomach strain'. Unusually for a self-certification form, this was not entirely untrue. Though, of course, the real reason for staying away for as long as possible was 'to hide', I did have stomach muscles that were not unlikely to give me the odd wince. I was prepared to let people think this was due to being caught in a window frame rather than, as I personally suspected, more closely related to BodyBox abuse. (And it didn't end there either, as unwanted yet tenacious worries about dealing with the Triads were also having an undesirable effect on my bowels.)

I still got dressed for work in the morning and strolled into the town during the late afternoon so I could return home at the usual time, however. (Quite obviously, I didn't want to let Ursula know I was not at work or she'd have set about devising all sorts of tedious things for me to do. Especially as the final legal bits of our house move had now been completed – she'd have had me doing the packing and all sorts of nonsense.) She wasn't especially sympathetic when she'd seen my picture in the local paper.

'Is *all* your energy devoted to embarrassing me?'

'In fact, no.'

'It is, though, isn't it? You're driven.'

'Look, you just don't understand how things work at the university – *anyone* could have become stuck in that window, it just happened to be me.'

'As if I don't have enough to deal with at work . . . What

do you think Vanessa's reaction was when she saw that photo of you?'

'Arousal? Yearning – she became wistful, right?'

'She had another excuse to have a go at me. I had to stand there defending you, and you know how I hate that.'

As the mechanics of moving house are designed around a model where an interminable period of inchingly slow progress suddenly turns into a frantic race against time, I had to go in to the university to sort out a few things that had instantly made the jump to pressing. Being in the area anyway, I decided to drop in to Patrick's for lunch and catch up with Tracey and Roo. (There was a danger of bumping into someone from work, but I reckoned an indicative clutch at my stomach and the pulling of a face as I stood up would answer any questions they might have.)

'What's better, to be clever or to be beautiful?'

'Well,' replied Roo, 'obviously, it's not a choice I've ever had to make . . . I'd hate to have to give up either, but being beautiful takes far less effort – you can be beautiful while you're asleep, even – and it's also easier to fake being clever. There's a fine line between genius and insanity, but the line between beautiful and ugly is really, *really* thick.'

'I think ugly people tend to be stupid,' added Tracey.

'Isn't that prejudice?' I asked.

Tracey forcefully rejected the suggestion.

'Oh, no. No.' She swept her hand around the table. 'Some of my best friends are ugly. Anyway, I meant they're stupid *about beauty*, specifically. They dismiss people who are born beautiful because, I don't know, they haven't worked for it or something. It was just an accident of nature. But no one sneers and says, "Pfff – he was just *born* with a natural musical talent" or "His brilliance at maths is simply innate" – they get *more* respect if they're like that, in fact. If they're athletes or chess champions or artists or whatever then everyone thinks they're dead good. If they enter

218

beauty contests everyone mocks them. You know why I think that is? Because "beauty" is a quality most often associated with women, so a male-dominated culture has devalued it.'

'Christ,' said Roo.

'Christ,' I echoed.

'How long have you been working on that, waiting for the opportunity to say it?' Roo asked.

'A little over three and a half years.' Tracey waggled her hand and scrunched up her nose. 'Give or take.'

'God . . . and all that time I thought you were just staring into the distance thinking about Antonio Banderas.'

'I was doing that too.'

'Anyway, enough of this chatter,' said Roo imperiously, 'there are more important things to talk about . . . According to the press, you were jammed in a lavatory window I understand, Pel?'

'Oh, you know how they exaggerate stuff in the papers. Did I tell you we can move into the new house soon? Right after we come back from Germany, in fact.'

'Really? That's great – so about this lavatory thing . . .'

'That's why I've come in, as it happens. I want to see some students who were keen to rent our house. Get . . .'

'And . . .'

'. . . everything . . .'

'. . . the . . .'

'. . . sorted . . .'

'. . . lavatory . . .'

'. . . out.'

'. . . thing?'

'Better make a start on tracking them down, I suppose. Before the lectures begin again after lunch.'

'He's slipping through your fingers, Roo,' Tracey warned, raising her coffee to her mouth.

'So much does,' he responded, grinning.

Tracey snort-laughed into her drink, showering coffee everywhere.

'Well,' I said, 'sorry I can't stay for the food fight, but I
have tenants to entrap.'

I left them trying to sweep the coffee off the table into an
ashtray using the laminated menu.

There's very little that puts as much strain on a relationship as
defrosting the fridge. I flatter myself that I am a wise enough
man to realise that hardly anything is worth the misery and
frustration of doing it; certainly the loss of the freezer section
to grappling, bulbous tentacles of ruthless ice is but a small
price to pay. However, Ursula ambushed me during tea.

'Ah-ah-ah . . .' I said, as Jonathan began to twist himself out
of his seat and head away from the table. 'Eat your peas.'

'I don't like peas.'

'Yes you do.'

'I don't. They're yuk. I hate peas.'

'Tch – you *used* to like peas,' I said (because I'm a parent
and am driven by primal urges, when at a meal, to say things
like that – see also 'What do you mean you don't like it? That's
the best bit').

'No I didn't.'

'You ate them when you were a baby.'

He gave me a withering is-that-the-best-you-can-do? look.

'Well, whatever,' I continued, chastened. 'Eat some of them.
I don't really like peas either, but I'm eating them. It's a waste
to throw them away, there are . . .' (By the narrowest of
margins I managed to pull myself up before continuing 'people
in the world who are starving.') '. . . only a few of them.'

'They were in the fridge.' Ursula shrugged. 'They needed
using up.'

'I like peas,' said Peter.

'A *few*?' huffed Jonathan, 'There are thirty-four – look.'

'I like peas.'

'Peter likes peas, give him the peas,' argued Jonathan.

'That's not the point.'

'What *is* the point?'

'The point is, we're your parents and we decide who has what peas.'

Sternly eyebrowed and with the straight back of authority, I sat looking across the table in dominating silence. While Ursula swept Jonathan's peas on to Peter's plate.

'Do you want to do some packing after you've washed up?' she asked.

'Oh, I don't think so. The trouble with packing is the temptation is always to do *too much*. You end up having to unpack it again because you need the things before you've moved.'

'There isn't much time before we move. Don't forget we'll be in Germany all of next week.'

'Yes, but all the same . . .' I finished the sentence with a wave of my hand.

'OK, that's fine. You're probably right.'

Her words sounded to me like the tiny, tiny click a soldier hears beneath his foot that tells him he's just armed a landmine.

'You can defrost the fridge, then,' she said.

'Nooooo,' I winced.

'It has to be defrosted before we move, obviously. I've made sure the freezer's free now too.'

'Why do *I* have to do it?'

'It's your turn. I did it last time.'

'Says who?'

'Do you think . . .' Ursula spoke with a chilled venom, enunciating each word slowly and precisely. 'I would *forget* my defrosting the fridge?'

'Ohhhh.'

I sagged.

'Get a move on,' prodded Ursula. 'There isn't much time.'

You know things are bad when you try to drag out doing the washing up, but that's what I did. I even washed up the grill pan. Ursula had evidently been planning this whole thing as the fridge had been switched off some time previously and tea towels placed – optimistically – at its base to soak up the dripping water. Though the run-off was certainly beginning to breach these tea towels and make its way over the kitchen floor, the vileness of the icebox was, of course, barely dented by having been robbed of the source of its evil power.

The usual extravagant madness that stalks the world of fridge defrosting began to take control of my mind. A bowl of boiling water was placed in the icebox, where I watched it grow cold. The solid icescape laughed, unaffected. I repeated this several times, partly to observe the laws of physics being mocked and also to put off the frontal assault that I knew I'd have to undertake sooner or (better) later. Because I thought it might help, and I couldn't see any way in which it might lead to sudden hospitalisation or death, I rigged up an electric hairdryer so that it dangled in front of the icebox, roaring out hot air on its highest setting. The fridge did not flinch; I got forty minutes older.

Finally, I did what we must all do. I searched through the kitchen drawer for a knife not too deformed by having been used as a screwdriver and took it up to use as an ice pick. When Ursula is doing work around the house, I have the simple good manners and decency to sit and watch television well away from her. When *I* do things, however, she's not comfortable unless she's at my shoulder, coaching.

'Don't use a knife, you'll damage the icebox.'

'No I won't.'

'Yes, you will.'

'No, I won't. I'm being careful.'

I continued to plunge the knife down with rapid, heavy stabs; great eruptions of fine shards spraying out over me with each rasping impact.

'There are wires under that ice, look. The ice has formed around the wires.'

'I can *see* that.'

'You'll snap them.'

I'd managed to hammer the knife under a gap in one of the ice sheets. I was levering at it with the aid of swearing. It strained and creaked but refused to come free.

'No I *won't*.'

'And don't bend the knife. That's one of the good knives.'

'I'll buy you another knife.'

'It's part of a set.'

'I'll buy another bloody *set*, then.'

'It's a special set my grandmother gave me.'

'Do *you* want to do this? If you do it, then you can do it your way.'

'Don't get bad tempered.'

There was melting ice all over me. My hands were wet and raw pink with cold. The stabbing was making my wrist ache. I could see I had about another hour of this ahead of me.

'I *am not* getting bad tempered!'

The first huge slab of ice came away. It fell on to the linoleum floor where it shattered into ten billion pieces which skidded away to cover the entire surface area of the kitchen.

'And try not to make a mess,' chided Ursula.

My fingers tightened around the knife.

'I'd like you to go away now.'

'Where?'

'Italy. Go to Italy.'

'I think it'd have been better if you'd started at the top.'

'Thank you. That's helpful.'

'You know we need to have some way to move our stuff to the new house? Have you arranged that yet? It's pretty urgent.'

'I'm *doing the fridge*. Do you want me to stop doing the fridge and go and arrange it?'

'No. I'm just mentioning it. In case you'd forgotten.'

'I hadn't.'

'What about finding people to rent this house?'

'That's sorted.'

'Is it? You didn't tell me.'

'There's nothing to tell.'

'I'd have like to have *known*, at least. You always do that. You never tell me anything.'

'I'll be telling you a few things in a minute,' I replied, stabbing with increased vigour.

'Who's going to be moving in, then?'

'Oh, just some women.'

'How do you know them?'

'They're students at the uni.'

'Why women?'

'Um – their genes, I suppose.'

'You know what I mean. Why did you choose women?'

'What? What do you mean? They wanted the house, the timing was right and they seemed OK. What does it matter that they're women?'

'It matters to *you*, obviously.'

'Eh?'

'Or why did you say they were "women"? You could have just said "students", couldn't you?'

'And you'd have asked what kind of students – I was making an effort to *tell you things*, see?'

'Are they attractive?'

They were *stunning*, all three of them. Colin Rawbone might have a continuous, three-year haul on his hands trying to advise and cajole art students into a remotely employable state, but they certainly brightened up the place while he struggled to dull them down. These woman were all shining eyes and wild, dark hair. Moreover, they fizzed coquettishly; smiles hinted, straps slid from shoulders – they looked capable of *anything*.

'I can't say I took much notice.'

'So, they are, then?'

'I said I didn't notice.'

'You – *you* – "didn't notice"? Pff.'

'I was just concentrating on renting the house, that's all.'

'Are they attractive?'

'I didn't . . .'

'Are they attractive?'

I let air escape from my lips and shook my head to combat the disbelief.

'Well, I suppose they're OK. You know – average.'

'You *git*. Some eighteen-year-old English women giggle up and you say, "Right – here's our house." Unbelievable.'

'I think they're about twenty, actually.'

'Oh, right, that's OK, then – sleep with them.'

'I have no intention of sleeping with them, they're just renting the house. Jesus. And, for that matter, why on earth would they want to sleep with me?'

'You work at the university, they're students; they might look up to you.'

'I work in the *library* – no one on planet Earth looks up to me. But anyway, for reference, a good reply would have been, "Because you're a man of wit and charm, Pel, and not without your fair share of sexual magnetism." Just so you know.'

'You're going to break that wire.'

'I *am not* going to break that wire.'

It had reached the point where the knife (which I noticed was horrifically bent – I'd be suffering for *that* later) could no longer be used to get at the ice. What remained were the most stubborn and wily sections, the icebox elite. They lay behind awkward plates of metal, lurked under the cooling elements or had taken hostages and bound themselves to delicate electrical components. Only hand-to-ice combat could be used to attack them. My fingers, straining and twisted into improbable configurations, reached into blind nooks, pulling, crushing, scratching and trying to flick hidden pebbles of ice into the open. These pockets of resistance were the most fanatical in the icebox – you could spend five minutes just weeding out a piece of ice the size of grape. Gelid water ran wriggling down my arm, paused at my armpit to gather its strength, then continued onward to the waistband of my trousers, where it spread out.

'You haven't forgotten the parents' evening, have you?' said Ursula.

'*Eh?*'

'Parents' evening. I *did* remind you last week. Only you're due there in fifteen minutes. You're cutting it a bit fine.'

'Oh, shitting demons – why didn't you tell me before?'

'I did tell you, I told you last week.'

'That was *last week*.'

'Well, I've just told you again now.'

'Cheers. Thanks. Fantastic pacing. You're *unbelievable*.' I threw the knife into the sink and frantically rubbed my head to expel the worst of the melting ice from my hair.

'Don't start taking it out on me because *you* can't organise yourself properly.'

I sprinted upstairs to the bedroom. Two minutes later I sprinted back down again. Ursula was still standing in the kitchen, leaning against a work surface with her arms folded. I could tell by her stance that she'd been waiting, with some degree of pleasure, for my return.

'Where are all my bloody clothes?' I half demanded, half wept.

'Packed. Of course. Either packed ready for the holiday or packed ready for the move.'

'*All* of them? You packed *all* of them?'

'Of course not.' She nodded to the T-shirt I had clenched in my hand, the only thing I'd been able to find.

'I can't go to the parents' evening in a "69 Instructor" T-shirt – *look at the cartoon, for God's sake*.'

'Well, I've a terrible feeling that all your clothes are packed right at the bottom of things. Perhaps if you'd done some of the packing then . . .'

'This is you making one of your points, isn't it? I'm adrift in a point-making exercise.'

'You can finish the fridge when you get back.'

'You . . . *you* . . .'

No one had invented the noun I needed, so I had to make do with a roar of exasperation before spinning round and racing out of the door to the car.

Ursula was identically posed in the kitchen when I ran back into it thirty seconds later.

'Where *the hell* are the car keys?'

I might have screamed along all the way to the school at dangerous speeds but, fortunately, every single set of lights on the way was on red. Which, naturally, as well as taking the risky edge off my velocity, also had a hugely calming effect. Still, because I'd been shrewd enough to sit behind the wheel shouting 'Come *on*!' at every car in front of me for the whole journey, I arrived only a couple of minutes' late.

I parked creatively.

Bursting through the doors into the school, I hopped around looking for any signs that might give the precise location of where I needed to go to. The walls were confused with terrible paintings; I made a mental note that someday, surrounded by gorgeous women and envious men, I'd have to nod towards one of them and say, 'Tsk – that painting looks like it's been done by a four-year-old' so that everyone would think I was great. At the moment, though, there simply wasn't time. Amid the stick figures with huge, circular heads and arms jutting out at hip level ('My Mom'), I caught sight of a sign bearing 'Miss Hampshire' and a helpful arrow. I ran in the direction it indicated (passing a young couple – the man calling out 'Ha! "No running in the corridors." Eh? Haha!') and finally came to a door marked 'Miss Hampshire's Class'.

It opened in front of me.

'Ah!' The smartly dressed woman started with surprise at seeing me there. 'Mr Dalton?'

I nodded.

'I was just coming out to look for you – we have quite a tight schedule tonight.'

She invited me into the classroom and we both took a seat around one of the tables on primary school chairs; we were about eight inches off the floor, our knees level with our chests. She glanced at my shirt quizzically.

'Oh – has it started to rain?'

'No.'

Averting her eyes, she began to sort through some reports.

'I've only fairly recently become Jonathan's teacher . . .' she began.

'Yes, I know. I was very sorry to hear about the explosion of Mrs Beattie.' I could have phrased that better. 'Um, that is, I mean, Mrs Beattie's explosion.' Ah, well, it seems I couldn't have.

'Thank you. For that. It was an extremely sad incident. The children seem to have coped very well, though. We did do some things to help; we had a special assembly, got the children to draw pictures – a surprising number felt they wanted to draw the actual explosion, it turned out. Children have a remarkable resilience, they aren't afraid to confront things if they're given support.'

'Yes.'

'Well . . .'

'So, how is Jonathan's work?'

'It's fine, Mr Dalton. Very good, in fact. He's achieving excellent results across all subjects and is especially good at mathematics.'

'Really? That's great. Great. Nothing to worry about, then.'

'Ahh, well, there are some aspects of his behaviour that are giving us a little concern, however . . .'

'He's disruptive?'

'Not in the sense you mean, no.'

'Oh.'

'But, yes, he is.'

'I'm not with you.'

'Well, the other day, for example, he was calmly telling his classmates that God doesn't exist . . .'

She gave me a pained face and let the silence widen across the table. I began to realise she expected me to reply.

'Oh.'

'Yes, that's right.'

'Um.'

'That's obviously rather inappropriate, and possibly distressing for the other children.'

'Er, well, but . . . well . . . God *doesn't* exist, though. I don't really know what I can do about that.'

Maybe it was just the water in my underpants, but I thought the atmosphere chilled a little.

'You're aware that this is a Church of England school, Mr Dalton? You *chose* to send Jonathan here, rather than the school closest to where he lives, I see.'

'Yes, yes of course. But that's just because C of E schools tend to be better. I didn't expect religion would become involved.'

'Did you not?'

'No.'

'In a Church of England school?'

'Well . . . no. You have children from different faiths, don't you?'

'Yes, of course. We teach that there are many different beliefs and all should be treated equally. Christianity, Hinduism, Sikhism . . .'

'But not atheism?'

She laughed and gave a chiding look.

'I think that would rather confuse the children, don't you?'

'Ummm . . .'

'The children are too young to really understand the concepts involved here. It's far simpler for them just to accept the existence of God. Perhaps when they're much older some of them may make a different decision, but the only fair and *caring* thing is for us to teach them God does exist until then.'

'Did you put that case to Jonathan?'

'In simplified terms, yes. Yes, I did.'

'And?'

'He said his position "was non-negotiable". His precise words.'

'Kids, eh? Where *do* they get it from?'

'I did wonder.'

I cleared my throat a few times to fill the gap.

'So, you'll speak to Jonathan, then, Mr Dalton? It *is* quite important. The school is legally obliged to teach children to respect religious faiths. You can see how Jonathan's attitude could easily be interpreted as overt ridicule, not just of Christianity, but of the faiths of *all* the children at this school. That is something we need to address both because of the ethos of the school itself and our national, legal obligations.'

'Anything else?'

'I think he's feeding our modelling clay to the hamster. But that's just speculation at this point.'

'So?' asked Ursula from the sofa as I shambled in through the door.

'You know Mrs Beattie's accident?'

'Yes.'

'I think God may have been behind it . . . I'll be in the kitchen finishing off the fridge.'

IT'S THE BREAK FROM ROUTINE THAT'S
SO REFRESHING

Ursula and I never travel to Germany together. This is no bad thing, as the two of us being confined in any sort of moving vehicle transforms it into a wrestling ring except without the rule prohibiting biting and gouging. The real reason for our going separately, however, is that I don't fly. I used to fly. I don't fly any more. You know the bit I hate about air travel? It's the plummeting from a mile up in a blazing, cartwheeling, tomb of shattering metal. That and the legroom.

It had been surprisingly easy to get my leave cleared by Bernard. When I'd originally asked he wasn't keen to authorise it because he felt it was a busy time and lots of things were happening or about to happen. In the end, though, he decided I really needed a rest and it'd be better for everyone if I had one. After Improvement Day, in fact, he virtually insisted I take a holiday. I was slightly concerned that, as I was both supervisor and CTASATM, things in the Computer Team might utterly fall apart in my absence (and I'd be blamed for it on my return). Accepting this nagging concern was, however, well worth the cost of having a week away from a different nagging concern – the one that suggested that, whenever the office door opened behind me, it would be to admit an angry Chinese gentleman whirling some kind of big, pointy sword thing. (I hadn't heard from the Triads since the day I'd paid them, but I couldn't believe the matter was now closed for ever.)

The plan was to stay with Ursula's folks for a few days and then go off skiing with her brother and his wife – they had a holiday flat in a small ski resort close to the Stubai glacier. Ursula arrived there before I did simply because, if you're lucky enough not to find yourself driven four feet into the earth and surrounded by a corona of smouldering wreckage, then a plane will get you to Stuttgart in about two hours whereas a coach takes around twenty-four. In reality, the coach journey isn't too bad, once you get to know the ropes. Make sure you take a cushion for your head, expect the toilet to be out of order, don't allow the seat next to you to be claimed by the voluble and pestiferous American student; follow these simple steps and you can get across half of Europe *and* enjoy a few hours of flimsy and fitful sleep for a bargain price.

Of course, I always looked like hell when I arrived at Ursula's parents' home, but that was fine. If I ever turned up appearing smart and successful I don't think I'd be able to forgive myself for the disappointment I'd cause her father. On this occasion his luck was really in because on top of the shuffling, dishevelled, dark-eyed, heroin-addict appearance that a coach journey from northern England to southern Germany will bestow on anyone, I'd also been caught in a downpour just before arriving at the door. Thus I was able to add a vagrant-like array of dripping and squelching, not to mention the distinctive chemistry of dampness and body heat acting upon clothes you've been wearing for a whole day and eight hundred miles.

He opened the door to me and shone with an inner light.

'Uschi,' he called over his shoulder to an unseen Ursula, 'Pel is here.' How he stopped himself from adding 'Come look at him, and tell me I was wrong,' I can't imagine.

'Hello, Erich,' I said to him. 'How are you?'

He replied that he was well apart from a problem with his circulation. As he spoke absolutely no English and my German is not faultless (being largely learnt from Ursula or studying the multilingual descriptions in the photo stories in some of the more forthright magazines imported from Scandinavia)

I couldn't pick up all the subtleties, but I didn't think it mattered. Germans blame anything from extreme torpor to a vague feeling of wistfulness on their circulation, in the same way that the French diagnose themselves, at the drop of a hat, as suffering from 'a liver crisis'. (I don't know what the equivalent English national illness is. Stress, probably; which actually means chronically suffering from, or having one's heels persistently dogged by, the spectre of embarrassment.)

I squished inside and dumped my bags down in the hallway. Erich led me through to the sitting room, where the children were playing with each other – using small wooden saints as makeshift guns – and Ursula was chatting to her mother, Eva, about underwear.

'Hello, Pel,' said Eva. 'Did you have a good journey?'

She was, inevitably, entirely naked.

'Um, yes, fine,' I mumbled, concentrating with fearsome intensity on looking at her at eye level. Unlike Erich's formal and clipped Hoch Deutsch, Eva's German had a strong Swabian accent. Swooping 'oi' vowels replaced bright 'i's and the ability to find a 'sh' wherever it tried to hide made her sound as though she were erratically losing air.

'Ursula has brought me some of your English underwear.'

'It's not *mine*.' I smiled.

Her eyebrows made uncomprehending Vs.

'Haha.' I added.

She looked at Ursula.

'He was attempting to make a joke.'

'Oooh.' She relaxed. 'A joke. Very good. You must explain it to me later, Pel.'

'Mmm . . .'

'I think your English underwear is much nicer than the German underwear. The brassieres, especially, please me greatly.'

The German word for 'bra' is literally 'bosom holder', and hearing it set up a chain of associations and images that meant

233

resisting the involuntary urge to flick my eyes down below her neck took all the mental energy I had. I let out a small squeak by way of reply.

'They are, I believe, far prettier than those we generally see for sale here. Look at this one . . .'

She turned away from me, and bent over to reach into a bag. Death spurned my open, beseeching arms.

'. . . this is both feminine and well made. Don't you think?'

'I need to go to the bathroom now,' I said. 'I haven't washed since Victoria.'

'Victoria who?'

'Victoria coach station.'

'Oh, naturally – please, go. You know where everything is.'

I did now, certainly.

'Your towel is the blue one. It's on the right. It is the blue one, on the right,' advised Erich. 'You remember how to work the shower?'

'Yes, you explained last time I was here.'

I left the room at a light sprint.

'Ursula tells me you've been promoted,' Erich said during dinner. He chose the intonation of a man who'd just discovered that his sock drawer was full of emeralds.

'Yes, that's right.' I pushed a spoon through my *Maultaschen*. 'I'm the CTASATM now.'

'What's that?'

'Um, it's like a computer manager.'

'Like one, I see. It pays well?'

'About two pounds a week more than his last job,' Ursula said.

'That's after tax,' I added.

'Well done,' said Erich.

'Would you like some fish?' Eva, now mercifully clothed, asked, lifting the jar of unskinned raw herring slices in brine towards me.

'No, thank you.' Not now or ever.

'Did you have to take any exams for the job? Study for new qualifications?' Erich enquired.

'No.'

'Really?'

'Yes. It's a management job, you don't need any qualifications.'

'In Germany you must be qualified to do any job.'

'Things are different in England.'

'Yes . . . Is football hooliganism still widespread there?'

'No, it's not so bad.'

'Ursula tells me you've been burgled. Again.'

'Yes.'

'That must be terrible. I can't imagine how disturbing that would be; we've lived in this house for thirty-five years and never been burgled. I don't know anyone who has been burgled, in fact. Apart from you. England must have many, many burglars.'

'Or better ones – perhaps they take exams.'

'They take exams? In burglary?'

'No. No, sorry, it was a joke.'

'Oh, Pel.' Eva clapped her hands together. 'Explain to me the joke about the underwear.'

'Um, it wasn't a very good joke. I was just saying that it wasn't *my* underwear . . . It was *English* underwear, but not *my* underwear.'

'Why would you have female underwear?'

'I don't. That's the joke.'

'I see.'

'As I said, it wasn't a very good joke.'

'No, it is good. You don't have female underwear. You're ironically regretting how your underwear, as an English man, is not so pretty.'

'I . . . Yes. That's right.'

Having satisfied Eva, I was handed back to Erich.

'You are going skiing with Jonas and Silke soon?'

'Yes.'

'There's no skiing in England.'

'Not a great deal, no.'

'You must see that the boys get the most from it. Boys love skiing, so it's good for them to get the most from it before they have to return to England where there is no skiing.'

'Well, Jonathan will go skiing, but Peter's only three.'

'Many children here ski at three years. It is unremarkable.'

'I'm sorry – I need to go to the bathroom again.'

Jonas and Silke rescued me after a day. Had the Red Army Faction turned up at the door with a hood for my head and gestured towards the boot of their car with automatic weapons I'd have happily gone with them, so Jonas and Silke caused my eyes to well up from joy. They are the two nicest, most selfless people you could ever meet. It's like hanging out with Mr and Mrs Jesus. I couldn't even bring myself to carry my own luggage to the car because of the pain I saw the denial of freeing me from this tedious inconvenience was inflicting on Jonas.

We drove down to the glacier in the huge people carrier Jonas had hired listening to the dreadful German radio ('*Ein Schönen Guten Morgen* – All right! *Jetzt ist es Zeit* to get Radical! *mit die neuen Single von* Janet Jackson – Wow! Check it out!') become dreadful Austrian radio (precisely the same except 'Janet Jackson' is replaced by 'Jefferson Starship' or 'Kansas'). The children fell asleep, unable to withstand the gentle motion and the soporific hum of the engine. Jonathan fought it valiantly but, at last, I was able to take the Game Boy from his hands so I knew his body must have shut down apart from his heart and lungs. I was feeling very tired myself too; the lack of sleep from the coach journey beginning to catch up with me. I rolled my jacket into a pillow and put it against the window, letting my unfocused eyes rest on the smear of colours whipping by outside. My eyelids fell, and opened, and fell. Each time taking longer to open less wide. Gradually I loosened and slid towards sleep.

'Why can't you make an effort with my parents?' Ursula said, a billionth of a second before I sank into a warm ocean of slumber.

'Um-nngh-ahg?' I asked, squinting at her through a rubbery headlock of almost-sleep.

'It's not like you see them very often.'

I washed my face vigorously with my empty hands, trying to rub some wakefulness back into my head.

'What are you on about? I *do* make an effort.'

'Tchah. Every time my father tries to talk to you, you make it quite obvious you can't be bothered to have a conversation.'

'That's bollocks. Your father . . .'

'He asks about you . . .'

'Your father . . .'

'Let me finish . . .'

'Your father . . .'

'Let me finish . . .'

'He . . .'

'*Let me finish*.'

'Go on, then, *go on*.'

'He asks about you and what you're doing. He does all the work – you never show any interest in what he's doing.'

'Finished?'

'Yes.'

'Your father *does not* ask about me . . .'

'Oh that's . . .'

'*Let me finish!* – I let you finish, didn't I? Let me finish.'

'But that's . . .'

'Ah-ah-ah, no, no, let me finish.'

Ursula folded her arms together violently and glared at me, her mouth shut and contracted into a tiny horizontal dash by what she made clear was a triumph of restraint over justice.

'Your father doesn't ask about me, he just makes comments about me in the form of questions. And even . . .

'He *does* ask . . .'

'I haven't finished.'

'Let me just answer that, because . . .'

'No, no, let me finish what I'm saying.'

'You've said that bit, let me answer that bit.'

'No, I need to say the whole thing.'

'I only said one bit.'

'You said one bit and I *replied*, now I'm saying a bit. You had the first bit, now I get to say a bit.'

'You just don't want to hear.'

'I'm *happy* to hear you, after I've said this bit. Now let me say this bit, because if you don't let me say this bit, I'm just not going to listen to you, OK? That's fair. Now . . .'

'But he . . .'

'I'm not listening . . .' I shook my head as I turned to look out of the window.

'He . . .'

'I'm not listening. You can say whatever you want, because I'm not listening to you.'

'He does . . .'

'Ta-ta-de-tah . . .'

'. . . ask questions. He . . .'

'. . . de-daaaah-de-dum-de . . .'

'. . . asks about your . . .'

'. . . te-dah-dum . . .'

'. . . job, shows an interest in your work.'

'He does *not*,' I said, spinning back to look at her and fanning out my hands – No! – to emphasise the 'not'. 'Saying to someone "Are you still crap, then?" is *not* showing an interest in them. And he does that thing where he switches me off. He'll talk to me as if I understand German perfectly, then he'll talk *about* me, *in front of me*, like I can't understand a word he's saying.'

'He's probably just saying something a bit complicated and doesn't want to overburden you with complex German.'

'Pff – I understand German fine, thanks very much.'

Ursula made a little snort and replied with a German sentence that didn't contain a single word I understood.

'*That*,' I said, bringing down a finger at her, 'doesn't prove anything.'

'Oh, you two . . .' Jonas smiled, giving us a glance in the rear-view mirror. 'Forget about it. You'll have no energy left for skiing if you carry on.'

'Tell *her*, Jonas.'

'Oh, right – it's my fault again, *of course*,' Ursula huffed.

Jonas brought his shoulders up, then let them fall again.

'It doesn't matter *whose* fault it is. I'm just saying you should forget about it now.'

'Suits me,' I said. 'I didn't want to have this conversation in the first place.'

'Well, no, you never do, do you? So you get to avoid the issue – again – and I look like the bad guy – again.'

'I'm going to let that stand. See? Just to keep the peace, I'm not going to reply to that, even though it's bollocks – I'm just going to sit here quietly.'

'I'm going to push you out of a gondola.'

It's a measure of just how beatific Jonas and Silke are that they *volunteered* to look after our children while we went skiing. Usually, only Ursula or I can go at any one time, the non-skier staying with Jonathan on the lower slopes and taking a short cut to collapsing exhaustion via Peter, a toboggan and the words 'Again! Again!'. This, as you can imagine, leads to a great deal of 'Where the hell have you been?' wristwatch-tapping, thin excuses about taking the wrong run accidentally (and having to work one's way back from the other side of the Tyrol using a MENSA test of interconnecting lifts) and piercing recriminations echoing around icy Austrian valleys. All this was swept away because Jonas and Silke were happy to look after the boys all day, asking only for half an hour while we broke for lunch to go skiing themselves (and *Langlauf* – cross-country skiing – at that; which isn't even proper skiing, it's just a way of tricking people into what's really exercise).

For the first time since Jonathan was born we were free to spend the days having entirely different skiing arguments. Given the length of time it had been since we'd practised them, I was impressed at how effortlessly we got up to speed on the old rows. On the drag lift, for example, it was as if we'd never been away.

'Get your skis out of my track! You'll trip me up.'

'I'm only there because you're dragging us over. Stop leaning.'

'I'm leaning to get away from your skis.'

'No, you're— watch your sticks! If you trip me up I swear I'll kill you.'

'Keep you skis together, damn it. I've got no space.'

'Look, we're at the top, get out . . . get out . . . *Get out of the way*!'

All the exhumed memories washed over me. Here in the mountains, everything melted back into the time Ursula and I had spent living together in Germany. Sharing a tiny apartment, in a tiny village, on the Rhine. Perforated by mosquitoes (*I* was; they didn't bite Ursula – they wouldn't dare) and hundreds of miles from the nearest proper loaf. Those were the days when we had arguments in epic surroundings, when our lungs were younger and more powerful.

'Come on,' Ursula said, leaning forward on to her ski sticks and peering back at me.

'I think we need to go over there.'

'No, we need to go down here.'

'That's a black run.'

'I know.'

'If I go down a black run, I'll die.'

'Just try it. If it gets too hard, you can take your skis off and shuffle down on your bottom.'

'I know what you're doing. Don't think I don't know. Just because skiing is the only thing you're better than me at, you're rubbing it in.'

'There isn't enough daylight left to list the things at which I'm better than you. In fact, even the thing you've practised for the longest and most diligently – masturbation – I'm clearly better at, or you wouldn't ask me do it for you, would you?'

'Nice one . . . Yeah, that's right – stick with that grin. It'll probably freeze on you up here and they'll have to free your lips with a chisel.'

'Look, there's no point going down *that* run, it's boring. And it'll just be crowded with complete beginners and families with young children and people who are blind, in leg casts or frail from age.'

'Did I mention that ski suit makes your arse look *massive*?'

We had several days of these discussions. Ursula generally agreed to go with me down the easier run in the end to 'Look after you in case you hit a slippy bit', but as time wore on her craving for glamour and excitement (that is, naturally, the same craving that drove her to be my girlfriend in the first place) lured her away for the odd go down a black run. Looking on from my vantage point amid parties of primary school children and flailing, squealing, middle-aged women from Kent, it seemed she always made a point of riding up to the black-run-only areas next to some confidently tanned bloke who defined the Olympic ideal. Laughing and tossing her hair about all the way up.

'Who was that?' I asked, nodding nonchalantly at a lightly stubbled tosser in mirrored sunglasses who'd made a little wave towards Ursula as they went in different directions at the bottom of the piste.

'Oh, just someone I travelled up with on the lift.'

'Uh-huh.'

'His name's Bernd. He's a doctor – he's got his own practice in Basle, but he spends half the year travelling; skiing, rock climbing, white-water rafting, that sort of thing.'

'I think I'll come up with you for a go down a black run.'

'You don't *have* to.'

'Yes. Yes I do.'

The start, just after you got off the lift, was dotted with people, paused, looking down at the run below. I joined them and, silently, we all thought 'Oh, Christ' in unison. It wasn't so much a run as a sheer drop; it blurred the line between skiing and skydiving.

'Wow! Look at the view!' said Ursula. She was referring to the wave after fractal wave of mountains stretching off in a shining carpet between us and infinity. All I could see was my own imminent death.

'Yeah,' I replied. 'I think I understand why people say you're closer to God in the mountains now.'

I bent down and ratcheted my boots up to the point of circulation-restricting tightness.

'Are you ready?' She was doing a little stationary dance of eagerness.

'Not quite.'

Two or three minutes passed.

Ursula's eyebrows appeared questioningly over the top of her sunglasses.

'Not quite,' I said.

I tightened my boots again.

'You go down first. Then I'll be able to see if you get into any problems.'

'OK.'

'Great.'

'OK.'

'Go on, then.'

'I'm *going*. Don't hassle me. I was just about to go then, and you put me off.'

'Right. I'll stay quiet.'

I drew a deep breath and blew it out long and slow from pursed lips. 'OK.'

Ursula coughed.

'OK.'

I gathered my thoughts for a minute or so.

'OK, this is it. This. Is. It. This . . . Hey, look at that guy down there . . . Is he waving his arms to say the run's closed or something?'

'No. He's just waving to his friend.'

'Are you sure?'

'Do you want to ride back down in the gondola?'

'Of course not, don't be stupid.'

'I'm just asking.'

'Right, this is it. This. Is *It* . . . It didn't look like the kind of wave you'd make to a friend to me.'

'I'm getting cold.'

'OK, OK, stop going on.'

I stomped my skis on the ground to shake off any loose snow. Think positive. Think positive and it'll be all right. I turned to Ursula.

'Tell the children I love them,' I said, and pushed off.

In a little over two seconds I was doing eight hundred miles an hour.

The air whipping past was a deafening growl in my ears and rushed over my face, chilling the skin numb. I continued to pick up speed and my skis began to shake. Not because my legs were wobbling – they were, in fact, locked rigid in absolute terror – but because, I imagined, of a vibration phenomenon similar to the one that shattered early planes when they approached the sound barrier. Ahead of me someone was showing off by turning. He weaved left and right across my path. '*Aus dem Weg!*' I screamed – the words almost certainly washed uselessly back into my mouth by my speed, but there was definitely no way I could risk changing direction so screaming was the only option I had. Then I saw Ursula slip into view by my right shoulder.

'Woooo!' she whooped, waving her arms in the air.

'Fuck off away from me!' I barked across, maintaining my constipated crouch.

'What?' she shouted back, skiing closer to hear me.

'Fuck off! Fuck *ooooff!*'

'I can't hear you!'

'Fu— arrrgggh!' I hit a patch of moguls – the small mounds of snow between which the highly skilled practise their technique and over which Pel careers in a knee-battering, spine-hammering straight line of warbling sobs.

When I realised I'd passed them and was still, somehow, alive and feet-nearest-the-ground I was swept by endorphins. Despite being aware that I was travelling at a velocity so close to the speed of light that my body probably now had its own gravitational pull, I began to laugh hysterically. A shoulder-shaking, teary, stream of ack-acking was master of me now. Ursula appeared at my shoulder again.

'Fu-ah-ah-ck-o-o-ahh-ff-ah-ah!' I tried to shout without the aid of breath.

'What? What are you saying?'

She slid across even closer to me. I tried to veer away, but before I'd really begun panicked that I was off balance and about to catch an edge and pulled back. The pulling back was achieved by means of vast overcompensation, and I slewed off in the opposite direction, cutting right in front of Ursula. As I crossed, she went right over the top of my skis. Then a miracle happened.

When you ski over someone's skis the most likely thing is that you have a bit of a shake – but carry on – while they'll crash and burn. Somehow, however, I managed to have Ursula go over mine and remain upright – I barely noticed it, in fact. I skied onwards, on my new course, and eventually crossed into a blue-run area where I was able to gradually slow down in perfect safety.

Oh – but Ursula fell in an explosion of flailing limbs.

I waited for her at the very bottom of the piste. Some minutes later she came into view and slowly skied over to where I was standing. I was just about to remark upon the unusual and intriguing switch in outcomes in which our collision had resulted when she punched me in the mouth.

On the up side, she had to use her left arm to land the blow, because she'd injured the right one in the fall. She mentioned.

'You stupid bastard *wanker*! You cut right across me, you stupid bastard *wanker*. What the damnly hell were you doing? I went right over and landed on my shoulder – I bet it's broken, I landed *right* on it.'

'I think you've chipped my tooth . . .' I had an index finger exploratively in my mouth. 'It's . . . Jesus! Stop it! Those sticks are metal! Ow! Stop it!'

'My *shoulder*! Are you listening at all?'

'Yes, of course. We'll get you to a doctor . . . Your shoulder was an accident, though, whereas you deliberately hit me in the mouth. Hypothetically, if it ever went to court, then . . . Jesus! Will you stop that? They're *metal*!'

This day, Jonas and Silke had stayed at the flat with the children – who were tired and unwilling to get dressed that morning – so I drove us back. It took only about three-quarters of an hour to get there, not nearly long enough, in Ursula's opinion, to impress upon me what a stupid bastard wanker I was. It's best to let her get it out sometimes. Because I'm so tuned in to her emotionally, I understand that when she's set to full-on rant it's crass and unhelpful to interrupt her flow with counter-arguments, facts, etc. I just allow her to release the tension, unstaunched. Making long sighs, shaking my head, clicking my teeth and letting out small, ironic laughs is OK, though; I think she finds that soothing.

When we got back to the flat, Jonas was on all fours, the children howling with laughter and climbing all over him, like lions trying to bring down an elephant. Silke sat reading a magazine on the sofa. She peered over as we entered and I could see the concern fill her face as she looked at us.

'What's wrong?' she asked.

'I think I've chipped a tooth.'

'Uschi, you're so *white* – are you OK?'

'It's my shoulder. I hurt it.'

'How?'

'There'll be time to go into that later,' I said. 'The important thing now is to have a doctor take a look at it. Ursula needs calming drugs.'

It being a ski resort, where injury is almost part of the whole holiday experience, a doctor wasn't difficult to find. Jonas and I stayed with the kids, taking it in turns to be attacked, while Silke went with Ursula to the local clinic. They were gone for about half an hour, and when they returned Ursula had her arm strapped into a bafflingly complex sling affair. In England, a doctor who'd been awake and at work since the previous week would have rigged up a simple loop of bandage, or perhaps just suggested she keep her hand in her pocket for a few weeks. Here the sight of an E111 English medical form had clearly made them set out to show how far Austrian medicine was in advance of its bumbling English cousin. There were plastic rests, widened sections of anti-chaff padding and a criss-crossing array of Velcro-fastened straps fitted with elasticated sections for a smoother ride. It was the kind of sling that could have its own specialist department at a hospital.

'Well? What did they say?' I asked.

'It's the tendon. I've torn the tendon in my shoulder.'

'Phew – so not a broken bone, then?'

'Snapping a tendon is worse that breaking a bone, you idiot.'

'Is it? So you have a snapped tendon. Did they give you any drugs?'

'It's not completely snapped, thank God. It's torn but not all the way through.'

'Phew.'

'No, not fucking "phew" – I still have a torn tendon.'

'But not snapped, we can be grateful for that.'

'Suppose, in the middle of the night, I were to flick my finger *really hard*, but only at *one* of your bollocks? How grateful would you be?'

'About the drugs – they did give you some, right? Because if they've just fobbed you off without some serious pain-killers, then I'm going right down there now to sort them out for you.'

'They gave me some, they gave me some.'

'Take them, then.'

'I don't want to take them.'

'You'll feel better.'

'I don't want to feel better, it's not satisfying.'

'Right. I see . . . Can I take them, then?'

'Oh, no – we're in this together.'

Possibly because she regenerates like some alien species you'd see gradually picking off crew members in a sci-fi movie, Ursula's shoulder improved rapidly on its own. Just as well, as she was adamant that she wasn't going to see another physiotherapist on her return to England – 'Go to a physio? You must be joking. They're all sadists and maniacs' – and attempting physiotherapy on one's own shoulder is, apparently, 'The stupidest thing anyone has ever said'. By the evening of the next day, though she still couldn't move it very much or without pain, as long as she didn't wave her arm around or lift anything she was in no discomfort. Ironically, because I *hadn't* torn my tendon, I had skied for the entire day and my legs hurt from fatigue. I mentioned this to Ursula, but instead of seeing the funny side she just stared at me and started to scratch her nails into the arm of her chair.

'When are we going back to England?' asked Jonathan as I put him and Peter to bed.

'In a couple of days.'

'I don't want to go back to school.'

'Why not?'

'They keep making you learn things. I don't want to learn any more things, I've learnt enough.'

'You have to learn things so that when you leave you can get a job and realise how well off you were being at school.'

'I don't want to go school. It's harsh – it's mega-harsh. I want to stay at home.'

'Yeah, well, I want to stay at home too.'

'I want some crisps,' said Peter.

'You can't have any crisps, Peter,' Jonathan said. 'You've brushed your teeth.'

'But I *want* some.'

'Well, you can't have any.'

'Quiet,' I said. 'Peter – you can't have any crisps. Jonathan – you have to continue in full-time education for, at the very least, another ten years. Now, go to sleep, both of you.'

'That's not fair. If I have to go to school I don't think Peter should have any crisps for ten years either.'

'But I *want* some.'

'Both of you, go to sleep now. Any more fuss and I'll make you watch the farming programmes on Bavarian television tomorrow.'

I left them in the bedroom trading threats and insults in acceptably low voices and went to make myself a drink. Jonas and Silke had gone out for a meal and probably wouldn't be back until much later, stunned by some dense local speciality. Ursula was in the bathroom. I clicked on the TV while I waited for the kettle to boil. A news programme was just starting and – during the brief introductory round-up – British politicians appeared in three clips and indicated that they were passionately set, later in the programme, on filling me with shame and embarrassment. I turned the set off again.

'Pel? Are you there?' Ursula called from the bathroom as I was about to go back to making myself some tea.

'Yeah.'

'Come here. I need you.'

I lumbered over, my shoulders dropping. When Ursula calls me into the bathroom it's generally to ask the question 'Were you just going to leave that like *that*?', so I was in no hurry to arrive. As it turned out, she had struggled out of her clothes, removed the many-strapped device at the cutting edge of sling technology, and was standing in the shower.

'I need you to help me,' she said, an admission that obviously caused her very real suffering. 'I can't do this properly with only one arm and it's still too painful if I move my other one very much.'

'I'll get soaked, and splash water everywhere. I'll have to get in with you ... or stand across the room and throw sponges.'

'Well, *obviously*. Hurry up, wasting all this water and electricity isn't environmentally friendly.'

I took my clothes off and stepped in beside her. Unfortunately, there was no proper soap in there, only shower gel. I squeezed a spit of the viscous amber liquid into my cupped hand.

'I've already done there,' Ursula sighed as I began on her left thigh.

'Oh, shit, sorry. You'll be *too* clean now – wait here, I'll go and find some soot.'

'Just hurry up. This water isn't channelled into irrigation, you know, it's just wasted.'

'Gosh.'

Realising that we had perhaps only minutes before we destabilised the water cycle, I quickened my pace. I knelt down and used sweeping ovals and darting, soapy fingers to methodically work my way up. Starting with her feet, I slid my cleansing hands up and around her legs – losing a few seconds to indecision when I arrived at her stomach, unsure about whether it was easier to reach my hands up to rub over it or stand up again and reach down (I went with the latter, but I'm still haunted by the possibility I made the wrong decision and thereby sacrificed a quarter of a litre of water through poor tactics).

Ursula, as you know, is blonde. Clearly, this is a terrible shame, but despite this and the matter of having had two children she is still quite remarkably attractive. Even after all these years of pernicious familiarity, I'll sometimes find myself just gazing at her in appreciation. She might, for example, be in Woolworths publicly belittling my lack of commitment to the acquisition of garden furniture and I'll notice – notice again – how clear and blue and expressive her eyes are. How soft and smooth her skin. How the light, gentle down on her forearms is picked up by the halogen beams from the no-plumbing-necessary pond fountain that is behind her, reduced to clear. How her shoulders curve 'just so'; the contours made for me to run my hands over them. Altogether a beauty to set you aching, she's quite the loveliest of explosive devices. A thankful smile will seep into my face and I'll be overcome, simply overcome, with priapism. Now, and let me say that this is in no way meant to denigrate the accepted eroticism of Woolworths, at this moment I wasn't in a department store on a Saturday afternoon with two plastic carrier bags of previous shopping turning the ends of my fingers white. I was in a shower. We were both naked, our wet bodies sometimes rubbing against each other as I ran my soapy hands over her skin. I mean, well, what do you expect?

'What . . .' Ursula brought her arm down like a barrier until her index finger pointed where she was looking. '. . . is that?'

'Um, well . . . I *think* it's an erection – but I'll pop next door with it and ask if you like.'

'And why the hell have you got an erection now?'

'I'm sorry. I didn't know I had to book them.'

'You know what I mean. I'm *injured* here. This isn't a sexual situation, you're just supposed to be caring for me, helping me wash because I'm hurt. That . . .' She pointed at it again (it pointed back). '*That* . . . well, it's like breaking the doctor–patient trust or something.'

'You live in the Land Beyond Mad, don't you?'

'I can't believe you're getting turned on in a situation like *this*.' She shook her head and made a huffy, humourless laugh. 'I have a torn tendon, you are helping me with basic hygiene, and it *turns you on*.'

'We're naked in a shower . . .'

'My God, shall I go and get my sling, eh? If I strapped myself into that would it be even better for you?'

Better be careful here. She's probably asking a rhetorical question, not making an offer.

'Um . . . No?' I said, hesitantly.

'You're just weird, you know that?'

'You're *naked*, you're a *naked woman*. It's not like you've just found me going through a My Little Pony catalogue with one hand or something.'

'It doesn't matter that I'm naked.'

'We hold a different opinion here on Earth.'

'When I used to be naked – in a sauna or sunbathing – here in Germany, do you think all the men around me had sexual thoughts?'

'Yes.'

'You *what*? It's not a sexual context. Are you saying that a man who sees me naked on a beach is going to be thinking anything sexual?'

251

'I'll be sticking with "yes" here, OK?'

'Humfff – that's nonsense. Or maybe it's like that with English men, but *German* men wouldn't find it arousing.'

'Yeah, right.'

'They *wouldn't*.'

'Whatever you say.'

'They *wouldn't*.'

'I'm not arguing with you, OK?'

'But they *wouldn't* . . . say I'm right.'

'Fine. They wouldn't find it arousing, you're right.'

'Not like that, say it properly.'

'That was properly.'

'It wasn't, you didn't mean it.'

'Look, we're wasting water. Let's just get you washed and finish. I'm tired.'

'Why have you still got that erection, then?'

'Never mind about that. It's harmless; please don't hand it over to the authorities in Germany, OK?'

'Weird, that's what you are . . . Soap my breasts now.'

I had to start back to England a couple of days before Ursula and the children because of the restrictions of the coach timetable. As we kissed goodbye at the station Ursula slipped an envelope into my hand. I started to look down at it but she shook her head and clasped her hands around mine to prevent me. I stared out through the glass at them waving on the pavement as the coach pulled out of the excellently-named 'ZOB' (Zentraler Omnibusbahnhof) and I waved back until the turning of the coach panned the window and they slid out of view. Slowly twisting my hand upwards, I flattened out the front of the folded envelope and saw that it had 'Do not open until you are home' across it. Well, I consider Germany my second home, so I began to open it as we passed under the bridge fifty metres down the road from the coach station. Inside was a slip of paper, folded twice. I unfolded it and smoothed it out on my knee. On it Ursula had written, 'Pel. Hoover the house, all over – mop the kitchen and bathroom. Dust the house, all over. Clean toilet. Arrange removal vehicle. Double-check gas, electricity and water payments at both houses. Contact people who are renting, get things in writing. Clean toilet. Dismantle beds. Dismantle garden bench. Pack both (carefully – label slats and screws). Sort out mail redirection. Get keys from solicitor. CLEAN TOILET.'

CAN SOMEONE HELP ME DOWN OFF
THIS DESK?

I suppose that after having a holiday to regain my strength it was almost inevitable that when I returned to work I'd fall down a big hole.

I am not talking figuratively.

The day I went back rain was pummelling at the world from a melted, twisting sky. And, splendidly, the only umbrella available had Barney the Dinosaur on it. Still, it was better than nothing so I snatched it up, petulantly setting myself against saying I loved him too, and set off.

A powerful, gusting wind threw the heavy streaks of water through the air right into my face as I rounded the corner close to the Learning Centre, so I angled the umbrella down in front of me and made a dash for where I knew the staff entrance to be. Head bent, running flat out, all I could see was my feet hitting the ground. Which wasn't too bad until the ground disappeared. Each footfall splashed against the pavement, then on the muddy grass, then the final one encountered nothing at all. It had crossed the edge of a pit and just keep on going down, followed – in a sort of plunging, semi-crouched dive – by the rest of me.

When my foot finally hit something solid it was the side of the pit, and the only effect it had was to fling me farther into the centre of the hole. I executed an ugly, three-quarter somersault to land on my back in three inches of brown, lubricious, muddy water. I had enough forward momentum to skid along for another fifteen feet in this position – it might have been farther, but fortunately my progress was halted by a thin, vertical metal pole striking me firmly in the genitals. I made a piteous groaning noise and rolled over into a testicle-nursing, foetal position on my side. In doing so, I finally let go of the Barney the Dinosaur umbrella, which, snatched by the wind, flew backwards. In passing, its handle hooked under my chin. So I lay there, gasping in the mud, the umbrella struggling to get free but caught under my jaw; it looked as if a giant angler had captured me for sport.

'What are you doing down there?' asked a voice.

I would have liked to have replied with something so pithy that the owner of the voice would have been forced to take his own life, but, what with the genital situation and the umbrella tugging under my chin, all I could manage was 'Fnngh'.

'What? What did you say? Why on earth did you run into the pit? Don't you see how dangerous it is to do something like that? I was watching you with Ted and Ted said, "Look at him, he's going to run straight into that pit," and I said, "No, he'd have to be *mad*," and Ted said, "He is, you know – look," and we watched, and Ted was right, you ran straight into the pit. Are you *mad*?'

'Fnngh.'

I reached up and pulled the umbrella free. While I was doing this the voice called down.

'Here, grab this rope.'

He threw a block of wood attached to a thick nylon rope over to me.

It hit me in the genitals.

'Gnngh.'

'You're supposed to *catch* it – are you *mad*?'

Keeping my left hand on guard by my crotch, I snaked out my right and picked up the rope.

'Ted! Ted! Give us a hand here. I'm trying to pull him out.'

Somewhere farther away, partially muffled by the wind and rain, I heard a voice call back, 'Is he *mad*?'

By the time I had, like a newborn foal, made my way across

the slippery earth to the side of the pit, Ted had arrived. The pit wasn't very deep – perhaps a little over four feet – but its walls were made of loose, wet, slippery dirt, and getting out on my own would have been quite tricky. I wound the rope around my forearm and scrambled up the side with the help of Voice and Ted pulling me and shouting keen advice like 'Try to get to the top' and 'Don't let go of the rope'.

'Thanks,' I said, out of breath, when I eventually got up beside them.

'No problem. But don't you go doing that again, OK? How are your nuts?'

'My pulse hurts.'

I scooped some mud out of my ear.

'Why is there a big bleeding pit there?' I asked.

'Foundations, squire. We're doing the foundations for the new building here.'

'Are you Bill Acton by any chance?'

'Mmmm – maybe. Who wants to know?'

'I'm Pel. I'm the CTASATM here. We've spoken on the phone.'

'Oh, *right*. You were on leave when we started. Had a good time? Never easy coming back to work, is it?'

'Generally it's easier than this. Shouldn't there be a barrier around that hole? Tape or something?'

'Oh, we took it off the other night. We had diggers all over the place, going like the clappers, moving all the . . .' He tapped the side of his nose and water splashed off it. '. . . stuff. We were going to put the tape back up this morning.'

'I was waiting until the rain stopped,' said Ted.

'Jesus,' I said, looking down at myself. 'Look at the state of me. I'd better get cleaned up. Not that I have anything to change into here.'

'I've got some spare oilskins in the hut, you can borrow those to get you by,' said Bill.

'Um . . . thanks. I suppose they'll have to do until I can get some proper clothes.'

I went inside to the staff toilets and Ted appeared a couple of minutes later with the oilskins – bright yellow, rubberised overalls with 'Bill Acton Constructions' written across the back.

'Thanks, Ted.'

'One size fits all. I've brought you some wellingtons too – your shoes must be soaked through.'

'Yes. Thanks.'

I washed as best I could using the tiny sink. One of the caretakers came in just as I was naked and bent over under the hot-air hand-dryer; however, he immediately turned around and left again without saying a word. The oilskins were very stiff and uncomfortable against bare skin, but, I thought, I only needed to wear them long enough to get home and change.

I was hurrying back out of the Learning Centre again, my wet clothes in a sodden and grubby ball under my arm, when Bernard spotted me.

'Pel?'

'Hi, Bernard.'

'I need to see you in the office for a moment.'

'Well . . .'

'It's rather important. It won't take long.'

'Well . . . OK. If it's quick.'

I followed him into his office, noting as I glanced out of the window that the rain had now stopped and Ted was putting a red-and-white striped tape barrier around the hole.

'They've started the building the extension, then?' I said, nodding outside.

'Um, yes. Turned up just as you went on leave. I wasn't really sure how much you'd spoken to them – and Keith said it was our affair and he hadn't been involved since the tenders – but Bill said everything was under control. I just let them get on with it. Have you been out examining the site, then?' He gestured towards my overalls.

'Yes. Yes, I'm very "hands on", Bernard.'

Other members of staff were beginning to arrive at work. Walking past the large window, pointing me out to each other and sharing comments I couldn't hear but which obviously amused them no end. I rustled in my big, yellow, rubber suit as I turned around to face away from them.

'So, Bernard, what's the problem with the building work that's so urgent?'

'With the work? Oh, nueeer, nothing – as I said, I've just let them get on with it. I think Nazim has been talking them through some things, I've seen him around. As far as I know, it's all going well. I've asked you here about another matter.'

I felt a ball of fizzing panic start to expand inside my head. 'Another matter' – it was the Triads; I couldn't kid myself it was anything else. Somehow things had got out while I was away and I was now at the bottom of a mountain, watching as an avalanche of crap started to thunder down towards me.

'Um . . . would you like to sit down?' Bernard said, clearly uncomfortable.

'No thanks. I'm experiencing some chafing. I think that might make it worse.'

'Chafing?' He seemed to notice the clothes under my arm for the first time. 'Oh. I see.'

'I . . .'

'Oh, nueer, it doesn't matter. You don't have to explain.'

'But . . .'

'Nueer, really. Let me just tell you why I wanted to speak to you now, that might help.'

'OK. Fire away.'

'I'm leaving.'

'*Leaving?*'

'Yes. Another reason for my not getting too involved with the building work is I had quite a hectic few days last week. I told Keith I was leaving the university – I've left now, in effect. I'm just here today to collect a final few things from the office.'

'Don't you have to give notice?'

'Well, they can't really make you work out your notice. Not really. Everyone knows that. What can they do? Bring you in under guard and force you to work? I'd got some leave left too, and a little TOIL, so I just told them I'd be gone by the end of the week.'

'It's very sudden.'

'It's been coming for some time, it's just that everything finally fell into place last week. No one else here knows I'm going yet. I haven't told them because they'd start asking questions and I couldn't face it; they wouldn't understand. Keith and senior management were keen I keep things quiet too. So it suited everyone.'

He dropped his eyes away from me and began collecting items from his desk in a couple of carrier bags.

'Are you . . . are you in some kind of trouble, Bernard?' I asked.

He laughed.

'Nueer! Good Lord, *nueer*! Quite the opposite. Everything is great, absolutely great.'

'Sorry. I thought . . . From how you were talking . . .'

'Oh, I see. I see. Not like that at all. Let me tell you the whole story.'

'OK . . . If you want to.'

'I think I should. I know you'll understand.' He scratched his ear for a moment. 'Have you ever met my wife, Fiona?'

'No, I don't think so.'

'Really? I thought you might have seen her at Tony's leaving do?'

'Tony left before I started here.'

'Did he? Yes, I suppose he did – doesn't time fly? Well, anyway, my wife works – *worked* – for the public library service. She was heavily involved with developing all the Internet access they have in public libraries nowadays. Knows her computers, does Fiona – not like me, eh?' He laughed. I wasn't sure how much it was appropriate to confirm that statement by laughing along with him.

'Ha-umm-m,' I decided.

'When she started doing this work she began using the Internet a great deal. Quite an eye-opener. For both of us. At first we just browsed, exchanged e-mails with people around the world and so on. Then Fiona began learning Web page creation skills and we built our own site – "Rock & Rita's Place". She took care of all the technical computer stuff, of course, but I've always done photography as a hobby and so I contributed on that side.'

An immobilising, icy chill seeped slowly down my back.

'We built up quite a following. I never realised that the UK swinging scene was so vast, Pel, I really didn't. But we became a sort of forum, a meeting place; and not just for UK swingers, but for swingers from France, Holland, Belgium . . . it was incredible. We're getting over half a million hits a month now.'

He paused for my response.

'Uh-huh.'

He was growing increasingly animated and enthusiastic as he continued.

'Of course, we never dreamt we could ever make a living out of it – we were just doing it for the . . . well, we were just doing it. But then there started to be a bit of advertising. Just small things at first – massage oils, condoms, butt plugs and so on – but it really took off. We began selling the items ourselves; we bought them from wholesalers, naturally, but Fiona and I modelled them on the page to make it seem more of a personal service.'

Oh sweet Lord, let me not be in this office.

'Then we made a subscription-based members section where people could put up their details, make requests and chat. The other week we got sponsorship from a *major* company that sells playwear, specialist restraints, toys and all the rest. That's when we decided to go full time. We organise all the records, liaise with suppliers, provide our clients with information – we can earn far more than we've been getting in the library service for using precisely the same skills. There's no reason for me to keep working here now and, with it getting so big, it's sure to come out sooner or later and I knew the university wouldn't be happy with the situation – and, of course, they weren't when I told them. Even if they had been, here in the Learning Centre people would have been uneasy with it. That's why I'm only telling you. I knew you would understand.'

My hands were clenched so tightly that my fingernails were digging into my palms.

'Ermmm . . . Why, exactly, do you keep saying that *I'll* understand?'

There was a tap of knuckles on the window. We both looked outside. Bill Acton was standing there. He performed a mime which involved indicating his own crotch, then pointing at mine, then raising his thumb – 'OK?' – questioningly.

I turned back to Bernard.

'I need to go home now.'

'Sure, Pel, me too. Well . . . I suppose this could be the last time I see you. Take care, OK?' He reached forward and grabbed my hand, shaking it vigorously, clasped in both of his. 'I know it's my own choice, and I'm off to better things, but I'll miss the old place . . . Perhaps when things have settled down you and Ursula can come round the house for a meal – Fiona does a marvellous risotto. We'd both be delighted to have the pair of you.'

'I *really* need to go home now.'

'Yes, yes. The chafing. You said. Well . . . That's it, then . . . Oh! Would you like the address of our website?'

'*No!* No, no, that's . . . No . . . No. I'm sure I'd be able to find it. I am the CTASATM, after all.'

'Yes, of course. You could do it with your eyes closed, I'm sure.'

'I'd certainly try it that way. Look – I have to go . . . Good luck, Bernard. Really, I hope it all works out for you.'

'It's in the bag.'

'Yes. It probably is.'

I went home and changed out of my rubber suit as fast as I possibly could – uneasily unable to prevent myself musing that Bernard had possibly gone home to do exactly the opposite.

Ursula fell between gears in the van and the engine squealed.

'Careful,' I said, 'you'll wake everyone up.'

She took down the air freshener that was dangling from the rear-view mirror and threw it at me.

'Ow! What was that for?'

'That was to keep me going until I have the time to set fire to your head.'

'You're so tetchy, you know? No one else would put up with you.'

'It's three o'clock in the morning. I've been moving stuff for ten hours. I'm very tired. And I still have to find somewhere to dump your body. You've only survived this long because I needed help lifting the washing machine, so don't you go pushing your luck.'

There had been a misunderstanding.

Ursula had given me the job of hiring a van to transfer everything to the new house. She didn't want to hire a removal firm because she didn't trust them not to break things and, in any case, doing it ourselves was cheaper. So, I'd hired a huge van. As commanded. The van was massive, the new house only about two miles away, so I'd thought the whole process wouldn't take more than two or three hours. Therefore, I'd collected the van around teatime and driven back to our house to meet Ursula and get started; I'd even been organised enough to arrange for my mother to have the children to let us get on with it. When I turned up Ursula looked at the van and then back at me.

'You bloody, bloody, bloody, bloody, bloody idiot.'

'What?'

'What have you got that van for?'

'You told me to.'

'I mean, why have you got it *now*? It's a weekday evening. I meant hire one for the weekend. How are we going to move all the stuff on a *weekday evening*? How many days do we have the van for? When has it got to be back?'

'Um, tomorrow morning.'

I saw her muscles flex and took a step backwards.

'It'll be OK. What's the time now? Five? Five-thirty? We'll have it all finished by eight. Nine – absolute tops.'

I couldn't see how, with such a large van and almost everything already packed, it would take any longer than that. But, well, there we were at three o'clock in the morning still driving stuff to the new house. You live and learn, eh?

'Look,' I said, picking up an olive branch, 'I'm completely prepared to admit I was wrong about the time it would take to do this. There – I've said it . . . OK? . . . Eh?'

'You can't just apologise and . . .'

'Woah, hold on. I didn't say I was apologising, as such. I just said I was wrong; it was an honest mistake, let's not go apportioning blame. Because, if we go down *that* road, then someone will start saying that if you tell someone to do something, rather than doing it yourself, then you can't really complain if they don't do it *exactly* the way you'd have done it. You told me to hire a van, I hired a van. Those are the facts.'

Actually, it was probably a good thing for me to walk home. I reflected that it was only a mile or so and it'd give her time to cool down.

'Oh, *Chrrrist* – turn that bloody thing off, Nazim, man.' George Jones held his hands over his ears as Nazim's mobile phone shrieked out a piercing ring tone. 'Not with *my* head this morning. It's like having frozen shite stabbed into your ears is that.'

I was swaying slowly in the VC's office after arriving at work, and barely having had time to satisfy Bill Acton's enquiries about the state of my testicles before a call had summoned me over. When I got there Nazim had welcomed me with a blokey slap on the back and George had briefly attempted a smile of acknowledgment as he raised a glass of Alka-Seltzer to his mouth. He'd drained it and then banged the glass back down on to his desk with a gasp, his face speckled with little water droplets from the fizzing. In the minute or so since then, Nazim had chatted rapidly about nothing whatsoever, George had groaned and belched, and I'd tried to catch myself before I fell both asleep and face down on to the floor. The only thing keeping me awake at all was fear; being abruptly summoned to see George and Nazim probably meant Triad trouble.

'Sit down, man,' George said finally. 'You look like crap. What's wrong with you? Were you on the Guinness last night too? You promise yourself it's just a quiet drink with the lads and you'll stop after five or six; next thing you know you come round lying halfway up the stairs with your bowels trying to escape from your body, eh?'

'I'm OK, George. I'm just a bit tired.' I'd had twenty minutes' sleep, in fact. Now every blink was inviting unconsciousness.

'You want to take care of yourself, Pel, you do. Your health's the most important thing, you know.'

'Look, guys, as everyone's a bit worse for wear today, let's just crack on with this, yeah?' Nazim said.

'Go ahead, man,' replied George painfully. 'You tell him. I'll just sit here and try to keep everything down.'

'No prob. You kick back, George. Pel . . .' Nazim slid a buttock on to George's desk and leaned towards me. 'Pel, have you any idea why we asked you to come here?'

'No. No, none at all,' I lied. Maybe if I affected innocent amazement at the announcement of whatever Triad-based horror they were about to reveal to me then I'd have more chance of not getting caught up in it any further.

'It's because we think you're a can-do guy, guy. The way you stepped into TSR's shoes and just got on with it without any fuss? That impressed us, Pel. We're a big, dynamic university here. Things move fast and we need people who can keep up with them. We believe you can see what needs to be done and do it; you think on your feet – that's what we need.'

I'd give a kidney for just an hour's sleep, I thought. On my feet.

'Now, as you may know, we have a bit of a situation here at the moment.' Nazim slipped on his serious face. 'Bernard Donnelly has hopped on his bike and left us a bit in the lurch. Do you know why he's gone?'

'Yes. He spoke to me yesterday.'

'Did he? Do you know who else knows?'

'Erm, Keith – Keith Hughes – I think. But other than that no one. That's what Bernard told me, anyway.'

'Good. Well, that's the way we'd like to keep it, yeah? The media love stories with sex in them and it's not really the kind of publicity the university needs.'

'Right. Fine. I won't say a word. That's no problem. I'll be off now, then.' So that I can go to sleep in the toilets.

Nazim laughed and slapped me on the shoulder.

'No, Pel, that wasn't why we asked you here. We knew

you'd have the nous to keep shtoom, we knew we wouldn't need to tell you that. Good God, no. We're here to offer you the post of LCM.'

'Acting,' added George from beneath the hands on which his face was resting.

'Yes, acting – Acting Learning Centre Manager. How about that, Pel? You up for it?'

There was, I felt, about an eighty per cent chance that I'd nodded off and was dreaming all this. I rubbed my eyes. When I'd finished, George and Nazim were still there.

'You want *me* to be LCM? You're aware, for a start, that I'm not a qualified librarian?'

'That's not something that should worry you,' replied Nazim, shaking his head and holding his hands up as though nonchalantly stopping traffic.

'I didn't say it worried me – I'd be swept by self-loathing if I *were* a qualified librarian, naturally. But it's sure to be an issue with the librarians in the Learning Centre. Appointing a non-librarian as LCM? They'll march through the streets, overturning cars.'

'It won't be an issue, trust me. You'll be an acting LCM and the very fact that you're *not* a librarian will reassure people that you're just steering the ship temporarily. We need someone to step in here really quickly, Pel, but we don't want them to think we've, de facto, appointed a new LCM without following procedures.'

'What about David, though? Why don't you ask David to do it? He's the senior librarian.'

'We'd rather not have David Woolf in the position, Pel. He's certainly not going to be given the post permanently . . .'

'Why not?'

'Well, for a start, it's traditional for David not to get the job. If we made him LCM after the number of times he's gone for the post and not got it, it'd look like we were letting our standards drop.'

'Also, he's an officious tosser,' added George, without raising his head.

'What George means is that David Woolf is a bit inflexible . . .'

'He's a prissy gobshite.'

'. . . and blinkered thinking isn't really useful or appropriate in a modern, forward-looking university like this.'

'Still,' I said, from beneath a leaden blanket of tiredness, 'I would've thought Keith Hughes might have something to say about it.'

Nazim smiled. 'Keith Hughes increasingly prefers a "hands off" approach to all but very specific learning support matters. I think he has management fatigue.'

'Rose Warchowski, then. It is her department, after all.'

George let out a laugh. It was followed by a moan and his grasping the sides of his head tightly.

'Pel,' said Nazim, resting his arm on my shoulder. 'There *is* no Rose Warchowski.'

'What do you mean? I'm not with you. She's the Prime Administrator of Learning Support – are you saying you *made her up*?'

Nazim laughed and shook my shoulder with his hand.

'No, no, of course not – get a grip, Pel. Rose Warchowski was a real person and was Prime Administrator of Learning Support. You even used to go drinking with her outside work, didn't you, George?'

'Yep.' George raised his head, at last, and appeared to become slightly distant and melancholy at the memory. He nodded, very slowly. 'Great arse for a woman of her age.'

'However,' continued Nazim, 'some years ago she just – poof!' He flicked both his upturned hands open; like little explosions or flowers blooming at high speed. 'Vanished. Simply stopped turning up for work. For a while we didn't think anything of it; quite a lot of George's drinking friends go missing for the odd few days.'

George shrugged towards me.

Nazim went on.

'But after a week or so we became concerned – some quite, erm, important things were happening here at the time that involved her – and so, naturally enough, we went to where she lived and broke into her house. No sign of her at all.'

'Did you call the police?' I asked.

'Yes,' replied Nazim. 'Yes, of course – for a while we thought about doing that. But then we asked ourselves what would be best for *everybody*. The publicity wouldn't be good for us. If she'd gone mad, done a Reggie Perrin or something, then that was her business and she'd want us to leave her to it. If she'd been abducted – and it didn't give us any pleasure to think this, guy, not at all – she was probably already dead by now. She'd got no family, so who was going to benefit? No one. No one at all. *However*, while we were going through her things we realised how organised she was; librarians don't have an "off" switch, it seems. All her papers were sorted and filed and her life was set to run with the minimum of fuss. The bills – mortgage, electricity, telephone, gas, council tax, etc., etc. – were paid by direct debit, from the account into which her salary was automatically sent each month by the university.

'Rose Warchowski's life could continue perfectly well without Rose Warchowski.

'The great thing about this, though, was it meant we had access to her salary. As long as Rose kept getting paid we could write cheques to whoever we needed, to help the university. I practised a little, and her signature wasn't difficult to copy. Banks don't check very much anyway; they just wait for any complaints – it cuts administration costs. They also automatically post you a new cheque book when your current one is running out. Marvellous. Rose was on quite an impressive salary . . .'

'And I've given her three, very generous, pay rises since then,' George cut in.

'That's right. So it was a perfect fund that didn't need any sleight of hand with the books to make cash readily available to us. In fact, since she disappeared, Rose has probably done more for the university than in all the time she was actually here . . . Pel? Pel, you have a nosebleed.'

'Yes,' I replied, quietly. 'Yes, I rather thought I might have.'

Nazim pulled a handkerchief from his trouser pocket and handed it to me.

'Thanks . . . But, erm, how can you do this? What about Rose Warchowski's work?'

'She doesn't really have any,' said George. 'Oh, I'm sure if she were here she'd find something to do, but she'd make it up herself, no one really sets you tasks when you're a departmental administrator. The only person you're answerable to is me. Hold your head back.'

'But, still, why doesn't anyone notice? Keith, say; Keith must wonder why he hasn't seen his boss for several years – they have neighbouring offices, for God's sake.'

Nazim shook his head.

'Keith Hughes, as I said, is "hands off". "Hands off", "head down", "eyes straight ahead". He simply doesn't want to get involved in anything that he might find upsetting and will never ask questions if he even suspects he won't like the answers. From time to time George and I send him – and other people – e-mails that "Rose Warchowski" has written or post documents through the internal mail. If there's an unavoidable meeting with some external agency then George or I will just step in to represent her, apologising for her sudden food poisoning or broken ankle. Once, at a SCONUL meeting, we hired an actress to play her – told her it was a corporate test, to see if anyone could spot she wasn't really qualified.'

'Best SCONUL meeting we ever had,' preened George. 'We'd have used the woman more, but she went and got a part in *EastEnders* and it would have been too much of a risk.'

'You don't need to bother about any of this anyway, Pel,' said Nazim. 'The point is, Rose Warchowski isn't an issue when it comes to your being LCM.'

I was so tired it almost made sense. 'But, if I'm LCM, who'll be CTASATM?'

'Well, you'll be a transitional LCM, Pel, yeah?' replied Nazim.

'Acting,' said George.

'Precisely. You'll be acting LCM so, as it's only a temporary measure, we'd like you to keep on the CTASATM role as well.'

'I'm also the Computer Team Supervisor.'

'Yes. That too. It's only for a few months. Filling the other positions at this stage would just be disruptive in the long run. We'll pay you the full salary, at the entry level, of an LCM . . .'

'An acting LCM,' clarified George.

'. . . of an acting LCM, of course. Your CTASATM salary is insultingly small, isn't it? It's laughable, really; I don't know how we get away with paying you it. For the time you're LCM . . .'

'*Acting* LCM,' said George.

'. . . for the time you're acting LCM, you'll be on almost twice that figure.'

'And you'll have your own parking space.'

'I don't have a car.'

'Fine – auction the space among the other staff. You'll get a good price, guy, I tell you.'

Perhaps partly because I couldn't think, I couldn't think of a good reason for turning down the offer. Sure, it meant taking on more responsibility, in a senior job – one that I had even less idea how to do. Yes, things *were* moving very quickly – and, more importantly, the pace was George and Nazim's, it seemed, rather than mine; but was that necessarily a bad thing? I was being offered a job, temporary or not, that paid nearly double what I earned now. We'd just moved into a new house, and it needed lots of work. I knew Ursula wanted to get things done there, buy new furniture – all sorts of stuff. It would really make her happy if we had the money available for her to do that. She'd be so pleased to be able to improve the house and get things just how she wanted them.

Or there was that home cinema set-up I'd seen. We could spend the money on that instead; wide-screen, sub-woofer, surround speakers – yeah, that was something for everyone.

'OK,' I said. 'I'm your new LCM.'

'Brilliant!' said Nazim.

'Acting,' said George.

'Who would you be if you could be anyone?' I asked, beginning on the first of the three black coffees I had lined up.

'That's tricky,' replied Roo. 'I'm not sure that if I had to trade all this in . . .' He swept his hands downward to indicate himself. '. . . that a single person would be sufficient incentive. Can I mix and match? Bill Gates's money, say, but with the singing voice of Isaac Hayes, the wardrobe of Julian Cope and Anna Nicole Smith's breasts to play with in the bath.'

'Maybe you'll revise that choice when I tell you I've just been made Learning Centre Manager. Be honest, Roo. Now – now more than ever – you want to be *me*, don't you?'

'Wow! Congratulations, Pel,' said Tracey.

Roo shook his head and sighed.

'You're excited about getting promotion within a library. This, Pel, is the moment you became old.'

'It's not a library. It's a Learning Centre.'

'Ahhh – you hear the words come out of your mouth, but you're not quite sure if you're being sardonic any more, are you?'

'Can I just ask a question?' said Tracey.

'That *is* a question,' I said. 'You've pre-empted my reply.'

'You're actually *pleased with yourself* for saying that, aren't you? Unbelievable. But what I was going to ask is, why don't you want to be Ursula?'

'*What?*'

'Well, you'd think that was the person you'd most want to be. If you love someone more than anyone else in the world and want to spend the rest of your life with them, you must think they're uniquely special – so isn't the natural person to want to be your partner? I'm asking, you know . . .'

'Rhetorically?'

'Yes, like that. I'm sure I've never wanted to be any of my boyfriends. But, if they're the person I respect and love more than anyone else, why not?'

'Perhaps because, if you *were* them, they wouldn't be there to be your partner any more. And that'd be too much of a loss.'

She shook her head. 'No, I don't think that's it.'

'Oh, I think you might find it is,' said Roo.

'Ooooh, I think it's actually not,' she affirmed.

'Whatever you say.' Roo sucked his teeth and looked out of the window.

'Good. Because I'm saying it's not.'

'OK.' Roo shrugged.

'It's *not*.'

'I wasn't arguing with you.' He sucked his teeth and looked out of the window again.

I cut between them both. 'I have no idea about most people, but – apart from the whole madness thing – I wouldn't want to be Ursula because of the awful world she has to inhabit.'

'Why is it awful?' asked Tracey. 'Your being in it aside.'

'Oh, it's a terrible, terrible place. Joyless.'

'How?'

'Completely.'

'*How?*'

'*Completely*. That's the point. Everything's had the fun taken out of it, right across the board. OK, look, for example, take our car alarm, right? There's a little fob on the keyring and you push a button to activate or deactivate the car alarm. This is *brilliant*. You can fire it backwards to activate the alarm as you walk away from the car, even over your shoulder. And when you're coming *back* to the car, it's even better. You can see how far away you can be and still manage to get a hit – sometimes, right, if you hold the fob way up in the air, you can deactivate it from right across a car park! Or you can wait until you're closer and just – pow! – fire from the hip; I wish we had central locking, so I got a fantastic "Chunk!" when I hit the target. Draw! Fire! Chunk! *Brilliant!* I've watched Ursula turn the alarm on and off, though, and it's like she's getting no buzz out of it at all. Imagine having to live in a world like that?'

'Roo? Hold my hand,' said Tracey. 'He's frightening me.'

I returned to the Learning Centre to discover a mob. They had gathered outside the LCM's office – now *my* office, of course – waiting for me to arrive. As I approached someone shouted, '*There* he is!,' and they all turned to look at me, the indistinct rumble of voices increasing in volume. I nearly ran for it. I'm sure if I had it would have triggered them to give chase and I'd have been pursued through the streets by angry librarians screaming 'Get him!' and 'Loose the dogs!' However, I had accidentally gained access to a surprising degree of bluster by floating extreme tiredness on caffeine. It was a curious combination of feeling both very sharp and yet also not really there, merely watching as a disinterested spectator.

'What appears to be the problem?' I asked, strolling over to them.

There was a movement, a bubbling, within the crowd and, like an ant emerging from beneath a heap of sand,

Karen Rawbone struggled out to the front. (That is, what was *now* the front, because it was where I was standing – power indeed.)

'This,' replied Karen, 'is the problem.' And she handed me a print-out of an e-mail. It was from Rose Warchowski; doubtless Nazim had been doing a bit of channelling.

'Congratulations to Pel Dalton,' the spirit Rose Warchowski had written, 'on being appointed Learning Centre Manager! (Acting.) I know his technical ability and management skills will be a useful asset at this particularly busy time for the Learning Support Department. As the LSD's Prime Administrator, I'm sure I speak for everyone in wishing him all the best in his new, well-deserved, temporary post.'

'That's very nice of Rose,' I said, handing back the print-out.

I actually felt the draught from a hundred thousand hairs bristling simultaneously.

'This is completely outrageous,' spat Karen. 'You may be accomplished in other areas, Pel – I don't want to make this a personal issue – but you've certainly got no technical abilities or management skills. Even putting that aside, appointing you without any form of consultation is totally unacceptable.'

'Because I'm not a librarian?'

'Well, for a start, yes.'

I noted that David was there, but he was standing at the back, not even looking at me. Karen had elected herself spokesperson.

Oh, caffeine and adrenalin, with the softening vapours of crushing tiredness just to take the edge off. I walked a few steps and caught hold of a desk, which I then dragged out in front of the mob. With one quick swing I jumped up to stand on top of it. (Ooooooo – head rush; now we're *really* on a roll.) In my mind, it was *Henry V*, Act III, Scene 1. (Outside my mind, it was a bloke standing on a desk in a library, but things outside my mind were not especially real at the time.)

I surveyed the crowd. They were a puddle of upturned faces below me. Karen was out in front, closer to the desk; her head – excellently – exactly level with my crotch.

'I'm just a simple man,' I began. 'I was born in this city, it's my home town. Just a short distance away from here is my home. It's my home – my house, my house home. But, in a very real sense, *this*, this Learning Centre, is my home too. All I want is to do what's best for my home and the people who share it with me. I didn't ask for the Learning Centre Manager's job, no sir. I didn't ask for it, but if senior management have decided, in their wisdom, to give it to me . . . then I'm damn well going to do my best to do it properly. Yes, I'm not a librarian – how many people are? OK, OK, put your hands down. That's not the point. Yes, I'm not a librarian, but does that mean I don't *care*? We live in a world where information technology is transforming education. We all recognise that it's altered the service beyond recognition and will continue to do so until, in perhaps five years' time, we'll recognise it even less than we don't recognise it now. Well, do you know what I say? I say "Yes!". And I make no apologies for that. That – *that* – is the context in which you have to view my appointment as LCM. A *temporary* appointment, let's not forget. I am merely a funnel through which time will pass to get to the permanent appointee. Those are the facts. Now, my friends, let's just focus on what we *all* want: to give our users the best goddamned service they've ever seen!'

'But you're not a librarian,' said Karen.

'And *you* need to bleach your moustache, OK? Because, at this angle, "Burt Reynolds", that's all I'm saying.'

An inner voice whispered to me, 'Well, Pel . . . you're losing it.' In reply I shrugged 'Yeah, but I've had a good run.'

'How *dare* you speak to me like that,' scorched Karen.

'I'm head of the Learning Centre now, Karen. I need to be concerned with the image we project to our users. Students have a right to study without the distraction of your sour, carking little face.'

'I'm going to get you done for harassment, that's what I'm going to do. I suppose you think you can talk to me like that because that's how you and your girlfriend speak to each other. But I think you'll find that people with proper relationships don't communicate like that.'

She thinned her eyes into a sarcastic smile and looked up at me with her lips pursed and twisting; like a tiny, twitching anus.

'Couples who are normal,' she continued, 'don't have rows when they're out shopping. Couples who are *normal* share the same interests and views. The children of *normal* couples behave in public. If you're unable to stop having trivial domestic disagreements with your girlfriend, then I think it's better you end your dysfunctional relationship so your anger doesn't spill over into the workplace.'

'Listen to me, Karen. *You* may have built your relationship from the instructions in magazines, *you* may hang on every bit of pop psychology spouted on a daytime TV show, and *you* may well believe that if a couple has an argument while parking the car then their relationship is rotten to the core, but I don't, right? Furthermore, I do not want to go through my life in the narrow, masturbatory dullness of spending it with someone who likes the same things and thinks the same things as I do. Ursula and I are *kept together* by irreconcilable differences, OK? If your creepy, ripple-free, Disney-approved marriage works for you, then that's great. But normal couples argue about who had the TV guide last. *Normal* couples jostle for position at the bathroom sink. *Normal* couples contain one person who is obsessive and furious about lights being left on and another who is fundamentally incapable of ever turning them off. Ursula and I are just normal . . . only lots more so.'

'Ha!' Karen briefly glanced round at the, completely silent, crowd behind her. 'I think we ought to leave the decision about what's normal to the normal people, yes?'

'Oh . . . *Fuck off*.'

You know, I don't want to appear immodest, but I think it's true that the best managers are born rather then created.

THE HAPPIEST DAY OF
SOMEONE ELSE'S LIFE

'Martha and Phill are getting married.' I passed the invitation across the breakfast table to Ursula and moved on to opening the rest of the mail, a good deal of which comprised bills. The fact that we were now in our new house meant that, pleasingly, many of them were addressed to the previous owner.

'What for?' asked Ursula, turning the invitation over and examining the back, as if the answer might be found there.

'How should I know? Maybe Phill's trying to prevent Martha testifying against him in a murder trial.'

A series of muffled thuds drummed down through the ceiling. Almost as if Jonathan and Peter were leaping on to the bed from the top of the boxes of as yet unpacked items, in almost precisely the way I'd especially told them not to do about five minutes previously.

'We'll lose a Saturday, though. There's so much to do here and the weekends are the only time we have to really get down to it.'

'Pfft – it'll be OK. We'll get everything done.'

'*I'll* get everything done is what you mean. You don't do anything.'

'That's *completely* untrue. But – unrelatedly – doing stuff is easier for you.'

'How on earth is it easier for me?'

'Oh, God; because you're naturally industrious, *obviously*. I'm not, so it's that much more difficult for me. It's the same as having no fear doesn't make you brave. To be brave, you have to be afraid, yet somehow carry on anyway. Doing even small things takes *much* more effort and willpower for me than doing very big things does for you.'

'I see.'

'You might creosote the entire fence, while I just watch TV and then, when you've finished, I'll rinse out the brush. But really – *really* – we've both given as much of ourselves to the tasks.' I paused and sat back. Then, looking down, continued, 'Oh, right – and that made you feel better, did it?'

'Significantly.'

'Well, I'm going to change these trousers now and you'd better hope this milk doesn't stain, I'm telling you.'

I stomped up the stairs, leaving Ursula to reflect on her actions.

'Is that pee?' asked Jonathan, pointing at my crotch as I walked past him to the bathroom. Peter appeared beside him in a flash.

'No, of course not,' I said. 'It's milk.'

'Milk? Why . . .'

'Have you been jumping on the bed?'

'No.'

'Why that milk?' asked Peter.

'Shhhh!' said Jonathan.

How daunting. I hadn't gone into my new office the previous day. Well, things had been said, tempers had flared and I thought it best to simply go home and let everything settle. Standing there now, it was all rather uncomfortable. There was the uneasy sense – sitting in Bernard's office, at Bernard's computer, surrounded by Bernard's paperwork – that somehow I had *become* Bernard. I gave in to a small shudder. But even more psychologically sapping was the sheer amount of stuff that appeared to be in need of attention. My Computer Team Supervisor's desk was made up of rolling hills of chaos, so the impression was of some work – a single layer, perhaps – confronting you, all else surely being rubbish or irrelevance. Then there was TSR, who didn't go in for much paperwork at all; also, what he did have was put safely out of view and, even if you chose to look at it, it was largely meaningless. Moving to TSR's office hadn't been all that bad, in retrospect. Bernard was a librarian, however. Things were arranged. Without moving from my seat I could clearly identify three massive columns of obvious work rising from neatly labelled trays. One was marked 'Staffing' – I wasn't about to go anywhere *near* that. Another bore the title 'Complaints and Incidents'. I didn't really want to reach into that pile either, but the only other one was labelled 'Misc.', which was a *truly* terrifying option. Anything could be in there. Maybe, filed away in puzzlement by Bernard, there were competitive tenders for student recruitment services from the Mafia and the Yardies. *Far worse* than that was the prospect of uncovering an unintentionally discarded photo of Bernard in a thong. In any case, I knew it was best to begin with the complaints as there was a university commitment to respond to them within seven days. We didn't have to *do* anything to resolve the cause of the complaint – fortunate, as most of the complaints came from lunatics – but we did have to respond to the complainer.

I leafed through the pile. The first half-dozen complained that more computers should be made available, the next that more computers should be made available and the second-floor toilets smelt of sick. Then came a note from Security saying that a vagrant had been discovered in one of the study carrels again – including another call that students should display their ID cards so that picking out vagrants was easier. Some more angry tirades about the shortage of computers. A vitriolic attack on the staff for not policing the use of mobile phones. A vitriolic attack on the staff for fascistically policing the use of mobile phones. Another four or five bitter calls for more computers. A report of a flasher in Semiotics. More computers needed. Theft of a handbag.

A transcript of a complaint to Security by a mature student studying economics part time who, it seems, had peered out through a window on to the lawned area to see two male students facing each other, their trousers down. Grasping a penis each, two, kneeling, female students were beside them, rubbing vigorously and 'apparently engaged in some kind of race'. Fines. Fines. Fines. Computers. A request that the Learning Centre employ some staff who weren't stupid.

The phone rang.

'Hello, Pel Dalton, Learning Centre Manager.'

'Hi, Mr Dalton. My name's Marie Pileggi . . .'

'I'm sorry?'

'What for? What do you mean?'

'Sorry, I meant, "I'm sorry, what's your name?" I didn't quite catch it.'

'Oh, I see. Marie Pileggi.'

'Erm, can you spell that?'

'Of course. You think I can't spell my own name? Of course I can.'

'No – sorry – no. *Could* you sp . . . *Would* you spell it for me, please?'

'M . . . A . . . R . . . I . . . E . . . P . . . I . . . L . . . E . . . G . . . G . . . I . . .'

'Thank you. What is that? Italian?'

'Yes.'

'You're one of our overseas students, I assume?'

'No, I'm calling from the *News*.'

The *News* was the local paper. I never read it myself. It was no more dreadful than any other local paper. Which is to say it was mostly full of local businesses promoting themselves – 'Derek Bromley, left, receiving the Employee of the Month award from Managing Director Jane Nabbs' – furious retired schoolteachers demanding to know when the council was going to fix that drain, and as many group photos (schools, clubs, reunions, etc.) as possible in the hope that everyone in the picture, and everyone who knew anyone in the picture, would buy the paper. More important than the fact that I never read the *News* was that everyone knew its editorial policy was to hate the university. It was hard to say why this was. Probably, it was simply because a newspaper has to hate something to have any stature whatsoever, but a local paper can't alienate the people who buy it. Thus hating the university and the city council was no problem; the people who worked for them hated them as well.

'You're a reporter for the *News*?'

'No, I'm just a researcher. I'm calling to ask about the building work you're having done. Apparently it's started, is that right?'

'Yes.'

'And there have been no incidents?'

'What do you mean, "incidents"?'

'Oh, anything really . . .'

'Well, I fell into the hole.' I laughed. 'I don't think that warrants a piece in the paper, though.'

'You *fell into the hole*?'

'Um, yes. I was running, and I had this Barney umbrella in front of my face . . . it's not important. Forget I mentioned it.'

'So, apart from your falling into the hole, it's been OK? No problems or discoveries or anything?'

'No. It's . . . dull. Very, very dull.'

'Well, thank you very much.'

'That's quite all right.'

'Goodbye.'

'Ciao,' I said, expressively.

'What?' she replied.

'Goodbye.'

I put the phone down, but it rang again almost immediately. It was George Jones's secretary.

*   *   *

'My guts are churning, man. Absolutely churning – red wine doesn't agree with me. I know it doesn't, that's the thing, I *know* it doesn't. Never again.' George sat back and let out a long, rumbling belch. 'Ooooh, that's better.'

As it happened, standing in his office watching George belch was preferable to being outside it. Because, out there, sitting on a chair and smilingly turning her head towards me when I'd passed, was Karen Rawbone; a woman less pleasant to be near than a middle-aged Welshman performing pretty much any bodily function at all, in my opinion.

'Anyway – Chrrrrist, Pel. We make you LCM one minute and the next you're standing on a table swearing at the librarians. You couldn't have waited a few days? Just for the look of the thing?'

'Yeah . . . sorry, George. I'm afraid I was brain-addlingly tired, and then I overcompensated with caffeine. And then Karen appeared.'

'Hateful little shrike, isn't she?'

'It would be unprofessional of me to comment.'

'As you can guess, she went straight to David Woolf, as her line manager, to have you disembowelled and your head put on some railings. Woolf, clenched sphincter that he is, followed the book and put in a written complaint to *your* line manager, Keith Hughes. Thankfully, Keith's natural instinct to stay well away from everything kicked in and "unable to get hold of Rose Warchowski at the moment" – he said that without a flicker, incidentally, you have to admire him – he passed the matter on to me. I've had the bloody woman in here for an hour, man. And my head could have done without having *her* voice ringing around it this morning, I can tell you.'

'Sorry.'

'Yeah, well, never mind that now. I think she's been warmed nicely by the idea that her complaint has gone right to the top.'

I nodded.

'That's me, by the way,' added George. 'I've convinced her that you've been under a lot of stress – which she didn't care about – and that I'd call you over here and give you the bollocking of the century – which wet her knickers so much she could wring out a glassful, I bet.'

'Er . . . right.'

'So, when I call her in here, I want you to look bollocked, OK? Look bollocked and mumble a quick apology and I think we can forget about it.'

He called his secretary and Karen entered the room, her face going 'Ner-ner-n-ner-ner' at me.

'Karen,' said George, 'I've spoken to Pel about this unfortunate event and *vigorously* reminded him of the behaviour we expect from a Learning Centre Manager at this university. He accepts that his conduct was completely unacceptable. That's correct, isn't it, Pel?'

'Oh yes.'

'As this has come to my attention, as Vice-Chancellor of the university, it can't but affect any decisions about Pel's future here that might be referred to me for approval or consideration. You understand that, Pel?'

'My actions were unjustifiable. I wouldn't expect you, Vice-Chancellor, to do anything but recall them should the situation make it appropriate – *I'll* certainly not forget my actions that day for as long as I live. I can only apologise, Karen. I am sorry for my unprofessional behaviour. I'm sorry for the disruption I caused, I'm sorry for any distress I have given to you personally by questioning your abilities and saying you had fat thighs.'

'You didn't say I had fat thighs.'

'Didn't I? Oh . . . I'm sorry – it's all a bit of a blur, I'm afraid. The emotion . . .' I waggled my hands on either side of my head to indicate that the emotion had muddled up my brain. 'Well, the point is, I'm truly, *truly* sorry.'

'You're very fortunate that Karen is mature enough to let

this matter go now and move on like a professional, Pel,' said George.

'Erm, well . . .' began Karen.

'You take note of her, Pel . . . *that's* the kind of conduct we expect here. No personal issues interfering with the smooth running of the university. Thank you, Karen. Thank you for setting such a fine example.'

'Erm, well . . . As long as this kind of thing *never* happens again.'

George rose from his seat and gently guided Karen to the door.

'No, I'm sure nothing like this will. I have a few more things to discuss with Pel. You go back to the Learning Centre now and we'll try to put this whole ugly incident behind us. Thank you for dealing with it all so well. Thank you. Goodbye – if you have any more problems, you just come straight to me, OK?' He closed the door behind her with an affectionate wave and then turned back to me. 'You had to do the thigh thing, didn't you?'

'Sorry.'

'Whatever, man. Bigger fish. I've had the *News* sniffing round my arse.'

'Really? They just called me.'

'Oh, shite. What did they want?'

'It was all rather vague. They asked if the building work was going OK.'

'And you said?'

'I said it was.'

'Good. They're fishing. If they call again, direct them to Marketing, let Nazim handle it. Don't get drawn into commenting yourself.'

'Why are they calling anyway? There isn't anything wrong, is there?'

'Wrong? No. Of course not. A few bodies – Acton got rid of them.'

'You said "bodies" then, didn't you?'

'Yeah, bodies – forget about it, man.'

'You said "bodies" again.'

George slumped back into his seat and sighed with some irritation, indicating that he thought it rather selfish of me to make him go into explanations when he was so badly hung over.

'They were just old bodies, Pel. You know there was some talk about the site being a graveyard? We managed to get the clearance from the local council to go ahead on the basis that it wasn't. Turns out it was. Just one of those things. Can't have everything brought to a halt because of a few corpses; it'd mean delay, cost, damn archaeologists poking around – don't want academics taking up residence in the university grounds, thank you *very* much. The only solution was to keep quiet about it and have Bill Acton get rid of the evidence quickly. Maybe some of his men have been talking in the pub, I don't know, but the *News* has obviously got wind of something. They can't prove anything, though, if we just keep our mouths shut.'

'Isn't this . . . um . . . well, wrong? Doing that with an ancient burial site?'

'What are you, man, a Druid?'

'No, I meant wrong scientifically, or culturally, or something. Wrecking an historical find like that?'

'Get a grip, Pel. We've got about five thousand years of history and already it's more than we can cope with. And that, mind, is the slowest five thousand years we'll ever have. In the seventh century – I don't know – two, maybe three, things happened. Every century has had more and more things happen, faster and faster. Five thousand years of history. The sun has been pencilled in to destroy the earth, but it won't happen for another *billion* years. We are *not short of history*, OK?'

'Righto.'

'Good.'

'And I won't get into any trouble?'

'You're a worrier, aren't you?'

Over the next couple of weeks the *News* did call me a few times. Always, as George had said, fishing. They never had any specific questions, and even if they had I wouldn't have answered; I just told them to phone Marketing, hoping a few conversations with Nazim would be dispiriting enough for them to give up entirely. I was thoroughly uneasy about the situation, having thought that, after the Triad affair, I might look forward to going through life without any more incidents until I died quietly, without fuss. On becoming LCM I'd prepared myself emotionally to, say, make some tough decisions about photocopier maintenance agreements, not to cover up the disposal of bodies. Things like that can play on your mind. I was in panic up to about my knees but, as I couldn't think of any attractive way to get out of it, all I could do was cross my fingers, roll up my trousers and continue wading in the hope that a dry beach would eventually appear. I noted that George was helping Nazim out on the PR front. He appeared on the local television news (wearing a hard hat) and spoke glowingly about the way the extension of the Learning Centre was merely one way in which the university was forward looking and proactive. Clearly it wasn't a day on which he was up to standing without swaying too much to remain in shot, but he delivered the lines well. Perhaps, as the interview was not conducted by the building work itself but instead at his office desk, it might have been a good idea to lose the hard hat, but if I understood these things I'd have had Nazim's job.

'That's my work,' I said to Ursula, pointing at the TV.

'*Your* work,' she said. 'Let me tell you what happened at *my* work the other day.'

*　　　*　　　*

'Diarrhoea! Diarrhoea! Comes out your bum like Pedigree Chum. Diarrhoea! Diarrhoea! Comes out your bum like Pedigree Chum. Diarrhoea! Diarrhoea! Comes out your bum like Pedigree Chum. Diarrhoea! Diarrhoea! Comes out your bum like Pedigree Chum. Diarrhoea! Diarrhoea!'

Jonathan was in the back of the car, singing. We were driving to my mother's – so she could look after the children for the evening while we went to Martha and Phill's wedding – and Jonathan had been singing for about ten minutes now.

'Diarrhoea! Diarrhoea! Comes out your bum like Pedigree Chum. Diarrhoea! Diarrhoea!'

'Stop that now, Jonathan,' said Ursula, wearily.

'Diarrhoea! Diarrhoea! Comes out your bum like Pedigree Chum. Diarrhoea! Diarrhoea! Comes out you bum like Pedigree Chum. Diarrhoea! Diarrhoea!'

Young boys seem to be drawn to repetition in some weird, Hare Krishna-like fashion. Jonathan's loudly singing this, over and over and over again, was fascinating in a very special way that made me want to lose my temper explosively.

'Diarrhoea! Diarrhoea! Comes out your bum like Pedigree Chum. Diarrhoea! Diarrhoea! Comes out your bum . . .'

I really am going to lose it in a second.

'Diarrhoea! Diarrhoea! Comes out your bum like Pedigree Chum. Diarrhoea! Diarrhoea! Comes out your bum like Pedigree Chum.'

Here it comes . . .

'Diarrhoea! Diarrhoea! Comes out your bum like . . .'

I can't hold it back any longer . . .

'Pedigree Chum. Diarrhoea!'

'SHUT UP!' roared Ursula. 'Will you stop singing that, for God's sake! You're driving me mad!'

I glanced over at her reproachfully.

'Steady on, Ursula – he's only singing, after all.'

I drove the rest of the way to my mother's in triumph. Sadly, my spirits didn't soar as high as they might have done because I was under attack from an enervating cold that had begun the previous night.

'Have you got a cold?' asked my mother, the instant she opened the door.

'No.'

'Yes you have. It's because you don't wear a vest. Why don't you stay here? You can't go to this wedding with a cold, and without a vest.'

'I'm fine.'

'You'll catch a chill; you'll catch a chill, *then* you'll know about it. Why do you keep making me worry?'

'Mother, are we Jewish? You know, because I'm thinking, either no one's ever told me we're really Jewish, or there's been a huge stereotype mix-up somewhere.'

'Fine. Mock me, go ahead – that's good.'

The kids were already on the floor in front of a video and beyond the range of our voices.

'Goodbye, boys – be good . . . Goodbye . . . Jonathan . . . Peter . . . *Goodbye* . . .'

Nothing.

'You've got the number of the hotel if you need us, haven't you, Mary?' asked Ursula.

'Yes. Watch how you drive. Don't go on the motorway – there's no need for those kinds of speeds. Oh, I can feel a migraine starting.'

The wedding ceremony itself went off pretty well. I spent the whole of the night's post-wedding celebrations slumped in a chair groaning, however. My cold had worsened; it felt as though one of those companies who do cavity wall insulation had secretly used their high-pressure equipment to inject my head with snot. I discovered that gravity hurt. When it was all over, I apologised to Martha and Phill for being such a poor guest and Ursula said she hoped 'they wouldn't split up within the year, like you often see happen when couples who have been living together perfectly happily for ages suddenly decide to get married' – they said they'd try. With that we heaved ourselves into the car and began to drive back.

I put the headlights on full beam to illuminate the twisting country road.

'That was fun, wasn't it?' breathed Ursula, peeling off her shoes with her feet and fanning her glistening face with a flat hand.

'Mmm . . .'

'What?'

'Nothing.'

'No – what?'

'I don't want to talk about it.' I changed into fourth.

'Talk about what? I don't know what you mean.'

I allowed myself a single, joyless mono-laugh: 'Heh.'

'*What?*'

'I don't want to talk about it. Let's just drop it, all right?'

Two hundred yards passed.

'OK,' I said, 'I'll just say this. I'm glad the kids weren't there to see you hurling yourself at Simon like that. I'm thankful for that, at least.'

'What *are* you on about?'

'Oh, come on – you were dancing with him all evening, all that wriggling; it was like an Amsterdam floor show.'

'Simon's *gay*, for God's sake.'

'I don't want to talk about it.'

'But he's *gay*.'

'Let's just forget about the whole thing.'

'I simply do *not* believe you.'

'Fine. Let's leave it at that.'

Two hundred yards.

'I felt embarrassed for you, as much as anything,' I said.

'He's . . . gay! Gay. Are the implications of that somehow eluding you?'

'Oh, sorry, my mistake. Throwing yourself at a gay man . . .'

'We were just dancing.'

'. . . at a gay man is far less humiliating for me, and . . .'

'Ahhhh, I see.'

'And what's *that* supposed to mean?'

'This is about *you*, it's a fragile-ego thing. I see. Mid-life crisis, tiny penis – it all goes together; you're bound to be vulnerable to jealousy.'

'Bollocks. That's not the issue at all.'

'You're so sweet.'

'It's – fuck off . . . don't . . . get off me . . . It's not about my ego, that's bollocks. It's about you slobbering all over someone, all evening, in front of an audience.'

'I wasn't slobbering, I was just dancing and, for the millionth time, he's *gay*. What have you got against Simon?'

'I haven't got *anything* against Simon – he's an excellent bloke, in fact. Shall I introduce you to some other blokes I like? You might fancy offering yourself to them too?'

'Are they gay?'

'Will you stop it with the gay thing? It doesn't matter that he's gay. That's irrelevant.'

'Maybe *I* should tell the kids about the birds and the bees, do you think?'

'It doesn't matter because we're discussing *you*. Do you think Simon is attractive?'

'Well, yes. He's physically attractive, obviously.'

'And do you think he's entertaining? Charming?'

'You know he is.'

'Ah-ha!'

'What "ah-ha!"? *What?*'

'I don't think I need to say anything else, then, do I?'

'Well, that would depend on whether or not you want to be hit in the throat with a rolled-up road map of the British Isles, wouldn't it?'

'You fancy him.'

'I do not.'

'You just admitted it.'

'When? I didn't. *When?*'

'Just now. You said he was attractive and charming.'

'That doesn't mean I *fancy* him.'

'OK.'

'It doesn't.'

'OK.'

'It *doesn't*.'

'Whatever you say, I'm not arguing with you here.'

'Stop that.' Ursula aimed a finger at me. 'Stop that right now – you *know* it makes me wild when you do that.'

'What? I'm not doing anything.'

'Just because I think someone is physically attractive and has a good personality doesn't mean I *fancy* him.'

'Yeah, right. Because that's not, like, *the precise definition of what fancying someone is* or anything.'

'No, it isn't.'

'OK.'

'It *isn't*.'

'OK.'

'I've told you. If you keep doing that I won't be held responsible if I lose my temper and do something horrifying. Fancying someone isn't just thinking they're physically attractive and nice. I mean . . . OK, take Silke – she very nice and she's pretty, right? But you don't *fancy* her, do you?'

'We're not talking about me here, all right? We're . . .'

'Oh. My. God. You fancy *Silke*?'

'Look . . .'

'Who else do you fancy?'

'Can we please stick to the point? Which is . . .'

'Do you fancy the women at your work?'

'Oh, for God's sake – half of them are librarians.'

'So you don't fancy anyone?'

'No, no, hardly anyone, now can we . . .'

'*Hardly* anyone?'

'Can . . .'

'Do you fancy Pauline?'

'No – of course not.'

'Geraldine?'

'No. I . . .'

'Siobhan?'

'No.'

'Emma?'

'Look, this is stupid . . .'

'You fancy *Emma*? My God, I don't believe this.'

'What am I supposed to do? It's not my fault if they're attractive. The point is I don't throw back half a dozen bottles of Australian wine and then publicly rub myself up against them at the first opportunity. *That's* what counts, *that's* acting on it, not just idly imagining them naked or something.'

'You *imagine them naked*?'

'No. I have *never* done that. I was just illustrating a point, I don't know where that came from. And the point is . . .'

'Wooh – that's weird. We've entered "weird" now, OK?'

'The point is, you were just completely out of order tonight. That's all there is to say, and I don't want to talk about it.'

'Does you mother know you go around imagining women n . . . Hey – where are we?'

'I have *no* idea.'

The *News* didn't seem to want to let go. Almost every day there was a piece in the paper. Superficially, they were about how the work was being funded – little graphs showing the proportions of money from each source – or speculation about whether the work would be completed on time or retrospectives charting the rise of the university to its present heights. Yet there was always a vague reference to 'rumours' or 'speculation' about 'other matters'. They still called me at work. Not a researcher any more, but their reporter – Jane Ash; on a couple of occasions even the editor. I always said nothing and directed them to Nazim, who, I imagine, said nothing far more professionally.

It was the same in the Saturday version of the paper I was reading. In a national newspaper the nothingness of the piece might have stood out as odd, but in the *News* it was inconspicuous. Yet it seemed to me to be a message hidden in full view; it was the *News* speaking to me directly and it was saying, 'We're still watching you.' A lesser person might have become edgy. I became jittery.

I heard the click of Ursula's key turning the lock on the front door. She'd been out to talk to the people who were going to do some work on our guttering. Jonathan had some friends round – all of them were dashing about the house, waving guns and calling out to each other in hammy American accents – so I'd stayed with them while Ursula went out.

'Haven't you hoovered?' The disbelief fell upon her like a physical thing for some reason.

'No. Of course not. I've been looking after the kids.'

I pointed, randomly, at a child to indicate his being not on fire or anything.

'When I look after the kids I somehow manage to clean as well.'

'Well, you obviously don't look after the kids as thoroughly, then, do you?'

'Yes, I do.'

'You can't. Not if you're doing something else too. It's simple logic. I just thought that the wellbeing of these small children was the most important thing.'

'Have you been reading the paper?'

'No.'

'Peter?! Peter, has Dad been reading the paper?'

'What?'

'*Pardon.*'

'What?'

'Never mind – has Dad been reading the paper?'

'Don't know. Dad? You been reading the paper?'

'See?' I said to Ursula.

'Hoover now,' she replied.

'Oooh – do I have to? I've been looking after the kids all morning.'

'It has to be done some time this weekend. The builders are coming to do the guttering on Monday.'

'Oh, right. And if they see we haven't hoovered they'll get right back in their van – people in the guttering trade are notoriously finicky that way.'

'So, in essence, your position is that we should aim to keep the house *just* clean enough so that it doesn't physically repel visitors?'

'It's a psychological illness, you know? When you have to keep cleaning? It's a mental problem, a compulsion – I saw a programme about it.'

'Except *I'm* not hoovering. *You* are. Off you go.'

I shuffled away in the direction of the vacuum cleaner.

'No other boyfriend would do this, you know. *God*, you're lucky you've got me.'

'Hello, Mr Dalton? This is Jane Ash from the *News*.'

I sighed ostentatiously.

'I'm sorry, Ms Ash, but – *as I keep telling you* – I don't have anything to say. Nazim Iqbal has all the information for you.'

'Yes, I know, Mr Dalton, and I'm really sorry to bother you at work again, it's just that we've had a development and I thought it only fair to ask you about it first.'

'Development? I don't know about any developments. I'm sure Nazim . . .'

'Don't you? Oh, I suppose not – it's only just come into our newsroom here . . . . Apparently, workers at the city dump have discovered plastic sacks containing over seventy skeletal remains. They haven't been tested yet, but the feeling is that they could be old remains, very old indeed. How do you think sacks full of ancient body parts ended up at the city dump, Mr Dalton?'

'Um . . . Kids?'

'Is that the university's official line?'

There appeared to be a siren going off in my head which made it quite difficult to think.

'No – no, of course – I mean – you need to speak to Nazim. I don't . . .'

'I'm sure many people will speculate that the bodies can only reasonably have come from the site of your building work there.'

I swivelled in my chair and looked out of the window. Bill Acton was pointing at various areas as he discussed something with his men. He glanced over, saw me looking at him and waved.

I snarled my face at him and silently mouthed, 'You *fucker*.'

'What?' he mouthed back.

'Oh, come – that's only one of any number of possibilities, Ms Ash.'

'As you admit it's a possibility, would you be prepared to halt the building work and allow independent investigators to examine the site?'

'That's not my decision. However, the work is at a fairly advanced stage now – the foundations have been fully completed. It would be hugely costly to dig them up again.'

'So the university would not accede to that?'

'No, I don't think so. But it's not up to me. Really, call Nazim. Call Nazim, Ms Ash. Please.'

'Thank you for your time, Mr Dalton. You've been very helpful.'

'How? Oh, no – call Nazim!'

But she was hanging up even as I began to beg.

I threw down the phone and raced outside to Bill Acton, dragging him out of the conversation he was having and over to one side.

'Tell me you didn't sling the bodies from here on to the city dump.'

'Well . . . where was I supposed to put them?'

'I don't know. Isn't the standard thing to embed them in motorway flyovers or something?'

'What? Seventy of them? In one night? You haven't had much experience of the construction industry, have you, squire? Look, TSR didn't discuss the details. We weren't even sure we'd find anything. He just slipped us a few quid to get rid of them if we did.'

'A few quid?'

'Yeah, a couple of grand, that's all.'

'Two thousand pounds?'

'Hey – you try getting someone to move seventy sets of remains across town, in a few hours, in the middle of the night – middle of the night, mind, that's double time *and* unsociable-hours bonus for all these lads. You think Jenkins Brothers would have done that for under two and a half thousand?' He laughed. 'Dream on.'

'Fine, whatever, but couldn't you have dumped them somewhere where they were less likely to have people stumble over them? The river, say?'

'There's a five-hundred-pound fine for tipping in that river.'

I made a face.

'No,' he continued, 'I'm just saying, squire. If anyone had seen us we'd have been banged with a half-a-grand fine on top on everything else. Look, when we found them TSR had left and you were on holiday. I had to use my initiative.'

'You . . .'

I was interrupted by someone shouting 'Pel?' from behind me. I looked around and Wayne was leaning out of the staff entrance of the Learning Centre.

'What is it?' I called over.

'Ursula's on the phone. Have you got a minute? She's made the builders cry.'

I rubbed my hand over my head.

'Oh, Jesus, not again.'

I didn't want to duck out of work and go home – really I didn't, not with this latest hot-coffee-into-my-lap episode going on. When I spoke to them on the phone, however, the builders were distressed and skittish and refused to complete their work unless I came home and kept Ursula away from them. Not long ago we'd had to spend a day with windowless holes in the front of the house because Ursula had frightened the people who were doing the double-glazing and I didn't want a repeat to leave us without guttering. If I could keep the catastrophes down to just work *or* home, maybe I could just about stay on top of things.

It's a cultural thing, really. Ursula, being German, assumes that a builder will be someone who has studied long and hard for the official qualifications of the trade; a person who has served a tightly supervised apprenticeship while they learn the skills that need to be acquired and demonstrated under examination conditions before the Staat Etwasgesellschaft. In Britain we just fully expect a builder to be some bloke and his brother-in-law. By extension, the whole business of getting quotes is seen from a different perspective. Everyone gets three quotes for any extensive piece of work, of course. There'll be an expensive quote (you're paying for the name of the company, but quality is assured), a normal quote (standard cash-in-hand affair) and a cheapo quote (the work will be crap, but it'll be cheap too – maybe you don't mind all the fence posts being different heights if you're saving quite a bit of money). Ursula imagines, however, that all work will naturally be of a good standard and that the difference in prices is merely a reflection of the relative efficiency of the companies involved. She'll have asked the cheapo company, 'How much to build a conservatory?', not 'How much to build a rubbish conservatory?', so she believes it will be just as good as the one built by the most expensive company. Thus, Britain and Germany are set on a collision course even before a trowel has been lifted.

On this occasion, the problem was that the builders had broken some things – half a dozen slates, a few paving stones, a garden chair – which they considered acceptable losses, simply par for the course, but which Ursula thought they ought to repair or replace before she returned the keys to their van.

'I've been in the trade fifteen years, Mr Dalton, and I've never had anything like this before.'

'I'm sorry, Mr Denby, but you remember I *did* tell you about Ursula when we offered you the job?'

'She was talking about going to the trading standards office, the tax people, the VAT man – things you wouldn't believe, Mr Dalton. It's not just me I'm concerned about either. Tony and young Eddie there are signing on. You can imagine how it shakes them up when someone starts talking like that. It's just not decent.'

In the end, they agreed to make a stab at doing some repairs and take the cost of the chair off their bill, if I stayed with them and they didn't have to deal with Ursula directly again. Ursula, rather bad-temperedly as she thought I'd made unjustifiable concessions, gave me the keys and, growling under her breath, went off to do some therapeutic shopping.

They had finished by the time she returned.

'They've finished,' I said.

'*That's* finished?' Ursula replied. 'And look at the mess, they haven't even tidied up. I'll have to sweep up all this rubbish myself now. Why didn't you make them do it?'

'Dunno.' It didn't look like much of a mess to me – a few good downpours and it'd all wash away. It would have washed away in fewer than that, in fact, if we hadn't had the guttering fixed. Irony, eh? Tch.

'And they've stolen the broom!' Ursula's eyes were flashing around the yard and, indeed, just flashing in general. 'They've *stolen our broom.*'

'Why would they steal our broom?' I asked, calmingly.

'Why were they trying to fix slates on the roof using Blu-Tack? How should I know why they stole our broom? They're mad people.'

'OK, whatever. I'm going to collect the kids now. You stay here and work on your blood pressure.'

Ursula looked off into the distance, focusing on some thought that I couldn't see.

'This isn't over,' she whispered.

'Chrrrrist, my head's got a pair of rhinoceroses fucking in it.' George threw a handful of paracetamol into his mouth and quickly swilled them down with a swig of milk of magnesia. 'I could have done without *this* today, man, I can tell you.'

Last evening's the *News* was in front of him. A few sentences of the main story were written, mirror fashion, across his forehead, suggesting he'd earlier been slumped on his desk, resting his head on top of it. Nazim reached over, picked it up and looked at it – as a prop; his wandering glances made it obvious he'd read it already.

'This is all a bit unfortunate, guy. This, you see, is *exactly* the reason you should never say anything at all to these people. I'm not blaming you – you know how highly I regard you, right? – but you shouldn't have said we didn't fancy the site being dug up again.'

'But we don't. Do we?'

'Of course we don't. That's why we should never say it. You never allow them the opportunity to say, "The university refuses . . ." or "Pel denied . . ." – you're giving them a target, yeah? You say, "That's a very interesting proposal, and one that will definitely be considered while reviewing the situation – we don't want to rule anything out at this stage." But you don't even do that, of course, you just pass them over to me instead and I say it. I'm a professional.'

'Have I got pupils?' asked George. 'Tell me honestly.'

'What are we going to do now?' I asked Nazim.

'Prevaricate.'

Nazim's mobile trilled, making George wince. He read the display, laughed, clicked his teeth and looked back up.

'I'll palter, hedge and equivocate, maybe take a few people out to lunch.'

'Yes . . .' I mused. 'I suppose the important thing is to get the council on our side.'

Nazim laughed

'The council, guy? They're no problem.'

'But they were concerned about giving permission for the building in the first place. They control all the planning and so on, don't they?'

'They were only "concerned" for the look of the thing,

yeah? Unless things get *really* gruesome, the city council won't do anything against us – the university *is* the city. We're by far the biggest employer here. We're the biggest landowner. The wages of our staff and the money spent by the students we bring here are vital, you must see that? The council would never embarrass us deliberately. They want us to keep a good image as much as we do. If the students don't come . . . well, I won't say the city's dead, but it's got a sucking chest wound and is locked in a cellar flooding with sewage.'

'Yes. Yes, of course. And nice image too – cheers.'

'You got it, Pel. You don't need to have things spelled out, that's one of your strengths. I'm impressed by that. Honestly, that's always impressed me about you. Education is a business now. *That's* the dynamic. Anyone thinks it's about some holy idea of learning, some mystical, pure, academic standard . . . good luck to them. Because in five years they'll be in an underpass giving lectures on cellular meiosis for coins and their university will be a Tesco superstore. We didn't create this. Students have to pay now and they expect to get something in return for their money. Start there; it begins with the money, so that's where it ends too. This thing with the bodies is a blip, we'll wait it out. We do have time on our side – you know Andy Warhol said everyone will be famous for fifteen minutes, guy?'

'Yes.'

'Well, we're halfway there now because the public has an attention span of only fifteen minutes already. If we can drag our feet, the whole thing will be killed by apathy. The most important thing is that *you don't say another word*. OK?'

'OK.'

'Chrrrrist, my *head*,' said George.

I went back to my office, but had barely even switched on my computer ('You have 1,224 new messages') when one of the library assistants working on the counter knocked on the door to tell me that some people from the local television news had arrived and wanted to do an interview. Turning up unannounced was a clear sign that they wanted to catch me unprepared. As I hadn't been prepared, for anything, at any point at all during the previous eight or nine years, the joke was on them. I gave instructions that they were to be told I wasn't available and directed towards Nazim in Marketing. I was comfortable with this for about two or three seconds, then, noticing the windows exposing me to the outside, I became nervous again. What if they filmed me through them? You can add any sort of commentary to a shot of a person sitting at a computer – 'Pel Dalton at work yesterday. Deleting evidence? We just don't know.' I stood up and went over to draw the blinds. However, wiser now, I realised that drawn blinds just bellow concealment and intrigue, so instead I left them open and hid under the desk. I stayed there until lunch-time and, excellently, found 50p.

'What's the most important thing to remember in the Britain of today?'

'For best results, cook from frozen,' replied Roo.

'I see you made the papers,' said Tracey. 'Again.'

Roo closed his eyes and recited from memory. ' "The discovery of the bodies sent shockwaves through the city . . ." '

'Hnk.' I twirled my eyes. 'They "sent shock waves" – *there's* someone not afraid of taking an unexpected turn of phrase. I bet they can't wait for "growing concern" to lead the police to "swoop".'

Tracey leaned closer to Roo.

'I suspect he's going to base his defence on the prosecution's lack of vocabulary,' she confided.

'It's not a lack of vocabulary, it's just laziness. They . . . oh, you're mocking me, aren't you?'

'If I may continue . . .' said Roo. '"It provides more ammunition for those who believe that something wholly unacceptable is going on at the university. Despite the mounting pressure" . . .'

'Hnk.'

'. . . "Mr Pel Dalton, the Learning Centre Manager who has operational control of the project, is digging in his heels" . . .'

'Hnk.'

'"He told the *News* that he didn't believe the university would ever accept any calls for a proper investigation of the site – which lies directly outside his office."'

'Oh, Jesus – don't. These gits have been hassling me on the phone for weeks, and I've spent this morning hiding from the TV people too. That on top of having three jobs, all the staff hating me, having to apologise to Karen bleeding Rawbone, trying to keep Bernard's new career quiet, Ursula heading for a charge of builder-worrying – and never mind the Hung Society.'

'The Hung Society? You mean the *Triads*?' asked Roo, pulling back into his chair slightly.

'How come you know that? Am I the only person who didn't know that?'

'The Hung Society is a Hong Kong comic-book staple.'

'Great. That's great. What a lot of embarrassment I'd have saved myself if only I'd taken a greater interest in relationships between big-eyed pre-pubescent girls and giant robots.'

'That's more Japanese than Hong Kong, really.'

'Lord. Don't tell the press I got them mixed up, eh? I look foolish enough already.'

'If I might prioritise here . . .' Tracey cut in. 'The *Triads*?'

'Oh, never mind about them. There was just some issue with them and the Pacific Rim students a while ago. I'm trying to focus on more pressing matters – compared to the *News*, the Triads are quite endearing.'

'Mmmm . . .' Tracey looked questioningly at Roo.

'Mmmm . . .' he replied.

'What?' I asked. They both moved unnecessarily in their seats.

Tracey poked her spoon around in her coffee.

'Um . . .' she began. 'We've been meaning to tell you something. But first we didn't want to mention it, in case it went nowhere . . . and then we didn't know how to say it . . . and then it went on so long we were worried you'd think we'd deliberately excluded you . . . Only now, as you seem to have much bigger things to focus on . . . Oh – *Roo?*' She looked at him imploringly.

He busied himself rolling a cigarette. 'You're doing fine,' he said, lowering his head further.

Tracey drew a long breath.

'The thing is . . . Roo and I are an item.'

I stared at her, and then over at Roo (who was now bent down so close to the cigarette he was rolling that his nose was interfering with his view), and then back at her. No words came.

Tracey looked back apprehensively, then her shoulders dropped with a sudden sigh.

'You're picturing us having sex, aren't you?' she said.

'Yes. Yes I am.'

'Well stop it.'

'Believe me, I wish I could.'

'We've moved in together, in Roo's flat. I was there all the time anyway, so it just seemed . . . you know.'

'But . . . I . . . I mean, I'm really happy for you both. And everything. But, well – what on earth have you got in common?'

'*Hello?*'

'OK, right, the Ursula and me thing, yes. But, um, Roo's a freakish mistake of nature and you'd buy shoes instead of food – seriously, you could *both* do better.'

'Oh.'

'He's joking,' Roo said to Tracey.

'Are you?'

'Yeah, of course I am . . .'

'Of *course* he is – "freakish mistake of nature"? Tch.' He lit his cigarette with a Bette Davis flourish.

'Of course I am. It's great. It's saved Roo's eyesight for a start, right?'

'He's joking again,' said Roo.

'Yeah, *right*.' Tracey smirked. 'So you'll be throwing away all those Batgirl comics, then?'

'Batgirl?' I lifted my eyebrows. 'The comic-book Batgirl?'

'She's *brilliantly* drawn,' replied Roo, with huge gravitas.

'His palms are *shiny*.' Tracey wiggled a thumb in Roo's direction. He rolled his eyes and shook his head wearily. With a laugh, Tracey reached across, put her hand on top of his and squeezed it. Roo continued to shake his head and make 'Why me?' eyes but, searchingly, his fingers slid in between Tracey's and I saw him squeeze her hand back.

Well – Roo and Tracey; a couple. I didn't see that coming at all. (Though, interestingly, when I told Ursula, she looked heavenwards and sighed, 'Phew – *at last*.') It was good news, however, very good news. And good news was just what I needed. Maybe this was an omen that things were going to get better all round.

'Don't you go silent on me,' warned Ursula, twisting her head to a more reprimanding angle. 'That would be the worst thing you could do right now.'

I peered up at our skeletal roof. The beams were still mostly joined by a lattice of plaster-covered wood, but in places gaps allowed a view straight through to the sky on the other side. Against the darker surroundings, these holes shone with the shifting shades of the clouds that moved past behind them – like kaleidoscopes mounted high in the air; it was really quite pretty.

So anyway. It seemed Ursula had quit her job, come home, and had a row with the roofers. On the up side, she still didn't know the launch codes for America's nuclear arsenal.

'Vanessa has just been unbearable.'

'Uh-huh.' I was still staring up at the holes, transfixed.

'You don't know what it's been like. She's bad enough normally, but she just wouldn't stop and I was simply not prepared to stand for it any more. All this in the newspaper and TV about you has given her the chance to make one snide comment after another. That's what did it – all these things about you and the university. So, in a sense, this is really your fault.'

'Ahhh – *my* fault. Surprise pulls at my face.'

What with all the scaffolding and the possibility of things falling down, we'd arranged for the kids to stay with my mother for a few days. That was something. At least, quite literally, they had a roof over their heads.

'I'll admit,' nodded Ursula, spreading her arms wide to

reinforce her openness, 'That when I arrived back here I might have been a little, um, "gereizt" . . .'

'Yes, "tetchy". Yes, I have the scene in my mind now.'

'But they were both sitting on the scaffolding *reading newspapers*. Can you *believe* that?'

'Well, you certainly taught *them* a lesson, eh?'

'You have no emotions at all, do you? None at all. You can see how stressed I am, but are you being even the tiniest bit supportive?'

'I rather think the roof needs my support more.'

'There you go, *there you go*. The roof is just a "thing"; it's just a *thing*. Don't you understand?'

'Yes. It's a thing that keeps the rain out of our bedrooms.'

'And again. Is this some kind of English male thing? Do you have your entire emotional repertoire edited down to a shrug at school or something?'

'Oh, bollocks. Really – bollocks. Don't start with the "English male" crap because that's complete rubbish; if I were any more in touch with my feminine side I'd be shagging myself. I'm not interested in televised sport, I have no idea what a carburettor does, I can look the checkout girl right in the eyes while buying tampons – I'm practically a lesbian trapped in a man's body, for Christ's sake. And I think I speak for all women when I say, Sisters Like Roofs Too!'

'Right, that's it. I just can't talk to you when you're like this. I'll be in the dining room when you've calmed down.'

'Arrrrrrrggggggghhhh!'

'Arrrrrrrggggggghhhh!'

'Ooh – don't do that, Mr Dalton. You scared me,' said Bennett.

I really should have gone home – one benefit of having no roof, I suppose, is that it can't fall in on you. But it was well past seven o'clock at night and I was still at the university. In fact, I had somewhere else to go too, before

I could fall into bed and hope for dreamless oblivion. The art student women who'd moved into our old house had been living there for quite a while now. We'd agreed that they could drop their rent off to me at uni, as I was there most days and they too occasionally came in for a lecture or to attend the special 'damage limitation' careers seminars Colin Rawbone ran for the art faculty. However, the day for payment had slipped past without any of them appearing in it. I phoned and was assured that they had the money ready, they had simply been unable to deliver it owing to a series of events that, the more I listened, sounded increasingly like tales of the adventures of young gods in some colourful Asian religion. Ursula – struggling against her instincts, naturally – had decided this was 'my fault'. She'd insisted that I go round to the house and collect the rent. I'd agreed to do so. Some while later, under renewed pressure, I made a commitment to do so 'soon'. Finally, in response to a frankly wounding display of faithlessness, I promised to do so on a specific day – today.

'Don't forget you've promised to collect that rent today,' Ursula had said that morning. Ursula likes reminding me of things I've promised to do. I think that building a map of my obligations and then reciting them to me over and over again gives her a sense of structure.

'I *know*. God,' I replied. By my weariness and irritation every time I'm reminded, I seek to reassure her I haven't forgotten. I generally have, of course, but it would be a terrible unkindness to trouble her with the uncertainty that such things happen.

I fully intended to go and sort out the rent at around five-ish, when I expected to be leaving work, but it didn't happen. The day went along normally enough until the early afternoon. I spent most of it ducking a camera crew from *North-East Now!* They almost got me at one point, when they spotted me returning from lunch – but before they could get the camera running I leapt the barrier on to the central reservation on the ring road and lost them in the undergrowth. What time I had available in between hiding from the television news I spent on the phone pleading with the roofers to come back. They were still very upset. They insisted that Ursula had rained a totally unprovoked barrage of insults and accusations upon heads that had stopped for a tea break mere seconds before she arrived. Possibly owing to a natural fear of the unknown, they were especially indignant that she had, at one point, paced backwards and forwards while indulging in a furious soliloquy in German. They had no idea what she was saying, they said, but it sounded brutal, bellicose and satanic. I pointed out that pretty much everything in German sounds like that – and she might well have been musing on the sparkling moisture gently curving the petals of nearby flowers – but they remained resolute. I phoned four, increasingly desperate, times; by the end my tone was the verbal equivalent of offering to give the foreman my watch, but I couldn't manage to get anything beyond an offer to talk about it again the following week, when time had been allowed to soothe their wounds a little. However, then I got a call from a Dr Heller in the Faculty of Biological Sciences.

'Is that Pel Dalton?'

'Mmmm . . .'

'Hello? Is that Pel Dalton? The Learning Centre Manager? I'm Bob Heller, from BS.'

'Oh, right – yes, this is Pel Dalton. I don't know you, do I?'

'No, but I need to meet with you urgently.'

'Erm, OK. I suppose I can come over now.'

'No, not now. Later.'

'You said urgently.'

'Yes?'

'Well, um, isn't now better then?'

'No, I need to wait for someone to arrive.'

310

'I see. So, "important", more than "urgent".'

'Are you taking the piss?'

'No, I just . . .'

'Because I'm the Dean of Biological Sciences, Pel. You don't get to be the Dean of Biological Sciences by taking shit from anyone, you'd better remember that.'

'I wasn't . . . It's just that "urgent" means . . .'

'Who am I?'

'You're the Dean of Biological Sciences, Bob.'

'Thank you. So stop with the bleeding semantics and listen. I need to see you later. I have someone coming here and we both need to talk with you. He should have arrived by half past six, so meet me in my office at seven.'

'Seven? But . . .'

'*Who* are you talking to?'

'It's just . . .'

'*Who?*'

'Well . . . OK. I'll see you at seven.'

Using available cover (the *North-East Now!* crew may still have been around), I made my way over to the BS building at seven and tracked down Bob Heller's office. Bob opened the door himself. His was a chubby, middle-aged man of five foot one, perhaps five-two, with two furry caterpillars above his ears being all that remained of his hair. His eyes appeared set in a 'I know your sort' squint and his mouth never opened farther than the minimum necessary to let the words escape.

'You're Pel?'

'Yes.'

He didn't reply, but opened the door wider in lieu of an invitation to enter. It was a smallish office the layout of which gave the impression that almost everything in it was hidden away. There were cupboards around the wall – possibly containing books and papers, possibly human heads; they were all shut and it was impossible to tell. A couple of closed filing cabinets. A desk bare apart from a phone. By the desk stood a man smiling shyly from inside a crumpled suit. His hands were together in front of his chest and he was picking at one thumbnail with the index finger of his other hand; making unevenly spaced clicks, like a slightly embarrassed cricket. How old he was I wouldn't have liked to say, but I'd reckon he'd spent at least the last forty years hunched diffidently.

Bob Heller closed the door behind me.

'What a mess. What the hell do you think you're doing?'

'What mess?' I replied.

'Don't you try and tell me there's not a mess, Pel; I won't put up with any bullshitting.'

'I didn't say that. I just asked which mess you were referring to.'

'How many are there?'

'Pfft.'

'I'm talking about digging up the foundations of the building again. Why did you start them off on that?'

'I didn't. I said we didn't want to.'

'There you go. Perhaps you'd like to tell the press you're not gay too? Deny any financial wrongdoings? Say you have no plans to resign? Are you bastard *mad*? We cannot have those foundations dug up.'

'I think it's unlikely they will be.'

'Unlikely? No, no, no. Never mind "unlikely". They must never be touched.'

'Mmmm . . . There's something you're not telling me, isn't there? What did Acton do? Leave half the bodies under there?'

'Bodies? I don't give a fuck about the bodies.' Heller indicated the man in the weary suit. 'This is Dr Bennett . . .' Bennett smiled at me uncomfortably. 'Dr Bennett works for the Chemical Defence Experimental Establishment at Porton Down in Wiltshire. How much neurotoxin do you think is under the Learning Centre extension, Dr Bennett?'

'Ooh, it's hard to say . . .' He shrugged, as though he knew the answer but didn't want to appear to be showing off. 'Certainly enough to kill everyone in north-western Europe.'

'Arrrrrrrggggggghhhh!'

'Ooh – don't do that, Mr Dalton. You scared me,' said Bennett.

The panic that had been at knee level was now lapping just under my chin. Speaking with extraordinary care, I asked, 'Why do we have nerve gas buried under our extension?'

'Dear me – it was far too dangerous to move it.'

I looked over at Heller. I was unable to say anything, so instead I struck a pleading pose of quite heartbreaking desperation.

Heller sighed impatiently. He clearly felt I had the basic facts now and wanted to move on. 'What does that matter? Can we please try to focus?'

'I need to know how enough poison to stage a biblical holocaust ended up outside my office. What can I say? I'm anal.'

'Oh, for Christ's sake. It really doesn't matter. We have to concentrate on our plans for the future.'

'I have a real suspicion that your plans for the future are going to involve a special lottery and a spaceship to take the lucky winners to another world beyond the stars – so I'd like to deal with one thing at a time, OK? How did it get there, you twat?'

'Watch your step. I *am* the Dean of Biological Sciences and I can have *your* arse kicked out of this university so quick . . .'

'Arrrrrrrggggggghhhh!'

'OK, OK . . . It's not a very interesting story. Really. You've built it up now, and when I tell you . . . OK, *OK*. Jesus. All that happened is that one of our students here decided to do his final-year dissertation on the chemical disruption of neurotransmitters – sounds harmless enough, right?'

'Gnk.'

'He put in a very vague proposal and was assigned a project supervisor, Dr Knowles. Unfortunately, a few weeks into the work Dr Knowles died in a bar fight . . .'

'About what?'

'Christ – do you want *the history of the world*? It doesn't matter to the story, all right? Right. So, anyway, he wasn't assigned a new leader.'

'Why?'

'We forgot, OK? You never forget things? And, I swear to God, if you interrupt one more time, I'm not telling this story.'

I held a hand across my mouth.

'*Thank* you. Because he didn't get a project leader, the first we really knew about it was when he'd finished, had eighty gallons of a powerful new nerve gas, and wanted to know who to hand it in to for marking.' Heller glanced over at Bennett. 'Annoyingly, he'd chosen to do it as a double-semester project, or I reckon he wouldn't have been able to produce a quarter of that amount. Still – that's the way it goes.' He turned back to face me. 'His personal tutor was frightened of how I'd react to the news and tried to hide the stuff in his room. However, some of it injured a cleaner . . .' Heller saw my eyes widen. 'No, no – the container fell on her foot . . . Broke two toes, mind. This got reported to me and it all came out. As usual, I called Dr Bennett here. He had a look . . .'

'*Hugely* impressive,' interjected Bennett.

'. . . and we decided we needed to get the stuff somewhere safe. Knowing the extension was going to be built, I got in touch with TSR, with whom I'd dealt before. We provided the money to oil the wheels and TSR saw to it that the builders were clued up about burying the stuff when they laid the foundations. When TSR disappeared, I was a bit worried. But he'd obviously arranged everything with Bill Acton and it all went off perfectly. Until *you* started a media campaign to get them to reverse the work so they could look for the bodies of dead nutters. Happy now?'

'Erm . . . I have got *just a few* questions.'

'Oh, for God's sake.'

'First, what happened to the student who did this? How do you know he doesn't have another eighty gallons back in his digs that he's too embarrassed to mention?'

'Oh, it's all sorted,' replied Heller. 'He's working with Bennett now.'

'He's very gifted,' said Bennett.

'Unbelievable,' I sighed.

'What?' laughed Heller, 'One of our students getting a job?' He shrugged. 'It happens.'

'The next thing I'd like to know about is the money. What did you pay? To whom? And where on earth did you get it from?'

'Oh, TSR came up with a price – fifty grand – and we paid that. We gave him all the cash and he sorted everything out. Steep, admittedly, but it was an important job.'

'Where did you get *fifty thousand pounds*?'

Heller waved a hand dismissively.

'That wasn't a problem. We'd been given a couple of research grants, so we had that money, for a start.'

'But what will happen when you don't deliver the research?'

'We *will* deliver it.' For the first time Heller looked genuinely hurt by my words. 'It'll say "Results were inconclusive" or something, but we *will* deliver it. The Biological Sciences faculty here has an international reputation, Pel. We're perfectly capable of faking research, thanks very much. Anyway, as usual, the bulk of the money was donated by Porton Down.'

That was the second time Heller had used the words 'as usual' and, again, I decided it'd be better for my nerves if I didn't ask.

'We were glad to help,' said Bennett. 'The rights to this

invention in exchange for helping with its disposal was an excellent deal. We could have spent many times that on research and never discovered it. This way we'll own the patent and . . .'

'You're going to patent a nerve gas?'

'Erm, yes, of course. We applied for patents for VX – which was the most deadly toxin known to man until your student came along – in 1962, though they weren't officially published until February of 1974. You see, um . . . Pel, is it?'

'Yes.'

'An unusual name.'

'You think so? No one's remarked upon it before.'

'Oh, perhaps it's me, then. You see, Pel, it's important to register the discovery. First of all, there's the professional pride, of course. But, just as important, many countries refuse to sign, don't ratify or renege on the various international treaties regarding chemical weapons. If some pariah state produces our gas we might not be able to charge them with breaking a treaty, but we can damn well get them for breach of copyright.'

'Yes . . . I think I'll be going now.'

Heller stepped in front of me.

'So you see why there must *never* be any investigation of the building work?'

'Yeah . . . But, frankly, if I can't stop it, this really is your fault.'

'And yours.'

'What are you on about? I didn't even know about it until just now.'

'It'd be hard for you to prove that, especially when I'll be saying you virtually forced us into the whole thing. I trust knowing this will give an extra boost to your efforts to avoid any investigation?'

I looked, stunned, at Bennett.

'Erm, yes . . .' He coughed and gazed down at his shuffling

feet. 'This is all rather awkward, but we would have to make sure you took the bulk of the blame and went to prison for an awfully long time. National security reasons – I'm sure you understand. I'm really sorry about that.'

I turned back to Heller.

'You *bastards*.'

'Hey, like I said – you don't get to be the Dean of Biological Sciences without being able to play rough.'

Ursula was really quite angry.

'You couldn't ring?'

'I tried. The phone was engaged.' Not true, of course, but a safe bet, statistically.

'What time did you try to ring?'

Pffft – nice try; do I look as if I was born yesterday?

'I didn't notice the time.'

'Roughly.'

'I have no idea.'

'Uh-huh.'

'Are you saying the phone wasn't engaged?'

'Well . . . Alison did ring.'

Yep; playing the odds has never failed me yet.

'How long did you talk to Alison for?'

'I don't know.'

'Roughly'

'I have no idea.'

'Uh-huh.'

The phone rang. Ursula and I looked at each other for a couple of rings, but she was always going to break first and it was only halfway through its third ring when she snatched up the receiver.

'Hello? . . . No, he's not here.' She put the phone down again and turned to me with a smug little smile. 'It was for you. *See?*'

'And I'm not here. Apparently.'

'Oh, it was just someone from *North-East Now!* They've called several times today wanting to speak to you. I think you're in enough trouble without worsening it by speaking. Anyway, you need to collect that rent.'

'What? *Now?*' I thought about telling her a few of the other matters that were competing for my attention at that moment. It wasn't the right time, however. For one thing, I couldn't trust myself to explain everything calmly – more likely my self-control would rapidly unravel to the point where I'd be trying to get the basic facts across while shouting, sobbing and clawing at my clothes. For another, the setting was completely wrong. If I waited a few days – until after the roof was fixed, maybe – I could suggest the kids had some friends round. While they all played I could quietly tell Ursula everything that I'd been up to. Yes, a kids' party – Ursula wouldn't *dare* try anything there.

'It's your own fault it's so late, I can't help that. I'll drive you over there, if you want,' said Ursula.

'I can drive myself, there's no need for you to bother.'

'It's no bother.'

'No, it's OK. I'll drive.'

'It's my car.'

'Oh, for God's sake – you don't trust me with those students, do you? You don't trust me to go round to see them during the evening.'

'No, in fact I've ordered a Chinese and I need to pick it up in five minutes anyway. That was the reason. *Now*, of course, I don't trust you either.'

We swung briefly by the takeaway to collect Ursula's food. There was enough for two as she'd ordered double portions of everything she liked.

'See? Despite sitting there, without having heard from you, I made sure I got enough for both of us.'

'Cheers. Though you could have ordered stuff *I* like instead of just getting everything *you* like twice.'

'I hadn't heard from you, remember? Suppose you'd been run over or something, I'd have been stuck with loads of stuff I'd never eat.'

'Just out of interest, suppose it was a choice between my being dead *or* having to waste food?'

'Oh, grow up. I'm not saying I *wanted* you to have been run over. I'm just saying that if you *had* been run over all the special fried rice in the world wasn't going to bring you back.'

It didn't take long to get to our former home. From the outside, the only difference now we were no longer there was that it was vibrating. Or rather, that it was vibrating owing to frantic, punchy drum 'n' bass music rather than a frantic, punchy argument about who'd had the TV remote last. As a muffled crackling under the music I could hear the wash of multiple, indistinct voices shouting and laughing. They were having a party. That wasn't good news; after every student party I'd ever had we'd had to move to new accommodation, shedding the old one like a scarred, peeling, vomit-splattered husk.

Ursula took the Chinese off my lap and began digging around in the bag, opening things and tasting the contents.

'Mmm – lovely. Go in there and get the rent. Hurry up, I want to get back home before all this goes cold.'

Repeated banging on the front door summoned a thing with a can of Tennents Extra.

I roared, 'Is Anna in?'

He roared back, 'What?'

We did this for a while.

Eventually we connected, and he leaned back into the room and roared, 'Where's Anna?'

'Upstairs. Who is it?'

'Some bloke.'

Another student appeared at the door.

'Who are you?' she roared.

'I'm the landlord. Can I see Anna?' I moved my head around, subconsciously trying to place it at a point where I guessed her eyes might be focused.

'Yeah . . . sure.' She beamed, the change in the position of her lips unbalancing her slightly so she danced sideways out of view. She fell back into the doorway, where I could see her again. 'She's up in the front bedroom. You can go up. It's . . .'

'I know where it is, thanks.'

She did a flailing pirouette out from in front of me and I entered the house. I walked through a depressing Hades of fun. Dancing, shouting, giggling, staggering, whooping; it was all deeply sad. *We* did the whole youthful excess thing when we were young, that was *our* thing. These students just going over the same ground now? Well . . . couldn't they see what a pathetic cliché they were? My generation had done 'partying', ages ago – *move on*, kids. I did glimpse a tiny group in the kitchen standing without smiles, flicking non-existent ash from their cigarettes. But they were attempting 'world weary' and 'seen things you people wouldn't believe'. You can't pull off 'world weary' at nineteen, for God's sake; you don't have the skin. Why couldn't these people just apply themselves to their studies, look after the carpet and pay their rent on time? That I could respect.

I hopscotched my way around bodies and ashtrays and cans until I reached the stairs. Remarkably, there was only one couple (whispering boy, wet-eyed, sniffing girl) having a Serious Talk on them, and I was soon up to the door of the front bedroom.

'Anna?' I said, as I opened it.

I twisted the handle on the 'A' and pushed the door open before me on the 'n', which meant I still had a full 'na?' left to say directly into a pair of buttocks. In the light from the landing, the buttocks glowed a sunless white between the tops of hastily pulled-down trousers and the bottom of an impatiently pulled-up shirt. Pointing outwards either side of the buttocks – like the 'Here I am – thank you, ladies and gentlemen' arms of a cabaret singer receiving applause – were the bare legs of a young woman. At the sound of my voice, the buttocks became immobile and their owner's head slumped on to the bed with exasperation.

'Je*sus*,' he said, his voice muffled by being shouted into the mattress, but still clearly, and understandably, full of irritation.

Anna's head popped out from behind his shoulder.

'Oh – hi!' she chirped.

'Sorry,' I replied, backing out. 'I didn't ... I'm terribly sorry.'

'I suppose you want the money?' she continued, ignoring me and apparently utterly unfazed.

'I . . .' I began. I did want the money, of course, but asking someone to break off, mid-shag, to give you the rent seemed, well, a bit mercenary.

'What bloody money?' her partner asked, pushing himself up on his arms to peer at her. 'What bloody money?' he asked again, twisting around to face me.

'Arrrrrrrggggggghhhh!' I said.

'Arrrrrrrggggggghhhh!' said Colin Rawbone, simultaneously.

Anna – her thin cotton dress bunched up into a band around her ribcage – wriggled out from under him.

'Hey, thanks, guys. It's good for a girl's ego but, really, only the one I'm having sex with needs to scream.'

She leaned over the side of the bed and pulled a poorly woven shoulder bag from under it. After poking around for a second, her hand came out full of notes.

'What's the money for?' asked Colin, his voice creaking as if his larynx was made of old, dry wood. I suspected he might be going to cry. 'D-d-did she pay you to be a witness?'

'What?'

'Because I'll double whatever you're getting, Pel. I can have it by Monday, I swear to God.'

'Erm, I'm just here to collect the rent, Colin.'

'Chill, Col – he's our landlord,' tutted Anna.

He rolled over on to his back, tugging up his trousers. I tried not to glance down (I didn't want to send out the wrong signals – the day had been complicated enough already), but I couldn't help myself.

Ha! *That* made me feel a little better, at least.

Colin continued to flap.

'Please ... Er ... This is ... Oh, God – you won't tell Karen, will you? Promise me, Pel, promise me you won't tell Karen. She wouldn't understand.'

I imagined even Karen would, in fact, be able to grasp the situation.

'It's none of my business, Colin.' I turned my head to the side and put up my hands, pushing them forward to show I wasn't going to let the scene in front of me get any closer. 'I'm just the landlord. I've got my rent. I'm off now.'

'So you won't tell Karen? You promise? Say you promise.'

'No, I'm not going to tell her.'

'Say you promise.'

'Do I have to spit too?'

'Just say it. I know, I know – but I need to hear you say it or I just ... I won't ...'

'OK, OK, I promise.'

'You promise *what*?'

'I promise I won't tell Karen.'

'You're a hero, Pel. Really. I'll never forget this.'

'Whatever.'

'I love male bonding,' said Anna. 'It's *so* sweet.' She was lying on her back on the bed, her dress still up. The fingernail of her ring finger was between her teeth and she was twisting it backwards and forwards determinedly.

'Seriously, Pel ... Cheers,' said Colin gratefully.

'Anytime. Anyway, I'd better be off now. Um – thanks for everything.'

'Yes, cheers, Pel.'

''Bye,' sang Anna.

I slowly backed out of the room. As I was closing the door, Colin turned back to face Anna and his hand reached down to begin undoing his trousers again.

'You took your time,' said Ursula. 'What were you up to?'

'I got chatting to Colin Rawbone.'

'Really? Was Karen there too?'

She dumped the semi-ravaged bag and Chinese food back on my lap and started the engine.

'I don't think there was room for her. Colin was having a one-to-one session with an art student – giving her the benefit of his input.'

'Eh? What do you mean?'

'Never mind.'

'Don't do that. You know I *hate* it when you make some stupid comment then, when I ask you to explain, you say "Never mind" or "It doesn't matter" – just *tell* me.'

'It's not important.'

'Are you *trying* to make me angry? It's important now, just because you didn't say it. Tell me.'

I sighed.

'It's nothing . . . Colin was with a girl. A student.'

'*With?*'

'Yes, "with".'

'*With?* What's "with". What does that *mean?*'

'Oh, for God's sake – they were *shagging*. OK?'

'No! How do you know?'

'Duh . . . Because his head was bobbing while he was talking to me. How the hell do you think I know?'

'You *caught* them shagging?'

'Yeah.'

'So the girl was naked, then? You've been in there, slack-jawed, leching over some naked, shagging, idiotic student?'

'Where'd "idiotic" come from?'

'*Wrong* fucking answer.'

'Calm down. *I* wasn't shagging her. I just went in to get the rent – and *you* insisted I did that today, remember?'

'Was she naked?'

'No,' I stated with great insistence, huge astonishment at this continued line of questioning, and absolute, literal, factual accuracy. 'And anyway, she was under him.'

'So you didn't see anything?'

I threw my head back and brrrrr-ed my lips in exasperation.

'Yes – she had her dress up to her armpits and was just, you know, *lying there* for me to see. It's a image burned for ever into my mind.' I was extraordinarily careful to say this in a mocking, singsong voice. '*God,*' I added, rolling my eyes. This wasn't the time for half-measures.

'What do you think will happen when Karen finds out?'

'I don't know. How would she find out anyway?'

'*You're not going to tell her?*'

'*Tell* her? Why on earth would I tell her?'

'He's her *husband.*'

'So? It's none of my business.'

'Right. Right – you'll keep it quiet because he's a man is what you mean.'

I was drawn back into my seat slightly by the car accelerating. I whipped my eyes across and noticed we'd hit fifty. If Ursula is driving, the speedometer is generally a rather good indication of her emotional state.

'What? No. Bollocks.'

'So you wouldn't tell him if you'd seen her shagging a male student either?'

'If I had seen Karen shagging a male student I'd need thirty years of therapy before I could speak at all. No, it's nothing to do with Colin being a man.'

'So, if someone caught you shagging a woman at a party, you wouldn't want them to tell me.'

'I wouldn't be shagging another woman in the first place.'

'But if you were.'

'But I wouldn't be.'

'But if you *were*. Just imagine the situation, for the sake of argument. Imagine you were shagging someone . . . Silke, say – as we know you've got the hots for her . . .'

'Oh, Jesus. Give me a break.'

'If you were caught shagging her, you wouldn't want the person who caught you to tell me?'

'Well, if – *if* – that happened, then no. I wouldn't.'

'Why not?'

'Because . . . it might be a stupid one-off – I was hypnotised, senseless from crack and an accomplice was holding the children hostage until I slept with her, say – in which case it should be left secret and that would be that; your knowing about it would be far more damaging to our relationship than this single slip on my part. Or, if I were sleeping with other women every night, then there'd be fundamental problems that it certainly shouldn't require a third party to jump in and point out. Either way, there'd be absolutely nothing to be gained by someone telling you.'

'So if someone caught me shagging a bloke you wouldn't want to know either?'

'That's different.'

'Ha!'

'Bollocks, "Ha!". Don't you go "Ha!"-ing, because that's just bollocks. It's a completely different thing.'

'Because I'm a woman.'

'No.'

'Yes. Somehow you think your shagging Silke is *completely different* to my shagging Brad Pitt because I'm a woman.'

'No, that's not— Hey! How come you're shagging *Brad Pitt* all of a sudden?'

'What does it matter who I'm shagging?'

'You got to choose, that's what matters. You set me up with Silke, but *you* get to choose, and you choose Brad bleeding Pitt.'

'It doesn't matter. It's just the principle.'

'If it's just the principle you can be shagging Lon Chaney Junior, then – OK?'

'Lon Chaney Junior's dead.'

'What the hell does that matter? It's the *principle*. Are you saying you have a realistic shot at Brad Pitt?'

'What does that mean? I'm ugly? Is that what you're saying?'

'I didn't say that.'

'Oh, no, I'm not *hugely* ugly. I might be able to pull Lon Chaney Junior, but *Brad Pitt*? Pfft – no chance. Thanks very much. Shall I live in the attic from now on, eh? I'll live in the attic and you can feed me through a grille.'

'You're hardly going to be hidden away in the attic, are you? We've got *no fucking roof*. And anyway . . .'

'Look!'

'What?'

'There. That van – there.'

I looked where she was pointing and there, turning off the road we were on, was the van belonging to the people who'd done our guttering. Ursula glared at it with an unholy intensity.

'I bet our broom is in that van,' she hissed.

She heaved the steering wheel around and the car swung into the road after the van.

'What are you doing?' I asked, trying to protect the bag of Chinese food from the G-force of the turn.

'I'm going to get our broom.' She was winding down the window as we sped closer to the gutterers. 'Are we supposed to let them steal stuff and just get away with it?' She stabbed at the horn and leaned her head outside. 'Give us back our broom!'

'Please. Please – I'll buy you a new broom.'

'I don't want a new broom. I want them to give us back the broom they *stole*.' She shot off the horn again. 'Give us back our brooooom!'

'Oh, Jesus.' I opened the top of the bag and let my head flop forward into it so I couldn't see. I could hear Ursula talking to herself next to me, firing herself up with thoughts on the subject of brooms and theft. Soon I felt the car come to a halt and I lifted my head out of the bag. We'd pulled up at some traffic lights, pulled up right behind the van. Ursula was unbuckling her seat belt and opening her door, banging her horn at the same time. I saw a face appear in the window at the back of the van. It had a vague 'Wonder what that is?' expression which jumped straight to one reading 'Oh, dear Christ!' when it saw Ursula. The head pulled back rapidly, out of sight; presumably to talk to the driver, because a second later the van's wheels squealed and it flung itself across the traffic lights, which were still on red. Ursula already had one foot out of the car. She froze in surprise for the briefest moment before bellowing after the van, 'Come back with our broom, you bastards!' and ducking back inside. She snatched the car into gear.

'Let's take a second to think about this . . .' I said, just before my head was flung backwards on to the headrest as she stamped on the accelerator.

As we flew across the junction, I registered a car coming in the other direction, straight towards the side of us. I saw the driver pull it into a violent swerve and heard the Doppler effect of his receding horn. Ursula didn't seem to notice – she was utterly focused on the van that was racing down the road ahead, desperately trying to lose us.

'*OK Jung's – laßt mal sehen wie gerne ihr diesen Besen*

wirklich wollt,' said Ursula with the kind of smile you'd expect to see on someone strolling into a government building with explosives strapped to their body. The pitch of the engine soared up like the rev of a buzz-saw and we began eating the gap between us and the van.

'Right,' I said, extending a finger and firming up the expression on my face. 'I'm serious now ... I *am* ... Stop ... Just stop the car right now ... Stop ... I'm not going to tell you again ... OK ... OK, I'll give you money. You can buy that carpet, we'll get it tomorrow. Whatever you want. Just – Arrrrrrrgggggghhhh!' Ursula mounted the pavement. The van had turned away to the left and Ursula, seeing that she could cut the corner off the turn by doing so, had swung after it by heading up across the pavement and the small stretch of grass that lay in between. The grass was formed into a gentle mound so it acted like a ramp as we drove over it – the car left the ground and leapt through the air. It wasn't a long jump and lasted only one, perhaps two, seconds at the most. To me, however, it was performed in the slowest of slow motions. It spanned countless miles and took hours to complete. Long hours during which nothing but the word 'Shiiiiiiit!' was in my mind. We hit the road again with a jolt and a 'Nggh!' and Ursula had a momentary fight with the wheel to reassert control. The van hurled itself off into a side road on the right, but Ursula was immediately after it. It was a track more than a road, really. Nothing but two bald tyre lines in the dirt with a hairy stripe of grass in the middle. Bushes rattled against the side of the car.

'Come on now – the food's getting cold.'

'So we'll microwave it.'

'It's in aluminium containers. You know you can't microwave aluminium.'

'Then we'll tip it out into dishes. It's not a problem.'

'That's more washing up. What's the point of buying take-away food then making washing up for yourself?'

'God – *I'll* do the washing up, OK? Stop whingeing.'

'It just that I don't want to die.'

'Tch. Who's dying?'

We slipped into a nauseating spin. The track had ended and we were on some kind of playing field. The council had clearly found itself with an area of land on it hands that it couldn't develop – maybe it was above disused mine workings or on the site of an old rat poison factory or something. So it had stuck up a couple of goalposts and designated it a public sports field; despite the fact that the pitch sloped noticeably in one direction, was like the surface of the moon and was also, probably permanently, waterlogged. The gutterers' van had come to the end of the track and turned left across this field. Ursula had tried to follow them, but turned too sharply and just sent us spinning across the pitch, spraying mud everywhere and tearing trails with our wheels like the scars of giant, pirouetting ice skates.

'It's OK, it's OK, I've got it now . . .' she called, fighting the car out of its acrobatics.

'I feel ill,' I whispered.

'I've got it now – we're not spinning.'

'I meant just generally.'

The van was making better headway than we were, but it too was having difficulty. Its rear swept from side to side on the slippery earth, causing the driver to make weaving direction changes to maintain control. He was clearly making for an exit, an opening in the tall bushes that rimmed the playing fields, but his van was achieving the kind of heavy, bumbling, panicky progress you experience when trying to flee monsters in a dream. Fortunately for them, we appeared to be spending an awful lot of time travelling sideways. Ursula punched the horn again.

'Flash your lights too,' I said. 'There's always the possibility they haven't noticed us.'

Two clumps of brown paper came away in my hands. My

sweating palms along with the cartilage-popping grip of my terrified fingers had dug holes in the Chinese takeaway bag. I grabbed it afresh; it was my only friend now.

The pitch looked like a First World War battlefield. Anyone hoping for a game of football on it was going to be at a huge disadvantage compared to those turning up for a spot of competitive root-vegetable growing. The confirmation of this came when, as they made their final lunge for the gap in the perimeter, the rear of the gutterers' van slipped out to the side and caught one of the goalposts. The post it hit snapped at ground level and fell, dead, to the ground, dragging its side of the crossbar down with it. The impact, however, stopped the van's back from skidding, it straightened up and shot out of the exit into the unseen road beyond.

Ursula made a noise like a lion that's seen its prey suddenly disappear from a playing field in a van. She swung the steering wheel around and dropped into a lower gear, speeding up our pursuit but yanking us off course. Worried that she'd lose track of them, she was obviously taking a more direct route to the edge of the field, but this skewed her off target for the gap.

'You're going to miss the exit,' I said.

'I'm going to make a new exit,' she replied, much as I suspected she was going to, but, well, it's surprising how long you keep clinging to hope.

I braced myself for the impact but, in fact, we punched through the hedge with hardly a sense of hitting anything at all. I think the way it didn't impair our momentum surprised Ursula too. Certainly, I can see no other reason for her smashing through it and, without making any attempt to change course, carrying on across the road, through the hedge on the opposite side, and into the ornamental rose arch in the garden beyond. The arch was uprooted and fell across the bonnet, half covering the windscreen. It swung around for a time, like a movie hero trying to cling to the car of the fleeing villain, as Ursula pulled around and curved back towards the road, cutting through a second garden in the process. Finally, though, it was too much for the plucky piece of garden decoration and the sharp turn to align ourselves with the direction of the road sent it sliding off on to the tarmac. Ursula glanced up at it rolling and twisting to a halt in the rear-view mirror.

'We ought to get one of those,' she said. 'They're a nice feature.'

Her mood didn't brighten for long, however, because the van was nowhere in sight. Worse, we quickly came to a cross-roads. They could have gone in any one of three directions and there was no clue as to which it might be. Ursula pulled up and peered, infuriated, down each high-hedged road. Nothing.

'*Scheißdreck!*' she hissed, banging the steering wheel with the heel of her palm.

'Still – it's been a ride out, eh?' I said.

She grumpily knocked the car into gear and began moving forward again.

'This is just a joke to you, isn't it?' she said.

'In fact, no. Looked like it was going to be a bit of a laugh, obviously, but then slipped imperceptibly into a seemingly ceaseless and harrowing dance with death during which I was only able to keep my sanity by focusing on the struggle to avoid soiling myself.'

'I'm going to have to go back tomorrow to explain and pay for that rose arch too,' she grumbled.

'I'll pay for it if you let me watch you explain.'

Our discussion continued to bob along nicely as she drove back home. Personally, I was delighted that we'd miraculously avoided destroying the car and killing us both. That's possibly the difference between us; I thought it was a good result, Ursula seemed to feel it lacked closure. Whatever the reason, she worked impressively hard during the drive back to stoke up her temper to the point where it was doing fifty-five miles an hour in a built-up area.

'So you're saying you should have the final say on my career, then, basically?' she said, gripping the steering wheel as if it were a throat.

'I didn't say anything of the sort. I simply said that you might have mentioned to me that you were going to quit your job before you did it.'

'I told you loads of times.'

'No, you said you *wanted* to quit your job. That's not the same as being poised to quit it *actually*. Everybody in the world wants to quit their job, but hardly anyone does it.'

'Well, pardon me for being deeply unhappy at work and having intolerable colleagues.'

'I'm just worried that we can't survive on my wage alone.'

'So I should have stayed whatever because of the money? Maybe you'd like me to put a card up in telephone boxes? Charge by the hour for dribbling businessmen to ride me like a pony?'

'See? *That's* what I mean. How the hell does what I say bear any relation to what you say back?'

'It's exactly the same thing.'

'*Exactly* the same, is it? So it's an irregular verb? "*He* has no money", "*She* has no money", "*I* want to let dribbling businessmen ride you like a pony"?' I pointed just ahead. 'This is our turn.'

'I *know* this is our turn. It's the same principle. The money is important, not my feelings. You just cannot see things on any sort of emotional level.'

'Your emotions never *are* level.'

We were looking each other right in the face now.

'And there you go again with a stupid, glib answer.'

My staring directly into her face was probably not such an important thing, but her staring right into mine arguably was, as she was driving; swinging round the corner into our street, at perilous speed, from memory.

'It's not stupid, it's— Arrrrrrrgggggghhhh!'

I won't reveal where it was, but there was a point in this sentence when I cast my eyes towards the road ahead and noticed a man and a woman standing in it. The man had a shoulder-held camera and both of them were squinting up at our bedroom window, as though trying to see signs of life. A second later they were looking directly at our car racing towards them and the lives that were flashing before their eyes were their own.

'Jesus!' shouted Ursula. She threw her whole body into yanking the wheel to the right. We skimmed past the couple, hit the kerb with an axle-shattering jolt, ploughed up our driveway and crunched into the front of our house – the impact lessened slightly by the decelerating effect of the scaffolding, which reduced our speed before collapsing on to the car, tubular steel pipes falling and bouncing around with a noise like the ringing of church bells on the day of the Rapture. My seat belt stopped me dead in a winding hug, but the bag of Chinese food shot from my hands and exploded inside the car. The contents plashed against the windscreen and the bits that didn't stick rebounded all over me. Noodles, pork ribs, Gung Poo prawns and several tasty sauces swarmed at my upper body.

I wiped a prawn from my eye and shouted across at Ursula, 'Are you OK?'

'Yes.' She squinted at me as though she were trying to refocus her vision. 'That wasn't my fault, right?'

'I didn't say a word.'

'Before you do. They were standing in the middle of the road, it wasn't my fault.'

I hurriedly pulled my seat belt off and half stepped, half fell, out of the car. The couple were running towards me. The woman, I saw now, was holding a microphone.

'Mr Dalton? Are you well enough to talk?' she shouted.

The cameraman, looking only through his lens, positioned himself in front of me as I steadied myself by the car wreck.

Then, presumably seeing for the first time the strings of slimy noodle and clumps of meat dripping from my head, he let his camera drop down to his waist, his eyes rolled up into his head and he fainted backwards into a forsythia bush. Ursula scrambled across and clambered out of my side of the car, behind me. She looked as if she was *just brimming* with things she wanted to say to the reporters, but the cameraman had disappeared from view completely, buried somewhere inside the bush, and the woman, after a second of wobbling indecision, had reached in after him.

'Derek! Derek! Get up!'

She was leaning over, delving into the bush right up to her waist, frantically trying to pull her unconscious companion out. Her grip on him obviously slipped because she suddenly shot back upright, having sacrificed her perfectly done hair in the process and re-emerging from the forsythia as the Bride of Frankenstein.

'You . . .' Ursula began to say to the woman, but I grabbed her arm and tugged her towards our front door. 'Oi!' she protested, I think because I was getting sauce on her sleeve as much as anything. Sweeping aside her 'That'll stain!' protestations, however, I managed to drag her into the house after me, slamming the door shut on the approaching woman.

'What the hell?' grimaced Ursula. 'What are they doing outside our house?'

'I don't know,' I replied. 'Maybe I've won an award.' I glanced at my watch. The national TV news would have just ended, which meant it would now be the local North-East report. Dripping Chinese food like Swamp Thing, I started for the living room, but the phone rang just as I passed it. Instinctively, I picked it up; it was obviously going to be *North-East Now!* calling again – the woman was probably outside on her mobile.

'Piss off!' I shouted into the mouthpiece.

'This is your mom,' replied Roo. 'Piss off yourself.'

'Roo?'

'Yes. Where have you been? I've been ringing for ages – I thought I'd *never* get to be told to piss off.'

'Sorry, I thought it was going to be someone else.'

'It's too late to apologise now. The damage is done . . . Listen, Pel, I sort of need a favour.'

'Things are a bit lively right now, Roo . . .'

'Tracey's thrown me out of the flat.'

'What? It's your flat.'

'I mentioned that. It just inflamed the situation. It's a bit of a long story and, quite frankly, I don't understand it myself. The bottom line is we were having a conversation about that girl who comes into the shop. Not even a conversation, really. Tracey was just casually asking a few questions, I was just shrugging back my replies – I was trying to concentrate on the TV, you know, not taking much notice. Next thing I know it seems I'm a terrible human being and she's hurling my clothes out of the window. What's all that about? Anyway, my money's on PMS, and I reckon she'll be OK again in a few days . . . but I need a place to stay until then.'

'It really is quite a bad time, Roo.'

'I wouldn't ask you if I wasn't pretty desperate. I mean, obviously, right?'

I sighed defeat.

'OK. OK, you can stay here. But can you give it a few hours before you come round?'

'No problem – I'm in the pub.'

'Right, come round later, then. Ring the doorbell three times, then wait a second, then give two long rings and a short one.'

'Ooooooo . . . K.'

'There are reasons.'

'No doubt. Thanks, Pel.'

'Yeah. Whatever.'

I hurried on to the television. Nazim's face glowed into being on the screen. He looked concerned, yet in control.

'. . . have to say about it?' the voice of the woman now outside our house was saying over a recorded report.

'Yes,' Nazim agreed, seriously. 'As I said in the announcement, the university sees itself as very much part of the city. Naturally, we're anxious to be responsive to the community and that's why we welcome this investigation by the council. Not by us, I must make that clear – this is a completely independent *council* investigation. I don't want to pre-empt that inquiry, but it's common knowledge that Mr Dalton has been behaving rather erratically. I believe he's been under a great deal of stress and, despite our efforts, he's been unwilling to seek help. He's become very uncommunicative . . .'

'Secretive, indeed.'

'Not a word I would have used, but I suppose, yes. Taking on more and more responsibilities, refusing – I understand from what people are telling me – to talk to the media. Almost obsessive, one might say.'

'Ursula?' I called – she was doing something that required noise and swearing in the cupboard under the stairs. 'Ursula? Come and look at this – I'm fucked.'

The attentive face of the reporter nodded on the screen as Nazim spoke.

'That's partly why we are pleased to have this investigation take place.' He smiled. Likable and concerned.

I felt Ursula come into the room behind me.

'Mr Dalton continued to refuse to be interviewed today,' said the reporter. She was speaking in voice-over; above the caption 'Library Picture', there was a photo of me half protruding from a lavatory window. 'With this council investigation it is unlikely he will be able to keep silent for much longer. Stella Fitzmaurice, for *North-East Now!*'

I turned round to Ursula.

'Ursula,' I began, 'I've couriered money to the Triads who

are supplying the university with foreign students. The Prime Administrator of Learning Support is missing and her wages, along with money skimmed off various other grants and schemes, are being used as a massive slush fund to buy favours and finance illegal activities. They built the new extension over an historical burial site and paid the contractor to dump the bodies during the night so no one would see. They've also hidden a devastating nerve gas – which they created – under the foundations with the help of the government's chemical weapons department.'

She looked at me impassively.

'I've been meaning to tell you this,' I added.

She cleared her throat with a small cough. 'I've found the broom,' she said. 'Just now, looking in the cupboard for something to clean up all that Chinese food you're dripping on the carpet. I forgot I'd put it in there before the gutterers came.'

'Mmmm . . . .' I nodded.

'Don't,' she warned.

I bit my lip.

'OK, broom thing aside – for the moment – this is the situation. I have no proof that all of the stuff at the university just sort of fell on me. Nazim, the Vice-Chancellor, the Dean of Biological Sciences, *everyone* will doubtless have a carefully prepared story and are highly respected figures whereas I have no proof and everyone hates me.'

'What are you going to do?'

'I'll do seven to ten, probably . . . Even if I don't get thrown into jail, I'll certainly be thrown to the media and lose my job. You've just quit your job. We have half a roof and, I'm guessing, about the same amount of car. What, therefore, does that leave?'

She looked around the room and shrugged, before turning to me.

'Same as always, I suppose . . . Us.'

The doorbell began to ring insistently and I could hear Stella

Fitzmaurice shouting, 'Mr Dalton? Mr Dalton – just a quick reaction?' from outside.

I looked in the direction of the door and then back to Ursula.

'It that going to be enough?' I asked.

'Enough? Jesus – that alone would *kill* most people. Anyway, if it wasn't enough, would everything else be?'

I shook my head. 'Nope.'

The doorbell and the shouting continued.

'But what are we going to do about all this?' I said.

'Aw, bollocks to it – let's go to bed.'

She began to walk out of the living room, towards the stairs. I followed, briefly losing my footing on a creamy mushroom.

'I don't really think I can sleep,' I said. 'I don't know why, but I'm a bit jittery.'

'I wasn't thinking of sleeping.'

'No?'

'No,' she replied, walking up the steps ahead of me slowly. 'The imminent poverty, public humiliation, possible criminal proceedings . . . the reporter outside waiting to crucify us, the missing roof, destroying the car . . . I don't know about you, but it's really turning me on.'

'Yeah . . .' I said. 'I've still got it, eh? Get into bed. I'll just take a quick shower to clean off this Chinese.'

'No,' she replied. 'Take your clothes off . . . leave the noodles on.'

LOUISE WENER

Goodnight Steve McQueen

'If you liked *High Fidelity* you'll love *Goodnight Steve McQueen*' *The Times*

'A sweet, optimistic tale' *Scotsman*

'A warm and funny debut' *Mirror*

Danny McQueen has dreamed of being a pop star since he was 13 years old. At the age of 29, he's still dreaming. Now he faces a dilemma. His girlfriend Alison wants him to sort his life out. She's given him an ultimatum: find a record deal by the end of the year or find a new girlfriend.

When is it time to give up on your childhood ambitions? When is it time to stop watching *Columbo* in your underpants and get a proper job? Is six months long enough for one last assault on the big time? Is friendship ever more important than love? Is it just your imagination or can your girlfriend always tell when you've been looking at internet porn?

With the help of the boss Kostas, his two best friends and an eighty year old Kung Fu enthusiast called Sheila, Danny McQueen is about to find out.

FLAME
Hodder & Stoughton

JASPER FFORDE

Lost in a Good Book

'This year's grown-up J.K.Rowling' *The Sunday Times*

'Don't ask, just read it. Fforde is a true original'
Sunday Express

'Let yourself be entertained by a witty romp' *Sunday Telegraph*

Thursday Next, literary detective and registered dodo owner, begins her married life with the disturbing news that her husband of only a month drowned thirty-eight years ago, and no one but Thursday has any memory of him at all. Someone, somewhere, *sometime* is responsible. Could it be the ubiquitous Goliath Corporation, who will stop at nothing to get their operative Jack Schitt out of 'The Raven' – the poem in which Thursday trapped him? Or are more sinister forces at work in Swindon?

Having barely caught her breath after *The Eyre Affair*, Thursday heads back into fiction to search for some answers. Along the way she finds herself helping Miss Havisham close narrative loopholes in *Great Expectations*, struggling for a deeper understanding of *The Tale of the Flopsy Bunnies* and learning the truth about *Larry the Lamb*. Paper politicians, lost Shakespearean manuscripts, woolly mammoth migrations, a flurry of near-fatal coincidences and impending Armageddon are all part of a greater plan.

But whose? And why?

NEW ENGLISH LIBRARY
Hodder & Stoughton